# The Pirate Ruse

# The Pirate Ruse

By Marcia Lynn McClure

*The Pirate Ruse* by Marcia Lynn McClure
**www.marcialynnmcclure.com**

©Copyright 2010 by M. Meyers
Photography by Xavier Marchant | Dreamstime.com
Cover Design by Sheri Brady

Published by Distractions Ink
P.O. Box 15971
Rio Rancho, NM 87174

This is a work of fiction. All characters in this work are fictional.
Any resemblance to persons living or dead is purely coincidental.

Library of Congress Control Number: 2010936924

Printed in the United States of America

ISBN 978-0-9827826-4-4

*To Sheri,*

*Good times ever seem so good with you!*

*Thank you for motivational counsel, hysterical witticisms...*

*And for leading me on the archeological dig to rediscover me!*

*Thank you...my cherry, cherry friend!*

*(I could go on and on...but there are only a few hundred pages in this book!)*

# 1814 Pirate Glossary

**Bring 'em Near**—A telescope.

**Jolly Roger**—A pirate flag with a black field emblazoned with emblems of death.

**Bloody Banner**—A plain red pirate flag, signaling death would come to all who saw it. The flying of the bloody banner meant pirates would offer no mercy in the ensuing battle.

**Bloody**—A mild, non-vulgar slang term used as an intensifier.

**Chemise**—A woman's undergarment—loose-fitting and fashioned as a long shirt or dress, worn against the skin and beneath a corset.

**Corset**—A woman's undergarment—close-fitting and stiffened with whalebone or similar material. The corset was worn about a woman's torso and often tightened by laced stays.

**Schooner**—American Privateers often favored topsail schooners. They were fast, fairly small ships and quick sailers.

**La Petite Grenouille**—Frent for "The Little Frog."

**The Cat or Cat of Nine Tails**—The traditional maritime whip. Often a sailor to be whipped made his own Cat o' Nine Tails by unwinding a rope into its three strands, then further unwinding and knotting each strand. Each Cat was used only once—for if used repeatedly, its bloody cords would infect the wounds it inflicted.

**Pieces of Eight**—The Spanish silver coin (dollar), minted by the Spanish Empire following a Spanish currency reform in 1497.

**Gold Doubloon**—The doubloon was a Spanish coin used from the mid 16th to mid 19th centuries. It was stamped from gold and commonly referred to as a gold piece. It weighed just under one ounce and was made from 22 karat (almost pure) gold.

# Chapter One

"The bring 'em near, Cap'n," Baskerville said, handing the telescope to his Captain. "What do you see? Who be the two tangled ships?"

The infamous pirate, Navarrone the Blue Blade, stretched the telescope to its length—peered through it to the ships battling on the horizon. He felt a pleased grin tug at one corner of his mouth as he recognized the pirate ship broad aside a British frigate.

"Hmm," Captain Navarrone mumbled. "It's The Screaming Witch. Her crew is swarming the deck of the Brit's Chichester." Navarrone lowered his telescope a moment. As the right corner of his mouth quirked into a pleased half smile, he nodded. "Looks to be Captain Bully Booth means to plunder British spoils before we do." Glancing to Baskerville, he allowed his smile to broaden. "Booth always has been the biggest imbecile to sail the seas."

"Aye, Cap'n," Baskerville chuckled in agreement.

Navarrone raised the telescope once more. "Still...Captain Booth is flying his bloody banner...he means to give no mercy."

"Ain't the Chichester the ship they was speaking of in New Orleans, Cap'n?"

"Aye," Navarrone confirmed. "And if any pirate is to have her bounty...it be us, Baskerville...not that fool Booth."

"Aye, Cap'n."

Again Navarrone lowered the telescope.

"We've carried false colors long enough," he said. "The Chichester will think a sister ship is coming to her rescue. Let's not give hope where there is none." Navarrone chuckled. "When Booth sees the figurehead

3

of The Merry Wench bearing aft at him…well, another Brit vessel wouldn't strike him near as threatening as we will. Eh, Baskerville?"

Baskerville smiled. "Aye, Cap'n."

Navarrone nodded—collapsed the telescope, handing it back to Baskerville. "Hoist the Jolly Roger, lads!" he roared. "We be plundering the bloody British *and* Captain Bully Booth today!"

He laughed as the crew shouted with approval and anticipation of battle. His own excitement mounted as he watched the men begin to race over the deck of his ship, The Merry Wench. He saw the false colors of the British Empire being lowered—watched the skull, crossed bones and winged hourglass on black rise, unfurl, and begin thrashing in the breeze. He inhaled a deep breath of sea air tinged with the barely discernable scent of cannon smoke. Battle was upon them! The bloody British would lose another ship and Bully Booth would lose whatever booty was cached in its hold. Navarrone the Blue Blade would see to that!

"We'll put the Wench starboard of the Chichester's port…board her and beat down both Booth's crew and the Chichester's on her own deck."

"Aye, Cap'n," Baskerville said. With a nod of understanding, Baskerville began to shout out orders.

Captain Navarrone's dark eyes narrowed as he listened to his quartermaster barking orders to the crew with the skill, ease, and respect of the crew afforded any quartermaster or First Mate in the regular Navy. Baskerville was not only a true friend, but an accomplished sailor. Navarrone admired his quartermaster—knew that if Flynn Baskerville had had the choice given him of life in the Navy as opposed to that of piracy, he would have made a fine and valuable Naval officer—a one-day-captain of his own ship, no doubt.

"Bully Booth will spill blood more willingly than he would a crock of grog!" Navarrone shouted to his men as he took hold of the ship's helm. "Let's make certain the right blood is spilled, lads!"

"Aye, Cap'n!" the men shouted.

Navarrone the Blue Blade laughed as he headed The Merry Wench to battle. The balmy sea breeze billowed the sleeves of his shirt and he was glad he wore only his long vest—for its brother frock coat would not have afforded such a sense of freedom.

Baskerville continued to bark orders to the crew and Navarrone's heart began to pound with excitement as The Merry Wench closed the distance to the battle between the bloody British and the pirate Bully Booth. He could see the British sailors on the Chichester's deck fighting to defend against the swarm of pirates boarding her from Booth's Screaming Witch. He knew Bully Booth—the bloodthirsty barbarian would take no prisoners—leave no man alive. Booth was a murderous blackguard and Navarrone was glad to finally have reason to match blades with such a devil.

The breeze blew Navarrone's dark hair across his face, momentarily distracting him. Frowning, he paused at the helm to pull a blue length of cloth from his baldric. Stretching it over his forehead he tied it at the back of his head, thinking he should have had Baskerville crop his hair shorter than merely at his jaw line. Almost unconsciously he felt for the cutlass he knew hung at his hip. There would be brutal cutlass play with Booth's men and the Brits and, though he knew the weapon was with him, he felt more readily assured in having tangible proof. The pirate Navarrone's skill with a cutlass had well-earned him the sobriquet, The Blue Blade. Yet, battle was always wild and fast—chaotic and wrought with peril. Best to know his cutlass was within reach, rather than to assume it.

Wielding the helm, Navarrone wondered that Lafitte had not happened upon the Chichester and taken her already. Still, word was Jean Lafitte was too busy smuggling goods into New Orleans to be having adventures at sea. He smiled. With Lafitte otherwise engaged, all the more triumph and booty for the crew of The Merry Wench.

As The Merry Wench drew alongside the Chichester, Navarrone could see that her crew was indeed being slaughtered by Booth's men. If any Brits hoped to escape with their lives, they had best surrender to Navarrone and let The Merry Wench's crew best Booth's.

He had been clever to bring his Wench to the Chichester's port—for their port guns were unmanned—already occupied by The Screaming Witch to her starboard.

"Board that bloody British boat, lads!" Navarrone shouted as Baskerville hurried to his side once more. Drawing his cutlass, Navarrone nodded to his quartermaster. "Keep her steady, and kill anyone who tries to harm her!"

"Aye, Cap'n!" Baskerville assured him over the roar of the battle.

Navarrone watched as his men swarmed onto the deck of the Chichester via planks and ropes. The crash of cutlass steel rang out like an eerie bell-song and Navarrone the Blue Blade felt his heart hammering with mingled excitement and dread.

He swung from a yardarm rope to the deck of the Chichester—fought off three sailors of the Royal Empire, then spied Bully Booth across the way—on the deck of The Screaming Witch.

"Coward," Navarrone grumbled in disgust. Taking the stairs leading to the Chichester's quarterdeck two at a time, Navarrone wounded two rival pirates, pausing to shout to Bully Booth, "As ever the coward, Booth!" Deftly crossing a boarding plank to the deck of The Screaming Witch, he added, "Too afraid to fight for your own plunder…too much a coward to join your men in battle?"

"I'm surprised to see ya with yar cutlass drawn, Navarrone!" Bully Booth shouted in return. "I never thought to see ya risking that pretty face of yars!"

Two of Booth's men advanced on Navarrone—and he easily cut them down.

"I'd rather have a pretty face on the front of my head, than a dog's arse the likes you've got on yours, Bully," Navarrone countered, smiling. Navarrone sneered—disgusted by Bully Booth's appearance. Long red hair—curly and somewhat matted—hung well to his waist. His eyes were small, green and bulbous—like those of a toad. His beard was wrought into long twisted lengths and Navarrone fancied he caught the stench of his rotting, yellow teeth upon the very air.

Booth chuckled. "Pretty face or none, I've already been aboard the Chichester," he said. "And I've already discovered the richest of her spoils."

Navarrone frowned as the vile, repulsive pirate Bully Booth reached down and drew a young woman to her feet. Navarrone had not noticed the woman before—for his attention had been fully arrested by Bully Booth. The Blue Blade felt the hair on the back of his neck prickle as Booth wrapped one hand in the young woman's dark hair and pushed her to stand in front of him—between himself and Navarrone.

Navarrone's frown deepened—for he had not expected to find a woman aboard either the Chichester or The Screaming Witch. Tears were streaming over the woman's reddened cheeks—yet, her mouth was set in a pose of defiance and bravery. As the question briefly flitted through his mind as to what a woman was doing aboard a British merchant vessel, the damnable streak of chivalry that was Navarrone's father's gift to his character was summoned.

Navarrone would not leave a woman—any woman. No woman on earth deserved to be sacrificed to the heinous torture Captain Bully Booth would exact. He had planned to take the Chichester—to raid her hold— to save her crew from the merciless pirates of The Screaming Witch and send them sobbing back to New Orleans as prisoners. He took no prisoners otherwise—neither sailor, pirate nor civilian. He never did. Yet, he could not leave a woman to be defiled by Bully Booth and his men. He scowled— growled with the vexation of owning a conscience. His men would have to battle on the Chichester's deck without him—at least for a time.

Navarrone ground his teeth as another of Booth's men advanced. Without so much as a flinch or blink, The Blue Blade ran his cutlass through the man's midsection. He looked back to Booth—watched as the vile pirate put his lips to the woman's ear, kissing her temple once before licking her cheek.

"She tastes as sweet as well-ripened fruit, Navarrone," Bully Booth chuckled. "Ya keep that Empire's gold…and I'll keep the wench."

"I'll take the bloody British gold and the girl, Booth," Navarrone said, smiling. "And I'll run you through, too…just for my own amusement!" Bully Booth was notorious for murder—for spilling the blood of women and children as well as sailors and pirates. Thus, Navarrone owned no hesitation in ridding the world of such a monster.

Suddenly, Booth pushed the girl aside, lunging at Navarrone. Navarrone easily evaded the strike however.

"Oh, Bully," he goaded. "Tsk tsk. Have you not heard of The Blue Blade Navarrone?"

Again Bully struck—again Navarrone easily evaded. He let his cutlass slice the air—offered a simple strike he knew Booth could defend. The clash of steel heightened his determination and the sword play began.

Navarrone had meant to give Booth false hope—to toy with the scoundrel and let him think he might triumph over the famed Blue Blade. Yet as he saw two of Booth's men swing from the Chichester's deck back to The Screaming Witch to attend their Captain, he knew time could not be spent in tarrying.

Quickly he ran his cutlass through Booth's plump midsection. "My apologies, Booth," he said, as the man's eyes widened. "But I have no time to waste on you. May your foul deeds on the sea find your corpse forever rotting with the fish in Davy Jones' locker." He glanced to the Chichester to see Booth's men abandoning its deck—the crew of The Merry Wench having quickly diminished their numbers and fortitude.

Placing a red-cuffed boot to Booth's thigh, Navarrone pulled his cutlass from Booth's belly, and let the dying man slip to the deck. Reaching down, he took hold of the young woman's arm.

Instantly, the pretty wench began to struggle.

"Let me go!" she demanded. "Unhand me, you filthy pirate!"

Placing the tip of his cutlass (still smeared with Bully Booth's blood) to the soft hollow of her throat he growled, "Come with me, wench, and you might live." He glanced to the advancing crewmen of The Screaming Witch, adding, "Or, you may remain here and surely die…but only after Bully Booth's men have punished you for the death of their captain." She glared at him and he admired her for her defiance. "Of course they may take pity on you and merely flog you with the cat o' nine tails first. Yet, I think not. Moreover you will wish for death after they…"

Navarrone flinched as the woman's expectorated saliva met with his chin. He chuckled slightly—for he admired her for having mustered the courage to spit on him.

"Think carefully, wench," he warned her, wiping her spittle from his face with the back of one hand. "Would you truly prefer a mob of angry pirates ruin, torture and kill you, when the dashing and merciful Captain Navarrone is offering to have you instead?"

Though he thought it impossible, the young woman's expression of determined boldness increased. "I see no difference in the vileness of pirates," she said.

Navarrone laughed—ran his cutlass through the throat of one of Bully Booth's men as he advanced.

"Oh, my sweet little pomegranate," he said as he took hold of her shoulders. "How naïve you women are in your knowledge of men." Turning her from him, he tore open the back of her dress. She screamed and tried to run from him, but he easily caught her. He could see Booth's men advancing and quickly stripped the dress from her body.

Securing his cutlass at his hip, he pulled the young woman back against him, wrapping his arms tight about her waist.

"Let me go! Let me go!" she screamed as she struggled. Navarrone was surprised at her strength—yet he held tight as he backed toward the edge of the ship.

"Oh, but you'll thank me one day, love," he laughed as he hurled them both over the side of The Screaming Witch and into the sea.

An instant before the sea swallowed her, Cristabel Albay gasped her last breath. She was certain it would truly be her last breath, and as the water consumed her she thought of her mother—prayed she would somehow be made happy. Yet, mere moments later, her head broke the surface of the sea and she exhaled the breath she had been holding—the one that had not been her last—gasping for another.

"Do you swim, woman?" the pirate Navarrone angrily inquired.

"Y-yes," Cristabel stammered. Her thoughts were muddled—for panic was her only ally. Yet, she was cognizant enough to know that her life was still in danger—not from pirates perhaps—but from the sea.

"Then swim!" the pirate growled. "If you want to live to see another sunrise, then swim for The Merry Wench."

Cristabel had only an instant to think—to consider. She glanced up to the Chichester, where pirates and British sailors yet battled. The Screaming Witch was already sailing, and Cristabel would rather have died than be the victim of the atrocities that would have met her aboard it.

Yet, to abandon one pirate ship for another? It was madness! Still, she could not fathom drowning—for drowning terrified her more than any other fate of death. Her only hope in surviving was to do as the pirate ordered. Perhaps she could beg mercy from the captain of The Merry Wench. She had heard tales of Navarrone the Blue Blade—tales of mercy. It was said The Blue Blade often showed clemency where other pirates showed none. Perhaps he would take pity on her—even return her to her home. Thus, with no other venue to follow, Christabel began to swim— to swim for The Merry Wench and whatever fate awaited her there.

The girl was falling behind. She was a strong swimmer—especially for a woman—but Navarrone knew she would not make The Merry Wench without assistance. He stopped his stroke toward the ship, treading water until she reached him.

"Lower the rope ladder!" Navarrone shouted as he saw Baskerville looking over the side of the ship to the water. "Quickly, mate!" Baskerville nodded and Navarrone knew the rope ladder would be waiting—if he could get the girl to it.

As she approached, he attempted to take hold of her in order to keep her head above water. Stubborn female that she was, however, she began to struggle.

"I'm not about to violate you here in the sea in the midst of battle, woman!" he growled. "I'll swim you to the ship…but if you determine to keep fighting me, I'll let the sea have you!"

She ceased her struggling at once and for the first time he saw true fear in the depth of her violet eyes.

"That's a good lassie," he said. "Now, take my belt…here at the back," he instructed, taking her hand and placing it at his belt. "I'll swim you the rest of the way."

Navarrone noted the manner in which the young woman did not simply go slack, allowing him to swim her on his own. She yet kicked her feet and stoked her free arm in rhythm with his. This girl was no dwindling lily. Again he wondered at what reason she had to have been aboard the Chichester. Perhaps she was its captain's wife. Yet what man would bring his wife aboard a ship bound for war-ridden waters?

Breathless, Navarrone reached up, taking hold of the first rung of the rope ladder. The girl bobbed up beside him and he frowned a moment. She was winded—but there was something more.

"Here," he said, awkwardly removing his long knee-length vest. "Cover yourself with this." He helped her to put her arms through the vest adding, "Else your health is compromised from the wet and lack of clothing."

"I have no clothing, because you tore it from my body," she said through chattering teeth.

Navarrone glared at her. "The wetted weight of those bolts of fabric you women deem attire, would have taken us both to Davy Jones' locker.

10

You should be thanking me for allowing you to keep your undergarments and not stripping you to the skin!"

Still she returned his glare with defiance. Navarrone admired her will. He felt a grin tug at the right corner of his mouth.

"Now, unless you want to board my ship in nothing but your white, now gossamer, underclothes…I suggest you secure those vest buttons," he said.

Cristabel frowned, even though as she clung to the bottom rung of the rope ladder and struggled to fasten the buttons of the pirate's long vest—she understood why he had stripped her before hurtling them both over the side of The Screaming Witch and into the sea. The weight of her dress would have easily drowned her. Yet, she was further suspicious— suspicious of a pirate who would take concern over her modesty. Perchance he was simply trying to avoid chaos among his men. No doubt a woman dressed only in her near transparent underthings would cause disorderly behavior among the sort of miscreants known to sail pirate vessels.

"Now up the rope with you, love," Captain Navarrone ordered. "I have plundering to attend to."

Cristabel endeavored to pull herself up onto the rope ladder. The strength of her arms and legs were spent from swimming, however, and she could not manage it. Furthermore, the pirate's long, blue brocaded vest was wet and heavy. Again she attempted to pull her body onto the ladder and failed. She gasped when she felt a strong hand at her seat as Captain Navarrone boosted her up.

"Grab hold, girl!" he growled, boosting her seat once more.

His strength indeed assisted her and she began to climb. Her arms and legs were trembling and weak—heavy. Yet she persevered—even for the group of pirates gazing down at her from the ship's deck.

"Pull her up, Baskerville!" the pirate Captain barked from below her.

"Aye, Cap'n," a weathered-looking man called, offering a bronzed, knurled hand to Cristabel.

She paused—for the man was a pirate. A pirate! She could hardly fathom how she had come to be climbing up the rope ladder of a ship straight into the hands of pirates. Yet, neither could she sort out the

11

events that had found her kidnapped and taken prisoner aboard a British merchant vessel.

"Give me your hand, lassie," the weathered man said, snapping the fingers of the hand he offered. "Come now. Ain't a beauty in all the world that wouldn't rather be ravaged by Captain Navarrone 'stead of ol' Bully Booth. Come aboard so's that the Cap'n can have his way with you."

Cristabel gasped—paused in her ascent of the rope. Yet, the weathered man only chuckled—as did the men on either side of him.

"Oh, come now, lassie…we was only havin' a bit of fun with you now," he chuckled.

Another hand boost to her bottom and Cristabel accepted the hand of the man called Baskerville.

"That's it, kitten," Baskerville said as he and another man pulled Cristabel onto the deck. She collapsed at once—too exhausted to stand.

Captain Navarrone stepped over the side and onto the deck then. Cristabel watched—still too weak to move—breathless from the exertion of escaping one pirate ship only to be taken aboard another.

"What say ye, Baskerville?" the pirate captain asked, stripping off his belt, baldric, and wet shirt and depositing them on the deck. He pulled the blue sash from about his head, tossing it aside as well. He was a large man—taller than Cristabel had surmised him to be in her few moments on the deck of The Screaming Witch. His revealed broad shoulders, and bronzed, sculpted torso presented a far more intimidating character, and Cristabel was again struck by the knowledge she was in the hands of pirates.

"Those bloody Brits have a hold full of goods, sir…but little ammunition," Baskerville answered. "Not the usual cargo for a merchant vessel…especially in times of war."

"No," Captain Navarrone mumbled as his narrowed gaze fell to Cristabel for a moment. "Not the usual cargo at all."

"Bully Booth's men scattered like fleas, Cap'n," a young boatswain chuckled. The others who had heard him smiled—chuckled and exchanged triumphant nods.

"As well they should have," Captain Navarrone said, patting the young man on the back. "The crew of The Merry Wench are not to be trifled with, eh?"

The pirates cheered and Cristabel watched as Captain Navarrone began to stride toward a plank leading to the deck of the Chichester.

"Lock the woman in my quarters, Baskerville," he ordered. He paused mid-plank, turned, and glaring at his men added, "Any man who entertains one thought toward her…will feel twenty lashes with the cat. I did not face and run through a pirate the like of Bully Booth to see my prize spoiled."

"Aye, Cap'n," the men said in unison.

"Come along, lassie," Baskerville said, taking Cristabel's arm and pulling her to her feet.

"Unhand me, blackguard!" Cristabel said, somehow managing to deliver a stinging slap to the pirate's face.

Baskerville's grip only tightened at her arm, however—painfully. The intensity of his applied seizure rendered Cristabel unable to offend him further.

"Oh, and Baskerville," she heard Captain Navarrone chuckle, "be wary. That one's got a bit of a she-devil in her."

"Aye, Cap'n," Baskerville grumbled, glaring at Cristabel.

"You're hurting me!" Cristabel cried as Baskerville pushed her toward the captain's cabin beneath the quarterdeck.

"The Cap'n's got arrangements to make, lassie," Baskerville said as he forced her into the cabin. "But don't you worry your pretty little head none…he'll be back." Baskerville's smile broadened revealing devious thoughts. "I'm certain Captain Navarrone won't keep the likes of you waiting."

"Please, sir," Cristabel began to beg. Perhaps this man Baskerville would take pity on her—protect her from Captain Navarrone and whatever he planned to do to her.

"You rest a bit now, lass," Baskerville said, however. "It won't be long. The Cap'n can plunder a ship faster than any man I ever sailed with."

With that, Baskerville closed the door behind him. Cristabel heard him bark out an order to a boatswain, that the door be barred and guarded.

She was trapped—held prisoner by blood-thirsty pirates! Exhausted, Cristabel crumpled in a heap on the floor of the captain's cabin. Sobbing wracked her tired, frightened body and soul—hopelessness and despair overwhelming her. She was lost—entirely lost! She would be beaten—seized, despoiled and finally murdered! Cristabel Albay would find her end in being tortured in the heinous misery inflicted by pirates! She again thought of her mother.

"Pray…help Mother to find happiness," she whispered, through her tears. "I beg thee…never let her gain knowledge of the circumstance of my demise."

Suddenly a strange, unexpected desperation began to wash over Cristabel. She could not perish—not at the hands of pirates! She could not! She would not! Brushing the tears from her cheeks, she pushed her weary body to kneeling at least. She brushed more tears from her face as she glanced about the cabin in which she was prisoner. She frowned—bewildered by the finery meeting her gaze. The desk and its chair—the blue velvet-cushioned chaise lounge to one side—a painting on the wall, the bedding of the captain's berth—all were wildly luxurious and of great worth. Yet, Cristabel was only momentarily dazzled—for she was indeed in a pirate captain's cabin—and no pirate captain would linger in his cabin without knowing weapons of defense were within his reach. Though pirate crews that were captianed by a man they respected were loyal to their leader—pirates were still pirates—and no captain of such a vessel as The Merry Wench could trust his men entirely. Thus, there must be weaponry at hand.

Hope began to swell in Cristabel's bosom. Perhaps she could find a pistol—a dagger—something with which to aid in escape—or at least something with which to defend her virtue. She tried to stand, but her legs were still too weak from the exertion of swimming. Still, she was not thwarted and began crawling toward the desk at the far side of the room. She would not forfeit her virtue or her life without a struggle. When the pirate captain, Navarrone the Blue Blade, came for her, she would defend herself—to the death if necessary. She would plunge his own cutlass into his belly—drive his own dagger into his heart—shoot him between the eyes with his own pistol before she allowed him to touch her.

Reaching up, she took hold of the desk top—at last pulling herself to her feet. She smiled as she saw a dagger enclosed in a bejeweled sheath lying on top of the desk. Smiling, she picked up the weapon—drew the sharp blade from its ruby-encrusted scabbard.

Remembering the words Captain Navarrone had uttered a moment before he had hurled them both from The Screaming Witch and into the sea, she whispered, "Oh, but you'll thank me one day, love," as she studied the lethal weapon in her hand. "Will I thank you one day, Captain Navarrone?" she questioned the air. She smiled and whispered, "I may indeed, love. I may indeed."

# Chapter Two

Navarrone stood before the Chichester's few surviving crew members. Bully Booth and his men had well-slaughtered the British sailors. Only seven remained. He was angry—angry that Bully Booth had come upon the Chichester before The Merry Wench had found her—angry that his boots were sopping wet for the sake of the swim necessary to save the woman now locked in his cabin—angry at the British sailors for being part of the Empire's tyranny. Independence from the British Empire had been hard fought for by the United States—many men died for the sake of it—and now the British were attempting to conquer, or in the least oppress, the fledgling country. For over two years—since June of 1812—battle had been waged between the states and territories of the United States and the bloody British Empire. Navarrone was weary of it.

Navarrone studied the uniforms of the remaining British crew—their bloodied lips and defiant stances.

"You men," he began, addressing the enemy. "You are fortunate to be alive. The pirate, Bully Booth, did not intend to spare you. Yet, I have." He glared at the men—pacing back and forth before the line of young British sailors. His eyes narrowed as he closely studied the uniform of one man. "You," he said, glaring at the man. "You're First Mate. Where's your captain?"

"Dead, you filthy pirate!" the man growled. Navarrone raised a hand—intent on striking the man for his disrespect and British alliance. He paused however—for it took courage to stand in defiance of an enemy to which one was forfeit.

"The woman that was aboard your vessel," Navarrone began, lowering his hand, "The one Bully Booth captured. Was she your captain's wife?"

His instincts whispered that he should not allow the Brits to know he had taken the woman from Bully Booth. Furthermore, he was pleased with his men—for as ever, they displayed solemn faces—revealed nothing to the Brits that might alert them to their Captain's trickery.

"No," the Chichester's First Mate admitted.

"Why was she sailing with you?" Navarrone asked.

"What will the pirate do with her?" the First Mate bravely inquired.

Again Navarrone's eyes narrowed. "Bully Booth is merciless," he answered. "He will keep no prisoner alive…not for long anyway. Tell me why she was aboard an Empire's merchant vessel and I may spare your lives. Was she of some value…other than the obvious that is? Speak…and with respect…or you will share the same fate as your dead brother sailors."

The First Mate swallowed. Navarrone knew the man was considering on whether or not to tell the truth.

"I warn you, Brit…I will know if you are lying," he growled.

The First Mate of the captured Chichester sighed—slightly shook his head. "I don't know," he admitted. "I don't know why she was aboard…but I do know she was not willingly aboard."

Navarrone's eyes narrowed. "Not willingly aboard? Do you mean she was forced aboard?"

"Aye," the man answered. "We weren't told nothing about why she was with us. The Captain only told us we weren't to…to touch her. A small ship brought her to us in the dead of night."

"Did she tell you anything? Speak to you of why she was on the Chichester?" Navarrone asked.

The First Mate shook his head once more. "No. Seems to me she didn't know why herself."

Navarrone glanced to Baskerville. Baskerville nodded—he, too, understood that there was something inexplicably strange about the presence of the woman they had found aboard the Chichester.

"Do you mean to hang us?" a British boatswain asked.

Navarrone looked to the lad—judged him to be no more than seventeen.

He did not answer the boy—simply spoke to his own men instead.

"Empty the hold of anything of value," Navarrone ordered. "Gather any logs, maps or parchments from the Captain's cabin."

"Aye, Cap'n," Baskerville agreed.

"Have Fergus choose ample men to sail the Chichester back to New Orleans," Navarrone said. He paused—glaring at the line of British sailors. "If they want to live, they will man their posts…and the Governor will decide their sentence when we arrive."

"Aye, Cap'n," Baskerville said with a nod.

"Give the orders, Baskerville," Navarrone ordered.

"Aye, Cap'n." Baskerville inhaled a deep breath then and began to bark out orders. "You heard the Cap'n men! Empty the hold! Haul that British booty to The Merry Wench! Quick as you can, lads! We sail for New Orleans for feasting and riotous entertainment!"

The men cheered and Navarrone had to fight to keep a smile from breaking over his face. He well-liked the sounds of his men when they were merry—he well-liked besting the British. Yet, as he crossed the plank to the deck of the Wench, his thoughts turned somber once more. It was not logical—the girl being aboard the Chichester—and unwillingly. His sixth sense told him there was more to her presence—something of worth about her—or about something she possessed—perhaps she owned a knowledge the Brits had deemed valuable.

Whatever the reason for her presence, Navarrone would discover it— use it to his advantage if he could. He remembered the look of defiance on her face—even as Bully Booth held her in threatening her virtue and life. Her courage was admirable. Yet, it revealed a stubborn nature—a strength that, though estimable, could be unpredictable and therefore dangerous. He would have to watch her carefully—read her expressions and movements if he hoped to extract information from her. Still, if she did hold secret some valuable or precious information, Navarrone the Blue Blade would reap it from her.

"Cap'n" Fergus said, as Navarrone stepped onto the deck of The Merry Wench.

Navarrone turned to see Fergus deftly crossing the plank toward him.

Lowering his voice Fergus whispered, "There's a trunk of women's necessities in the Chichester's cap'n's cabin." Fergus—The Merry Wench's First Mate—was a man to be trusted. Navarrone ever admired his quick wit and ability to solve riddles. "Might it belong to the lady?"

"Most likely, Fergus," Navarrone mumbled.

"Should we bring it aboard the Wench, Cap'n?" Fergus inquired. "Allow the lady some dry clothes?"

Navarrone's eyes narrowed. "Bring the trunk aboard...but do not take it to the woman," he answered. "No one is to touch its contents until I have seen to them first."

"Aye, Cap'n," Fergus said.

"In fact...have it brought to me at once," Navarrone said. "There is something strange in all this. It unsettles me somehow. Best we root out whatever knowledge we can before we reach New Orleans."

"Aye, Cap'n."

Perhaps the contents of the woman's trunk would reveal her purpose aboard the enemy's vessel—or in least her identity. Navarrone's eyes narrowed. Yes—something was greatly amiss where the Chichester and its woman passenger were concerned.

Cristabel glanced about the cabin. She held the dagger at her back, yet she wished for some alternate weapon to aid her. She saw none easily accessible, however, and knew the captain of The Merry Wench would return soon. She must prepare—convince herself that death may be at her door—yet likewise persuade herself that she could survive—even triumph. Her eyes fell to the captain's berth—strewn with linens and clothing. She considered snatching up one of the shirts she saw abandoned there, in order to rid herself of the weight of the sopping brocaded vest. She knew the vest would inhibit her movements, yet she feared there was not time for such considerations.

Cristabel glanced up then. She was instantly intrigued by the large painting on the wall near the cabin door—a portrait of a beautiful raven-haired woman. The eyes of the woman in the portrait were as blue as the sky—her lips as crimson as summer cherries. She wore a dress of peacock blue and an expression of contentment. She was, by far, one of the most beautiful women Cristabel had ever seen. She fleetingly wondered if the portrait had been painted from the artist's imagination or from the sitting of a living woman. The woman bore a small, straight nose, high well-defined cheek bones, and a dark beauty mark at the crest of her right cheek beneath the corner of her eye.

Glancing back to the captain's desk, Cristabel realized that the portrait was placed so that any moment the captain was at his desk or in his berth—or even perhaps reclining on the nearby chaise—the view before him would ever be the portrait of the striking woman.

"A lover?" Cristabel inquired of the air. "Only such a rare beauty could be your equal I suppose," she whispered. For it was true—bloodthirsty pirate or not, Captain Navarrone was fully as handsome as the tales told of him claimed. Yet, the devil often masked evil with beauty—and though Cristabel Albay had never seen a more handsome and alluring man, she was not so easily swayed to think good of him as some women had been. The stories of the pirate Navarrone's conquests of women were many—and wildly scandalous! In Charleston it was rumored he had seduced the Governor's wife. Fair half the pirate wenches in New Orleans claimed to have fallen prey to his charms. It seemed the entire coast of the Gulf told tales of Captain Navarrone the Blue Blade and his carnal escapades.

Cristabel wrinkled her nose—disgusted with the notion of pirates and their riotous, wanton ways. She swallowed a lump of fear that rose in her throat—for only in that moment did the true desperation of her circumstances seep into her thoughts. When she had been bound, gagged and taken—hauled aboard a British ship with no knowledge of the reason—knowing she was the only woman on board—indeed she had known fear—sheer terror! However, when the Chichester had been attacked by pirates—by Captain Bully Booth and the crew of The Screaming Witch—her terror had increased one hundred fold. As the pirate Navarrone was known for his exploits with women, so the pirate Bully Booth was known for his lack of mercy—his methods of torture and murder.

Thus (though only silently admitted), Cristabel had known an odd sense of hope when Captain Navarrone had appeared on the deck of The Screaming Witch to spar for her. Her good sense told her that a pirate was a pirate—whether heinous to look up on as was Bully Booth, or handsome as was Captain Navarrone. Yet, in the depths of her soul somewhere, a whisper breathed to her thoughts that fortune had smiled upon her in delivering her into the pirate Navarrone's hands.

Cristabel gasped—startled from her thoughts as the cabin door burst open to reveal a looming, and obviously perturbed, Captain Navarrone.

As he tossed his belt, baldric and cutlass to the floor, she could not help but take two steps backward—even though she had previously determined to appear courageous when he returned. Yet, he was such an imposing figure! His dark, jaw-length hair hung wet and still dripping—and he raked a strong hand through it from his forehead, back over the top of his head. His well-groomed mustache and goatee were also darkened from the moisture still clinging to his whiskers. His massive form was sailor-bronzed—the muscles in his shoulders, arms and torso rigid and tensed. The simmering anger in his dark eyes pierced her resolve at bravery like unto some medieval knight's broadsword and she again swallowed the trepidation in her throat.

As he aggressed toward her, Cristabel heard the sloshing of his sea-saturated boots—saw the determination in his countenance—and it unsettled her far more than she had hoped. Acting too quickly—for he approached with the power and rage of a hurricane—Cristabel drew the dagger, wielding it at the advancing pirate. He did not even slow his gait—simply reached out taking hold of her wrist in such a vise's grip that her hand involuntarily opened, releasing the dagger. She watched in astonished horror as the weapon clattered to the cabin floor.

"Why were you aboard the Chichester, woman?" the pirate Navarrone growled. "Who are you? Are you some treasonous wench conspiring with the bloody Brits?"

"No!" Cristabel managed. She was angry that he should so accuse her. "I am no traitor!"

"No traitor to whom? To the States…or to the crown?" he bellowed.

"I was born in South Carolina, sir!" Cristabel answered through gritted teeth. "I am no traitor…though I do not know what right a pirate has to question my loyalty."

"South Carolina is it?" he asked, releasing her hand. "Then why were you sailing with the British?"

"I was taken," Cristabel hatefully informed him. "Stripped from my step-father's home in New Orleans in the dead of night…bound, gagged and dragged aboard a small ship which sailed me into the dark and finally to the Chichester."

She watched as the pirate's eyes narrowed. "Why?" he asked. "Who are you that you should be taken by the British."

22

"No one, I assure you," she told him. She could feel the emotions of fear and confusion torrid within her. Yet, she struggled to keep them hidden. She could not let this fierce pirate see her weakness.

She watched as he pulled a nearby chair to position in front of her. He took his seat in it and began struggling to remove his sopping boots.

"Did they mean to ransom you? Who is your father? " he asked.

"I do not know…and my father is dead," she answered curtly.

She heard him growl as he stood and began unlacing the ties at the waist of his trousers.

"Then who is your step-father, wench? The one with the house in New Orleans from which you were taken?" he grumbled. He paused in untying the laces at his waist and glanced up to her. A smile tugged at the right corner of his mouth and he said, "Make your choice, girl…avert your gaze and trust that I am otherwise occupied with changing these wet trousers for dry and will not descend upon you…or do not trust and offer yourself a lesson in pirate anatomy."

Understanding his implication, Cristabel gasped, covering her eyes with both hands.

"Who is your step-father?" he repeated.

"William Pelletier," she answered—still covering her eyes.

"A wealthy man?"

"A terrible man," she said.

"I did not inquire of his character, woman," the pirate growled. "Is he a man of wealth or position in government? Perhaps both?"

"Both," she answered.

"Then the British meant to ransom you, no doubt. And you may uncover the innocence of your eyes, love."

Tentatively, Cristabel lowered her hands and opened her eyes. The pirate Navarrone the Blue Blade was once again somewhat modest. She watched a moment as he tied the lacings at the waist of a pair of black trousers, produced another pair of boots from beneath his berth and sat down on the chair before her to pull them on.

"William Pelletier would not pay a ransom," she said. "Not for anyone."

"Is your mother still living?" the pirate asked.

"Yes."

"Then he would pay it."

23

"You do not know him," Cristabel assured him. "He would be glad to see me gone." She caught herself only a moment before she might have confessed to the pirate that the thought occurred to her that her loathsome step-father, William Pelletier, might indeed be the composer of her abduction.

She watched as he tugged on the long black boots, folding over their cuffs below his knees.

"You're keeping secrets, love," he said, rising to his full height. He raked a hand through his hair once more. Several lengths of hair cropped shorter than the rest, tumbled over his forehead to linger over his eyes— resting on his cheekbones. Cristabel noticed then the well-groomed condition of not only his mustache and goatee—the perfectly trimmed triangle of whiskers below his lower lip that met with those at his chin— but also the angled grooming of his side whiskers—the manner in which they bordered his face before each ear to angle to each mid cheek. She frowned—thinking surely not all pirates were so well-kempt.

"Keeping secrets, love," he repeated.

"I-I have told you all I know," she said, still distracted by his unusually attractive and striking appearance.

"Do you truly expect me to believe that you…the step-daughter of a wealthy New Orleans politician…were abducted in the dark of night, sailed to an enemy British ship, and put aboard for no reason you can fathom?"

"It is the truth," she said. Oh, Cristabel Albay had suspicions as to why she had been taken—or in the very least suspicions of who was behind her abduction. Yet, she would not share them with a pirate! "I do not own the suspicious nature of a pirate, Captain," she told him. "I have told you all I know."

Navarrone grinned. "No you haven't," he said.

He turned and strode toward the cabin door. Opening it, he called to a crew member who handed him some white garments. He closed the door and returned to her.

"There," he said, tossing the garments to his berth. Cristabel recognized the clothing as her own—a chemise, corset and pantaloons. "Strip yourself of that wet clothing."

"No dress?" she inquired.

"No," he answered. "I will allow you a measure of dry clothing so that you do not contract disease and die before I discover exactly why you were aboard the Chichester, consorting with the enemy."

"I was not consorting with the enemy!" Cristabel defended.

"However," Captain Navarrone continued with a scolding glare, "you will not be allowed to properly attire yourself until I am satisfied…either with the information you have finally revealed, or…" He paused, studying her from head to toe with a wanton expression, "until I have had my fill of perusing your appearance while so immodestly garbed."

Navarrone chuckled at the astonished expression of indignation on the girl's face. He fancied she blushed, and was further amused. Allowing her to attire in only her undergarments would keep her pliable and compliant, until he could determine what she was keeping secret concerning the circumstances which found her aboard a British merchant vessel. Still, he found her indignant expression wildly entertaining. He would have to remember to provoke it again.

"You…you blackguard!" she growled at him.

Navarrone chuckled. "I am a pirate, love," he said. "Did you expect me to be a gentleman?"

She was furious—entirely overcome with indignation. It was again amusing. However, he could not be distracted—for he somehow knew the girl's presence on the Chichester was significant. He snatched a previously discarded shirt from his berth, pulled it on over his head, neglecting to tie the laces at his chest.

Cristabel watched as the pirate Navarrone gathered a long red sash from the heap of clothes on his berth, positioned its middle at his forehead, securing it at the back of his head. Picking up the dagger she had dropped, he retrieved its sheath from his desk, securing both at his waist in the back of his trousers. He took a baldric down from a hook on the wall and secured it over one shoulder. He retrieved a belt he had sometime previously discarded to the chaise and fastened it at his waist. At last, he drew his cutlass from the sopping belt on the floor and secured it at his hip.

An intimidating presence indeed was the freshly garbed, well-groomed pirate Navarrone. Still, Cristabel maintained an air of defiance. He could not know how truly weak and vulnerable she felt.

"Change your garments, girl," he ordered. "We set sail for New Orleans."

"We are returning?" she gasped. At once she was horrified—confused by the fact that she was nearly as afraid of returning to New Orleans as she was to be in the company of pirates.

"The surviving crew of the Chichester must atone," he growled. "Furthermore, there is something you're hiding, love…and I intend to discover it. Thus, since your part in this event began in New Orleans, then to New Orleans we will sail."

"You plan to simply sail into New Olreans? Pirates?" she scoffed.

Captain Navarrone smiled, however. "It's New Orleans, love…and we're at war with the British. Pirates come and go nearly as they please. Perchance you have even brushed shoulders with Jean Lafitte himself while strolling past Saint Louis Cathedral or the Cabildo in the Place d' Armes. Besides, I have a captured British ship in tow, its seven surviving crew members as prisoners…and the lovely daughter of a wealthy New Orleans politician…whom I saved from certain despoilment and death. There will be vast rewards and commendations no doubt."

"Step-daughter of a wealthy New Orleans politician," she corrected. "And I assure you…he will pay no ransom. Moreover, you are still a pirate. They will hang you." She frowned, mumbling, "And I am certain I would have remembered brushing shoulders with Jean Lafitte."

Captain Navarrone chuckled, and Cristabel was intrigued that she had amused him. Perhaps her wit could work to her advantage somehow.

"Now," he began, "I have told you my plans. Therefore, reveal to me what you know about your abduction and placement aboard the Chichester. If you do, perhaps you will be returned to your *step*-father's home as virginally unspoiled as you left it."

His threat reduced her confidence once more and she stepped back from him.

"I have told you everything I know of assurity," she said. "I was taken and put aboard an enemy vessel. They would tell me nothing. That is all I can tell you."

The pirate's eyes narrowed. "All you *can* tell me…or all you *will* tell me?" he growled striding toward her.

"P-perhaps I am mistaken in thinking my step-father will not pay a ransom," she said, stepping further back from him. She had been too brazen in her defiance of the pirate. Suddenly she thought that if he believed William Pelletier would indeed ransom her, then perhaps Navarrone the Blue Blade would not ravage her. "Perhaps he will ransom me…for my mother's sake…if I am unharmed."

Captain Navarrone's chest rose to its full breadth as he inhaled deeply. His eyes narrowed—he studied her for a moment.

"You're still keeping secrets," he said. "Yet I will allow you a measure of time to consider your situation. Cooperate with me…tell me all you know of the British ship, Chichester…of your suspicions where your step-father is concerned…for I know you own them…it is obvious. Thus, reveal your full knowledge to me…as well as a sampling of your feminine charms perhaps…as thanks for my rescuing you from the appetites of Bully Booth…and I may return you to New Orleans…essentially unscathed."

"I have told you everything I know," Cristabel insisted.

He was upon her at once—her chin gripped firm in his hand.

"No! You have not!" he roared. His eyes flamed with fury—his teeth clenched tight. "Do not lie to me again, love. Do not lie to me again."

Even for the discomfort caused by his strong hand at her face, Cristabel quickly reached around him to where the dagger lay sheathed at his back. Drawing it quickly, she gasped when his free hand deftly took hold of her wrist, causing her to drop the dagger once more.

"And pray…" he growled, "cease in trying to best me. If you persist…it will not go well for you." With one final glare and a slight push, he released her. He retrieved the dagger, returning it to its scabbard at his back. "Now change your clothes, girl. I'll not have you dropping dead of pneumonia before my purposes in rescuing you are satisfied…all of them," he growled at her, turning and striding toward the cabin door.

"Baskerville!" he shouted as he opened the door.

"Yes, Cap'n?" the quartermaster asked, nodding as he appeared in the doorway.

27

"Keep the wench guarded," Navarrone ordered. "No food or drink until I give the order."

"Yes, Cap'n," Baskerville said. "James Kelley!" he shouted.

Captain Navarrone left the cabin. Cristabel heard his heavy footsteps ascend to the quarterdeck overhead.

"Aye, Mister Baskerville?" a young man said, appearing behind the Quatermaster.

"Cap'n wants his cabin door guarded, lad," Baskerville instructed. "You're to keep the woman inside. All right, boy?"

"Aye, Mister Baskerville," the young man said. The boy was small, blonde—Cristabel thought he could not be more than fourteen. She thought it sad that his life was in ruins. After all, he was so youthful—and already mixed in with pirates.

"Enjoy yourself, lassie," Baskerville said to Cristabel. "At least yar not lingering in the likes of Bully Booth's cabin." He closed the door then and she heard him give the boy named James Kelley further instructions.

Cristabel was frightened—indeed she was terrified! However, instead of allowing fear to conquer her, she determined to let indignation and hope be her allies.

"Bloody pirate," she grumbled as she stripped off her boots and stockings. Angrily she threw one sopping boot at the door. Yet, the boy guarding her did not even glance back through the small window in the door to look at her. "Arrogant blackguard!"

Quickly she stripped herself of Captain Navarrone's heavy, blue brocaded vest. She began to discard it to the floor—but paused.

"Hmm," she said, holding the knee-length vest up in front of her. She studied it for a moment. "Excellent stitching…beautiful brocade. A very fine garment, indeed…and no doubt it owns a corresponding frock coat…both very costly, I'm sure. Hmmm."

Walking to a nearby porthole, Cristabel opened it, stuffing the opulent brocaded vest out to tumble into the sea. She closed the porthole, dusting her hands together with satisfaction, and returned to changing her sopping undergarments for the dry ones Captain Navarrone had supplied.

"And there goes yar finest vest, Cap'n…swept away on the waves of the sea," Baskerville chuckled, leaning on the quarterdeck railing and gazing into the sea below.

Navarrone growled. "I wonder that the British did not keelhaul her. She's a stubborn little vixen."

"Indeed," Baskerville agreed. "It takes a strong will to risk provoking Navarrone the Blue Blade."

"She only possesses the will of defiance because she is an innocent," Navarrone said. "She has heard tales of pirates no doubt…tales of sword play, treasure and rum. Yet, I know…I know she has no conception of what her fate would most assuredly have been at the hands of Bully Booth and his men. She could not know…else she would not be so stubborn…so brave in defiance of me."

"Aye, Cap'n," Baskerville said, nodding his concurrence. "Aye."

Navarrone felt the familiar nausea rise from his gut to burn in his throat. He ground his teeth and turned, striding to the helm.

"We sail for New Orleans, Baskerville," he snarled. "Signal Fergus to keep the Chichester at a close distance…port." Shaking his head he added, "I will discover what is amiss…whether treason, treachery or trifle! And while we're about it…we will venture with Governor Claiborne and become even richer men!"

"Aye, Cap'n," Baskerville said. "All hands to the deck and rigging! We sail for New Orleans and glorious bounty!"

As Baskerville barked orders to the men, Navarrone stood at the helm. Closing his eyes a moment, he tried to vanquish the heinous vision from his mind. It was not the ever lingering sensation of the cat on his back that anguished him—not the beating, the starvation, nor the memory of the stench of the hold. Rather it was the vision of Vienne that haunted him—his beautiful Vienne. It was the vision of her being taken that devoured his mind—the vision and the knowledge—the knowledge he owned of all she had endured before her merciless, savage death.

"Vienne," he breathed as he took the wheel. He glanced aft—to the Chichester behind—and hatred boiled in his veins. He loathed the British for their part in it all—and for a moment, considered setting the seven surviving British sailors adrift. Let the elements take them! Let Bully

Booth's crew torture, flog or keelhaul them! They deserved no better treatment! They were the enemy!

Still, for all his rage, Navarrone knew there was treason afoot. Someone was bartering with the British—and the girl—with Cristabel Albay. Navarrone had never asked the vixen her name—for he knew she would simply have lied to him. Yet, Cristabel Albay—it was the name on the trunk his men had found aboard the Chichester—her trunk.

"Cristabel Albay," he mumbled. "Are you a victim...or a traitor?"

Navarrone sneered—infuriated—filled with hate. He would discover the truth concerning the bloody British Chichester and its passenger, Cristabel—even if he had to drive his own hand down her throat and rip the truth from her lungs!

Cristabel stood before the looking glass secured to the cabin wall. She wondered what disease she might contract in using the bone comb she had found in Captain Navarrone's desk drawer. Yet there had been no evidence of lice among the teeth of it, and she could not endure matted hair. She was thankful the pirate had brought one of her long chemises. Perhaps her shoulders were bare—save her corset straps—but at least her feet and ankles were fairly covered. She wished there had been stockings included in the items Navarrone had allowed her. Yet, she was grateful to be dry and warm—and somewhat more modestly attired.

She heard his voice outside the cabin—heard Captain Navarrone speaking to the boy, James Kelley. A wave of sudden terror rippled through her and she dropped the comb. It clattered to the floor and she hurriedly retrieved it, tossing it to his desk top and raking a hand through her now dry, smoothed hair. Would he keep to his threats to sample her feminine charms? Would he truly return her to New Orleans? And what if her step-father would not pay ransom? What then?

Cristabel had no more time for thoughts—for Captain Navarrone burst in upon her in the next moment. He closed the door behind him and Cristabel stepped back. His presence filled the room as fully as breath filled the human bosom.

"You have had hours to consider your predicament," he said, striding toward her. "Therefore, being that you appear to be an intelligent young woman...will you now tell me all you know?"

"I-I have already told you all I know," she answered. "I have no more to tell."

"There is always more for the telling, love," he said. "I think you well know that." He cocked his handsome head to one side—considered her for a moment. "Are you not hungry? Do you not thirst? Reveal your secrets and I will have you fed and your thirst quenched."

It was not difficult for Cristabel to ignore the appetite in her stomach—yet her mouth was so in want of drink she could not swallow.

"I have no appetite in your presence," she bravely ventured.

She watched as the right corner of the pirate's mouth curled. His eyes narrowed and he approached. Cristabel stepped back from him, but his desk foiled her retreat.

"And what of thirst?" he asked, standing directly before her. He reached out raking a powerful hand through her hair from her temple back over the top of her head. "Is there nothing I can offer to quench your thirst? Is your mouth parched, love?" He bent toward her and in a lowered voice purely provocative in nature, mumbled, "For mine is moist...and will quite eagerly lend its moisture to yours."

Cristabel was breathless with fear—fear and something akin to elation—something she did not understand. Yet, she would not be bested by the pirate's use of intimidation and lewd coquetry.

"If that is the only choice you offer," she began. He grinned—yet she continued, "Then I will wait until I may quench my thirst with your blood!"

He continued to grin, however. "Ah, I think not, love. I think not," he said. "Hunger may not drive you mad...I see that in you. But thirst will, woman. Thirst will have you begging to tell me your secrets. That I promise."

He turned and strode from the room. "Give her nothing, James Kelley," he ordered the boy as he closed the door.

Cristabel attempted to moisten her burning lips and throat—but there was no saliva in her with which to dampen them. Captain Navarrone was right. She would succumb to him—reveal her suspicions regarding her step-father—else she would go mad!

Going to the chaise lounge, she sat—raking her trembling fingers through her long dark hair. Perhaps she had run the length of belligerence. Perhaps the only hope she now had was concurrence. Captain Navarrone

31

had not wounded or killed her, and he had not even made to ravage her—though pirates were notorious for ravaging innocent women. Yet, she well knew that had she remained in the clutches of the pirate, Bully Booth, she would surely have been dead already.

She thought then of Navarrone's obvious loathing for the British. Yet, her mind fought to believe a pirate could own loyalty to anyone or anything—especially a country. Still, it seemed his anger was provoked by thoughts of traitors and treason—and Cristabel knew no alliance with either. Thus, perhaps her best chance was to tell him her suspicions of William Pelletier, her step-father. Perhaps then, even if William did not pay the ransom Navarrone demanded—perhaps he would take mercy on her and release her all the same.

Cristabel's thirst was near excruciating! She wondered that she was not so thirsty a moment before Captain Navarrone had inquired if she was so. She must find water. Yet, she knew water was a rare commodity on ships. Still, she must quench her thirst before her mind could settle on what to do further—on whether to barter with the pirate captain or continue to defy him.

Desperately she rose from the chaise and began to look about the room. She had already perused the captain's belongings—his comb, his clothing—several drawers in his desk that held nothing but meaningless trinkets. However, as her gaze fell to a small wooden crate in one corner of the room, her hopes brightened—for she recognized the markings on the box.

"Oh please...please let it be," she breathed as she went to the crate. Quickly, she removed the lid—near giggled with triumphant delight as she saw what lay within. "Marie Blanchard Biscuits!" she said, recognizing the small tin of sweet biscuits. "Complete with an accompanying bottle of rum," she whispered pulling the bottle from the crate.

Cristabel had never drunk rum—nor beer or port. Still, she knew Navarrone would not allow her water—even if The Merry Wench had it in her stores. She must not faint of parchedness—and she must survive the nights and days aboard the The Merry Wench if she hoped to be ransomed.

Thus, with continued existence as her ambition, Cristabel nourished herself with Captain Navarrone's stash of Marie Blanchard Biscuits and a bottle of pirate rum.

"Aye, Cap'n," James Kelley whispered. "But how long would you have me wait before I am to pretend to slip her the flask of water?"

"No more than half the hour, James," Navarrone answered. "I do not want her thirsting long, yet she must not know I ordered it. She must think you are disobedient to me...giving her water without my knowledge."

"Aye, Cap'n," James said, smiling.

Navarrone patted the boy on the shoulder—though he thought for a moment that tousling his fair hair might be a more appropriate gesture. James Kelley was so young—too young for the life of a pirate.

"Good lad," Navarrone said. Handing James the flask of water, he strode away. The men must be told of what little he had learned from Cristabel Albay. All must be prepared before they reached the bay—for this was not to be the normal visit to Governor Claiborne to settle shares of booty. No. There was far more to this visit to New Orleans—and the crew of The Merry Wench must be at the ready.

# Chapter Three

Captain Navarrone allowed an hour to expire before returning to his cabin. His thoughts were that the girl would have had the water James Kelley had provided and would perhaps be hungry enough to reveal more information to him. He well-believed she knew little about her abduction—yet he sensed she owned suspicions of who had orchestrated it. He further surmised that whoever the blackguard was who had her taken aboard the Chichester, was involved in treasonous activities. Thus, he wanted to know more about Cristabel Albay and her suspicions—for she indeed seemed an intelligent and observant woman—very beautiful as well.

Navarrone paused outside his cabin door to speak with James Kelley.

"Did you give her the flask of water as I asked?" he inquired of the lad.

"Aye, Cap'n," James whispered. "She thanked me for it, sir…said she'd be saving it for a moment of desperation."

Navarrone frowned. "Moment of desperation? But I left her already thirsting."

"She was quite happy to see it, Cap'n," James explained. "She's a very merry sort of woman, isn't she?"

"Merry?" Navarrone asked. "What do you mean, merry, James?"

"Smiling and giggling, she was, sir…like she was off on a holiday, instead of locked up in your cabin as your prisoner." James smiled, adding, "And she offered me one of them biscuits you left for her, sir…them Marie Blanchard ones. I thought it was right kind of her to offer."

"Marie Blanchard biscuits?" Navarrone mumbled. "I did not give anything to…" He winced with realizing his own stupidity. Of course! The crate of Marie Blanchard Biscuit tins and rum Governor Claiborne

35

had gifted him weeks before. He had placed it in his cabin upon sailing from New Orleans and never more thought of it.

"I fear the little vixen has bested me, James Kelley," Navarrone growled as he opened the cabin door. "I just hope the rum doesn't kill her."

"Captain!" the girl cheerily greeted as Navarrone entered his cabin, securing the door behind him. "Good evening, you naughty, naughty pirate!" The girl sat on the chaise—a bottle of rum in one hand. Her cheeks and nose were rosy already, and as she raked a dainty hand through the softness of her long hair, she winked at him.

Sloshed—the girl was entirely inebriated. Navarrone's heart near skipped a beat when he saw she had consumed at least a third of the bottle of rum. It was no doubt she did not indulge in spirits as habit—thus it was fortunate he had not tarried in returning. Had she consumed the entire contents of the bottle, he may well have returned to find her dead!

"I see you found the rum," he said, striding to her.

She wrinkled her nose—grimaced and nodded. "Vile stuff it is." She shrugged. "Yet, what was I to do? For you refused to offer me anything to drink."

Cristabel drew the bottle to her lips, yet Navarrone snatched the rum from her.

"Rum is not for those of a tender constitution, love," he said. "And I see you've been into my tin of biscuits as well."

"Aye, Captain," she giggled. "I adore Marie Blanchard biscuits. My mother and I often stroll down near the river to sample the biscuits and sweets in her shop. She's very old, you know…Marie Blanchard." She sighed with reminiscing.

"Is she?" he mumbled.

Navarrone felt the corner of his mouth curve into an amused grin. She had found one of his discarded shirts and put it on over her corset and chemise. He was pleased in her efforts to find means of defying him. He had not allowed her a dress—thus, she had obviously decided to best him by donning one of his shirts for modesty. Naturally, it was too large for her—sagged off one smooth, porcelain shoulder—hung near to her knees.

"Why, yes," Cristabel answered. "Mother says the woman must be near seventy years." She winked at him once more, adding, "It must be why her biscuits are so delectable…eons of practice."

"Indeed," Navarrone said. Again he pulled a chair from its secured position and placed it before her. Sitting down, he leaned toward her and said, "You say you and your mother often visit Marie Blanchard's shop."

"Yes," she said. "Quite often."

Navarrone's eyes narrowed. Marie Blanchard was not only a skilled baker of biscuits, but a loyal patriot. The fact that Cristabel and her mother often visited Marie Blanchard greatly intrigued him.

"Tell me about your mother," he begged. "She sounds like a good woman."

Cristabel nodded—her balance wavering slightly, even for the fact she sat on the chaise.

"My mother is an angel, Captain," she sighed. "She so loved my father. He was wounded fighting the bloody British the first time, you know…but survived to marry my mother. She was much younger than he, of course…but they were so in love." She smiled—exhaled a wistful sigh. "Her name is Lisette…Lisette Ines Chachere Albay. Isn't it a lovely name?"

"Very lovely," Navarrone agreed. "Yet, would she not be Mrs. Pelletier now?"

Cristabel's smile faded. She frowned—her lovely brow crinkling with disgust.

"Yes," she admitted. "Lisette Ines Chachere Albay Pelletier. I loathe William Pelletier. I do not know why Mother ever married him. I suppose she felt an obligation."

"An obligation?" Navarrone inquired.

She sighed. "You know," she began—her expression that of irritation. "When Father died…William Pelletier purchased our house in South Carolina. Mother said we would have been driven to destitution without his help."

Navarrone's eyes narrowed. "I see," he said. And he did. Cristabel's mother had found means to take care of herself and her daughter—by marrying a wealthy New Orleans politician.

"But I do not wish to speak about William Pelletier," Cristabel grumbled. "The thought of him causes my stomach to churn."

Navarrone smiled. He well-doubted it was thoughts of William Pelletier causing Cristabel's stomach to churn. He only hoped he could glean a bit more information from her before the rum she had consumed found her unconscious.

"Would you speak of pirates?" he inquired.

"Pirates?" she asked, her pretty brow furrowing with curiosity. "What might I know that you do not already know when it comes to pirates, Captain Narr…Narravone?"

He chuckled—amused by the easy manner the rum had washed over her.

"Oh, I know plenty of famous pirates," he began, "Of Jean Lafitte, Bully Booth, Henry the Merciless, and the like."

"Narravone the Blue Blade?" she asked, smiling and winking at him.

"Yes," he chuckled. "Certainly Navarrone the Blue Blade."

"Then why ask me about pirates?"

"Because I am a pirate…and I think you own a knowledge of pirates that I do not."

Cristabel's eyes narrowed as she studied him a moment. "How long do you spend in grooming your mustache and goatee of a morning?" she asked. Reaching out, she pressed her index finger to the small triangle of whiskers beneath his lower lip. "It all must be quite time-consuming…for it is perfectly manicured."

Brushing her finger from his chin (for her touch had caused goose flesh to ripple over his arms), Navarrone continued in leading her into possibly illuminating conversation.

"The pirates you have knowledge of that I do not…those who took you from your home in New Orleans and sailed you to the Chichester…"

"They weren't pirates, silly man," she said, shaking her head with exasperation.

"Who were they then? If not pirates? British?"

Cristabel Albay's soft, berry pink lower lip began to quiver. Navarrone saw moisture rise to her eyes.

"I-I don't want to speak of it," she whispered.

"Of course. Of course," he said. He was in danger of losing her reciprocity. He must be patient—glean what he could before she realized she was offering information to him she might not share when clear-minded once more.

"What would you like to speak of, love?" he offered. "Anything at all. What would you have us discuss with one another?"

Instantly, her frown curved into a smile—the tears in her eyes retreating.

"Anything?" she asked.

"Yes." He nodded his assurance, adding, "In fact, it does not take so long as you think to maintain well-groomed facial hair."

She giggled and he was pleased—she was with him once more.

Her eyes narrowed and she studied him a moment—still smiling. "Is it true you seduced the Governor's wife in South Carolina?" she asked.

"The truth?" he countered.

"Yes," she assured him—though he thought she looked somewhat uncertain—as if she dreaded hearing the answer.

"Then, no," he confessed.

She sighed with visible relief. "Oh, I like that answer," she whispered to herself.

"Do you have more questions for me?" he prodded.

"Will you answer each one truthfully?"

"Yes," he chuckled. "You have my word."

"Have you seduced many women?" she asked.

"Seduced them to what, love?" he volleyed.

"To romance," she answered plainly.

Navarrone frowned—bewildered. "Romance? Do you mean to ask if I have seduced them to flirting...or do you mean to ask if I have seduced them into my bed?"

Cristabel gasped and Navarrone chuckled as she reached out, clamping a hand over his mouth.

"For shame, Captain!" she scolded in a whisper. "You must know I mean to flirting...to allowing you to steal a kiss." She frowned. "I would not like to think you would take women to your...to you otherwise."

He was flattered that she should be so sweet—so pure and, he sensed, somewhat jealous.

Removing her hand from his lips—though keeping it clasped in his—he answered, "I'm a pirate, love. Of course I've seduced women to...romance, as you put it."

"To kissing you?" she asked—concern still evident in her expression.

"To kissing me, yes," he said. She sighed—smiled with relief. He was glad—for he knew it was the answer she most wanted to hear.

"If I was not your prisoner," she began, "would you then try to seduce me to romance?"

He smiled. "Oh, most certainly, love," he admitted. "Most certainly."

She giggled—blushed—pulled her hand from his grasp.

"I've always dreamt of romance, you know," she sighed. "I suppose all women do." She frowned. "But I daily grow more doubtful of its existence." She was pensive and Navarrone sat silent—a feeling of sympathy for the fairer sex. "I've always thought it odd...the way God made women such creatures of the heart, when men are so very carnal in nature."

"Do you think all men are born without hearts in their breasts?" he asked. He thought of the pain in his own—of the agony of loss—of Vienne.

"No...but I think many are," she admitted. She smiled then. "Not my father, of course. He loved well. He loved me and he sorely loved my mother...I could see it in his eyes...in the way he touched her cheek. My mother knew romance...once. My father romanced her...but William Pelletier..." she shook her head, frowning once more. "He loves nothing...nothing but power and money." She looked at him—lowered her voice and began, "Do you know...the night I was taken...I thought perhaps he...that perhaps my step-father..."

She paused—bit her lower lip as if she was uncertain as to whether she should continue.

"You're a pirate, you know," she told him.

Navarrone understood at once. He was a blackguard—a man not to be trusted. She was reminding herself of this—not him.

"I am a pirate," he said, smiling at her. "And that is why you have so astounded me tonight."

"Astounded you?" she inquired.

40

"Yes, love," he told her. "For you hold your rum as well as any pirate." He could not help but grin—for the girl was as weak for the drink as a pirate was to wenching.

"I do?" she asked with obvious delight. She hiccoughed and he chuckled. "That's astosh-astoshining…for I've never drunk a drop before."

"No!" he exclaimed with dramatics. "Are you certain?"

She nodded, smiling. "Not a drop." She reached up, running her fingers through his hair—tugging at one strand at his forehead until it tumbled down over one eye. "Yes, indeed!" she said, gently slapping his cheek twice. "You are a handsome devil, are you not?"

He chuckled as she continued, "If I was a pirate wench and you came wenching into the inn one night…I might romance you first."

Though he smiled, Navarrone experienced an unsettling discomfort at her confession. She was his prisoner—possibly a traitor to the country. He could little afford to risk attachment to her of any sort.

"Now tell me, love," he began to prod, "tell me the tale of how you came to be aboard the Chichester."

Cristabel shrugged—sighed. "There's not so very much to tell, really" she slurred. "The men came for me, they took me…put me aboard the Shishester…" She winked at him and sighed, "And then you rescued me from that Bully Boof." She giggled. "He was a loathsome creature, was he not?"

"Yes, he was," Navarrone agreed—for it was true.

"His breath was effluvial…like rotting fish heads," she mumbled.

"You say men came for you…took you," he coaxed. "What men?"

She shrugged. "Men. Men are men. Aren't all men the same?" She winked at him, adding, "Except in your case."

Navarrone endeavored to ignore her growing flirtation. She was not in her right mind—nor was she the first pretty woman to compliment him.

"These men…were they British or American?" he asked.

"Men," she answered. "They all had gruff voices and Adam's apples at their throats. You know, Cap'n…men."

"Very well…they were men. Yet, think hard…were they British or American? You heard their voices…did they speak as American's or British?"

41

Cristabel frowned—obviously struggling to remember through the cloud of confusion the rum had caused in her mind.

"French!" she exclaimed, suddenly. "They spoke French...Acadian French."

Navarrone smiled and sighed, "Acadians. So...they were Americans."

"Americans that spoke French," Cristabel corrected.

"Not British," Navarrone mumbled. "Yet, they took you to a British ship. They were traitors."

"Or employed by traitors...mercenaries," she suggested, winking at him again.

"Yes. Perhaps employed by traitors." He smiled—for he admired the cunning she retained while sloshed by rum. "And they took you to..."

"To a boat!" she interrupted. She frowned—tears suddenly filling her eyes. She reached out and placed an unsteady hand on his forearm. Her touch was far too affecting—yet he attempted to ignore it. "They bound me...my hands at my wrists...my ankles." She gasped as an expression of true horror leapt to her face. "They touched my ankles!" she exclaimed in a whisper. She bit her lip—covered her mouth with one hand. "I am a ruined woman now!" she breathed as tears spilled from her eyes.

Navarrone's inclination was to laughter—but he would not glean information from her if he did not show pity.

"It was not your fault," he said, stifling a smile. "They were bad men."

"Worse than pirates," she told him. She shook her head. "Even pirates would not touch a woman's ankles!"

Navarrone ran a hand over his mustache and goatee to conceal his smile. "No. No I suppose not." He must distract her from her humiliation over her ankles having been sullied. "They took you then to a boat?"

"Yes," she said, brushing at her tears with the back of her hands. "And sailed out into the night."

"To meet the Chichester."

"Yes! The Shishester!" she confirmed. "It was swarming with those bloody British sailors!"

Navarrone bit his lip to keep from chuckling once more.

"Only the Shishester's captain spoke to me...no one else would," she continued. "He said very little...only that I should be well fed and watered…as if I were no more than a dog! Do I look like a dog to you, Captain?"

"No," Navarrone said. "Not in the least."

"He said we were sailing for the Empire…that I was to be taken there to wait."

"To wait for what? Ransom?"

She wept again—shaking her head. "I do not know. Only that I was to be taken to England to wait."

"To England to wait," Navarrone mumbled. He knew no more than when he had begun and frustration caused him to feel hot and angry. He pulled off his shirt, tossing it behind him to his berth. "To England to wait," he repeated—still thoughtful. Suddenly, something about her tale did strike his curiosity. "You say the men took you…how did they take you?"

She frowned—confused. "With their hands and lengths of rope," she said, rolling her eyes as if his question had been purely asinine.

Navarrone smiled—a breathy chuckle escaping him. "No, love…how did they so easily gain entrance into the house? Did you not tell me…before this…that they came into your step-father's house and took you?"

She nodded. "Yes. They came in and abducted me."

"No one heard them enter? No one sounded a warning? Does not your step-father have servants about at night?" he asked.

"Of course." she grumbled.

"So these men simply came into the house and took you? Did you scream or cry out for help?"

Again the girl rolled her eyes with exasperation. "Of course, you ninny!"

"And no one came to aid you?"

"No one. Naturally, the abductors promptly gagged me for screaming."

"But yet, you did cry out," he reminded her, "and no one came to you."

"No. No one." She shook her head and giggled. "As you know I've suspected all along that my step-father, the gentleman William Pelletier, had something to do with it all. He loathes me, you see."

"Why is that?" Navarrone asked—wildly intrigued with her revelation.

"I suppose for the sake that I loathe him," she giggled.

"And you are sure you were not to be ransomed?" he asked.

"Quite certain, my bonny pirate captain," she slurred, again winking at him. "I heard one of those bloody British sailors inquire of the Sh-shishester's captain. 'Is she to be ransomed?' the sailor asked. 'No. She is to be taken to London…to wait.' That was all I ever heard concerning myself."

Navarrone inhaled a deep breath—exhaled it slowly. "A wealthy politician's daughter is taken from his home…without one alarm having been raised."

"*Step*-daughter," Cristabel corrected him.

"Step-daughter," he said. She nodded with approval. "Abducted, taken out into the Gulf and boarded onto an enemy merchant vessel."

"You forgot to mention that I was violated," she whispered.

"Violated?" he growled. He could feel the rage welling up within him. "They…they violated you?"

She nodded. "Remember?" she asked. Then lowering her voice, tears welling in her eyes, she added, "My ankles were touched."

Navarrone sighed. "Oh, yes. Yes, I forgot. Your ankles were touched."

"Y-you're not planning to…to touch my ankles are you, Captain?" she wept, suddenly fearful. "It's not why you rescued me from Bully Boof's clutches is it? To violate me by touching my ankles?" She brushed tears from her cheeks and again, Navarrone had to struggle to keep from bursting into laughter.

"No, love," he assured her. "When I flung us both from the deck of The Screaming Witch and into the sea, it was not your ankles I was thinking of."

"Oh, good," she breathed—and he was amused by her profound relief. She was silent a moment and then began to study a ring she wore on her right ring finger. "I feel impressed to give you this, Captain Narr-Narravone," she said pulling the ring from her finger and offering it to him. "It must serve as my thanks to you…for saving me from the clutches of Bully Boof. I am surprised you did not plunder it before this."

Navarrone had indeed noticed the large ring on her right ring finger. It was a valuable piece—fashioned of gold and diamonds. Yet he and his men did not plunder from civilians as a rule.

44

"Do not thank me for taking you from Bully Booth's ship to mine," he told her. "We pirates are akin…the lot of us."

She smiled at him—wagged a scolding index finger. "But that is not true, now is it? Did you not hear your quartermaster tell me that it would be far better to be ravaged by you, than it would have been to be ravaged by Bully Boof?"

"Yes…but," he began.

"Well, then…shhh…let me tell you a secret, Captain," she said lowering her voice. "I'm certain he was correct. You are ever so much more handsome and virile than that heinous Bully Boof! But do not tell yourself that I told you that…it's a secret that only I can own."

He chuckled as she took his palm, pressing the ring into his hand.

She began to weep once more then, and Navarrone's chivalry and guilt heightened.

"So take the ring, pirate. I want you to have it. It means little to me anyway…only a betrothal gift from my fiancé."

"Fiancé?" he asked—astonished. "You are engaged to be married?" If she was to be wed, why then did she not wear the ring on her left hand as was tradition?

"Yes. To Richard," she sighed.

"Richard? Richard who?"

Cristabel puffed a breath of exasperation and rolled her eyes. "Richard. Richard my fiancé," she answered.

"Tell me about Richard," he urged.

Cristabel shook her head—as if disgusted. "He is my fiancé and he's ever so irksome."

"And yet you are betrothed to him?"

"It was not my choice…not really."

"Tell me. Whose choice was it?" he asked—but she melted into tears.

"I feel so hopeless suddenly, Captain…so fearful," she wept. "As if…as if I'll never feel joy again…as if the sun will not rise on the morrow."

Navarrone exhaled a breath of self-disgust. He was a vile devil to trick her so—to take advantage of her intoxication. He silently cursed his father for the conscience and silver streak of chivalry he had inherited from him.

"The sun will rise on the morrow, love," he said, cupping her fair, soft cheek in one hand. "Yet, I fear you might feel ill as the day dawns even so."

She gazed at him a moment and Navarrone felt his heart begin to hammer—his mouth begin to water. She was far too tempting and vulnerable. Her eyes were glassed and he could see the weariness mingling with the rum. She would soon be overwhelmed and unconscious.

Unexpectedly, she leapt up from the chaise—frantic!

"My ankles!" she cried. "They're entirely exposed! Any man may touch them! Any man!" Sobbing, she fell to her knees. Placing her head on his thigh she wept, "Oh, help me Captain! Please! Don't let those men touch my ankles! I cannot endure it again!"

Navarrone was unsettled. He wondered how the girl could endure abduction, kidnapping, being put aboard a vessel of men bound for England, and falling into the hands of blood-thirsty, lustful pirates, only to worry about her ankles being touched.

"Here, love," he said, slipping the ring she had given him onto his smallest finger and stripping off his boots. "Here. Wear these. Your ankles will be well protected this night."

She smiled and whispered, "Thank you, Captain Narravone," as he helped her pull his boots on where she sat on the floor. "Thank you," she repeated as he helped her to stand. "I feel quite protected now."

"Good. Now tell me of this Richard," he said.

The ship pitched slightly to one side however, and the girl lost her balance. Navarrone caught her easily enough in his arms and she smiled at him.

"Remember, Captain," she whispered. "Do not tell yourself that I would rather be ravaged by you than...than...whoever that other pirate was. Keep it secret." Raising an index finger to her lips she slurred, "Sshhh."

Navarrone swept her into the cradle of his arms then as unconsciousness claimed her.

The Blue Blade shook his head as he placed the intoxicated woman on his berth. For a woman to be so concerned over the touching of her ankles—a woman who was brave enough to have weathered what Cristabel Albay had weathered—it was inconceivable that such a trifle should worry her. Awkwardly, he removed his strewn clothing from beneath her—laid her out straight and as comfortable as he could. It was not very difficult—for she was limp as a cloth doll.

He chuckled as he studied her a moment—his shirt enveloping her—his large boots on such tiny feet. Her hair was spread over the pillow and linens like midnight waves of the sea and he smiled as she suddenly sighed. He would fetch another chamber pot for her—in case she woke to the contents of her rum-filled stomach manifesting itself all over the floor. He frowned, angry with himself for leading her to believe he would truly have denied her food and drink. If she survived her encounter with the rum, he would approach her more agreeable in order to glean information. Such a courageous and beautiful woman deserved better treatment than he had exacted thus far—any woman did for that matter.

Navarrone thought of Vienne and the ache in his heart caused him to double over a moment—to gasp for breath.

Glancing to the portrait hanging near the cabin door, Navarrone whispered, "I do not ask your forgiveness, Vienne. I am not deserving of it. Thus, do not forgive me…never forgive me…tell the angels I do not merit any mercy."

He glowered at Cristabel Albay, peacefully asleep on his berth. Mercy from the angels or not—forgiveness from his angel Vienne or not—yet he would not allow traitors and treason to linger in New Orleans. If the pretty wench he had found in the clutches of Bully Booth owned some knowledge that would lead him to one traitor or more—and his guts pure boiled with the sense that she did—then he would retrieve it from her.

Growling with self-disgust and frustration, he retrieved a discarded shirt from his desk. As he slipped it over his head, he frowned, however—glancing about the room. Navarrone the Blue Blade kept more shirts about him than the average pirate. As he looked to his clothing spread over the floor, the chaise, his desk—he realized the girl must have tried every shirt he possessed before settling on one to wear for modesty. Striding across the room, he settled himself before the door—rested his arms on his knees.

"Bothersome little vixen that you are, Cristabel Albay," he grumbled. "I was looking forward to those biscuits."

# Chapter Four

The sunlight seemed to scorch her eyes—even for the fact they were yet closed. Cristabel was certain the hammer and anvil causing the throbbing ache in her head were indeed penned up inside it. Her throat burned—nausea engulfed her stomach—her limbs were so weak, she could hardly move. Had she been beaten? Tortured? Was she ill—poisoned? As her mind struggled to comprehend the miserable state of her being, Cristabel vaguely remembered Captain Navarrone's threat to deprive her of food and drink until she confessed all she knew.

An image of a crate—of a tin of Maria Blanchard Biscuits—mingled with a vision of the young pirate James Kelley. Had he, in secret, gifted her a flask of water—or had she dreamed it? She tried to move—for her lips felt parched—her throat continuing to burn—and she was desperate for water. Yet her arms and legs felt as if they were made of lead! The excruciating pain in her head was near unbearable, and when she opened her eyes, the light caused them to tear.

"The best remedy is to take your time, love."

The pirate's voice echoed though her mind—causing the brutal aching in her head to increase. Tears escaped her eyes, spilling over her cheeks.

Cristabel opened one eye—a tiny slit—to see Captain Navarrone hunkered down next to his berth on which she lay.

"You did this to me," she breathlessly accused.

"No, love," he said. He shrugged then, adding, "Well, perhaps in a manner. But you are the one whose belligerence found you sipping at a bottle of rum."

"Rum?" Cristabel breathed. "What are you saying?"

"You went and got yourself sloshed, love," he answered. He was grinning with amusement and she wanted to slap him—but she lacked the strength.

"You did not beat me into feeling this way?" she asked.

He shook his head—chuckled. "No. You did this to yourself."

Cristabel then owned a rather misty memory—a bottle of rum—in the crate with the tin of biscuits.

"I-I have never had a drink of it before," she said. "I did not think it would be so...so miserably affecting...even for it being so loathsome to swallow."

The handsome pirate sighed. "Most of us learn a hard lesson or two. Sometimes we make a wrong choice and there's not so much harm done." He frowned, adding, "More often, one decision can change the entire course of a life. You remember that, love...before you take to drinking rum again."

"Lessons in morality from a pirate?" she grumbled. Even the sound of her own voice increased the pain in her head.

"Lessons in morality are of value no matter where they come from," he said.

He took hold of her arms at her shoulders and she meant to struggle—but she could not. "Here now," he said, pulling her to a sitting position. "Sit up and we'll get some food into you. Water, too. It will do you good."

"Ow!" she moaned as the hammering in her head augmented. A wave of nausea overwhelmed her, and she feared whatever contents were in her stomach, might make an appearance out through her mouth. "I'm sick!" she sobbed.

"There you are, then," Navarrone said, placing a pot on her lap.

"A chamber pot?" she whispered as heaving nearly overtook her.

"Not to worry...we scalded it."

Cristabel looked beyond the chamber pot in her lap—to the black boots projecting from her knees where her calves and feet should be. She

50

wiggled her toes and was disturbed to find that she did, indeed, wear a pair of pirate boots.

"No doubt your feet were cold," Captain Navarrone offered.

"Yours?" she asked, nodding toward the boots.

The pirate studied the boots a moment. "It would seem so," he answered.

Cristabel looked at her hands—for they were trembling and somewhat numb. It was then she noticed the far-too-long sleeves at her arms—the lacings at her bosom where her only her chemise and corset should be. She gasped as realization washed over. She wore his shirt?

"Yours?" she breathed—more tears escaping her eyes. "Oh no!"

"Correct," Navarrone said. "Apparently you were in need of further attire…being that I kept yours from you. That is all…nothing more to it than that."

"Swear it!" she begged.

"I swear it," he assured her.

Still she wept. "But you're a pirate. I cannot trust your swearing."

"Oh, when it comes to my swearing, love…believe me…you can trust in it," he chuckled.

Cristabel frowned—suspicious of her captor. He seemed a great deal more congenial in manner than he had the previous day. Yet she could not fathom why.

"You shared a great deal with me last night, love," he said, rising to his feet.

"I did?" she asked—tremulous with dread.

"Information, girl. Merely information." He smiled and she was angry with him for finding entertainment in her misery.

There was a knock on the cabin door.

"Enter," Navarrone said.

"Cook sent the eggs, Cap'n…and quite a pile of bacon," James Kelley said as he entered carrying a plate heaping with food in one hand—a large tankard in the other. "A bit of fresh water, as well."

"You're fortunate the Chichester had fresh stores, girl," Captain Navarrone said. "Else you'd have nothing but hard tack to eat…being that you devoured my treasured tin of Marie Blanchard Biscuits."

51

"You threatened me with starvation and thirst," Cristabel managed. She watched as James Kelley placed the plate of food on the berth next to her—handed the tankard of water to his Captain.

"Thank you, James," Navarrone said.

"Aye, Cap'n," James Kelley said, smiling at his leader. "Good luck, miss," the lad added to Cristabel before turning and leaving the room.

"I did threaten you with starvation and thirst," Captain Navarrone admitted. He grinned. "Though if you remember...I likewise offered to quench your thirst myself. There was no need to swim in the devil rum."

"I did not know I would be so...so overcome by so little," Cristabel confessed.

"Sometimes a spoonful of wickedness leads to a mountain of regret."

Cristabel grimaced—gritted her teeth, though it pained her head to do so. She glared at him—wondering what right a pirate had to churn ethical metaphors.

"Yes, I know...no more lessons in morality...especially preached by the immoral," Navarrone chuckled. "I'll leave you to your convalescing then. Eat a small portion of eggs then bacon. If your stomach does not refuse it...then eat more. Sip the water, as well. Do not be greedy." He set the tankard of water on the berth.

"I suppose I should thank you for not...for not..." she stammered.

"For not despoiling you when I had the chance last evening?" he finished for her. She frowned—unsettled—and he continued, "Fear not, love...the only parts of you revealed to me last night, were memories of your abduction and journey to the Chichester."

Cristabel gasped as Captain Navarrone then took hold of the heel of each boot she wore, stripping them from her feet in one swift motion. "Forgive me, but I am in need of my boots, wench." He chuckled. "Ah! How many times have I uttered that phrase, eh?"

"You're vile," Cristabel growled with disgust.

"Oh, you have no idea, love," he said, pulling on the boots. "Hmm," he hummed, looking at her. "Fancy that...they're still warm."

Perhaps he was not so congenial after all—still a vulgar pirate—only less ill-tempered.

"Now, eat up, love," he said, striding for the door. "For you and I have matters to discuss before we reach New Orleans. Though you revealed much last night, you are still keeping secrets…and I mean to harvest them from you." He paused—glowering at her over one shoulder. "By whatever means necessary."

Captain Navarrone closed the door and Cristabel melted into sobbing.

಄

By the warm, orange light in the cabin, Cristabel knew she had been asleep for hours. Very groggy and still weak, Cristabel sat up. As full consciousness was hers, she yet paused—remembering the miserable state of her being when last she had awakened. After a moment, however, she began to feel that her head did not ache so painfully as it had—that she did not feel overwhelmed by nausea. Carefully, she moved to stand—bracing herself against the wall with one hand for a moment—uncertain as to how long her legs would support her. When she did not collapse, she was reassured.

The most vile taste lingered in her mouth, and she remembered the tankard of water. She hoped she had not already drunk it all. She glanced about for the tankard, surprised to see a small glass vial sitting on the floor next to the tankard. Picking up the vial she removed its lid and was immediately met with the strong, rather frosty scent of peppermint.

"Peppermint oil," she whispered—and she could not help smiling—for Captain Navarrone had proved his intelligence once more. Peppermint oil was rare—wildly expensive—and very effective in treating nausea and ailments of the stomach and bowels. Cristabel knew the vile taste lingering in her mouth would also be vanquished with a drop of the oil derived from the leaves of a species of herb plant. Carefully, she tipped the vial, allowing two drops of the oil to alight on her finger.

Placing her finger to her tongue she smiled and sighed, "Mmm!" Lifting the tankard lid, she allowed several drops of peppermint oil to mix with the water it contained. Gripping the tankard handle, she swirled the water and oil a moment before drinking of its heavenly refreshment.

Cristabel sipped the peppermint-laced water as she combed her hair with Captain Navarrone's bone comb. She removed the pirate's shirt she'd slept in, straightened her chemise and corset, and even dabbed some of the water from the tankard beneath her eyes and on her neck to freshen herself. Within half the hour, Cristabel felt much recovered. She likewise considered that it might be best to dwindle of thirst before ever pilfering

53

rum again. It was no wonder rum was referred to as the demon drink. Cristabel was inwardly disgusted with herself for owning such ignorance— in owning such thorough belligerence that she had attempted to best Captain Navarrone by drinking rum when he had threatened to let her linger in thirsting.

She thought again of his threats—as well as his vile offering to quench her thirst with the moisture of his own.

"Blackguard," she mumbled. Yet, in the next moment, she wondered how many pirate wenches had known such a manner of thirst quenching from him. "Filthy pirate!" she exclaimed to the air.

Cristabel went to a porthole near the berth—opened it and inhaled a breath of salty sea air. She had survived her first night as captive aboard The Merry Wench, and it was more than many men had done.

She frowned—remembering then that Navarrone had claimed she had revealed information to him—information regarding her abduction and journey to the Chichester. She tried to remember exactly what she had told him—what had transpired the night before—but she could not. There were only wisps of memory—and those were clouded and nonsensical.

Navarrone had promised he would return to extract further information from her, and Cristabel knew she must own far more wisdom in dealing with her captor than she had previously. Thus, she contemplated— reviewed the events that now found her, yet alive, aboard The Merry Wench and on her way back to New Orleans.

The abduction was terrifying! In fact, Cristabel mused that enduring abduction was most likely why she was not as astonished as she perhaps should be at lingering in the company of pirates. Strangers had come in the middle of the night, dragged her from her bed, bound her, gagged her and carried her to a small boat. As remembered fear began to wash over her, she chose not to linger on those moments—but to think instead of her time aboard the Chichester.

"Are you feeling better then?"

The sound of his voice startled her. Still, she looked to him, feigning courage—as ever she did. Oh, but he was handsome! A weak-minded maiden might well be seduced by his physical allure alone. Cristabel was thankful she was not a weak-minded maiden—though she further mused that were he not a pirate—were he a gentleman—she might allow herself a morsel of weak-mindedness. She gritted her teeth—inwardly scolding herself for thinking any good thoughts of a pirate.

"Yes," she admitted. "And thank you for the peppermint."

He nodded. He then turned and called out, "James Kelley…bring the trunk."

Cristabel watched as James Kelley and another member of the crew, carried in the trunk she recognized as being her own. She looked to the pirate captain and he nodded to her once more. Thus, she made her decision. In that very instant, she chose to be compatible with the pirate—not combative. After all, had he wanted her dead, he would have killed her already. Had he wanted to ravage her, he would likewise have ravaged her already. Therefore, in those brief moments, Cristabel Albay began to believe that perhaps she did know something of worth to Captain Navarrone. Furthermore, if she did own some knowledge he desired to glean from her, it may well be the further saving of her life.

James Kelley smiled at Cristabel before taking his leave, and she sensed he was a kind sort of boy. After all, he had also in secret slipped her a flask of water the night before. She thought him brave—for he had defied his captain's orders—risked a no doubt harsh reprimand in the least.

Captain Navarrone closed the cabin door, then turned to her and said, "I am allowing you to have your things."

"May I dress?" she asked. Oh, she would not be combative—but she would not be too demure and agreeable—lest he think she was weak.

She felt a blush rise to her cheeks as Captain Navarrone cocked his head to one side—studying the length of her.

"You are dressed, love," he said. "As modest as any other woman of my acquaintance. No need to cause yourself discomfort in this balmy air by adding another layer of attire."

Cristabel must proceed with care—this she sensed. She must not attempt to best him in constancy—yet she could not forever lean to forfeit.

"You make a point," she said. "The air is balmy…and you are used to women donning less attire. Furthermore, I do not sense that you plan to allow me to leave this room in the near future…thus I will remain comfortable as I am."

Cristabel was far from comfortable lingering in the presence of a man (any man) dressed only in her undergarments. Still, she would not allow him to know he yet intimidated her. Even for the intoxication that had overtaken her from drinking the rum—even for the weakness and vulnerable state it had forced her to—Navarrone knew he could not easily bully her into obeying his will. She must keep the pretense that she would not be bullied.

"Still, I would like my hairbrush," she said, going to her trunk. "Since you are allowing me the freedom of accessing my things."

"Of course," he said. He stood near her, watching as she opened the trunk.

As she lifted the trunk's lid—as she saw the ransacked state of its contents—she sighed, "I see you have already taken inventory here."

"We took inventory of everything we brought aboard from the Chichester," he said. The right corner of his mouth curved. "Though admittedly, I did not trust that you might try to kill me with some feminine article buried in its belly. Thus, I took the liberty of making certain there were no sharp items within."

"Well, it's certainly obvious pirates do not own the organizational concerns or care for clothing and delicates that British sailors do," she said. "All my things were perfectly ordered...all my clothing well-folded when I first opened the trunk aboard the Chichester."

Navarrone frowned. He thought of the tale of her abduction—the one she had shared so openly while intoxicated the night before.

"You say...all your things were in order?" he asked. "The clothes neatly folded?"

"Yes," she said—and he saw the bewilderment on her pretty face.

"Yet you told me it was not the British who took you from your home...but men speaking French...Acadians," he said. "Mercenaries would not pause to pack a trunk...especially with care." He saw the understanding begin to wash over her. "The trunk was..."

"Prepared before I was taken," she finished.

"Cristabel Desiree Albay...you are aligned with traitors," Captain Navarrone said.

She gasped. "I never revealed my name to you...nor am I aligned with traitors!" she insisted. Doubt puckered her brow then, and he knew she

56

was thinking she had revealed her identity the night before—influenced by the devil's rum.

Navarrone pointed to the inside of the trunk's lid—to her name printed there. Her gaze followed his indication and she breathed a relieved sigh.

"Still, I am no traitor," she reiterated. "I have told you before that I…"

"Yet, you will not tell me all you know concerning the Chichester…your abduction," he reminded.

"You're a pirate!" she exclaimed.

"Even so, I am an American…American bred, American born, American raised…and I protect her," he growled.

"American born, eh?" she asked. "And where might you have been born, Navarrone the Blue Blade."

Navarrone knew he must win her trust—at least a measure of it. He knew that he could expect her to share nothing if he did not offer something in return.

Thus, he answered, "Salem."

"Massachusetts?" she asked, smiling. "Salem, Massachusetts? The township of the old witch trials a hundred years ago?"

"Over a hundred years ago," he corrected.

She laughed—and he fought the urge to enjoy her laughter.

"Well, of course! A pirate…born of witch country. I should have guessed at it," she giggled.

"Puritan country as well," he interjected. He was pleased by her enthusiasm—though somewhat astonished.

"Indeed…though I think history will find those accused and hanged for being witches owned the better character."

"Then you should be comforted to know that I am descended from the condemned…and not those who sat in ignorant judgment," he confessed.

"Truly?" she asked. He could not keep from smiling—for her face purely radiated with interest. "Are you in earnest?"

"Of course, love," he assured her. "A pirate I may be…but why would I have reason to deceive you over such a trifle thing?" He wagged a scolding index finger at her. "You however…you I found aboard a bloody

British ship! Your trunk was neatly packed and ushered aboard as well. Thus, how can I believe you are not aligned with the enemy?"

Navarrone watched as she bit her lower lip—pensive. He had her! She would tell him the full breadth of all she knew—at last.

"What will you do to me once you know my thoughts...my suspicions...and they are only that, Captain," she said. "I only have thoughts and suspicions."

Navarrone's eyes narrowed as he considered her a moment. "In truth, I cannot say, love," he confessed. "For if you are a traitor, I will give you over to Governor Claiborne...just as I will the remaining crew of the Chichester. If you are not traitor..." He shrugged. "I can promise only that I will not kill you."

She was silent a moment—appeared suddenly awash with anxiety.

"If you determine that I am not a traitor...which I am not...will you give me your word that you will not take me to Governor Claiborne...even if you think it would be in your favor to return me to New Orleans?"

Navarrone was wildly intrigued. The girl did know something.

"I promise," he agreed.

"Then ask your questions, Captain Navarrone," Cristabel Albay sighed. "And I will tell you all I am able."

He was astonished—for it seemed she was truly resigned to speak to him. He watched as she retrieved a hairbrush from the depths of the trunk, sat down on the chaise and began brushing her hair.

"Why do you not wish to be returned to New Orleans?" he began. "In particular to Governor Claiborne?"

"I-I..." she stammered. She paused—inquisitively frowning at him. "How could you return me to Governor Claiborne? How can you expect to take your captured British ship and sailors to him? You're a pirate! He would have you hanged!"

She was quick witted—perhaps too quick witted. He must proceed with care—else he reveal too much of himself.

"It's a British ship, love," he answered. "And seven bloody sailors. Do you really think the Governor would refuse such prizes simply because a pirate offers them? We are at war, Cristabel Albay. Or didn't you know?"

Cristabel considered Navarrone for a moment. She had heard of such things—pirates entering New Orleans without fear of punishment simply because they owned information or goods desired by New Orleans citizens. Her thoughts lingered on the matter of weeks before—when commodore Daniel Patterson set out aboard the USS Carolina to Barataria Bay—the bay south of New Olreans where Jean Lafitte and his brother Pierre anchored a fleet of privateers and smugglers. The Carolina and six other gun ships attacked Jean Lafitte's Baratarians, scattering or capturing Lafitte's men and ships—though Jean Lafitte himself escaped.

"Are you a Baratarian, Captain?" she asked. "Do you sail for Jean Lafitte?"

Captain Navarrone smiled in obvious admiration of her inquiry.

"Ah!" he said. "So you know of Jean Lafitte and Barataria Bay."

"Of course."

Captain Navarrone chuckled. "Though I know it may disappoint you, love...I am not a Baratarian...nor do I sail for Jean Lafitte. I make my home port...well, not in Barataria Bay." He smiled and asked, "Are you allies with Jean Lafitte, Cristabel Albay? Is that why you do not wish to be returned to Governor Claiborne?"

"Don't be ridiculous," she said, frowning.

"Then why?" Navarrone asked. "What reason would you have for lingering with pirates when your home is nearly within your grasp?"

Cristabel swallowed the lump of trepidation in her throat. Again she reminded herself that Navarrone the Blue Blade had neither killed or ravaged her. She must confide in him if she hoped to keep it so.

"M-my mother will know more safety if I am not near to her," she answered.

"What?" Navarrone asked.

"William Pelletier is a monster! And, I think, a traitor!" she confessed. The words continued to spill from her lips. "My mother married him for obligation's sake I am certain...and her life has been miserable because of it...because of me. It is why I agreed to marry Richard...though I do not love him...I do not even like him! Yet, William was determined that I should marry him...Richard is his distant cousin...Richard Pelletier. Therefore, I agreed...for my mother's sake...for it seemed William was always angry with her concerning me...ever arguing...threatening to turn

59

her out. I think it is for the sake that I hear things…notice things. Mother notices them, too…yet she stays silent…out of fear of William. But William knows I am not so easily frightened as Mother."

Navarrone smiled—with sarcasm asked, "Is that so?" He was not surprised the young woman was less afraid of her step-father than any other woman may be—for did she not stand in perfect composure, dressed only in her undergarments and revealing secrets to a pirate?

"Yes," Cristabel continued without realizing he was perfectly aware of her daring.

"What did you hear?" he asked then. "What notices did you take?"

Cristabel shrugged. "Words…words one does not normally hear in patriotic conversation. Things such as, 'King George is a worthy monarch'…names of ships I know are not of our navy. There is a man that visits often…and he is never presented to mother and I…even when we are in the same room as he arrives. I saw him give William a sealed letter once. William read the letter, then tossed it into the hearth and left the room. He did not know I was hidden behind the draperies and I rushed to the hearth to retrieve what he had tried to destroy, but the letter was too far in the fire. Yet, a part of the seal was there…outside the grate. It was only four words I saw…but…but…"

She paused, and he sensed she feared he would not believe her.

"Go on…four words…" he urged.

"King of the Britains," she whispered.

Navarrone inhaled a deep breath—exhaled it slowly. "King George's seal reads, George the Third, by the grace of God, King of the Britains, Defender of the Faith."

"Yes."

"Perhaps it is all a ruse," Navarrone mumbled. "Perhaps you are involved with treason. Perhaps your story of abduction is simply that…a story. Perhaps you are truly the Chichester Captain's lady and…"

"No! No!" she argued. There was desperation in her countenance.

Certainly Navarrone knew she was a prisoner aboard the Chichester. He had known it at once—even before the Chichester's surviving crew had confessed it. Still, he had learned the night before that the lovely Cristabel Albay easily took any bait that would champion her character.

"Then tell me...how long were you aboard the Chichester?" Navarrone asked.

"Six days and nights," she instantly answered.

"And you heard them say they were to take you to England?"

"Yes...to London."

Navarrone was thoughtful. "And you think your step-father was behind it?"

"He is a traitor...I am sure of it," she said. "I may not have tangible proof...but in my heart I know it is true."

Navarrone nodded—for he too, understood the power of the sixth sense.

"But why not simply have you murdered?" he asked—speaking his thoughts aloud. "Why not simply kill you? Why send you to England...even if he is loyal to King George...unless...for profit?" He paused—his thoughts too disturbing to share with her.

"Profit?" she asked, frowning. "Profit? I am certain William had to pay the men who took me...the captain of the Chichester. What profit is there in that for him?"

"Slaving is a profitable business, love," he said. "Bloody Satan pays his slavers well."

"Slavery?" she asked. Navarrone was touched by her innocence. "But..."

"It's called white slaving, love...and we'll leave it at that," he interrupted. He turned from her—somehow ashamed he had spoken of such an evil to one so lovely. His gaze, however, fell to the painting of Vienne on the cabin wall—and he winced with the pain his memory brought to him.

"Y-you think William meant to have me...sold?" she asked, breathless with astonished disgust.

"I think William Pelletier is a conspirator," he answered. "I think he knows you are quick to observe and far too clever for your own good and sought to rid himself of you."

"But I have agreed to marry Richard," she offered. "He would be rid of me soon enough."

"No he would not. You would be out of his house, perhaps...but you would not forget what you have already seen and heard," he explained.

61

He heard her moan and turned to see her bury her face in her hands. "Oh, why did Mother marry him? I can make no sense of it."

"You told me it was to save your family home," he offered. "To keep you from poverty."

"That is what she tells me," Cristabel said. "Though I would rather have endured poverty than knowing my mother submits to one such as William Pelletier."

"What happened to your father?" Navarrone asked, suddenly curious.

"He died," she answered—tears escaping her eyes.

"How?"

She shook her head. "No one knows how it happened. He was found dead...drowned in the Ashley River near our home."

Cristabel looked to the pirate captain. He seemed lost in his pensive thinking. Yet, she could not keep the question from escaping her lips.

"Do you really think William Pelletier meant to have me sold, Captain?" she asked.

The reality of what might have become of her had Navarrone the Blue Blade and his Merry Wench not come upon the Chichester and The Screaming Witch, was grim and ghastly—horrid in its terrifying nature. Had Bully Booth's crew not succeeded in wholly taking the Chichester, its captain may have taken her to England—there to be sold to what unfathomable end she would not ponder! Yet, The Screaming Witch surely would have taken the British ship. Thus, if Navarrone had not intervened, her fate would have been just as heinous. In truth—though she would not show weakness and confess it to him—Cristabel owed Captain Navarrone a greater debt than could ever be repaid. Not simply the debt of her life saved—but of her spirit's rescue as well!

"Yes, love," he grimly admitted. "I know that someone is white slaving in New Orleans. I just did not know who...until now."

Cristabel covered her mouth with her hand—for she was certain what little contents of breakfast remaining in her rum-ravaged stomach would present itself at any moment.

He exhaled a heavy sigh as he studied her a moment. "Where's the vial of peppermint oil then?" he asked.

With a trembling hand, Cristabel pointed to his desk. The pirate Navarrone retrieved the tiny vial, removing the lid. She watched as he poured several drops onto the back of his hand, licking them off with his tongue. He nodded to her and she held out her hand. He took hold of her fingers, turned her hand to place several drops of the oil on the back of it. Quickly Cristabel licked the oil form her hand in the same manner. At once her stomach began to settle a bit.

"Cheer up, love," Navarrone said, replacing the vial's lid and tossing it to land on the chaise next to her. "I could be wrong after all. Your step-father could be quite innocent in all this, and it is merely someone else at the helm, composing your abduction in hope of acquiring ransom or reward."

"William Pelletier will not pay a ransom for me," she reminded him.

Cristabel watched as Navarrone smiled—reached into the pocket of his rather tight-fitting trousers and produced Richard's ring. She frowned—confused as she watched him toss it in the air, then catch it as if it were some thing of significant value beyond that of the obvious.

"Perhaps not," he said. "But Richard Pelletier might, eh?"

At the thought of Richard, Cristabel's stomach churned once more.

"Fear not, love," Navarrone chuckled. "I promised I would not kill you and I won't. Furthermore, I will not return you to Governor Claiborne...but tell me why you do not wish to see the Governor?"

She had told him everything she could think to tell him. Thus she saw no reason not to answer.

"William watches him...closely," she said. "He often visits with a man I know to be in Governor Claiborne's employ."

"Good enough, love," he said, stuffing the ring back into his pocket. "I will have James Kelley bring a plate of food to you. Eat slowly and take your rest. We are three days from Lake Borgne. You should be well recovered by then. Ripe for ransom or reward I would think."

"You really are a blackguard," Cristabel said—the sting of disappointment heavy in her bosom.

"I'm a pirate, love," he reminded. "Not an angel."

He left her then—left her somehow more weak, hopeless and miserable than she had been when he had come to interrogate her.

"See that she eats James Kelley," Navarrone mumbled to the boy guarding his cabin door. "Pray tarry a while in conversation with the lass. Her spirits are low…and your cheerful countenance will do her far more good than my glowering Vulcan's brow, eh?"

"Aye, Cap'n," James agreed.

"Good, lad," Navarrone chuckled. He paused—feigned concern. "But remember, boy…if anyone's to ravage her…it's to be me. Do we have an understanding?"

James laughed. "Yes, Cap'n. No ravaging of the pretty prisoner."

Navarrone nodded. "As you were, James Kelley."

"Aye, Cap'n."

The sun was sinking on the horizon. As Navarrone climbed the stairs to the quarterdeck, he felt empathy for Cristabel Albay. No doubt the lingering effects of the rum would heighten her anxiety and despair over her circumstances. He would stay close to her through the night—watch her—guard the door from within just as he had the night before. He could sense he was on the brink of discovering a nest of traitors and treasonous mercenaries—and it bred desire in him—desire to crush their cowardly conspiring beneath his boot. Cristabel Albay bred desire in him as well— of a different sort, of course. He thought of her hair—the way it seemed to harbor glistening illuminants among its soft, dark tresses. He fancied it was the color of spice—of cloves—and he wondered if it smelled as rich.

"Cap'n!"

Baskerville's shouting startled Navarrone from his pleasant thoughts of the prisoner in his cabin.

"Aye, Baskerville? What is it?" Navarrone asked looking to the deck.

"It's them smaller barrels you were suspicious of, Cap'n," Baskerville explained. The quartermaster smiled. "You was right…it ain't just provisions they're storing."

As a smile tugged at the right corner of his mouth, Navarrone asked, "Silver? Gold?"

Baskerville nodded. "And far more, sir. Far more!"

As Navarrone returned to the deck, Baskerville said, "And we ain't got to the crates yet, sir."

"We intercepted something conspiratorial where the Chichester is concerned, Baskerville," Navarrone said.

"Indeed we did, sir!  Indeed, we did!"

# Chapter Five

"James Kelley!" Cristabel exclaimed in a whisper. "Are you attempting to convince me that your captain is some sort of rogue saint?"

"No, miss," James Kelley said. "I only said he don't go wenching when we're in port."

"He's a pirate, James," Cristabel reminded the boy as she offered the remains of her supper to him. "All pirates ever do is plunder, pillage, fairly bathe in liquor and chase after tavern wenches."

James shook his head, however. "Now that ain't fair, miss…that ain't fair for you to say. I'm a pirate and I don't take spirits or chase after women," he said.

"But Captain Navarrone is infamous for his skill in seducing even the most innocent of women," she reminded him.

"Yes, miss."

"Are you telling me, James…that I am perfectly safe in his company?" she asked. "For he ever and always threatens to…to despoil me."

"I ain't saying he wouldn't, miss," James said. He smiled—a purely mischievous smile. "I'm only saying he don't go wenching while we're in port."

The moment of hope and safety Cristabel had experienced was vanquished.

"None of the crew does," James added. "Most of the men of our crew…they have families…and they're loyal to them."

Cristabel laughed. Was the boy truly so naive as to believe his captain and shipmates were moral, loyal men with untarnished souls?

"It's true, miss," James assured her as he quickly devoured the remains of her meal. "They have families…and though the lot of them do swallow

67

a drink or two while we're in New Orleans…there ain't no wenching goes on."

Cristabel quirked one eyebrow in lingering, powerful disbelief. Suddenly, an unsettling thought traveled through her mind. "Captain Navarrone the Blue Blade…he has a family? A wife…children?" For some strange reason, she felt oddly jealous. Likewise she was even more discomfited by his threats and flirtations.

James swallowed his food. "A mother," he answered. "No wife and little ones…but a mother." James smiled and Cristabel was delighted when he said, "She's like a mother to me as well. Treats me like her own."

"You've met Captain Navarrone's mother?" she asked—though wildly relieved to hear he did not own a wife. The boy's story was astonishing—too astonishing to possibly hold an ounce of truth.

"Oh, yes, miss!" he answered. "Whenever we…"

"James Kelley!" Navarrone growled from the open doorway.

"Aye, Cap'n?" James said, leaping to his feet.

"Return to your post, boy," Navarrone ordered. The scowl on his face showed plainly his irritation with having found James in such comfortable conversation with his prisoner.

"Aye, Cap'n," James said. He nodded to Cristabel—his cheeks pink with humiliation.

Cristabel watched James hurry away. She mused he looked like a scolded puppy.

As Navarrone closed the door behind him, she began to worry that perhaps James' punishment for speaking so casual to her might be far more severe than she liked to imagine. Would Navarrone have the lad flogged? She could not bear the burden of knowing she may have brought the boy to such a punishment.

"He only told me you have a mother, Captain," she began. "Please do not harm him. He's only a boy."

"He's a pirate, love," he mumbled. "And as such, he is subject to all the punishments any of us are."

"But please…" she began to plead.

"Even Black Beard had a mother. Thus, so do I. So settle your concerns, love…I'll not flog James Kelley for telling you I have a mother."

68

Cristabel sighed with relief. She could not have endured watching the boy be punished simply for being kind to her.

Navarrone did not stride to her—did not take his seat on a chair. Simply, he sat down on the floor with his back against the door. His eyes narrowed as he studied her and Cristabel began to feel overly warm. As ever, Captain Navarrone's alluring presence disconcerted her. She considered for a moment that perhaps something was wrong with her—that she had somehow been overcome by an illness of the mind—for what decent woman experienced such an overwhelming attraction to a villain?

"Tell me, pretty pomegranate," he began then. His eyes narrowed as he studied her. She remained where she sat on the chaise—attempting to appear indifferent to his presence. "How wealthy is your step-father...this William Pelletier? And from whence comes his great wealth?"

"He is very wealthy," she answered. "Immorally so...though I do not know from whence he derived it." She blushed, remembering a matter included in their previous conversation. "Though you may well have stumbled upon one venue of his collecting it."

"White slavery," he mumbled, nodding. "Yes...and that would perhaps explain..."

He paused—as if he had not meant to muse aloud.

"Explain what?" she asked, however.

Navarrone sighed. Cristabel watched as his strong, squared jaw clenched and released several times. He was in obvious considering whether or not to answer her.

"You understand that I am a pirate...that I keep what I plunder," he said.

"Of course," she affirmed. Yet as a tiny flicker of anxiety began to flame in her mind she added, "Meaning things of value...not people."

"People are of much greater value than things, love," he told her.

Cristabel rolled her eyes. "Another moral lesson from The Blue Blade of righteousness? I only meant...you do not keep people...you will not keep me."

"I have not decided whether or not I will keep you," he said. "That remains to be seen. What events transpire in New Orleans will determine your fate. Meanwhile, I was speaking of the fact that the crew of The

Merry Wench and I, have captured a British ship…and the ship and the contents of its hold, are mine to do with as I please. Do you understand?"

"Yes. But what has that to do with…"

"We found small barrels and crates aboard the Chichester," he interrupted. "The men thought them filled with only grain and trinkets. Yet, they seemed heavy to me…too weighted for mere trinkets and food stores. Therefore we opened each one…sifted through its contents."

"And what did you discover?" she asked.

Navarrone tried not to be amused by the sudden light in her eyes—her obvious voracious curiosity.

"Jewels," he answered. "Gems. Spanish pieces of eight…gold coin as well. A fortune…all hidden in barrels and crates marked New Orleans."

"Do you think William was attempting to transfer his riches to England? Perhaps planning to follow?" she asked.

Navarrone shrugged. "I do not know what his plans were. Yet, I will be interested to hear of his reaction when he discovers that the crew of The Merry Wench has plundered the Chichester. That is why I will send a boat ahead of us…to spread the news that a British ship has been captured, and send a message to Governor Claiborne to schedule our meeting to discuss it. If William Pelletier is as close to the Governor as you say he is…it might well be that he may manage to have himself invited to the assemblage."

"You want to see his face when he hears the Chichester's hold is empty," she said.

"Yes," Navarrone confirmed. "The Governor will be so pleased by the acquisition of ship and prisoners he will not suspect that the Chichester carried any more than merely the expected supplies. Yet, William Pelletier…if he is the traitor behind your abduction and the owner of the treasure cached in the Chichester…William Pelletier will be enraged."

"Yes! He will!" Cristabel giggled then. Navarrone was pleased by the expression of pure delight on her face. "Oh, I wish I could see it! I would love nothing more than to witness William Pelletier being bested! Perhaps he will be so angry, he will reveal himself as a traitor before Governor Claiborne! For he cannot suppress his temper." She sighed—overjoyed with hopeful dreaming. "And then you will ransom me to Richard…and

70

he will pay the ransom…and I will return to Mother…and they will hang William Pelletier for treason and she and I will be free of him!"

Navarrone worried for her in that moment. He was certain events would not unfold so ideally as she imagined.

"I have not decided whether or not I will ransom you, love," he reminded her. "Perhaps I will keep you…for my own amusement."

Cristabel Albay laughed. "You do not intend to keep me. Especially not when the price I would bring as ransom is within your reach. And if you wanted to amuse yourself at my expense…you would have done so already."

Navarrone scowled. In his youthful naiveté, James Kelley had revealed too much to the little vixen. He sensed he was losing his hold over her. If she did not remain intimidated by him, she could well unravel his plans.

He stood—strode to her—grinning when he saw her eyes widen.

"What has James Kelley told you, love?" he asked.

"That you do not go wenching when the ship is in port," she answered without reserve. He could see the confidence in her eyes. She did not fear he would ravage her or ill-treat her in any manner. He had been too soft with her—too careful—and it may have already jeopardized the lot. He remembered the night before—something she had asked while she had been overcome by the rum. She had asked him if he had indeed seduced the wife of South Carolina's governor. He told her the truth of it—that he had not—but he was certain she did not remember speaking to him of seduction and romance.

"That is true," he said, taking hold of her arm and pulling her from her seat on the chaise. "I do not go wenching in taverns and back alleys. I prefer much more delicate women than are found there. Wealthy women…the neglected wives of politicians…the wife of the governor of your home state in fact."

Cristabel gasped. Were the rumors indeed true? Had the pirate Navarrone the Blue Blade truly seduced the wife of the governor as she had heard the gossips whisper? She put her palms to his broad chest, pushing at him as his strong arms encircled her waist.

71

"Stop it!" she said, attempting resistance. She struggled, but he simply turned her body in his arms, pulling her back against him. Taking hold of her wrists, he easily crossed her arms over her bosom and held her tight.

"You see, love…I prefer women who are soft and warm," he whispered into her ear. He pressed his cheek against the place—allowed his whiskered chin to lightly brush her neck. She tensed, struggled—yet he did not miss the goose flesh breaking over her arms.

"Unhand me!" she growled.

Still, he held her tight—placed a lingering kiss to her shoulder.

"I prefer women who would not normally think of taking a man like me to their bosom," he whispered. He smiled—for he could feel the trembling in her. "Women like you, love." He again kissed her shoulder. He wondered then why had she not taken the time to put a dress over her chemise and corset. He had allowed her to have her trunk, and he knew it held several dresses within. "Pretty women who own a sweet fragrance to their skin…who tremble in my arms…who dress to please me…or in your case, love…undress to please me."

"I have not remained immodest to please you…vile blackguard that you are," she growled through clenched teeth. "In truth…I-I neglected to dress for the sake that James Kelley arrived with a plate of supper for me before I was able. Release me and I will gladly dress…though not to please you."

Navarrone sighed—relieved that she was once again intimidated by him—and he knew she was—for she was combative once more. Yet, he hesitated in releasing her—for she was indeed soft and warm in his arms—the fragrance of her skin that of some whimsical nectar. His considerations were fast moving from holding her for the purpose of intimidation and control, to that of heightening desire to have her. He must seal his dominance quickly, and set her away from him—before his heart found some attachment to her that might interfere with his purpose.

"How can I release you, love…when it is so very obvious that you delight in my attentions?" he baited her.

"Delight in your attentions?" she near squealed. He was amused by her riled indignation. "Your attentions churn a nausea in me that even the rum could not equal!"

"Oh, but that is not true, is it, Cristabel Albay?" he teased her. "For you're trembling."

"Because I am angry!"

"So you claim," he began, allowing his lips to travel over her shoulder—to her neck—to her tender cheek. "And yet you are found out, love...for you are riddled with goose bumps...a certain evidence that your flesh savors my touch. Thus, though your mouth will not speak the truth to me...your body does."

"Oh unhand me! Unhand me!" she cried.

Cristabel was frantic to escape him—not for the fact she feared he may indeed ravage her—but for the fact her trembling and goose flesh were evidence of her pleasure at his attentions.

Navarrone the Blue Blade was a rake! A rogue, a blackguard and a pirate! There was nausea churning in Cristabel's stomach—nausea born of the sudden knowledge that she was as affected by his charm and allure as easily as any other woman he had endeavored to seduce. Yet, she would not be as weak-minded as the others—as weak-willed as the wife of South Carolina's governor.

He raised her wrists—somehow spun her in his arms so that she faced him—her hands pinned at her back in his strong grip. Her body was flush with his, and she was breathless as she glared up into his face—breathless with fear, morbid desire to be kissed by a rogue and self-disgust in even owning attraction to him.

Cristabel felt tears fill her eyes—though she struggled to keep them from escaping—to show no further weakness. Still, her heart was aching—for she had hoped there was some measure of good in his character—entertained notions that he might not own so black a heart as it was said he did. Yet, now—now she knew the truth of it—Navarrone was a pirate. Whether or not he went wenching in taverns while in port—he was a seducer and defiler of woman—and the disappointment frothing in Cristabel's stomach was insufferable.

"Do not struggle so vehemently, love," he said. The soothing tone of his voice drew her attention and she frowned at him—did cease in her struggles. "It will go better if you simply choose to..."

"Is that why you returned?" she interrupted. "After all I've confided in you…after all your proclaiming that you wish to ransom me for a price…to best the traitor that is William Pelletier? You returned to your cabin to…to…"

"Ravage you?" he finished when she could not speak the words.

She nodded—frustrated with herself for not being able to hold back her tears.

"No, love," he said. He still held her hands at her back, but she felt his grip loosen. "I returned to take rest in my berth. But opportunity presented itself…and you are a tempting little morsel after all. What man would deny himself such a savoring of succulence?"

"Please, sir," Cristabel begged in a whisper as near panic overtook her. "Please…I am certain Richard will pay you well to have me returned…unharmed."


He had her! Navarrone had her in his power once more. Certainly he felt sickened with himself for having been so brutal—at having threatened her with despoiling. Still, he yet sensed much was at stake—much more than simple wealth gained in besting one British ship—and Cristabel Albay was too willful and undaunted a woman for him to allow her to own much confidence—else she endanger herself and the crew of The Merry Wench.

He chuckled—released his hold on her—certain she understood she should yet fear him.

"I would not have harmed you, my ripe little pomegranate," he told her. He leaned forward—whispered in her ear, "I would simply have bathed you in such ambrosial bliss that you…"

He startled as her slap stung his cheek.

"Enough!" he growled. The little vixen was too pertinacious for her own good. "I'll bed you this moment or slice your throat and forsake any ransom you might bring!"


Cristabel gasped—cried out as the pirate Navarrone stooped, scooping her up onto one broad shoulder.

"Don't you dare to touch me!" she cried. "Don't you dare!"

She gasped once more as he indecorously dumped her onto the berth. She began to evade him—to try to move from the berth—but the blade of his cutlass was at her throat in an instant.

"Do you know why I am christened The Blue Blade, love?" he asked. He stood looming over her—his dark hair tumbling over his forehead to slightly shade one eye. His scowl was intense and Cristabel knew she was bested by his will.

"Y-yes," she stammered, breathless with dread.

"It is for the sake that I am as quick with a blade as blue lightning is at striking," he explained nevertheless. "Therefore, remember this, girl...I am weary...for the bloody Chichester and its troublesome female passenger have robbed me of my sleep for two days and a night. Thus, I will take my rest now...there on the chaise." He nodded toward the chaise lounge. "And you will not move from this berth. You have spoiled my appetite for ravaging you this night, love...but I still wish to rest. Hence, remain where you are...else you provoke my temper again and I keep good my threat to slit your pretty throat."

"Aye," she whispered. She had vexed him too far. She sensed he would tolerate no further obstinacy from her.

Navarrone sighed—returned his cutlass to its place at his hip.

"Here is another moral lesson taught you by a pirate," he said, glaring at her. "Strong will...it is a strength in character. However, pure belligerence leads to foolishness...recklessness for the sake of pride. Do not let your pride keep you from your righteous goals, love. You and I own the same desires." His eyes narrowed—a mischievous grin tugged at one corner of his mouth. "That is to say, our desires own congruence where the outcome of the mystery of traitors and the Chichester is concerned. Consequently, it would bode well for you if you were to cease in attempting to do battle with me at every turn. I want the bloody bastard who is aligned with the British and selling women abroad. You want to return to your home...to your beloved Richard. Then do not let your arrogance and determined defiance defeat you."

Cristabel said nothing—for she could see there was wisdom in his sermon. She was at the mercy of pirates—and yet she did naught but provoke her captors. In that moment, she again realized how fortunate she was to be the pirate Navarrone's prisoner, instead of the vile Bully

Booth's. She frowned—wondering why it was she could not hold her tongue and remember her good fortune whenever he provoked her.

"You have nothing to say?" he asked. "No retort dripping with sarcasm?"

Cristabel only shook her head—brushed the tears from her cheeks.

"Good…for I am very worn and need my rest," he mumbled.

She watched as he turned toward the painting on the wall—seemed to study the image of the beautiful woman it owned.

"And do not disturb me while I sleep," he said. "I would hate to be startled and accidentally run you through."

Cristabel watched as he sat down on the chaise—raked a strong hand through his dark hair. He removed his boots and stretched out on the chaise. He was, of course, too large to fit on it properly, and she owned a moment of guilt for his discomfort.

"This bloody day is nearly over," he mumbled. "I expect you to be asleep before the green flash of sunset, love."

He closed his eyes and Cristabel lay down in his berth. She rolled to her side—watched him for long moments as the light in the cabin further dimmed—until the sun dipped below the sea's horizon and only the moonlight shown through the portholes to illuminate his form lying in pure masculine repose on the chaise.

She did not know how long she wept—though it seemed hours. Cristabel Albay wept for the sake of the anguish and fear she had kept buried in her bosom. She wept at the horror of what might have been had Bully Booth bested Navarrone and the crew of The Merry Wench. She wept for the revulsion welling in her at what may have become of her if the Chichester had reached England. She wept for her mother—a pawn in the hands of a treasonous monster. She wept and wept—until, at long last, her tears were spent and sleep claimed her.

❧

"Cap'n!"

There was a pounding on the door.

"Cap'n Navarrone!" the anxious voice called.

Cristabel opened her eyes to see Captain Navarrone sitting on the cabin floor in front of the door—his back resting against it—his head drooped forward.

76

"Cap'n! The Screaming Witch is at us aft!" Baskerville called from beyond the cabin.

Navarrone roused then—raised his head and ran a hand through his hair.

"What's that, Baskerville?" he asked, as he rather struggled to his feet—as if there was a stiffness about his limbs that was not familiar to him."

"The Screaming Witch, Cap'n," Baskerville answered as Navarrone opened the door. "She's followed us, she has. She's gaining on the Chichester at our back!"

"Her crew knows ours is split between the Chichester and the Wench," Navarrone mumbled, rubbing the sleep from his eyes. "The crew of the Witch is fewer than before we met her...yet we are only half a crew on each ship."

"Aye, Cap'n," Baskerville agreed. "What are your orders?"

Again Navarrone rubbed his eyes—raked a hand through his hair. He glared at Cristabel a moment—as if to place the blame of The Screaming Witch's reappearance on her.

"Since Bully Booth is dead, The Screaming Witch has a new captain," he said. "Thus, does her new captain mean to avenge Bully's death? Or did he have some knowledge of the riches aboard the Chichester?" He paused a moment—seemed to study Cristabel. "Signal Fergus to move aport of us," he ordered. "Have Fergus make for the bay, send the schooner out to us...then take the Chichester to the place we determined. We'll see who the Witch follows and make our plans accordingly."

"Aye, Cap'n!" Baskerville agreed.

Cristabel startled as the quartermaster then began barking orders to the crew.

"Looks to be Bully Booth's men were not so easily bested as we supposed, love," he said. "So think hard, Cristabel Albay...in whose arms would you rather spend your last night of life? Mine...or whoever the crew of The Screaming Witch elected as their new captain?" When she did not answer, he arched one eyebrow, adding, "Think quick, love...for your answer may determine how boldly I defend you if they board us."

"Yours!" she spat with writhing resentment, though no tears welled in her eyes—for she had spent them all the night before.

77

He smiled—nodded. "That's a good lass. Now, you best get dressed...we may be entertaining company."

He was gone then—shouting orders at Baskerville's heels.

Hurriedly, Cristabel left the berth. She quickly brushed her hair, braiding it into a long plait. Using the water left in the tankard James Kelley had brought to her the night before, she refreshed her throat and face—placed several drops of the peppermint oil on her tongue and attended to other necessities. She chose a dress from the trunk—blue—and hurriedly pulled it on. She could hear the men racing about the deck—saw the Chichester pass The Merry Wench on the port side.

It did not take her long to realize that no one was guarding the cabin door. The members of the remaining crew were too busy in preparing for battle. Cristabel went to the back of the room—looked with utter terror upon the bow of The Screaming Witch fast approaching. Her figurehead was a maiden as Cristabel would have expected. Yet the maiden's hair was a flaming red—her mouth agape to display sharpened teeth and the protruding tongue of a serpent.

Terror instantly washed over her! What if Navarrone was harmed? Or James Kelley? Or any of the others aboard The Merry Wench? What if she was taken by Bully Booth's vengeful crew?

"Oh, God, please!" she pleaded in a whisper. "I know he is a pirate...but please...please see him the victor once more!"

She startled—nearly screamed as the cabin door burst open. James Kelley entered, strode to her, took hold of her arm and began pulling her with him.

"The Cap'n says you're to remain in here, miss...until the fighting's over," James Kelley explained as he went to a panel in the wall near the front of the cabin and pushed on it. Cristabel was astonished when the panel separated from the wall by the tiniest margin. James then pried it back with his fingers to reveal a space just large enough to cache one person.

"I hate to shut you in, miss," James said. "It's awful close-looking in there...but it's the Cap'n's orders."

None too gently the lad pushed her into the space then—pressed the panel into place once more.

"Not to worry, miss," he said. "The Cap'n says it'll all be over soon enough...one way or the other."

Cristabel could hear it then—shouting—pistol fire—heavy footsteps racing across the deck over head. The Merry Wench was under attack.

# Chapter Six

"Seems it's revenge they're after, lads!" Navarrone shouted as the Screaming Witch drew broadside of The Merry Wench. The Witch had not fired her guns, and he surmised she had spent her ammunition stores on taking the Chichester. "They'll swarm our deck...but we're the crew of The Merry Wench! And Hell itself could not defeat us!" He smiled as his men roared with cheering—even in the face of battle—at being out-numbered at least two to one. "Strike swift and hard, lads! Show no mercy...for they fly the bloody banner and will surely show none!"

He watched as the crew of The Screaming Witch climbed her rigging—began to swing over to the deck of The Merry Wench. He thought of Cristabel Albay hidden in his cabin—hoped she would not allow her stubbornness to rule her actions.

"Stay there, love. Stay there," he whispered as two members of the Witch's crew advanced on him. He grinned as the two pirates suddenly realized who was before them—paused—trepidation evident in their yellow eyes.

"Come on then," Navarrone challenged them. "There're two of you after all. Don't tell me you're afraid to draw cutlass against The Blue Blade when you have the obvious advantage."

His goading was sufficient to provoke them and they advanced. With lightning speed and skill, Navarrone ran his cutlass through one man's chest—withdrew it and watched the second man drop to the deck—Navarrone's blade slitting the blackguard's throat before he could blink.

"Bully Booth always did sail with idiots and fools," Navarrone grumbled as he rushed at a pirate advancing at James Kelley's back. He easily dispatched the villain with one broad stroke—then took up the dead pirate's cutlass and turned to face more. Wielding two blades, Navarrone fought an onslaught of attackers. One managed to strike him—at his back—and the wound was deep. Still, he took naught but a moment's notice of it—for he would not see Cristabel Albay fall into the hands of the crew of The Screaming Witch—nor would he see one of his men cut down—not one.

Out of the corner of his eye, he saw then a pirate skulking toward his cabin.

James Kelley was at his back and he shouted, "James Kelley!"

"Aye, Cap'n?" the lad asked. The boy was strong—yet young—and Navarrone could hear the fatigue in his voice.

"To my cabin, boy! Quick! I will hold these four...but you must best that one!" He nodded toward his cabin.

"Aye, Cap'n!" James Kelley shouted. The lad was off then, leaving Navarrone at sword play with four pirates about him.

Cristabel gasped as she heard the cabin door burst open. She clamped a hand over her mouth to keep from crying out in terror. She could hear the battle raging on the deck of The Merry Wench—wept for her own fear and for the sake of the men doing battle.

"Where are you, wench?" a low, threatening voice growled. "I saw that murdering Navarrone take hold of you and jump from the Witch and into the sea...after he'd killed our captain Bully Booth to have you. I'm sure he ain't done with ya yet...so where are you, you trollop?"

Cristabel attempted to hold her breath—but the great sobbing born of dread was wracking her body and she had to breathe. Would he hear her?

"Get out!"

It was James Kelley's voice—and suddenly Cristabel's concern was not for herself.

"How dare you enter the Cap'n's cabin?" she heard James growl.

The pirate whose voice she did not know, laughed.

"What? They sent a boy to face me? The Devil Wallace...pirate...and captain of The Screaming Witch?" the stranger roared with amusement. "A boy? This is who Navarrone sends to protect his wench? Where is she, boy?"

Cristabel heard James cry out—heard the clash of cutlass blades.

"What wench?" she heard James ask. "Cap'n Navarrone don't keep women. And besides he'll run you through for stepping foot in his cabin."

"Where is she, boy? Where is the woman who cost Bully Booth his life?" the enemy pirate growled. "Bully Booth was my brother...and I will have my revenge on that woman...and Navarrone!"

There was more sword play. Cristabel tightly squeezed her eyes shut—ground her teeth—for her instincts were screaming in her mind—begging her to run to James Kelley's aid.

"Ah, you're a fair swordsman, boy," the evil pirate chuckled. "Would it be The Blue Blade himself who instructed you?"

"He taught me how to kill idiots, if that's what you mean," James growled.

"I'm weary of nursery games, lad," the pirate growled.

Cristabel heard James cry out in agony and she could not bear it!

"Stop!" she cried as she pushed at the panel in the wall and revealed herself. "Stop it! He's only a boy!"

Plethoric tears sprang to her eyes—drizzled over her cheeks as she saw James lying on the floor, writhing in pain.

"Ah, there you are, trollop," the hideous pirate mumbled.

Cristabel grimaced at the sight of him—Bully Booth's brother—for it was plain obvious they shared the same lineage. The pirate who bore an uncanny resemblance to Bully Booth—long red hair, matted beard, yellow teeth—studied her through small, protuberant eyes resembling those of a rat.

"My brother is dead because of you!" he roared.

"Your brother is dead because h-he was weak!" she bravely countered.

The pirate lunged for her, but Cristabel quickly evaded him. Dashing to the back of the room, she stood behind Navarrone's desk. Each time the pirate The Devil Wallace attempted to circumvent it she moved—keeping the broad desk between herself and a certain morbid end.

"My brother is dead because Navarrone is a coward!" The Devil Wallace shouted. He was enraged—his face near the color of his dirty red hair. "He did not even face down my brother...simply murdered him for the want of a woman."

The Devil Wallace turned his head—expectorated the contents of his foul mouth onto the cabin floor as a gesture of disrespect and disgust. Cristabel screamed as he slammed the blade of his cutlass on the desktop.

"I'll have you, girl!" he roared. "I'll have you if it costs me my ship and crew…I'll have you yet!"

"You'll never have her," Navarrone growled.

Cristabel gasped, wept with relief as she glanced to see Navarrone standing just inside the cabin. His white shirt was splattered with blood, yet he stood as handsome—as calm and as confident in appearance as ever. Even for the danger lurking just at the other side of the desk and out on the deck—the thought traveled through Cristabel's mind that the pirate Navarrone was as astonishing to look upon as ever any Greek or Roman God might have been. He tossed one of the two cutlasses he wielded to the floor—to James—then ran a hand back through his hair. Cristabel watched as several of the shorter lengths of it tumbled back over his forehead.

"You'll never have her…*and* you will lose your ship and crew," Navarrone growled, as he advanced. "Your life will be spent as well, if you dare to match blades with me, Wallace Booth!"

"I will match blades with you, Navarrone!" The Devil Wallace bellowed. "And when I've run my blade through your bloody heart…I'll cut it out and boil it in my stew!"

Cristabel gasped as The Devil Wallace lunged at Navarrone. Yet, Navarrone easily evaded.

"You're bested before you've begun, Wallace," Navarrone taunted. Again Wallace advanced—enraged to murder. Again Navarrone easily evaded.

Cristabel glanced to James—to where he endeavored to move himself from the center of the room. She wanted to go to the boy—to aid him—with all her being she wanted to aid him.

She glanced to Navarrone—but he glared at her—shook his head in indicating she should not make to move. She understood his unspoken warning—that she may well cause distraction enough to give The Devil Wallace an opportunity to strike—at either her or Navarrone. Thus, she swallowed the lump of fear and anxiety spurring her toward rushing to James—and waited.

"Is that the best you have to offer, Wallace?" Navarrone goaded the enemy.

"Not by a fathom!" Wallace growled, advancing once more. This time blade met blade as the two pirates engaged in a battle of strength and skill. Cristabel covered her ears as the crash of steel rang in them.

The door to the cabin burst open and two more pirates from The Screaming Witch entered.

"Aye, lads! Get the girl aboard the Witch!" The Devil Wallace shouted.

"James!" Navarrone growled.

Cristabel looked from Navarrone steeped in violent cutlass battle with The Devil Wallace, to where James had been lying on the floor. She gasped when she saw that he had somehow managed to rise to his feet and was facing the two pirates. Her instincts drove her to attempt to make her way past The Devil Wallace and Navarrone in order to aid James Kelley.

Drawing a deep breath she began to sprint toward the wounded boy.

"No!" Navarrone shouted. Yet her feet carried her forward. Navarrone increased the measure of his aggression on The Devil Wallace and Cristabel dashed beyond the two pirates locked in battle.

Without thinking, she reached down retrieving the spare cutlass Navarrone had discarded upon entering the room. Wielding the weapon clutched firm with both hands and braced at one shoulder, she ran straight for the two pirates advancing on James.

"Leave him be!" she screamed. One pirate was startled into looking at her—stared at her as if he could not believe what he was seeing. The other however, was intent upon James—intent upon James until Cristabel drove the cutlass blade into his chest.

Instantly, Cristabel released the cutlass—sickened as she saw the the manner in which it remained in the man's body—as he looked at her in utter astonishment and sank to his knees.

"Why you little…" the other pirate began, raising his cutlass to strike.

Cristabel screamed as she felt her body being yanked backward—saw Navarrone lunge forward from behind her and drive the blade of his cutlass into the man's gullet.

"They're running like rats, Cap'n!" Baskerville called as he hurried past the open cabin door.

"Aye!" Navarrone said.

Cristabel could not move. Her body was still—unable to fathom the sight before her—at what she had done. She stood paralyzed with horrific awe.

"James Kelley!" she heard Navarrone say. "Are you able?"

"Aye, Cap'n," James panted. "Nothing a little stitching won't solve, I hope."

"Then attend the girl while I see what other damage has been done us."

"I've killed a man," Cristabel whispered. She could not yet move—felt as if she were sculpted from stone and would never move again.

She felt Navarrone take hold of her chin—looked at him as he turned her face toward his.

"You ran through a pirate that meant to murder James," he said, scowling at her. "And he would have tortured and murdered you had he been given the chance. Do you understand?"

Cristabel nodded—even though she could make no sense of Navarrone's words.

"She is experiencing shock, James Kelley," Navarrone told the wounded boy. "Baskerville! Baskerville!" he shouted.

Baskerville appeared at the doorway once more, "Aye, Cap'n?"

"Are they gone? Is the Witch setting sail?" Navarrone asked.

"Aye, Cap'n." Baskerville chuckled. "Them that's still alive anyway."

"And our crew? How many lost?" Navarrone was concerned for his men—yet he knew Cristabel's mind was failing her. James Kelley was wounded and could not care for her if her shock worsened.

"None, Cap'n. Not one," Baskerville answered, shaking his head with awed disbelief. "Some's pretty cut though." Baskerville looked to James then. "Yep. Looks to be we'll be having us another stitching-up festival."

Navarrone nodded. "See to James Kelley, Baskerville," Navarrone said. "I'll be on deck in a moment more."

"Aye, Cap'n."

"Have the able men strip these bloody pirates and toss their corpses into the sea," Navarrone growled.

"Aye, Cap'n."

"I-I killed that man," Cristabel whispered.

Navarrone frowned—steadied the girl as she swayed in slight.

"Looks as if she ain't taking it all too well, Cap'n," Baskerville observed as he placed one of James' arms around his broad shoulders to assist him.

"Aye," Navarrone mumbled. He knew Cristabel might indeed lose consciousness, and he wondered if it would not serve her. He admired her bravery. She had charged a pirate—run him through—and it was astonishing.

"Here, love," he said, lifting her into his arms. "Sit down a moment." He carried her to the chaise—attempting to ignore the alluring fragrance of her hair—the manner in which her body was so forfeit in his arms. Gently he sat her on the chaise—hunkered down before her.

"I killed that man," she breathed as tears spilled from her eyes.

"Yes," he told her. "And James Kelley lives because you were brave for his sake."

"I feel…I feel ill," she panted. "Dizzy…as if…"

"Too much rum and too much adventure, love," Navarrone said. He watched anxiety overtake her as the shock began to abandon her mind to make way for realization.

"I'm spinning," she breathed. She began to panic for the sake of her muddled, whirling senses. "Help me! Help me!" she breathlessly begged. She reached out, taking hold of his shirt—fisting its fabric in her tiny hands. "Help me, help me, help me!" she cried.

"Hush now, love," Navarrone soothed. She did not fight him when he laid her down on the chaise—only clung to his shirt—still whispering her pleadings for help.

"I killed that man!" she wept as perspiration sprung to her fragile brow.

"You saved the boy," he reminded her.

"Oh, no! Please, no!" she gasped. "Oh, no! I've become a pirate!"

Unconsciousness overwhelmed her then—blessedly.

Even for the dead men being dragged from his cabin by his own men—even for the deep wound at his back that now pained him—he chuckled. He did not know what to make of a woman who would worry over her ankles being assaulted when she had only hours before been stripped to her undergarments by a pirate and thrown into the sea. He did not know what to make of a woman whose last thought before fainting would be that, because she had killed a murderous, blood-thirsty pirate to save the life of an innocent lad, she had somehow involuntarily converted to piracy. Moreover, he did not know what to make of a woman who drew such an intense interest from him—a woman who evoked such a desperate protective nature from him—a woman who had awakened such a ravenous desire in him as to cause him to entertain thoughts of genuinely ravishing her in pursuit of quenching it.

Navarrone glanced to the painting of Vienne on the wall. As ever, the dagger of guilt, regret and self-loathing plunged into his heart. He did not deserve the affections of a woman the likes of Cristabel Albay. Even if he were not a pirate, he would not deserve her—should not even fancy she would find in him any worthy thing to adore.

Still, as he studied her now peaceful face, he thought of the feel of her flesh against his face—beneath his lips. The very center of his being began to quiver in slight at the memory of holding her to him—of placing soft kisses to her shoulder and neck. He wondered then that if her skin felt as velvet as a rose petal to kiss—how much more sweet and succulent would be her mouth?

"She's a pretty one, ain't she, Cap'n?"

Navarrone did not startle at the sound of Baskerville's voice so close behind him. He was a pirate after all—and what ever in the world could startle a pirate?

"She is that, Baskerville," he agreed.

"I see the incident overwhelmed her in the end," the quartermaster observed. "Poor little thing. Yet, I don't know that I've seen such bravery in a genteel woman."

"Nor I," Navarrone admitted.

He stood then—turned to face his quartermaster.

"The crew of The Screaming Witch ought to do a might more considering when electing their next captain, eh, Baskerville?" he asked, forcing a triumphant smile.

"Aye, Cap'n!" Baskerville chuckled. "We may be bleeding…but there's fifteen dead men on the deck of The Merry Wench…and not a one of them from our crew."

"Aye…but did you expect any different?" Navarrone asked, heartily slapping his friend on the back.

88

"Not when we're sailing with The Blue Blade, Cap'n!"

Navarrone smiled. "Then let's swab the deck and be on our way to our meeting with the Governor."

"Aye, Cap'n," Baskerville said. He paused in following Navarrone out of the cabin, however—studied Cristabel Albay a moment. "Do you think she'll be out long, sir?"

Navarrone frowned. He was concerned for the girl—yet he knew swooning was most likely the best recourse for her frantic mind.

"No," he answered. "And do not worry, my friend. She'll be awake and pricking my temper soon enough."

Baskerville chuckled. "Oh! Is it your temper she pricks then, Cap'n?" he teased.

Navarrone grinned. "Among other emotive sensibilities, yes."

Further amused, Baskerville said, "Emotive sensibilities. I like the way you put things, Cap'n. So polished and refined."

Navarrone smiled. "I'm glad I can amuse you, Baskerville. Now let's see to the men and the ship, eh?"

"Aye aye, Cap'n."

❧

Cristabel slowly opened her eyes. She felt dizzy—disoriented. Still, her bewildered state quickly passed and she gasped, sitting up quickly as memory washed over her. She looked to the other side of the room—to the place where the man she killed should be. Yet there lay no dead pirates there, or anywhere about her.

For a moment she mused that perhaps she had simply dreamed it all up—the return of The Screaming Witch—The Devil Wallace wounding James—her hands running a cutlass through a man's body. She knew she had not dreamt it, however—for the horror lingering in her soul was too genuine.

Glancing around the cabin, she found that she was alone. Navarrone was not near. Instantly, her concern was for James Kelley—for he had been terribly wounded. Captain Navarrone had been well—but was James Kelley?

Ignoring the dizziness still clinging to her mind, Cristabel stood—made her way to the cabin door. She was surprised to find that no one guarded it from without. In fact, as she opened it, and for the first time in days stepped into the open, no one was there to halt her.

Timidly she made her way forward—for she saw Captain Navarrone, the quartermaster Baskerville, James Kelley and several other men, sitting in a circle together mid-deck near the mast. It seemed they were engaged in some kind of intensive conversation. She glanced to one side to see a boatswain near.

She gasped, but the man only nodded, greeting, "Feeling better, miss?"

Cristabel nodded—managed a polite, "Yes, thank you."

Though she was yet distrustful, it seemed she was not to be barred in the Captain's cabin any longer. With great hesitation, she moved toward Navarrone and the group of men sitting on the deck. Yet, as she approached she could better see their activity. She gasped once more— covered her mouth in astonishment as she realized the pirates and their captain sat stitching one another's wounds!

The quartermaster glanced up catching sight of her.

"Cap'n," he mumbled. Navarrone looked to Baskerville and the man nodded toward Cristabel.

The moment his attention fell to her, Cristabel Albay began to tremble. It was strange to be outside the cabin and see him. She somehow wished she had stayed on the chaise—waited for him to return to her.

"Feeling better, love?" he asked as he knotted a thread at the wound of a crewmember.

"I-I suppose," she stammered. She watched as Captain Navarrone drew the dagger from its place at the back of his trousers waist to cut the thread he had used to sew the man's wound closed.

"There you are, Cap'n," Baskerville said as he cut a thread at Navarrone's back. "A might nice job of stitching, too…if I do say so myself."

Cristabel felt tears welling in her eyes once more.

"Thank you, Baskerville," Navarrone said, rising to his feet. He strode toward her—shirtless—the lacings at the front of his pants loosed.

Cristabel blushed and cast her gaze to the deck as he approached.

"It's all right, girl," he said, taking his stance directly before her. "All the men are well. A little scratch here and there…but we're well stitched up now. Nothing to concern yourself over…your James Kelley is fine."

She looked up to him then—for she had been ever so worried for James.

"Assure the lady of your health, James Kelley," Navarrone ordered—though he still looked at Cristabel.

"I'm fine, miss," James called from the stitching circle.

Glancing up to Navarrone for reassurance, Cristabel stepped around him and hurried to James.

"Oh, James!" she breathed as she saw the deep, still seeping wound at his side. "I-I am so sorry!"

"Sorry, miss?" James asked. He smiled—even chuckled a little. "You saved my life, miss…and I ain't ashamed to admit it. Thank you, miss."

"I-I did nothing…nothing but bring this upon you," Cristabel whispered.

"The crew of The Screaming Witch brought this upon us, miss," Baskerville reminded her. "Not you."

"Were…were any of you lost?" she asked. She remembered then that James had told her most of the men had families. The thought horrified her—that perhaps some husband, father, brother or lover had been lost in the battle with the Witch.

"No, miss," James Kelley answered, smiling. "But we heaved twenty bodies into the sea…including The Devil Wallace and the one you killed, miss."

"James!" Navarrone scolded.

Cristabel felt nausea begin to rise in her stomach at the memory of having forced the cutlass into the torso of the enemy pirate. Yet, as she glanced up to James Kelley—as she saw the life and delight in his young, cheerful countenance—the misery in her stomach subsided a little.

"Are you recovered then?" Navarrone asked.

Cristabel turned to answer him—gasping and covering her mouth with one hand at what met her sight. He stood turned away from her—gazing up in seeming scrutiny of the rigging. Yet it was not the long, freshly stitched wound at his lower back that took her breath from her in horror—but the evidence of many, many old and now healed lacerations there.

When she did not answer his question, he did turn—to see her standing with tear-filled eyes—aghast at the scars on his back.

91

"Ah, yes," he mumbled, craning his neck in an attempt to look where her gaze was fixed. "It seems few men endure the cat of nine tails without a few scars to keep their memories fresh. Eh, Baskerville?" he said.

"I-I'm so sorry, Captain," Cristabel stammered. She was not horrified by the existence of the scars—where Navarrone the pirate was concerned, the scars served only as further evidence of his powerful masculinity. It was the notion—the knowledge he had been whipped by a cat of nine tails that horrified her.

"Do not apologize for a wound you did not inflict, love," Navarrone said, smiling. "Look at her, Baskerville…one would think she was the wielder of the cat."

"Turn 'round, Cap'n," Baskerville suggested. "Your front is still as pretty as any man's."

Navarrone did turn—but Cristabel blushed and glanced away—for the lacings at the front of his trouser were still loosed.

"Oh. Forgive me, love," Navarrone chuckled. "I suppose we must attend to our modesty, lads," he called to the crew. "For there is a lady on board The Merry Wench after all."

"Aye, Cap'n," went up the unanimous agreement.

"There," Navarrone said. Cristabel looked to see him tie the lacings of his trousers in a knot. "Modest once again."

He moved to her—stood looming before her. Cristabel was certain she could feel the heat radiating from his body—for she felt overly warm—thirsty.

"And whilst we are discussing modesty," he began, "for your bravery today in the face of certain death…for the fact you defended James Kelley as if he were indeed a member of your crew and not mine…I have decided to relent…to allow you to wander the deck during the day, if you please."

Cristabel Albay looked up to Navarrone at last and he could not keep from smiling at her. She wore an expression of profound bewilderment. He knew she was yet overcome with having killed the pirate—that she was more uncertain of herself then ever she had been since he had acquired her. His heart softened a bit, and he fought to keep it unfeeling.

"James Kelley," he said.

"Aye, Cap'n," James replied.

"Have you gathered the clothes for our prisoner that I requested?"

"Aye, Cap'n! The best I own, they are," the boy said with excitement.

Cristabel frowned. "Clothes?" she asked. "But you already allowed me my trunk."

"If you are going to wander the deck, love...parade before pirates and whomever we might encounter otherwise...I think it best you do it dressed...differently than you are now."

"What?" she asked—entirely confused.

Navarrone snapped his fingers and the poor boy—whom he knew was enduring the worst pain of his life thus far—got to his feet and gathered the clothing.

"Your pirate togs, love," Navarrone said as James offered the pile of garments to her.

"Pirate togs?" Her expression was delicious—that of entire ignorance.

"Yes, love," Navarrone explained. "Trousers, a shirt, boots and even a hat...all contributed by James Kelley."

"Trousers?" she asked, wrinkling her nose. Baskerville and the others chuckled—amused by her expression of distaste.

"Yes. This way you can roam the deck without offering too much distraction to the men...or to any ship we might encounter," he explained. "Agreed?"

Still she frowned—and Navarrone struggled to keep from bursting into laughter.

"You wish me to dress as a man?" she asked—the indignation he liked in her so making its reappearance.

"Yes, love," he answered. "That is, until your Richard pays the ransom and I return you to him...if I return you to him."

She sighed—unconvinced.

"It is the only way I will allow you to roam the ship," he added. He leaned forward, lowering his voice and provocatively whispering, "Let us save your delicate curves for the Captain's pleasure, shall we? No need for all the men to relish the delights of your feminine figure."

Her eyes narrowed and he knew he had her once again.

"Very well," she said. He fancied her posture straightened. "It will be well worth it...to have some semblance of freedom from being isolated in your company."

Navarrone chuckled—amused by her dramatics.

She looked to James. "These are yours, James Kelley?" she asked.

"Yes, miss," James replied. "The best and cleanest I own."

"Then I thank you, James." She turned to Navarrone—glaring at him. "If you will excuse me, Captain Navarrone. It seems I must attend to my wardrobe."

"Of course, love," he said. He bowed slightly and gestured she should move past him. He smiled as she lifted her nose to the air with her now familiar determination, grasped the clothing and boots James had offered to her bosom and started toward the cabin.

His eyes widened when she paused, quickly taking hold of one of his trouser laces and tugging on it to release the tie.

"You're an appallingly immodest man, Captain Navarrone," she scolded.

"I'm a pirate, love," he told her. "I have no need of modesty. It's the nature of my trade." He reached out taking hold of her arm and pulling her close to him. Leaning toward her ear he quietly spoke, "As is plundering ships…and seducing women."

Her eyes narrowed and he knew he had got her temper up. She puffed a breath of disgust and hurried toward his cabin.

"Now who's pricking whose temper, Cap'n?" Baskerville asked, smiling with amusement. Navarrone grinned and nodded to his friend. The quartermaster chuckled to himself and mumbled, "Emotive sensibilities. What a way with words you have, Cap'n Navarrone. What a way, indeed."

# *Chapter Seven*

Cristabel leaned on the railing of the quarterdeck—gazed over the side of the ship into the waves of the sea. Baskerville had told her only that morning, that Navarrone's schooner should be nearing them at any moment—sailing out to meet them from 'the bay'. In the five days she had been aboard The Merry Wench, Cristabel had gathered enough information from Navarrone, James Kelley, Baskerville and the others to surmise that the crew of The Merry Wench made their homes and community on an isolated shore somewhere in Lake Borgne. She knew the ship had already entered the mouth of the lake—that one of Navarrone's schooners was sailing out to meet them. The schooner would take Navarrone and several of his crew to the secret meeting with the Governor, regarding the Chichester and the British sailors.

Navarrone had explained to Cristabel that she would wait aboard The Merry Wench. He would meet with Governor Claiborne, perceive if William Pelletier was in attendance, and then decide how to proceed where ransoming her was concerned. She sighed—discouraged at having to wait. She wondered if Richard would pay a ransom for her. Part of her hoped he would not—for she held no affection or esteem for him and did not wish to return to marry him. In truth the thought made her nauseous. Yet, she had decided weeks before that for her mother's wellbeing she would endure a life with Richard Pelletier—forsake any home of true love and happiness herself. Still, what would become of her if he did not pay the ransom Navarrone would demand? She owned Navarrone's promise that he would not kill her—but what would he do with her?

With all her heart Cristabel wished she could attend the secret assembly between the pirates and the Governor—if not to simply observe the goings on, then at least to set foot on dry land. Yet she most wished to attend in order to witness William Pelletier's response when he discovered there was no longer any treasure cached aboard the Chichester.

Cristabel smiled—giggled in slight—as she thought of Navarrone's clever plan to best William Pelletier. Navarrone had ordered the crew to remove the jewels, gems, gold and silver from the barrels and crates—to replace them with stores from The Merry Wench. Thus, when Governor Claiborne's men opened them to investigate their contents, William Pelletier would either reveal his treasonous ways in inquiring after the riches he knew were once there—or keep silent and live all his life in knowing he had been well-bested by a pirate!

Cristabel thought of her mother again—as ever she did—and struggled to keep from weeping. Oh, how she hoped her mother was well and safe—that perhaps William's ill-treatment of her had lessened since Cristabel had been taken. Shaking her head, she determined she would not think on it. She would anticipate only one event at a time. The schooner would arrive soon and take the pirates to meet the Governor. Then, if Navarrone was able to locate Richard, the pirate captain might collect a ransom and she would be freed. Again she felt discouragement threaten to overwhelm her at the thought of marrying Richard Pelletier— but she would see her mother again—and she so longed for that.

It was then that thoughts of Captain Navarrone intruded her musings. She gritted her teeth with aggravation—for it seemed the rogue was ever lingering in her mind. In truth, Cristabel had begun to wonder if she truly wished she could accompany the land party in the schooner in order to see William Pelletier bested and to discover her fate—or for the sake that she was wildly unsettled each time she thought of being without Navarrone's presence.

"Bloody pirate," she mumbled as she thought of him—as she felt a blush rise to her cheeks at the memory of his lips caressing her shoulder when he had held her bound in his arms in his cabin. She closed her eyes—determined to cast the scoundrel from her thoughts. Yet, with no more visions of the sea before her, her mind was pummeled with images of the handsome rogue! She thought of the breadth of his shoulders— the sun-bronzed tone of his torso when he was roaming the ship without his shirt (which he did often). She thought of his finely trimmed mustache, goatee and side whiskers—of the charming manner in which his dark hair would tumble over his forehead to veil one smoldering eye. She thought of his adeptness with a cutlass or other weapon—of how he had now twice saved her life.

"Miss! Miss!"

James Kelley's enthusiastic call drew Cristabel from her disquieting thoughts. She turned to see James ascending to the quarterdeck—a jolly smile on his youthful face.

"Hello, James," she greeted, smiling at him—for he was a cheerful boy.

"The Cap'n's allowing me to go...to the meeting with the Governor!" he exclaimed.

Cristabel giggled. The boy fairly beamed with delight.

"That's wonderful, James!" she said.

"Yes, miss," he sighed, nodding with pure pleasure.

Cristabel wistfully looked to the horizon. "I wish I could go, as well," she mumbled.

"You, miss? Why, whatever for?"

"To witness the dumbfounded expression on William Pelletier's face when he realizes he has been bested by Captain Navarrone," she explained. She looked to him, adding, "And to see if my fiancé will truly pay a ransom for me."

"Oh, there's no doubt in that, miss," James assured her. "Why...any man would give all his earthly possessions to win you back."

Cristabel giggled—touched by James' earnest and very complimentary declaration.

"You're so good to me, James...so kind and thoughtful."

"It's you who's good to me, miss," James said. His smile faded—he seemed thoughtful for a moment. "You saved my life."

Cristabel shrugged. "You would have done the same for me. You were doing the same for me, in fact...facing pirates...risking your life."

"Naw...it was Captain Navarrone who saved you, miss...not me."

Cristabel put a hand on James' shoulder. "You championed me first, James...I heard you from my place behind the panel in the wall. You battled The Devil Wallace for my sake. I can never repay you for that."

James frowned—again thoughtful. Cristabel wondered what was in his mind—for his jaw was clenched—his brow deeply furrowed.

"I might be able to repay you though, miss," he mumbled.

"You have nothing to repay me for, James. You owe no debt to me."

"Yes I do, miss," he argued, however. His expression had turned very solemn, and Cristabel was saddened that it had—for he owned such delight a moment before.

James studied her—his eyes narrowed. He carefully considered her from head to toe—and more than once. Yet, it was not a lustful sort of perusal—rather one of ponderous scheming.

"Dressed as you are, miss...I'd wager you could pass for me in low light...if the brim of your hat was pulled low on your brow...and your hair hidden down the back of your shirt...maybe a sailors scarf wrapped 'round your neck," he mumbled.

"What are you suggesting, James?" Cristabel asked—nearly taking offense that he had suggested she resembled an adolescent boy.

His face brightened—his cheerful smile returning.

"I've thought of a way to repay my debt to you, miss," he said.

"James...I told you...you are in no way obligated to..."

"Cap'n Navarrone says he's never seen a woman as fearless and wild for adventure as you," he interrupted. He lowered his voice—his eyes fairly gleaming with excitement. "Are you up for it then, miss?" he asked. "And be sure of your answer before you give it...for the Cap'n will have me and you both flogged with the cat if we're caught."

"Am I up for what, James?" she asked—though the anticipation welling in her bosom already whispered to her of what James was planning.

"I think you should take my place on the schooner tonight," he whispered. "Cap'n has told us we won't sail until the sun's set. They always set sail at night...so it ain't so easy to be seen. They're to meet the Governor at a small settlement north of here in order to gift him the Chichester and the British sailors while The Merry Wench waits near Alligator Bend."

"James," Cristabel began, lowering her voice to a whisper, "are you suggesting that I pose as you in order to accompany the away party tonight?"

"Yes, miss," James admitted, still smiling.

"Oh no, James," she said. "I could not possibly do it!" Yet, in her thoughts and heart she was wildly provoked to attempt it.

"Oh yes you could, miss!" James assured her. "I've heard tell they don't speak a word...none of the crew...not while they're sailing to such an end. It will be very dark and you won't be allowed to speak. Cap'n Navarrone will give over the Chichester to the Governor, set the terms of his ransom for you, and come straight away back to The Merry Wench. No one will be the wiser."

The excitement spreading through Cristabel's body and limbs was near overpowering! To stand witness to it all? It would be marvelous!

"But if we're caught, he'll have us both flogged. You said so yourself, James," she reminded him.

James shook his head. "We won't be caught," he assured her. "Even the lanterns on the Wench are put out before we board the schooner. It will be easy as eating pudding."

"James...I just don't know if..."

"We can do it, miss," he interrupted. "I'll let you knock me cold if it will help. Then if the Cap'n questions me, I'll just say you hit me over the head. We'll need to exchange clothes, of course. You can't be wearing my best or they'll know."

"James...I-I cannot possibly..."

"Think of it, miss...you'll be witness to it all!"

Cristabel bit her lip—considered the plan a moment. It was too tempting to refuse—yet she was concerned for James.

"But you were so delighted about being chosen," she offered.

He shrugged. "I don't mind missing it, miss. I think it means more to you. And besides, if you do well in my stay, I'll be invited to go next time."

Cristabel smiled. "Very well, James. When do we exchange our togs?"

James chuckled. "I'll come to you, miss...when the time is ripe...I'll come to you and we'll swap them. All right?"

Cristabel nodded. She knew she should refuse—that it was dangerous to deceive—especially pirates and traitors. Still, she could not neglect the opportunity to witness William Pelletier's defeat.

"Good," he chuckled. "Then I'll come to you when the time arrives. And remember, miss…you must not speak…to no one…at all. I give you the same instruction the Cap'n gave me."

"I understand," Cristabel agreed.

"Now I must go," he whispered. "Cap'n Navarrone has the eyes of an eagle, he does. If he sees us speaking in hushed voices, he might suspect our conspiracy."

Cristabel nodded—bit her lip with barely-restrained enthusiasm. "Thank you, James…truly."

"Thank you, miss…truly," he countered before hurrying away.

Navarrone leaned against the mast—watched as James trotted down the stairs in descending from the quarterdeck. He wondered what James had said to Cristabel Albay to make her smile with such obvious delight. In secret he wished she would smile such a smile for him—yet he was her captor—a villainous pirate captain who did not deserve to be the recipient of such virtuous charms. He swallowed his rising jealousy—silently reminded himself that James Kelley was no more than a boy. James had not made Cristabel smile for the sake of his wooing—but more likely for the sake of his boyhood wit. Navarrone determined he would not fester over it—that he would drive the unwitting vixen, Cristabel Albay, from his thoughts. Though in truth, he had been unable to cast her from his waking mind for any length of time longer than an instant—not since the moment he had come upon her aboard The Screaming Witch. Even his unconscious mind was not free of her feminine wiles—for during the few hours of sleep he struggled to capture each night—she was there—haunting him like some siren temptress of legend.

Navarrone sighed—raked one strong hand back through his hair. He was perturbed with himself for once again entertaining quixotic sentiments of his prisoner. Perhaps if he had been born a different man—or at least maintained the man he once had been before Vienne. Then perchance he might entertain fancies of winning the heart and hand of the fair Cristabel Albay. But he was not the man he had been—nor would he ever be that man again—and he owned a deep, aching regret in the knowledge—for Cristabel Albay was unlike any other woman he had theretofore known.

She was strong-willed, witty, brave and a beautiful. She was feminine, yet not fragile—a woman of rare worth.

He growled—turned his back on the quarterdeck in attempting to divert his thoughts. Yet they would not be diverted, and his mouth began to water as the sudden memory of the feel of her soft flesh against his lips broke over him.

"Ship, Cap'n!" a man in the crow's nest shouted.

"The schooner?" Navarrone called.

"Aye, Cap'n," the man confirmed. "Looks to be Mr. Fergus at the helm."

"Aye!" Navarrone smiled—nodded with approval. Fergus was as prompt as ever he had been, and Navarrone was glad. The more quickly he discovered the depths of the intrigue and treason surrounding Cristabel Albay, the more quickly he could release her and continue about his business.

"If I was a better pirate, I'd ravage her whilst I had the chance," he mumbled to himself. But Navarrone was not a better pirate—for he was, in truth, a supreme patriot instead.

☙

"Now remember, miss," James Kelley whispered as he helped Cristabel on with his boots. "You mustn't utter one word…not one…not for any reason or no matter what happens at the assembly."

"I won't," Cristabel assured him.

"You cannot," he reiterated. "Else it will be both our heads on a post."

Cristabel nodded—even as the nausea of trepidation and uncertainty rose within her.

"The Cap'n told me to be the last one in the schooner and the last one off each and every time we board or disembark. All right? Last…always last," he said. "It will work to our advantage…for you will never be in front of anyone."

"I understand," she said.

"And when you're at the assembly, we stand apart from each other in two rows…like sentries lined up on either side of a pathway in ushering in the Governor," he continued. "We face opposite directions every other man…so that we can see all sides of the place where we are meeting and not be ambushed. If you are able, position yourself with your back to the meeting. Then there'll be little risk that they'll even see your face."

"I-I am a bit frightened, James Kelly," Cristabel admitted. She was, indeed, trembling. In that moment, she was uncertain as to whether or not she had made the correct choice in accepting James offer and plan.

Suddenly, the words of Navarrone the Blue Blade echoed in her mind, *"One decision can change the entire course of a life,"* he had told her. Navarrone was wise—she knew it—especially at that moment. What if her self-serving decision to accompany the away party found both she and James under the furry of Navarrone's cat of nine tails? What if she made a mistake during the meeting with Governor Claiborne and was recognized?

"There's the Cap'n's whistle, miss," James whispered. "It's too late now to change your mind…even if you wanted to."

"But James I-I…"

"Hurry, miss! Cap'n Navarrone will be suspicious if you're not in line," he said.

In the next moment, James blew out the lantern that had been lit nearby. "The whistle means the lights are to be extinguished and the men going ashore are to board the schooner," he explained. "Go! Go, miss…now!"

Without further thought or hesitation, Cristabel hurried out onto the deck. All was dark—only the moon and stars to show her the way. As she quietly made her way toward the rope ladder that would take her to the sea and the schooner, she thought how uncanny the silence was. There was no sound but the sea—no voices—nothing but the rocking of wood in the water—and waves.

Anxious, she watched as Navarrone disappeared over the side of The Merry Wench. Baskerville followed—Fergus nodding at him in assurance that the able First Mate would guard the ship well. Four other men disappeared over the side—then another. It was Cristabel's turn and she did not pause.

As deftly as possible (considering James' boots were far too large for her), she descended the rope ladder—stepped into the small boat waiting there. Two men began to row toward the schooner. Not one man spoke—not a word. The night was dark and even Cristabel could not ably discern the faces of the men in the boat with her. She knew Navarrone, of course—for his size set him apart from the others. Likewise his powerful allure drew Cristabel's awareness. She thought that if she could not see at all—could not even see the shadows and shapes of the men in the boat—still she would know where Navarrone was seated—for his very essence educed her—like a moth to a candle flame.

The schooner was not far and in a matter of mere minutes, all the men were aboard—Navarrone at the helm. The ship slipped through the darkness and water as an imperceptible spirit—a ghost—the breath of a ghost.

Near an hour they sailed—silent. James had instructed Cristabel that Navarrone had set him as Stern Watchman. Thus, Cristabel stood her post well—strained her eyes to see through the darkness and ensure they were not being followed.

At last the anchor was dropped. Navarrone lit a lantern and began to swing it in signaling someone on the shore. The lantern was quickly extinguished, however, and Cristabel exhaled a sigh of relief—for the small flame in the lantern light had illuminated the night with such brilliance, that she had feared she might be found out. Yet, she was not, and—save two men who stayed aboard to guard the ship—she was last to leave the schooner for the small boat with two occupants that rowed them to shore.

Still they did not speak—even as they disembarked and followed the two men who had rowed them ashore. They were led past several buildings—two of which were tavern inns. Cristabel glanced in through one of the warm-lighted windows of the nearest tavern—felt her eyebrows arch as she witnessed drunken men and scantily-clad women cavorting within. People dressed in dark clothing watched them proceed with suspicion. Cristabel heard several men speaking in hushed tones—Acadians. She did not speak fluent French, yet she understood enough of the words and phrases being exchanged to know the local inhabitants suspected there were pirates in their midst.

Cypress trees grew tall—fairly dripping with Spanish moss—darkening out the stars and moon. Cristabel found it difficult to find her footing at times—could only follow the line of pirates before her with blind trust that each man owned for the one ahead of him. The smells of the bayou were strong—water, moss—prolific vegetation. And yet, there were sweet and spiced scents as well—and Cristabel's mouth watered at knowing there was good food cooking somewhere nearby.

At last they approached a large building. There were lanterns lit within and the old house glowed with an inviting warmth. Cristabel thought how very deceptive a thing could look. To the random wanderer approaching the place, the house looked no different than any other— restfully alluring with its glowing orange windows. Yet the truth was that pirates and traitors were meeting within. Yes—deception at its finest.

Cristabel followed the pirates into the building. Her eyes widened as she saw the seven British sailors, shackled and standing in one corner of the room. Apparently Navarrone had not revealed all the details of the instructions he had given his First Mate concerning the Chichester and her remaining crew—for, indeed, the British prisoners had already been delivered to the Governor.

"Captain Navarrone," Governor Claiborne greeted. "What a fine service you have rendered in defending your country."

Cristabel had recognized the Governor at once—recognized William Pelletier standing at his side—and Richard Pelletier standing against one wall. So distracted was she in fact by Richard's presence, that she nearly neglected to align herself with her brother pirates in the manner in which James had instructed.

Quickly she fell into position—between Baskerville and a man whose name she remembered as being Elias. She was fortunate to be in place with her back to the goings on between the two rows of pirates, as James had instructed—for the astonishment of seeing Richard in attendance had thoroughly scattered her thoughts.

"Thank you, Governor," Navarrone said. "And you found the Chichester and her remaining crew where I indicated she would be?"

"We did," Governor Claiborne said, nodding. "It was a wise man who issued you your Letters of Marque, Navarrone. The Chichester will make a fine addition to the navy fleet of these United States. I believe she is the seventh ship you have captured and contributed."

"Yes, Governor," Navarrone said—bowing in slight.

Cristabel almost gasped aloud. Letters of Marque? Of course! She was disgusted with herself over her own ignorance. How could she not have fathomed it? How could she not have seen that the pirate Navarrone was, in fact, a privateer! Letters of Marque had been issued for hundreds of years—and though she had no previous notion the United States had ever issued them—Navarrone the Blue Blade stood as pure example.

"Privateer," she mumbled in a whisper, shaking her head.

"James!" Baskerville scolded in a quiet breath.

Cristabel stood astonished at it all—in particular, her own blindness. Having been abducted and taken aboard the Chichester, attacked by pirates and Bully Booth, flung into the sea by Navarrone, intoxicated with rum— all of it was certainly reason enough that her mind might not have been as quick-witted as usual. Even so—she could not fathom how she had not thought of it before.

When dispatched, Letters of Marque granted the bearer permission to attack the enemy of the country from whence it was issued. Enemy ships were often then gifted to the issuing country as fortification for the naval fleet. Some Letters of Marque required privateers to divide other booty captured with the issuing government or monarchy. Cristabel wondered if Navarrone was in breach of his letter by not declaring the treasures the crew of The Merry Wench had found aboard the Chichester. Still, she wondered if the circumstances—there being traitors so close to the Governor—allowed him pardon for not revealing the existence of the treasure.

"May I inquire as to whom these men are who accompany you, Governor?"

"Of course, Captain Navarrone," Governor Claiborne answered.

Navarrone's question had drawn Cristabel's attention away from her astonished realizations. Having momentarily forgotten she was in disguise, Cristabel glanced over her shoulder toward William and Richard Pelletier.

"Straight ahead, James!" Baskerville scolded in a whisper. "Are you mad, boy? The Cap'n will have your head for..."

Baskerville's words stopped cold as he glanced down to Cristabel the very instant she glanced up to him.

"Oh, sweet Mary Murphy!" Baskerville exclaimed. Cristabel fancied his face grew pale as death as he stared at her. He frowned then—and she could see his jaw clenching with fury. "Keep your hat low...James," he instructed. "And your gaze straight ahead."

"Aye," Cristabel whispered. She was found out! What punishment would be inflicted on she and James? Would Navarrone truly put them under the cat?

"This is William Pelletier," Governor Claiborne then explained to Navarrone. Cristabel tugged at the brim of her hat—hoping to shade her eyes more thoroughly. "And his nephew Richard. They have a particular interest in the Chichester."

"And what might that be?" Navarrone asked.

Cristabel listened with more intent than ever she had listened before.

"Would you allow them to address you concerning the matter, Navarrone?" the Governor inquired.

"Are they to be trusted?" Navarrone queried.

"Of course, my friend!" Governor Claiborne assured him. "I have known William Pelletier for years now. He is a true patriot and defender of the people."

"Then allow them to speak, of course."

Cristabel closed her eyes—gritted her teeth in resisting the temptation to look over her shoulder once more. Oh, how she wished to see William Pelletier writhing with rage over his lost treasure! Yet, suddenly, she realized how selfish she had been in accepting James Kelley's place in the pirate away party. If she were found out—a battle may ensue—Navarrone and the other crewmen of The Merry Wench may be injured or killed!

Cristabel opened her eyes once more—fought the panic quickly rising in her. What had she been thinking? Where had her good sense gone? Why had she agreed to such a ruse? Yet, it was not James' fault—for he was only a boy—and she should have been wiser.

Nevertheless, it was too late to choose differently. The only course was to remain calm—unnoticed.

"Navarrone...I am William Pelletier," Cristabel heard William say. "This is my nephew, Richard."

"And what is your matter concerning the Chichester?" Navarrone inquired.

Cristabel held her breath—waited for William's response. Would his temper flare, revealing him as the traitor she knew him to be?

"Governor Claiborne has told us that the Chichester carried only the expected stores and supplies in her hold," William answered.

Cristabel bit her lip to keep from smiling. He would reveal his treachery—there before the Governor of Louisiana—she was certain of it! Boundless joy swelled in her bosom—for he would be hanged as a traitor and her mother would be free of him.

"Yes," Navarrone deceived. "The expected measures for such a ship and crew."

"Yet, tell me," William began, "did you find any evidence of..." He paused, and Cristabel's joy heightened.

"Of what sir?" Navarrone queried.

"Of a woman, sir," William finished.

Cristabel's heart leapt into her throat. Her anger was suddenly full aflame! He was not going to admit to owning knowledge of the treasure?

"A woman, Mr. Pelletier?" Navarrone asked.

"A young woman," Richard interjected. "We are in search of a missing young woman of our acquaintance."

There was a pause. Cristabel knew Navarrone was as astonished as she was—or at least, closely as astonished. Could it be that William Pelletier was not a man to sell women into slavery? Could it be he was not behind her abduction and the vast riches found aboard the Chichester? Could it be he was no traitor? Yet, Cristabel knew he was vile and treasonous.

"Hold," Baskerville mumbled.

Cristabel inhaled a deep breath—attempting to calm herself.

"I have heard nothing of a missing young woman," Navarrone said. "And why might a woman of your acquaintance be found aboard an enemy ship, sir?"

Oh, but he was clever! Navarrone had posed the question before the Governor—it was a thinly veiled accusation. Yet, he could easily claim ignorance.

"She is Cristabel Albay...Richard's betrothed," William answered. "It appears...loath as I am to utter it...Richard and I have recently discovered evidence that has led us to believe that Cristabel Albay may be a traitor."

"What?" Governor Claiborne exclaimed. Cristabel was thankful the Governor had himself exclaimed, for the sound had masked her own exclamation of the same word.

"Hold your temper, miss," Baskerville growled.

"It is true," Richard said. "I found letters...correspondence between Cristabel and a childhood friend...a man...a British man. It seems they have kept their communications open these long years."

"We believe Cristabel conspired to meet this bloody Brit...to off with him to England," William added.

"In his correspondence the enemy sailor mentions his duties as boatswain aboard the British Chichester," Richard supplied.

"Indeed," Navarrone said—and Cristabel sensed a new panic rising in her. What if Navarrone believed Richard's tale? What if he determined Richard to be the truth-teller and Cristabel the liar? Yet, surely he was too wise, too smart and clever for it. She knew he was. Her confidence in Navarrone's wit was unwavering. Still, she feared his confidence in her character was not so strong.

"Did you find evidence of a woman aboard the ship?" the Governor inquired.

"In fact, we did, Governor," Navarrone admitted.

Cristabel was rendered breathless with disappointment, fear—and heartache! He had given her up! She would hang for treason—but in that moment she was most disturbed by the fact that Navarrone had given her up.

"You did?" Richard asked—frantic.

"Yes," Navarrone confirmed. "I believe the woman you are seeking may have been this Cristabel Albay. Though I do not think she was there of her own free will."

"What do you mean?" the Governor asked.

"When we boarded the Chichester," Navarrone began, "she was already under heavy attack by The Screaming Witch."

"So these bloody Brit seadogs were telling the truth of it," Governor Claiborne said.

"Yes," Navarrone confirmed. "Captain Bully Booth's men had slaughtered many of the Chichester's crew...though Booth himself...coward that he was...remained on his own quarterdeck. I glanced up during the battle to see a young woman in his clutches."

"A dark-haired young woman?" Richard inquired.

"Yes," Navarrone said. "Bully Booth was killed and The Screaming Witch set sail."

"And the girl? She was aboard when they set sail?" William asked.

"She was aboard The Screaming Witch," Navarrone replied.

"Yet how can we be certain it was Cristabel Albay they took?" Richard queried.

There was silence a moment—and then Navarrone answered. "After we had taken the Chichester, my men were seeing to the dead. I was summoned, for one of the wounded Brits had a tale to tell. He told me that a woman had been brought, against her will, to the Chichester in the dead of night days before. The crew was ordered not to speak to her."

"Taken against her will?" Governor Claiborne pressed.

"Yes. The lad said she was brought aboard by men...French Acadians...Americans."

"Impossible!" the Governor exclaimed.

"So it is easier then to believe that a young woman would herself make the arrangements to meet an enemy ship when we are at war?" Navarrone offered.

"That is all the proof you have of her?" Richard asked. "The testimony of a dying Brit?"

"That, and the severed finger we found on the Chichester's deck," Navarrone said.

"Severed finger?" Governor Claiborne mumbled.

"Yes," Navarrone said. "I hope you are not angry, but I kept it as a souvenir...being that I was gifting you the ship, Governor."

There was silence. Cristabel remembered then that Navarrone had taken the ring Richard had gifted her as an engagement endowment.

"We found the finger in the British Captain's cabin," Navarrone said. "There were three others with it...a woman's fingers."

"The bloody Brits cut off her fingers?" the Governor asked with disgust.

"Or Bully Booth himself," Navarrone suggested. "Though...Booth would never have left such a trinket as this behind him."

"Indeed, it is my ring," Richard said. "The one I purchase and gifted Cristabel."

"I think, perhaps, you know then, sir...the whereabouts of your missing young woman," Navarrone said.

"She is aboard The Screaming Witch then," William offered.

"Or perhaps sold into white slavery," Navarrone suggested. "There are white slavers operating out of New Orleans, Governor...as you, no doubt, are aware."

"No," the Governor admitted. "I was not aware of it. How came you by such a knowledge?"

"Privateering, sir. One must have ears in all places to succeed," Navarrone said. "Cheer up, lad," he exclaimed then. "Perhaps your lady bled to death from the loss of her fingers and was not sold into slavery. Keep the ring. It is yours after all...and a reminder of your beloved."

"And you found nothing else in the hold?" Richard asked. "In the barrels and crates of stores? Only food and other necessaries?"

"Inquire of Governor Claiborne, Richard Pelletier," Navarrone said. "The ship and all her riches belong to him now."

"May we see the stores, Governor?" William queried.

"Why of course," the Governor agreed. "But what could you hope to find to offer further information about this Cristabel?"

"Perhaps more fingers?" Navarrone suggested. He was baiting William and Richard—implying he knew what they would not find in the barrels and crates stored in the Chichester's hold—for he had already taken it.

"Perhaps," Richard said.

"By all means, investigate, William," the Governor said. "My men will escort you to the Chichester in the morning. Meanwhile, you are dismissed, for I must speak with Captain Navarrone without any citizens present...in order to conclude these matters."

"Yes, Governor," William nearly growled. "Come along, Richard. I believe we have the information we were seeking here."

Cristabel was near to bursting into flames with frustration! All that had transpired—all that had been revealed—she heard every word of it, yes! But she had seen nothing!

"You may dismiss your men, Navarrone," the Governor said. "We will conclude our business and you may join them then."

"Yes, sir," Navarrone said.

"There are taverns down the way, men," the Governor called to the pirates. "Your captain will join you forthwith."

Cristabel grew rigid—for she felt Navarrone's approach. She did not hear his footsteps, nor his voice—yet she felt the warm allure of him at her back.

"Baskerville," he began in a lowered voice. "Take the men to the tavern, La Petite Grenouille and wait."

"We ain't all of us men, Cap'n," Baskerville mumbled.

"Oh, I am well aware of that, Baskerville," Navarrone growled. Cristabel glanced up to him to see him glaring at her with the full fury of Hell itself. "I recognized that charming little bottom the moment she turned her back to me!" He leaned forward, whispering in her ear, "James' trousers could never completely disguise your enticing curves, love. Just be glad it is only I that am so familiar with them as to have recognized you."

"Captain, I-I…" she began.

"Off to La Petite Grenouille, lads," he said loudly. "And keep a wary eye on our young James here, Baskerville…else he finds himself in more trouble than he can manage."

"Aye, aye, Cap'n," Baskerville grumbled. "Come along, lads. The Cap'n will settle with the Governor from here."

Taking hold of Cristabel's arm, Baskerville pushed her ahead of him. "You're a daring wench, miss…not a soul can deny that."

"Will he kill me, Baskerville?" she asked as they stepped outside once more. "Will he flog me with his cat, do you think?"

"I don't know, miss," he said. "The Cap'n was pure furious, he was."

"And what of James? I-I smashed him over the head with a bottle of rum," she stammered. "None of this was his fault…only mine."

Baskerville chuckled—still holding to her arm as he pushed her along. "Oh, you smashed him over the head with a bottle of rum, undressed him all by yourself, and set out with us, somehow already knowing our ways for going ashore to meet the Governor. Is that it?"

"Exactly," she lied—though she knew he knew she lied.

Baskerville tugged her hat—pulling its brim lower still.

"Well, if you can convince Cap'n Navarrone of that story, I can learn to fly like a bird, girl," Baskerville chuckled. "Now, let's have us a drink at the Grenouille, lads," he called to the pirates ahead of them. "It's best we all be ready when The Blue Blade arrives to deal with this pretty pirate, eh?"

The men all cheered and laughed—but Cristabel was only further terrified. What would Navarrone do to James? What would he do to her? She tried to envision the excruciating pain inflicted by the cat at flogging— yet she knew even her vivid imagination could not fathom it.

"Don't worry, lassie," Baskerville said as he opened the door to the tavern and ushered her inside. Lowering his voice, he whispered, "Perhaps the Cap'n won't flog you…in exchange for certain delights you can offer."

Cristabel gasped—mortified by his inference. But Baskerville merely chuckled.

"You sit here and wait for Cap'n Navarrone," he said pushing her into a chair at a small table. "He'll be right along. Indeed he will, and I have the feeling this will be a night you'll not soon forget, Miss Cristabel Albay."

Cristabel tried to restrain her tears, but several escaped over her cheeks despite her willful efforts. Slowly she began to reconcile herself. Her fate would be what it would be—and she fairly deserved it.

Again Navarrone's warning echoed in her mind. *"One decision can change the entire course of a life,"* he had said. In that moment, Cristabel thought there had never been truer words spoken—not in all the ages of the earth.

# Chapter Eight

"And you suspect treason is afoot? And close to me?" Governor Claiborne inquired.

"I fear I more than merely suspect it, sir," Navarrone answered.

"But who? Who would be in league with King George?"

Navarrone paused—for he was not yet certain he should reveal what he knew as yet. The Governor obviously held great trust in William and Richard Pelletier—or at least in William. He did not think Claiborne would easily accept an accusation against his friend. Thus, Navarrone simply fed him broth—instead of stew.

"I am certain I will be able to trap the traitors," Navarrone said. "I am certain of it, sir. But I ask for your patience…as well as your own wise and wary eye. I must give my men their respite. We have been at sea much longer than I had originally planned, and I have promised them time with their families. Thus, we will take our rest…and I will strategize as we do. For you know there is nothing more repulsive to me than a traitor."

"Yes," Claiborne agreed. "I own the same feelings."

Navarrone watched as the Governor frowned—was pensive for long moments. He was afraid Claiborne would press him further—that he would not own the patience necessary in waiting for Navarrone's trap to spring.

Governor Claiborne inhaled a deep breath of resolve—nodded. "I trust in your character, Navarrone," he said. "And your judgment where the character of others is concerned. Take your rest…let your men renew their strength. Then inform me as to how I may assist in revealing these treasonous traitors and bringing them to the feet of justice."

"Yes, sir," Navarrone said. "We will prove them to be worthy of hanging for their crimes."

Claiborne frowned. "And you believe these same men are running the white slavery operations?"

Navarrone nodded. "I believe they are the foulest form of men...those who abduct innocents from the coast of Africa for sale into bondage here...then abduct our virtuous young women to sell in other countries, yes. Any trade and sale of human beings is contemptible and depraved."

"And you believe the woman my friend William was seeking was taken from New Orleans for this purpose?" Claiborne inquired.

"I think it very likely."

Claiborne sighed. "As I said, take your rest, Navarrone...then root out these traitors among us."

"Yes, sir."

"Now see to your men."

"Thank you, Governor," Navarrone said as he struck hands with Governor Claiborne.

"Thank you, Captain Navarrone," Governor Claiborne said. "I have never fully approved of the concept of issuing Letters of Marque...but in your case, I am glad of it."

Navarrone nodded. He turned, striding from the old house. He had never favored Governor Claiborne—not in the least. Still, he knew the Governor's loathing for traitors was nearly as thoroughgoing as his own. In this they were allies—and he was glad of it.

Still, as he hastened to La Petite Grenouille his vexed indignation where Cristabel Albay was concerned smoldered in his chest like catching kindling. She could have been found out and somehow harmed! Furthermore, she could have ruined everything where his plans to trap the traitors were concerned. And how ever had she convinced James Kelley into allowing her to take his place in the away party? He felt as if he might literally bend her over his knee and spank her round little bottom when he had her in his hands again. In truth, he was so awash with relief that she was well and unscathed, that perspiration gathered at his brow— his strong hands still trembling with residual fear for her safety. Yet, he could not allow his thoughts to linger on his relief that she was yet well. He could not allow tenderness of thought to distract him from his purpose. Cristabel Albay was a pawn of war—a game piece desired by each player. He must remember it. She was no more than a pawn—a beautiful, tempting piece of his gambit and he must remember it—no matter how thoroughly the thought of her put his mouth to watering with desire.

❦

The waiting was torturous. Cristabel wondered if indeed the anticipation of being flogged was worse even than the flogging itself would be. She thought—yet she was utterly terrified. She thought about dashing from the tavern—about leaping from the chair where Baskerville had ordered her to stay, and racing out in search of assistance. After all, she was being held captive by pirates. Yet, to whom would she run for help? The people of the small town who were obviously friendly to those who held her captive? To Governor Claiborne who was deceived by William Pelletier? To Richard? She thought then of all her ears had witnessed, frowning—for it was obvious that Richard was as steeped in treason as his uncle. It had been Richard who had spun the lie of Cristabel's false correspondence with a non-existent British sailor. Yes—Richard was a traitor, too. Thus, where could she run? Nowhere.

Cristabel sighed—discouraged, frightened and confused. Perhaps she could convince Navarrone not to flog her. Perhaps—as Baskerville had suggested—there was something she could offer in return. Yet, she was not so naive as that. She knew what Baskerville's insinuation had truly been—and that was not a consideration.

"Privateer," she whispered then. Full understanding had washed over her during the exchange with the Governor. She had perceived it all quite clearly then—Captain Navarrone and his crew were privateers. Pirates of a sort, yes—but not blood-thirsty and murderous the likes of Bully Booth and others. In truth, Navarrone's offering of the Chichester was near an act of loyalty to country! Pirates would have simply commandeered the British ship—fit it with a crew—most likely forcing the British sailors to join them—thereby doubling their chances to plunder. Giving the Chichester over to the Governor supplied another ship to the United States' defense.

"Do not romanticize it all, Cristabel Albay," she whispered to herself. "He's a pirate! For pity's sake, he's kept you captive…means to flog you!" She gulped as the anticipation of brutality returned.

Desperate for distraction, she glanced up—to the barmaid standing in conversation with a man at a nearby table. Frowning, she looked up once more.  From beneath her pirate's hat Cristabel stared at the woman—felt her mouth fall agape as she sat in utter astonished disbelief.

"It cannot be," she whispered to herself.  All thoughts of flogging emptied from her mind as she studied the woman.  "It truly cannot be!" she breathed.  Yet, as she continued to scrutinize the barmaid, the truth was only more and more evident.  The woman was beautiful—even for the dark circles of fatigue beneath her eyes—even for the fact her hair was ratted and unkempt.  Even for all her disheveled appearance—the woman from the painting in Navarrone's cabin was as beautiful in the living flesh as ever she was in oils and canvas!  The tavern inn light was low, yet the woman's blue eyes glistened like sapphire stars.  The unique dark beauty mark on her lovely face was indicative of her person, as well—there at the crest of her right cheek—just below the outer corner of her right eye.

"Indeed, it is her!" Cristabel said.  Quickly she glanced about.  Where was Navarrone?  Had he not yet entered the establishment?  The men of the away party still sat where they had a moment before.  Yet, where was their Captain?  Should not he have arrived by now?  Cristabel's first instinct was to rush out of doors to find him.  Surely he would want to know that the woman, whose portrait hung in his cabin ever in his view, was standing not five feet from Cristabel.  Still, with her next breath she paused.  An odd sort of jealousy—or perhaps protectiveness—was rising within her.  The woman was no doubt Navarrone's lover—or once had been—and the thought caused Cristabel's teeth to tightly clench.  She shook her head—disgusted with herself.  Why would she own jealousy where Navarrone was concerned?  He was a pirate—a privateer in the least of it!  Therefore, she chose to be more attentive to the feeling of protectiveness she was experiencing—for there was safety in that.  Had the woman spurned Navarrone—once broken his pirate's heart?  Or was she yet his lover?  Was the woman in the tavern the reason Navarrone had chosen the place for the meeting with Governor Claiborne? Was it why he had sent his men ahead to wait for him at La Petite Grenouille?  She briefly wondered why the establishment had been named The Little Frog—but ignored the trivial thought—for Navarrone's lover stood before her!  Still, she mused her considerations were intolerable.  What care should she have for Navarrone's heart—for his lovers? Furthermore, she thought it more likely Navarrone had broken the woman's heart—instead of the reverse.

"May I offer you anything, sir?" the woman from the painting inquired as she approached.

Cristabel glanced to one side—then the other. "Me?" she asked, pointing an index finger to herself.

The woman from Navarrone's painting smiled. "Yes, sir," she said, nodding. "May I offer you a drink?"

Cristabel cleared her throat—lowered her voice in an effort to sound somewhat masculine. "No thank you, ma'am," she said—wondering if she sounded too polite for a pirate. Still, James Kelley was polite to her—thus, why should she not be polite to a barmaid?

"What ship do you crew with?" the woman asked. "There are several of you here tonight that I do not recognize."

"The Merry Wench," Cristabel answered. She slightly gasped—instantly realizing she had only just named a pirate ship! Not simply a pirate ship (though publicly claiming to be a pirate was dangerous enough—even near New Orleans), but Navarrone's ship! It was certain the woman was acquainted with Navarrone—most likely well acquainted with him—intimately acquainted with him. Oh, why had she spoken?

"The Merry Wench?" the woman asked in an awed whisper. Sensing the near panic in the woman's voice, Cristabel looked up in time to see the woman's lovely face grow pale—her blue eyes fill with tears. "Pardon me, will you?" the beauty said. "Celestine! Celestine!" she called. Another disheveled woman quickly appeared.

"Oui?" the woman called Celestine asked.

"Please…I-I must go…for just a short time," the beauty from the painting explained. "Quickly!" she added, handing Celestine the crock of beer she had been holding. "I will return when…when I am finished."

"You can't leave now!" Celestine argued. "Cristophe will be very angry!"

"Tell him I'm sick…very ill. I-I will return as soon as I am able."

Without another word, the beauty from Navarrone's painting was gone—vanished through a door in the back of the room.

Cristabel was assured then—assured that Navarrone and the beauty were entwined—their lives entangled. She wondered at the circumstance

117

of their connection—or at least how they had once been associated. It was plain evident the woman did not wish to cross the path of anyone from The Merry Wench—did not wish to cross Navarrone's path. Had the woman from the portrait been one of Navarrone's many conquests? Or perhaps this woman had somehow escaped him. Thus, he kept her portrait ever in his attention—determined he would one day have her. Whatever the tale was, it was apparent that Navarrone the Blue Blade obsessed over the woman—but that she would ever run from him.

"You little rat!"

The hair on the back of Cristabel's head stood on end at the sound of his angry voice behind her. The woman had momentarily distracted Cristabel from her ponderings of her fate. Yet, she suddenly remembered she was about to be flogged. Leaping from her seat, she meant to dash from the place—avoid Navarrone's wrath. Yet he was too quick and she felt him take hold of the back of her shirt.

"You might have gotten us all killed!" he growled into her ear. His breath on her cheek and neck caused her flesh to ripple with goose bumps.

"I am sorry, Captain," she whispered as she felt one of his powerful arms band round her waist. "I only wanted to…"

"Killed, love! Dead! They would've hung us on the spot if they had seen you…known we were lying…that I had kept a woman captive!" he interrupted. "And what of James Kelley? What is his part in this?"

"Nothing! I swear it!" she whispered. "I knocked him over the head with a bottle of…"

"Enough!" he grumbled. "And do not even contemplate attempting to escape. There is something malicious at work here and you are at the center of it. I may not have ransomed you, love…but neither will I free you. You are my possession until I say otherwise. Do you understand, Miss Cristabel Desiree Albay?"

"Aye, Cap'n," Cristabel managed.

He released her—taking her by the collar. "Then come along, lad. All sailors must learn to hold their beer—no matter how young. Am I right?" he roared.

A general agreement from all the men in the tavern went up in cheers.

"Drinks all around, barmaid!" Navarrone laughed, tossing a handful of pieces of eight to the woman called Celestine. "Drink up, lads! The

118

Blue Blade would see all the patrons and wenches at La Petite Grenouille happy this night!"

Again a general uproar of well wishing and thanks erupted.

As the men in the tavern began staggering toward the bar and demanding drinks be brought to their tables. Navarrone growled, "Come along, love," as he pushed Cristabel out of the tavern. "It's back to the ship with you."

"Are y-you going to flog me?" she asked.

"You know the rules of being ashore for a purpose such as we had tonight," he growled. "No talking. None whatsoever."

"B-but,"

"Silence, vixen!" he ordered. "Else I strip and flog you here this moment!"

Cristabel gulped—tried to keep the tears in her eyes—but they escaped to cascade over her cheeks.

"Now come along, Miss Albay," he whispered. "You have much to answer for.'

He took hold of her arm, storming toward the small boat waiting to ferry them back to the schooner. Cristabel glanced up to the stars and moon—wondered if it was the last time she would ever see them winking at her from the heavens.

⁂

Not a word was spoken—no conversation exchanged between the crewmen. The hour sail back to The Merry Wench seemed an eternity to Cristabel. Anticipating torture was more heinous than ever she had imagined. Though she did not break into sobbing—tears trickled over her cheeks at varying intervals all the way back to The Merry Wench. The only comfort offered her came from Baskerville. Just before they reached the ship, the weathered man placed a knurled hand on her shoulder—nodding reassurance when she looked to him. Yet she was little comforted. Furthermore, she worried for James. He would surely be flogged alongside her—perhaps cast away from the crew.

Oh, why had she been so selfish—so rash in her decision to accompany the away party?

The schooner arrived—the smaller boat took the crew to The Merry Wench—and Cristabel Albay climbed the rope ladder to meet her doom.

119

"James Kelley!" Navarrone roared once they were on deck. "James Kelley!"

Cristabel's tears renewed when she saw James bravely appear on deck. It had been agreed he would wait for her below deck—yet, she was certain he knew they had both been found out. The anger in Navarrone's voice was unmistakable.

"Aye, Cap'n?" James greeted as he stood before Captain Navarrone.

"I'm sorry, James," Cristabel began.

"Do not speak, girl!" Navarrone growled—and she bit her tongue.

"Cap'n," James began, "It ain't her fault, Cap'n. I…"

"She claims she struck you over the head with a bottle," Navarrone interrupted, however. "Is that true, James Kelley?"

"No, Cap'n," James admitted.

"James, please…" Cristabel whispered. She gasped when Navarrone took hold of her chin—forced her to face him.

"I said, do not speak!" he reminded her. He released his grip on her and returned his attention to James. "How did this come to be then, James?" he asked.

Cristabel shook her head—silently pleading with James to keep their secret—to save himself from flogging.

But he was a good boy—and loyal. "I suggested it, sir," he admitted. "To pay my debt to her for saving my life."

"Did you think of the danger, James?" Navarrone asked. "If not to her…to us? If we had been found out…I told the Governor Bully Booth had her, James!" he shouted. "They would have stretched our necks if they had found her! And then they would have come for The Merry Wench, James! For everyone!"

"I-I'm sorry, Cap'n Navarrone," James stammered. "I…I did not think. I acted rashly and I am sorry."

"There are rules here, James," Navarrone said. "Punishments must be inflicted for such crimes as these. Do you understand? Do you know what I must do? I cannot allow this to simply fade away, James Kelley."

"I understand, Cap'n. And I will accept whatever discipline you name," the boy said.

"Please, Captain," Cristabel began. She turned to him—her desperate gaze pleading with his infuriated one. "Please…whatever punishment you name for him…I will take it in his stay."

Navarrone's eyes narrowed. "You have your own punishment to bear, love. You would not survive both his and yours."

"I know," she breathed—terror breaking over her. What did he mean to do to her and James? What could be so brutal that she could not live through it? "Yet, is there no way I can barter with you? Is there nothing I can offer to lesson his pain? It is, all of it, my fault and only mine."

Navarrone's dark eyes narrowed. He seemed pensive a moment.

"Oh there is something, love," he said. "There is definitely something." Cristabel wept as he said, "Are you willing then to barter for James' health then, Cristabel Albay?"

Frantically Cristabel's mind fought for rescue. She knew she had only herself to offer—yet she could not sacrifice her virtue. But what of James Kelley? It was her fault he was to be flogged. She could not let another human being suffer pain and perhaps death for her mistake.

Thus, she nodded—brushed tears from her cheeks and nodded.

Navarrone inhaled a deep breath, exhaling it slowly.

"What say you crew?" he bellowed then. "Do you love James so much as to allow our fair prisoner to save his hide from the cat?"

"What terms, Cap'n?" Baskerville asked.

"My terms, Baskerville," Navarrone said. "If Cristabel Albay offers me what I intend to have…then I may be swayed to spare James Kelley the flogging he most certainly has coming to him. What say you crew of The Merry Wench? Would you see your captain have the fair Miss Albay's affections, in exchange for James Kelley's well-being?"

"Aye," came a unified rumble of agreement.

"No, miss!" James Kelley argued, however. "It's my fault, Cap'n Navarrone! Only mine!"

"Silence, James Kelley!" Navarrone roared. "You are in no position to barter…but she is…so silence." He took hold of Cristabel's arm and began roughly dragging her toward his cabin. "And do not disrespect her sacrifice for you by arguing further, boy!"

As Navarrone opened the cabin door, forcing her inside, Cristabel's tears increased—for it was only then that she realized she would not be able to barter—that she would truly be sacrificed. She had somehow forgotten, until that moment, that she was no longer of any worth to Navarrone. He had not ransomed her to Richard—for it had been revealed

121

that Richard was somehow involved with his uncle's treasonous activities. Why else could it have been Richard who invented the lie concerning her and the non-existent British sailor? Therefore, she no longer had hold over Navarrone—for he had no reason to return her to anyone—especially unspoiled.

"The Governor would have hanged all my men, Cristabel!" he growled, once the door was closed. Glaring at her he said, "And what would've become of you, eh? With your traitorous fiancé and step-father taking possession of you? You might not have been so fortunate as to have an honest privateer come upon you again. Though we may have hanged, your fate might have been far worse!"

"I-I'm sorry," Cristabel sobbed. "I did not think of it. I did not think I would be found out."

"Deception is always uncovered, love…one way or the other," he told her. "In time, all lies are revealed."

She gasped as he swiftly stripped off his shirt and advanced toward her. His eyes smoldered with mingled desire and rage.

"No, no…only wait!" she begged. "Please…I-I…"

He paused—his brows arching in an expression of daring. "Shall I put James Kelley to the task of fashioning a cat of nine tails for himself?" he asked.

"No! No! Only…only give me a moment," she said. "I-I only need time."

"I have allowed you plenty of time, woman!" he growled. "Since the moment I pulled you off that bloody Screaming Witch I've given you time." His massive chest rose and fell with the labored breathing of fury. "Do you know what your fate would have been if Bully Booth had succeeded in taking you?" he asked. "Do you have any flicker of a notion of what they would have done?"

Cristabel was confused—for it seemed his rage was only increasing. She could not guess why—he had defeated her after all. Why then was he yet so enraged?

"And how would you have defended yourself against him? Against his crew?" he asked. He shook his head. "You could not have. You would have been lost…ravaged…then killed."

"I am perhaps not so weak as you think," she ventured. "I-I have kept you at bay this long, have I not?"

He shook his head. "You have kept me from nothing, love. I thought you might bring me riches. That is why you remained aboard The Merry Wench...untouched. However, now...now..."

"Now I yet know things. Perhaps more...for I did not suspect Richard...and now that I do..."

"I will not be swayed by your promises of traitors and secrets, vixen," he interrupted. "I have kept from you long enough. Furthermore, I will not be collecting a pretty sum for your ransom...therefore I must collect something from you for my efforts and patience."

"But you are a patriot...not a pirate," she said—desperate to dissuade him.

"I am a privateer, love," he corrected. "And most of us are not so distant of cousins from pirates."

# Chapter Nine

As Navarrone stepped toward her, Cristabel put up a hand in a gesture he should not aggress. Oh, how he prayed she would fight him off. He had no intention of truly ravaging her—only meant to terrorize her into owning more wisdom—into keeping out of harm's path in the future. Yet, he would play the lustful pirate a moment longer—if only to know that she would not actually sacrifice herself for James Kelley's sake. Still, it was an honorable gesture—and he further admired her for her strength and selflessness.

"Only wait," she begged, stepping further back from him. "Is there nothing else you will accept?"

"Nothing," he said.

"Wh-what of the ring? Richard's ring to me? It is worth a small fortune, is it not?" she asked—desperate.

"You forget...I returned it to him," he reminded her. "As proof of your morbid end."

She shook her head. "I do not believe you actually mean to..."

"I do mean to," he interrupted—though he thought he saw as much hope in her eyes that he would not take her as there dwelt in his heart that she would not allow him to. "And will you fight me as you tried to fight Bully Booth?" he asked. "You did try to fight him, did you not?"

"Of course!" she answered—her indignation rising. "I fought with all I had in me."

"And yet he captured you...took you aboard The Screaming Witch...and all for the sake you did not know how to defend yourself from him. Am I correct?"

She frowned. "I fought him," she said. "I struggled...I beat at his chest with my fists...but his strength was too great for me."

Navarrone shook his head—thought of Vienne—knowing she had not been strong—could not have defended herself even as well as Cristabel Albay might have.

"A woman must know how to hurt a man," he said. "There are ways to defeat him. Perhaps the chance is small...yet the chance is greater if she knows what to do."

Cristabel's frown deepened. What was he about? His threats had turned to near warnings—tutoring of sorts. Had he changed his mind about ravaging her? Cristabel owned an odd sense of offense in musing it.

Navarrone's eyes began to glow with an intensity that was near to mesmerizing then. Anger was in him, yes—but there was such an expression of determination in his countenance suddenly, that Cristabel was awed to wonderment.

"Defend yourself, girl!" Navarrone growled. "A pirate aggresses...and what do you do?" he asked striding toward her. "His intentions are vile...your virtue and your life are at stake. What do you do in defense of them?"

Cristabel's quick wit told her he was indeed challenging her—not that she could avoid being ravished by him—but rather that she should endeavor to keep him from it. Reaching toward her, he attempted to take hold of her throat with one hand—but she ducked—dashed aside, successfully evading him.

"You're quick," he said, nodding with admiration. "But you cannot evade him forever. What will you do when he takes hold of you?"

"I'll worry about that when he takes hold of me...*if* he is able to take hold of me," she said as he lunged for her. Again she moved aside and his hand missed grabbing her arm.

"Oh, he is able, love. Well able," Navarrone growled. "Perhaps he is only toying with you...like a cat toys with a mouse before devouring it."

Cristabel gasped as Navarrone did indeed easily catch hold of her arm.

"What now, love?" he asked—his eyes still smoldering with anger.

"I escape," she said, trying to yank her arm from his grasp. Yet he was too strong and she could not free it. She pulled at his fingers with her free hand, trying to pry them from her arm—but to no avail.

"And if you cannot?" he asked, still holding her arm.

Cristabel attempted to use her weight to free herself—sunk to her knees, pulling on her own arm. Yet, still he held tight to her.

"I can," she argued, standing once more. Placing one foot to his thigh to leverage herself, she again tried to pull her arm free of his grasp.

"And if he has both your arms restrained?" he asked, taking hold of her other arm—sliding his powerful grip to her wrists. Before Cristabel could draw breath once more, Navarrone pushed her back against the cabin wall—pinning her wrists at either side of her head. "What now, love?"

Gritting her teeth with indignation, Cristabel allowed her own eyes to narrow.

"A knee to his..." she began. She gasped however when she felt his body press against hers—further trapping her against the wall—rendering her unable to lift her knee to meet with the place on his body that might have offered him enough discomfort to free her.

"Ah ah ah," he said, shaking his head in a manner of scolding. "Not there, love." A grin of mischief tugged at the right corner of his mouth. "We're only sparring, after all. You wouldn't want to damage something of me you might come to regret later, now would you, love?"

"Oh! You're disgusting!" she exclaimed.

"Am I?" he asked. "Then escape me...lest you be spoiled for some petal-soft politician you may wish to call husband in the future."

She resented his sarcasm—was greatly disturbed by the fact his nearness to her—his touch—was wildly invigorating—overwhelming to her senses—both physical and otherwise. She knew she could not evade him— he was too powerful—too strong and capable. She could not evade him— no. Yet, she could, perhaps, best him at wits.

"What if I do not wish to escape you?" she asked. "What if I wished to be ravaged by the pirate Captain Navarrone?"

"Oh, you wish me to ravage you, is that it, love?" he asked. An amused smile spread across his handsome face, purely enchanting Cristabel for a moment. He chuckled. "All this...all this evasion and escape you've been attempting was what...a lure? Feminine chicanery meant to tempt me?"

"Perhaps," she said. She was disappointed he did not at least consider the possibility that her stratagem was in earnest.

"Ah, yes...I see it now," he began. His breath was warm on her face, and somehow caused her mouth to water. "You are the proverbial debutant...restricted and controlled by wealthy parents...forced into a loveless betrothal...void of any carnal desire or passion. Thus, you wish to know the wanton lust of a pirate...feel his hands on your skin...know the sense of his mouth met with yours."

Cristabel swallowed the lump of nervous exhilaration gathering in her throat. "P-perhaps," she breathed. Already his hands were on her skin— at her wrists—and even that aggressive, brutal touch delighted her somehow.

She was astonished when Navarrone laughed. "Enough flirting, love. Now evade me...escape. You have tried to match your wits to mine...and failed. Now, think hard...I have dominant strength, yes...yet, pirates can be made to feel pain...even injured...allowing you a moment in which you might escape. Think. How can you hurt me?"

Cristabel grimaced as he moved her arms—lowered them—still holding to her wrists. She began to struggle and managed to strip one wrist from his grasp. Instantly she tried to slap him—but he easily caught her hand in his.

"Good!" he said, smiling at her. "Yet a slap will do nothing. Pirates experience more painful events manning the helm during a coastal rain." He took her hand, placing her palm to his right cheek so that her thumb lingered just below his eye. "Here is where you place your hand...and then...do not scratch...but press your thumb with as much force as you can muster into the socket of the eye."

"What?" Cristabel gasped.

Closing his eye, Navarrone placed her thumb over his eye. "Do not dare to injure me, of course...but were I another pirate about to despoil you...you would push as hard as you were able...causing me pain by way of my eye. Gouging it out would be best."

Quickly she pulled her hand from his face—horrified at his suggestion.

128

He caught her hand once more. "There...as quick as that, you lost your chance of escape." She struggled as he bound her arms at her back, tightly clasping her wrists in one hand as his other went to her throat. "You must strike quick, for you cannot waste such an opportunity, love," he said. "For you may only be given one...and once it is gone...it is gone...and you are then at his mercy." His hand at her neck caused goose flesh to prickle her arms—caused her breathing to quicken. His thumb pressed her chin—traveled downward in a soft caress to linger at the hollow of her throat. "Here is another place of weakness," he said. "Should you have a hand at his throat, drive a finger through his flesh and he will..."

"Stop it!" she exclaimed. "Stop! I could never do such a thing! I could never gouge out an eye...or...or tear the flesh at a man's throat!"

Navarrone frowned. "Yes...you could," he growled. There was an odd desperation in him she did not understand. "For the sake of your virtue and your life...you could! Tell me you could!" There was more to his tutoring than his anger—more than the fact she had been caught in dressing like a pirate and accompanying him to the secret assembly with Governor. She was certain of it.

Cristabel frowned as she studied his expression. There was anger—fury in his eyes. Still, there was something else—anguish, despair—pain?

"I could not," she whispered.

"You could...just as I could attempt to ravage you here and now...you could keep me from it if you tried," he growled.

"Perhaps I do not want to keep you from it," she said.

His eyes narrowed. "Do not mock me, love," he warned. "I am a pirate...and I own a pirate's ways."

"You are a privateer...and if you wanted to harm me, you would have done so already." She paused—an odd, painful disappointment pinching her heart. "I'm still worth more to you for the knowledge of traitors I own...then I am as simply a woman with which to...to amuse yourself."

His eyes narrowed, smoldering with emotion. "Perhaps I'll amuse myself, as you term it...as well as benefit from your worth in other regards."

His handsome face was level with hers—she could feel his breath on her cheek. He was so wildly attractive—like some mythical man who owned a power over women that could not be eluded. She studied his dark eyes—the long lashes that shaded them. She studied his nose and strong chin—his perfectly manicured facial hair—his lips. Her mouth flooded with the warm moisture of desire, and she could no longer resist his incomparable allure. Impulsively she leaned forward, pressing her lips to his in a brief but ardent kiss. The sense of his lips against hers snatched the breath from her bosom! A tingling bliss traveled through her limbs and she felt as if her stomach was filled with some sweet, balmy air rising up within her to heat her entire being!

She drew back from him—ashamed at her own weakness and wanton desire. Navarrone did not move—kept her hands pinned at her back with one of his—his other lingering at her throat. She could see his jaw tightening—clenching and unclenching with restrained rage or some other sensation.

Quickly he released her, turned and strode across the room toward the cabin door. Cristabel's emotions vacillated between pride in triumph and disappointment that he was leaving her company. Her disappointment was fleeting however—for as swiftly as he had left her, he turned and was upon her once more.

His hands at her waist, Captain Navarrone pushed her back against the cabin wall. He was breathless—his broad, bronzed chest rising and falling with the labored breathing of anger—or desire. He took her face between his strong hands—allowed his thumbs to trace her lips a moment.

"Ravaged is it?" he growled. "Then so be it."

Cristabel gasped—melted into enchanting, breathless quivers as his mouth ground against hers. He offered no tender beginning—no tentative kiss in testing her acceptance or refusal of his attentions. Rather he took her mouth with his in a driven, heated, demanding kiss that caused her thoughts to scramble—left her uncertain as to how to respond.

"Succumb to me, Cristabel," he mumbled against her mouth. "It is as easy as waking to a sunrise, love."

He kissed her again—with less brutality perhaps—but with pure as much sensuous allure.

"Submit, my ripe little pomegranate," he breathed. "You cannot tempt a pirate the likes of Navarrone the Blue Blade and not expect to pay the price." He kissed her—softly—playfully. "Come now, Cristabel Albay. I endeavored to teach you to evade me…let me now endeavor to teach you to kiss me."

"I know how to kiss you," Cristabel whispered—breathless and blanketed in goose flesh.

"Do you, love?" he teased.

"Yes," she breathed, allowing her hands to grip his muscular forearms as her knees began to weaken.

"Then prove it," he mumbled.

He released her face—dropping his hands to his side and straightening his intimidating posture to his full height. He was taunting her—challenging her—and did not think she had the courage to spar with him. Yet, she was Cristabel Albay—Cristabel Albay who had weathered kidnapping—who had escaped the pirate Bully Booth. She had killed a man, dressed as a man and lingered in the presence of traitors. Surely Navarrone the Blue Blade did not think her determination to survive would be so easily vanquished. Yet, it was not her instincts of survival that had led her to kissing him—but her pure desire to know what it was to feel his lips against hers.

Still, she could not be found out. Judging that he may be obstinate in her efforts to prove herself to him, she glanced around the room in search of something to better heighten herself. The crate that had once contained a bottle of rum and a tin of Marie Blanchard Biscuits stood against one wall. Quickly, she pulled it to a position directly before the pirate Navarrone, turned it over and stepped up onto it.

Folding his muscular arms across his broad chest, Navarrone's eyes narrowed with daring.

"I am not afraid of you, pirate," Cristabel said. She had uttered a lie—but only in part—for she did assuredly know one thing—that if the pirate Captain Navarrone the Blue Blade had truly meant to harm her, he would have done so already. Furthermore, her mouth was watering for want of kissing him again. She surmised there must indeed be some terrible, reckless creature lurking in her if she were to know such desire. Yet, her pride was at stake—as well as her craving to kiss him.

"I am not afraid of you," she repeated, reaching forth to capture his squared, strong jaw between her hands. She allowed her thumbs to gently trace the line of his well-groomed mustache—from its center—down over the corners of his mouth—to rest finally at the goatee at his chin.

"You should be, love," he mumbled—and she trembled as her hands followed their own will, to slide over his cheeks and into the soft, dark length of his hair.

She would waste no more moments on consideration—else the courage she fought so bravely to retain would be lost.

Leaning forward, Cristabel pressed her lips to Navarrone's. She had not been kissed so many times before. Yet, she had spent many hours in secret observation of her step-father's servants engaging in the playful, sometimes impassioned, exchange of kisses—in the woods, near the river, or in various stables and barns. This, combined with the euphoric example of alluring, ambrosial kisses Captain Navarrone had only recently applied to her mouth, offered Cristabel ample instruction on how to proceed—or at least she assumed it did.

Again she dared to kiss him—to tenderly press her lips to his—and her heart leapt when she sensed his tentative response. He unfolded his arms from across his chest, and when she felt his hands come to rest at her waist, Cristabel Albay was undone! Instantly, her arms encircled Navarrone's neck as she kissed him once more. Her lightly parted lips met his and a sudden fire ignited within her as he pulled her body against his, wrapping powerful arms around her waist. His warm, moist mouth captured hers as he then became the captain of not only The Merry Wench—but of their savory exchange of desire. Again and again he kissed her—mingled the flavor of his mouth with her own in a rhythmic, impassioned cadence that mirrored the breaking waves of the sea.

Cristabel was undone—helpless to resist him! As his hands roved over her back, caressed her shoulders, and again grasped her waist, lifting her down from the crate to pull her into his powerful embrace—her body grew weak and pliable to his will. Tears filled her closed eyes—for he was a privateer! Captain Navarrone was not a captain in the regular navy—he was a privateer—a mercenary! He was a scoundrel—a rogue and rake! Yet, her body begged for his touch—her mouth watering for want of his continued kiss—her heart silently crying out an admission that she cared for him—cared for him in a manner she should not!

Desperate to salvage her pride—her heart—perhaps her life—she allowed her arms to slide around his waist. She felt his body tremble from the caress—wanted to weep for what she was about to do—what she did not want to do, but must.

Grasping the hilt of the dagger he kept sheathed at the back of his trousers, she quickly unsheathed it, gently drawing the blade to his throat.

At once Navarrone broke the seal of their lips, chuckling as he released her. Struggling to restrain the tears brimming in her eyes—tears of regret—tears of something akin to heartache—Cristabel stepped back from him.

"I-I could have cut your throat," she stammered, feigning intention. She had not meant to best him at his own game—but fear of the emotions that had near overcome her in his arms had forced her to it.

A grin tugged at the right corner of his alluring mouth and he said, "Well played, love. Well played." He smiled then—breathed a chuckle and added, "Though do not attempt to convince me that you would have been so agreeable in Bully Booth's cabin."

"S-so certain, are you?" she countered—though her innards were a chaos of knotted desire and regret.

He smiled again. "Yes, love," he answered. "Remember...I'm a pirate. I can taste desire on a woman's tongue as surely as you can taste sugar on yours."

"Why are you keeping me?" she asked—humiliated as a tear managed to escape her eyes to travel over her cheek. Their tryst was over—as was the competition of wills he had set in motion. Thus, she offered him the dagger and he accepted it—sheathing it in the back of the waist of his trousers once more. "There will be no ransom to collect. Why keep me a prisoner?"

"Perhaps to satisfy my wanton, pirate lust," he grumbled, frowning at her.

"It is obvious that is not your reason," she said. She glanced to the portrait hanging on the cabin wall beyond him—wondered if the beautiful woman in the portrait had known the warm wonder of his kiss. The thought of his kiss caused her mouth to water. Another tear escaped her brimming eyes.

"Very well," he said, inhaling a deep breath. "I do believe you are still of worth as a pawn in my hand." Navarrone's frown deepened—his breathing became rapid with restrained anger. "We fought hard to forge this country...and not so long ago. Still, the British are yet moved to test

133

us! Many men died for our freedom…and I will not stand idle by and watch more men wasted under the British thirst for power! I will see your bloody Richard hang with William Pelletier at his side!"

Navarrone had not known she could hurt him—wound him so deeply as she had when she had feigned pleasure in his kiss only to best him at his own game. He had been nearly certain he had sensed a desire in her—a desire for him that was nearly as powerful as his desire for her was. Yet, he had been mistaken—fool that he had become. Even yet he trembled within—his innards quivering with hope and desire. The feel of her caress still lingered on his arms—his face—in his hair.

"And I will gladly witness it as well," she said. She looked to him and he fancied there was pain in her eyes. "But if you do not want me for any…for any carnal purpose, Captain Navarrone," she began, "then I have nothing to offer in exchange for James Kelley's flogging."

He frowned—for it near seemed she was disappointed that he was not going to attempt to ravage her further. He thought for a moment—reflected on her involvement in their kissing—on the fact that she indeed kissed him first. Could it be there was more to her reasons than the simple besting of him?

"I promised I would not flog him if you gave me what I intend to have," he said. "And I intend to see the Pelletier's stretch their necks for treason and slaving."

She still seemed disappointed somehow and he began to wonder if perhaps she had more attachment to him than he surmised. Hence he added, "Thus, come at me again…as if I were your lover and you meant to seduce me…and I will stay his flogging."

"D-do you mean that I should kiss you again?" she asked. He grinned when her cheeks pinked with something akin to delight.

"Indeed," he confirmed. "Kiss me as you would kiss your lover, Richard…though I suppose he is no longer your lover, is he?"

"I-I never kissed Richard."

"What?" Navarrone exclaimed in disbelief.

"I told you before…I never liked him."

Navarrone chuckled. "Then kiss me the way you would kiss a man you wished to coax into being your lover…and I will stay James Kelley's flogging."

"Do you promise?" she asked, tears welling to her eyes. Oh, how loath she must be to kiss him again. He knew it—yet he would have the flavor of her mouth to haunt his dreams—once more he would know her kiss—even for her loathing of him.

"I do," he said.

He watched then as she pulled the old crate to position before him once more—took her place upon it.

"F-for the sake of James Kelley," she whispered as she took his face between her soft hands.

"For James Kelley, love," he mumbled.

Cristabel's body trembled with desire—her arms and legs engulfed in goose flesh at the anticipation of knowing his mouth once more. Tentatively she pressed her lips to his in a soft kiss—grew breathless as she felt his lips begin to meld with her own—felt the piloting of the exchange transfer from her will to his.

"Aw, but I want a lover's kiss," he mumbled against her mouth. "For James Kelley's sake…it must be your lover's kiss you gift to…"

She silenced him with her kiss—melted against him as his arms encircled her. Again he was captain of their exchange—sailing her on waves of bliss with the heated moisture of his mouth. She could feel his whiskers at her chin, her cheek—against the flesh of the perimeter of her lips and she shivered with pleasure at the knowledge the pirate Navarrone was kissing her!

His hands went to her waist and she gasped—drew away slightly when his hand inadvertently slipped beneath her shirt a moment. His palm was warm—his touch purely vitalizing!

She blushed and he grinned. "Why, you're not wearing a corset, love. Not even a chemise, for that matter," he mumbled.

"I-I was afraid I might be found out if…" she stammered.

His hand left her skin—returned to the outer of her clothing and she frowned—relieved, yet somewhat astonished at his not taking advantage of her immodesty. Instead, his hands slid up her back and he pulled her against him as he ravished her mouth in one last driven drink of her.

"I'll stay James Kelley's flogging, Cristabel Albay…and yours," he mumbled against her mouth. "For now."

He released her and she stumbled off the crate, leaning against the wall for support—for he had quite weakened her knees with the rendering of such impassioned kisses.

"Change your pirate's clothes for your own now," he commanded, turning and striding to the chaise. "We sail for the bay and a period of respite and planning."

"Do you mean I am to accompany you to your home?" Cristabel asked.

"Yes, love," he said, stretching out on the chaise. He chuckled. "I suppose you could say I'm taking you home to meet my mother."

"My own mother will think I'm dead by now," Cristabel mumbled as the thought occurred to her.

"Yes, love. I suppose she will," Navarrone said. "Now exchange James Kelley's clothes for your own. I will avert my gaze." He exhaled a heavy breath of fatigue and mumbled, "James Kelley…poor lad. I suspect his misery will be punishment enough."

"His misery?" Cristabel said.

"Yes…for I intend to allow him to believe you indeed sacrificed yourself to me on his behalf," Navarrone explained. "He must learn that each choice offers a consequence. Mustn't he, love?"

"I suppose so," Cristabel mumbled—knowing full well Captain Navarrone was again playing moral tutor to her.

# Chapter Ten

Cristabel could sense the crew's excitement. As they rowed the boats to shore, the men chuckled with mirthful anticipation—exchanged conversation concerning their delight in the prospect of seeing their loved ones. She gathered they had been at sea for much longer than was usual, and were desperate for shore and family.

Then—all at once it seemed—women, children and a few men, began to appear on the shore. They waved, calling out to the boats.

Cries of "Papa!" and "Darling!" filled the air—and tears filled Cristabel's eyes—for she knew the families of the crew of The Merry Wench were desperate to see those they so adored.

The boats were brought ashore and all those aboard them disembarked to be met with squeals of joy, tears—hugs and kisses. Cristabel stood aside, smiling as she watched small children throw their arms around the necks of their privateering fathers. Wives kissed their husbands and wept. Pirates kissed their wives and children—held them with desperate embraces. It was a tender scene to witness—such rough, sea-weathered men displaying gentle, loving hearts. Upon witnessing the affectionate, loving exchanges, Cristabel was once again joyous for the sake that none of the men had been lost in the battles with The Screaming Witch. Tears escaped her eyes, rolled over her cheeks at the realization that, had the battles waged with different consequences, some families might have watched The Merry Wench's return only to know suffering and unbearable heartache at being told a husband and father had been killed. Even James Kelley was greeted with smiles, warm embraces and kisses—though it was obvious he had no family of his own. Once welcomed, James stood near Navarrone, smiling as a beautiful older woman owning silver-streaked, raven hair, threw her arms about Navarrone's neck.

"Oh, my darling boy!" she wept. "You were gone so long this time…so very, very long!"

"I am sorry, Mother," Navarrone said, holding her fast in a firm, affectionate embrace. The woman kissed each of his cheeks—held his face between her hands, gazing into his dark eyes with boundless motherly love.

"And everyone is well?" she asked.

He nodded. "And here?" he queried. "All is well here?"

"Yes, love," Navarrone's mother assured him. "The men have kept us safe and well cared for." She smiled—caressed his cheek with the back of her hand. "How long will you stay this time, darling? Please tell me this is to be a longer stay than the last."

"Perhaps several weeks," he said. "For I am weary…and have much to plan."

"Oh! I am glad for it!" the woman exclaimed embracing Navarrone again. "And you, James Kelly," she said, embracing James then. "Have you kept yourself from mischief?"

"I attempted to, Mrs. Navarrone," James said.

The woman held James at arms length a moment, smiling at him. She kissed his cheeks and giggled, "Well, that's all we can ask for, isn't it?"

"Yes, ma'am," James said as she hugged him again.

The woman glanced aside and caught sight of Cristabel then. She released James, took hold of Navarrone's hand, gasping and offering a broad smile.

"At last, Trevon!" she exclaimed. "At last!" Cristabel was astonished when the woman suddenly threw her arms about Cristabel, embracing her! "At last you have found her!" The woman released her embrace, but kept hold of Cristabel's arms—studying her from head to toe with a purely delighted expression of approval. "She's lovely, Trevon! Exactly what I would have expected you to choose for yourself. Are you already wed? Or have you yet to…"

"She is my prisoner, Mother," Navarrone interrupted.

His mother's smile faded—a frown puckered her exquisite brow.

"Your prisoner?" she asked. "Trevon Navarrone...what mischief are you about?" She released Cristabel—and Cristabel was somehow disappointed that she did.

Navarrone sighed—raked a hand through his dark hair. "It is a woefully long tale, Mother," he answered. "Cannot we simply rest a while, enjoy a meal...then I will tell you all about it. I promise."

Navarrone's mother returned her attention to Cristabel. "Have you been ill-treated in any manner, Miss...Miss..."

"Albay," Cristabel offered. "Cristabel Albay, ma'am."

"Cristabel is it?" Navarrone's mother inquired.

"Yes, ma'am."

"Well, I am Claire Navarrone...the mother of your apparent captor." Cristabel smiled when the woman cast a scolding glance to Navarrone. "And I would hope that you have been treated as a lady should be treated."

"In truth..." Cristabel began. Yet, instantly, Navarrone was upon her—at her back, pulling her against him—his strong hand suddenly covering her mouth.

"Trevon!" his mother scolded.

Still, he kept hold of Cristabel—continued to cover her mouth with his hand. Cristabel was unsettled by the wild delight rising in her. To be held by him—even for the sake he was merely trying to silence her—it was ferociously enlivening!

"She has been treated far better than any prisoner may expect, Mother," Navarrone said. "Especially for one who owns a tendency to be a nuisance."

"Oh, for mercy's sake, Trevon! You release that young woman this minute!" Claire demanded. She stamped one foot on the sand of the shore, wagged a reprimanding index finger at her son, and repeated, "This minute!"

"Mother," Navarrone began, "she is aligned with traitors and treason."

Cristabel began to struggle—for she did not want the woman to think badly of her—but Navarrone held her fast.

"Traitors?" Claire gasped, frowning at Cristabel. "She is a traitor to the country?"

"No," Navarrone answered. "But she holds information regarding traitors...in the least, one. Furthermore..." He paused—sighed as if resigned to some sort of defeat. "Furthermore, she is believed dead…and if it is found out she is yet living…it will not bode well for any of us."

Claire still frowned—studied first Navarrone and then Cristabel.

"I will hear this tale, Trevon," she announced. "Yet I know you are weary. The men need time with their families, and you and James Kelley need nourishment. Thus, I will wait to hear of it all…but only as long as it takes you to be fed."

"Very well," he resigned. "Allow me a moment of respite, and I will tell you everything I know concerning this little vixen." He removed his hand from Cristabel's mouth, yet taking hold of her chin as he placed his mouth close to her ear. "My mother will be your companion while we're here, love," he told her. "But I will never be far…so do not attempt any of your usual tomfoolery."

"Tomfoolery?" Navarrone's mother inquired.

"Ah, yes, Mother," Navarrone chuckled. "You'd best keep the rum hidden from Miss Cristabel Albay if you do not wish to find her tinkered up and gallivanting about in her undergarments."

"What?" Cristabel gasped—horrified that Navarrone would misrepresent events.

"Gallivanting in your underthings, is it?" Claire asked. Cristabel was certain she saw a twinkle of amusement in the woman's dark eyes. "Well, it's no wonder Trevon has held you captive."

"I swear to you, Madame…on my father's grave I swear…" Cristabel began in defense of herself.

"No need to swear, darling," Claire interrupted, however. She looked to her son—cupping his chin in one hand. "I am certain Trevon will see to any swearing that needs doing." Taking James Kelley's hand, she said, "Come along, James Kelley…you're far too thin for my liking."

"Yes, ma'am," James said, smiling with the gleeful anticipation of a child on Christmas morning.

Navarrone chuckled—kissed his mother on the temple.

"Come along then, love," he said taking hold of Cristabel's wrist. "I'd wager it has been a long time since you enjoyed a meal as fine as the one my mother will provide for you."

At the thought of good food, Cristabel's mouth did begin to water. As she followed Navarrone into the tree line, she glanced about at the others.

140

All were advancing to the trees, or had already disappeared into the safety of their cover. The only people remaining were men who were already boarding the small boats—obviously preparing to row back to the ship. However, these men were not the crew members with which Cristabel was familiar.

"Those are other members of The Merry Wench's crew. They stayed back to protect the families whilst we were out," James explained. He smiled at Cristabel. "When The Merry Wench sets sails again they will go with her, and some of us will be chosen to stay until she returns once more."

Navarrone stopped—turned to face James Kelley. "Heaven preserve us if you're to reveal every secret we own, James Kelley," he reprimanded, glaring at the boy.

"Sorry, Cap'n," James said, looking like a scolded puppy.

"Here," Navarrone said, offering Crirstabel's arm to James. "I'm weary. Lead her home, lad. You know the way."

"Aye, Cap'n!" James smiled at Cristabel and took hold of her arm.

Cristabel watched as Navarrone placed a strong arm about his mother's shoulders as they walked together. She smiled—pleased by his obvious affection for the woman.

"Them two is thick as mud," James whispered. "I'm grateful they treat me so well."

"So am I, James," Cristabel whispered, smiling at him.

James' smile faded, however. She watched as a wave of something akin to discouragement seemed to wash over him.

"What is it?" she asked.

"I'm sorry I led you astray, miss," he mumbled. "I'm sorry I led you into…into sacrificing your…yourself to the Cap'n for my sake." He frowned—as if puzzled. "Though I will say…your spirit, at least, don't seem damaged."

Cristabel's smile broadened. Navarrone had been correct—James' guilt was worse punishment than a flogging might have been. She glanced ahead to where the pirate captain and his mother were steeped in conversation.

Lowering her voice she spoke to James, saying, "Do you feel that you know your captain well, James Kelley?"

141

"Aye, miss," the lad answered.

"And you, yourself, told me he does not go wenching, yes?"

"Aye." He was puzzled and she giggled.

"Then do you truly think he would despoil me, simply as punishment…simply to be cruel?"

James thought a moment. Cristabel watched as understanding caused an expression of pure delight to capture his features.

"No, miss!" he exclaimed in a whisper. "Indeed, I do not think him capable of it."

Cristabel giggled again. "Then you have proven you do, indeed, know him well. For I am as unharmed as I was when first he found me on board The Screaming Witch."

"Oh!" James sighed, placing his free hand on his chest in a gesture of profound relief. "Oh miss…I am so comforted. I have been having nightmares…carrying such awful and burdensome guilt."

"I know," she said. "It was to be your punishment…finding no respite from the matter."

"I understand," he said. He shook his head with admiration, saying, "Cap'n Navarrone is a wise man indeed…for I might well have endured less pain under the lash of the cat." He chuckled. "At least, less pain of the mind."

"Yet, this must be our secret James," she whispered. "I could not allow you to linger in misery…but I owe Captain Navarrone my life…just as you felt you owed me yours. But you are young and…"

"And still learning from my own mistakes, miss," James finished for her.

"We are both young and still learning," Cristabel offered.

"It's like Cap'n Navarrone is always telling me…one decision…"

"Can change the entire course of a life," she finished.

"Yes, miss," James chuckled.

"She is our prisoner, James," Navarrone growled, glancing back over one broad shoulder. "Not our court jester."

"Aye, Cap'n," James called.

Navarrone shook his head with frustration—raked a strong hand through his dark hair.

Cristabel bit her lip to keep from giggling as she exchanged amused glances with James Kelley.

"You're our prisoner, miss," James whispered. "Not a court jester."

Cristabel covered her mouth to stop the laughter bubbling in her throat from escaping.

"James Kelley!" Navarrone bellowed.

"Aye, Cap'n. My apologies," James said.

They stepped into a clearing then. Cristabel gasped as she saw the wondrous vision that greeted them. There—built into the limbs of an ancient and enormous bald cypress tree, was a vast and finely crafted tree house. Looking quite like a large, brown gazebo with shutters, the house's center was founded around the tree's massive trunk. A smaller enclosure—looking the exact miniature of the first—was poised just above its counterpart. It was obvious that the shutters—though propped up and open in that moment—could be lowered and fastened in cases of inclement weather. Yet, for all its functionality, the pure craftsmanship and enchanting nature of the tree house, fairly took Cristabel's breath away!

"It's magnificent!" she breathed. "Like something from a dream!"

James Kelley smiled. "Aye. And it's home."

Cristabel watched—still awed—as Navarrone and his mother climbed the two flights of steep stairs.

"After you, miss," James said. He stepped aside and gestured that she should precede him.

A delighted giggle escaped her throat as she did, however, and Navarrone glanced down at her.

"It's like inviting an imp in and asking it not to cause mischief," he mumbled, glaring at her.

"Prisoner or not...you treat her as a lady should be treated, Trevon" Claire told her son.

Navarrone nodded to his mother—turned his back to the railing of the stairs—and motioned that Cristabel should precede him.

As she passed him, her shoulder brushed his broad chest and he mumbled, "Watch your step, love." Cristabel tried to ignore the thrill of breathless euphoria racing through her limbs as he put a hand at the small of her back, allowing it to linger as she reached the platform at the top of the stairs.

"Here we are," Claire cheerily exclaimed, smiling as she turned to Cristabel. The woman sighed—placed a tender, warm hand to Cristabel's cheek. "Oh, but you are lovely, dear. However has Trevon kept his hands from you?"

"I haven't," Navarrone said. Cristabel looked to see him striding toward a nearby hammock. He climbed into it—sighing with obvious fatigue and closing his eyes. "Nor have I known a decent moment's sleep since taking her aboard The Merry Wench."

Claire Navarrone sighed with exasperation—shook her head and rolled her eyes with impatience. "I will choose to ignore your insinuative remarks, Trevon. You are so like your father sometimes."

"Thank you for having me here, Mrs. Navarrone," Cristabel said, dropping a polite curtsy.

Claire smiled—brushed a stray strand of hair from Cristabel's cheek. "You're welcome, dear," she said.

"Mother!" Navarrone exclaimed from his place in the hammock. Cristabel looked to see him scowling at them. "She is my prisoner...not my playmate!"

"Prisoner or playmate...she will be treated well in my home, Trevon Navarrone," Claire said. "Now, sit down and have a bite to eat, dear." Cristabel nodded as Claire offered her a chair near a small table. "You must be famished! I know they could not have possibly fed you well with what stores they might have had left. The Merry Wench was at sea so very long this time. James? Darling...sit here with our lovely prisoner and I will prepare something savory for you both. Trevon? Darling? Oh, don't sleep yet, love! You must be famished!"

Yet, Trevon Navarrone kept his eyes closed—allowed the overwhelming fatigue that had been chasing him for weeks to overtake him. At last he could rest. The men guarding the ship would warn those ashore of any intruders or danger. His mother would see to Cristabel Albay and James Kelley. Suddenly, his body ached with weariness.

"Yes," he heard his mother say—though it was as if listening through a dense fog. "Trevon is named for my brother who was lost as an infant." He should scold his mother for revealing his given name to his prisoner—

yet he was too exhausted to care in that moment. "And you are quite sure he behaved with the utmost propriety?" he heard his mother ask.

"Of course, ma'am," Cristabel lied. "I owe him my life…more than once over. And what a thankless harpy I would be, if I did not defend his good character."

Navarrone grinned through his fatigue. She was a clever little vixen. He was, in fact, astonished she had not exposed the truth of all that had passed between them. His mouth flooded with excess moisture at the thought of hers—of her warm, ambrosial kiss. He grimaced—forcing his thoughts to return to the extreme weariness of his mind and body. He would leave her in his mother's care and rest—rest from privateering—from worry—from the growing desire in him to simply cache Cristabel Albay away in his tree house and never return to the sea. War was afoot—and treason—and neither could be ignored.

Navarrone forced his tired mind to other venues—to memories of childhood—to visions of the rural beauty of the fields and foliage surrounding Salem. The leaves of the trees would be changing just then—turning from green to brilliant crimson and orange. The old churches would be framed by the glorious flames of gold, ginger and scarlet leaves gently dancing in the breeze. It soothed him—the beautiful images of his home—visions of fields of ripening corn and pumpkin—visions of children at play in the cemetery where generations slumbered in peaceful repose.

"He is over-weary, as always," Claire said.

Cristabel smiled as she watched Trevon Navarrone sleeping in the hammock nearby.

"I have not seen him sleep…not since he found me," Cristabel muttered.

"That's because he ain't hardly done no sleeping since he brought you aboard, miss," James said, gratefully accepting a small loaf of bread when Claire handed it to him.

"Now, tell me, dear," Claire began, taking a seat at the small table, "how did you come to be Trevon's prisoner? And what is it you know that is so important?"

Cristabel paused, however—fearing Navarrone's wrath should she reveal too much. She now knew that each decision she made would have consequences, and though she could not foresee what consequences any particular choice would bring—she was wary.

"Don't worry, miss," James Kelley said then. "He'll be snoring in another minute."

Cristabel smiled at James—accepted a piece of bread when he offered it.

"In truth, your son saved my life…more than once," she began.

"Indeed?" Claire prodded. "Tell me the whole of it, Cristabel Albay. Oh, I do so favor that name! Cristabel…it's lovely…like the tinkling of tiny silver chimes."

Cristabel smiled, mustering her courage as James nodded to her with encouragement.

"Well, I suppose I must begin with my abduction from New Orleans," she began.

"Abduction?" Claire exclaimed, obviously unsettled.

"Not by Captain Navarrone, ma'am…by mercenaries," she explained.

"Oh, thank heaven!" Claire sighed. "I should drop dead if Trevon ever stooped to abduction."

Cristabel smiled—delighted with Navarrone's mother's apparent admiration of her son.

She spilled out the remainder of the tale then—of how she had been taken to the Chichester—of The Screaming Witch. She told Navarrone's mother nearly everything—leaving out only her experience with the rum— and she and Navarrone's tryst in his cabin. James Kelley interjected here and there—describing events or occurrences he felt might be of worth. Through it all, Navarrone slept—slumbered nearby in the comfortable hammock, stretched within the walls of the wistful house nestled in an ancient bald cypress tree.

"So," Cristabel began as she watched Navarrone enjoying the fine meal his mother had prepared, "Trevon is it?"

A grin tugged at the right corner of his mouth, causing butterflies to flutter in her bosom. He was ever so handsome! Even more so now that he lingered in a state temporarily void of angst and battle.

"Yes," he admitted. "Trevon Navarrone. Mother does not consider before she speaks at times."

"No secondary name? No mid-name?" she inquired.

He chuckled. "Oh, it must needs be I retain some secrets, love," he answered.

Cristabel sighed—somewhat perturbed that he would not reveal his middle name.

"And how long have you lingered here…on this island or inlet or whatever it is?" she asked.

"Two years," he answered.

"Who constructed this house?" she queried, glancing about the house.

"A pirate named Don Gabriel…he was a Spaniard," he mumbled.

"*Was?*" Cristabel whispered.

"Yes…was. He died…not four months ago."

"Was he your great friend?" she asked.

"Yes…and a master carpenter."

Cristabel paused to press Navarrone further—for she could see the agony of loss suddenly apparent in his countenance. Don Gabriel had been someone Navarrone cared for deeply.

"I'm so sorry," she mumbled.

"I miss him…but he was near ninety years when he gave up the ghost," he said. "A good long life for an outcast Spanish Don turned pirate, eh?"

Cristabel smiled as she saw a grin of remembrance spread over his lips. "Indeed."

"Do you plan to riddle me with questions and prodding all through my meal, love?" he asked, winking at her.

She blushed—suddenly ashamed that she was pestering him. "No, of course not," she answered—though still continuing to stare at him.

He shook his head—obviously amused. "James Kelley!" he called.

"Aye, Cap'n," James said, quickly removing himself from the hammock which had only a short time before served as Navarrone's respite.

"Have the men brought the Chichester's treasure ashore?" he asked.

"Aye, Cap'n," James said. "Whilst you was asleep."

"Good. Then would you be so kind as to escort my mother and the Spanish inquisition here, to see it?" Navarrone asked, nodding toward Cristabel. "You would like to see the wealth that was hidden aboard the

147

bloody British ship, wouldn't you, love?" He did not wait for her to answer—simply added, "Mother always enjoys sifting through jewels, and gold and silver coin." He winked at Cristabel again and she felt her cheeks pink with delight. "Once you've settled our prisoner and my mother 'midst our plunder, return to me, James…I have an errand for you."

"Aye, Cap'n," James agreed. "Come along, miss," he said, taking Cristabel's hand. "It's quite a jolly thing to sort through the plunder."

Cristabel was disappointed—almost wounded of the heart—at being so perceptibly dismissed by Navarrone. Still, she could see he was in want of solitude. Furthermore, the treasure did intrigue her—as well as did the idea of being in company with Navarrone's mother once more.

"Off with you now, love," Navarrone said as she stood and followed James Kelley. "Enjoy your game of sorting jewels and coin."

"As you enjoy your meal, Captain?" she could not help but tease.

"Exactly," he chuckled.

She followed James then—down the stairs leading to the ground—to the place where they found Claire visiting with other members of the crew.

"The booty is ashore, Mrs. Navarrone," James said as they approached.

"Oh, wonderful!" Claire exclaimed, clasping her hands together in delight. "Has Trevon given permission for me to see it?" she asked.

"Yes, ma'am," James said smiling. "And Miss Albay as well."

"Lovely!" she said as she fell into step beside Cristabel. "It's one of my favorite delights," she began to explain as they walked, "sifting through whatever treasure the men gather on their voyages. It will be divided evenly of course…and a fair percentage gifted to the poorhouses and asylums. Still, I do so love to see what rare and wonderful things have been collected."

"The poorhouses and asylums?" Cristabel asked.

"Oh yes, dear. Of course," Claire assured her. "You did not think we kept all the plunder gathered from other pirates and the bloody British all to ourselves, did you?"

"Well…well, yes," Cristabel admitted.

Claire laughed—then sighed. "Oh, I suppose Trevon would not have told you that…especially if he wishes for you to tremble with fear whenever he advances. God forbid you should mistake him for a philanthropist instead of a pirate, eh?"

"God forbid," Cristabel mumbled as she mused over what had only just been revealed to her concerning the captain and crew of The Merry Wench. She followed James Kelley and Claire Navarrone while lingering in a near trance-like state. Poorhouses and asylums? The privateers of The Merry Wench were charitable as well as patriotic? It was near inconceivable! Yet as her mind reviewed all she had witnessed, she felt as if she was indeed painfully ignorant not to have conceived it before.

As James led them into a thick outcropping of cypress and onto a dilapidated house boat, Cristabel pulled her thoughts from that of curious wonderment over Navarrone's character, and to the vision before her. There, strewn throughout the entire interior of the house boat, were piles of jewels, gems, gold coins and silver pieces of eight!

Baskerville greeted Claire as she gasped and giggled with merriment.

"We was quite surprised and well-pleased when we opened them barrels and crates from the Chichester's hold to find all this, ma'am," he chuckled.

"I have no wonder of it!" Claire exclaimed. She glanced around a moment, and then asked, "And Trevon thinks it all belonged to this William Pelletier?"

"Aye, ma'am," Baskerville said. "A treasonous traitor who deals in bartering human flesh as well."

A shiver of horror traveled up Cristabel's spine. To think she had been dwelling in the home of such a man—to think her mother still lingered near to him—it sickened her.

"Well, I'll sift through it a bit…and then you boys can dole it out as you see fit," Claire said.

"Yes, ma'am," Baskerville chuckled.

"The Cap'n allows his mother to search through the plunder…choose a few items to keep or give as Christmas gifts to the wives and children of the crew," James whispered aside to Cristabel. He smiled as she looked to him, adding, "Last year she gave me a gold doubloon…minted in 1751 it was."

Cristabel smiled—for it was sorely apparent that the fact Claire had presented James a gift for Christmas was far more valuable to the boy than the coin itself.

"She seems a very kind and worthy woman," Cristabel whispered.

"Aye, miss. That she is," James agreed.

"Come along, darling," Claire called to Cristabel then. "Come and sift through the treasure with me. Oh, it is such fun!"

As Cristabel joined Claire in looking into a chest filled with pieces of eight, she heard James Kelley say to Baskerville, "The Cap'n asked me to return to him at once, sir. Says he has an errand for me."

Baskerville chuckled. "Then it seems you did not linger long under his temper, boy. Count your blessings in that."

"Aye, Mister Baskerville...I will!" James said with a nod before exiting the house boat.

"It is a clever place to cache treasure," Cristabel said as she glanced around the one-room house boat.

"Yes!" Claire agreed, handing a fistful of silver pieces of eight to Cristabel. "Trevon is a clever boy...after all, who would think such a thing as this old floating house would secret such riches, eh?"

"Indeed," Cristabel giggled.

"Now, I like best the old pieces of eight, darling," Claire said then. "Help me search out a few older coins, will you?"

"Are the oldest coins rare...more valuable in some regard?" Cristabel asked.

"Not as the world sees them, love," Claire began, "but to me they are. The old ones have character. They have been weathered by adventure and experience. I like to sit and ponder them...wonder where they have been and what they have seen...whose hands once held them."

Cristabel smiled—delighted by the woman's dreamy sentiments.

"You see...here's one, dear," Claire said, offering Cristabel a worn-looking coin. "1739 is its date...see it there?"

Cristabel gazed at it—studied it with intrigued interest. The arms of Castile and Leon were hardly discernable on the reverse of the coin—as were the Pillars of Hercules on the obverse. Still, the date was there.

"1739," Cristabel whispered.

"And where do you think this coin has traveled in nearly 100 years?" Claire asked. "Has it been held in the hands of kings or queens? Paupers and pirates? What was it used to purchase? Rum? Food or clothing?"

"Your pondering of this simple coin…I find it fascinating," Cistabel mumbled as she studied the coin with even more intent.

Claire giggled. "So do I," she agreed. "But think of the truth in it…that very coin you hold was most likely first held by a man or woman who has long since gone to heaven. What mark did that person leave upon the soul of that coin?"

Cristabel smiled at Claire—entirely intrigued by what she had submitted to her thoughts.

"So this treasure…all of it," Cristabel began, "it is not the monetary worth of it that intrigues you…but rather it's value as a thing that has traveled through history as an adventurer."

"Exactly!" Claire exclaimed, smiling. Her eyebrows arched as she said, "Though do not misunderstand…for I do find the gems and jewels very, very beautiful. I own several pieces of unfathomable beauty…gifts from Trevon. Yet, even with rubies and sapphires set in silver and gold…it is their sequence of existence I adore imagining." She paused, sighed as she studied a particularly shiny gold doubloon. "I own a necklace crafted from silver and set with diamonds and sapphires. There is an inscription on the back of the middle gem's silver setting. Can you guess what it reads?"

"Never," Cristabel truthfully giggled.

Claire arched one eyebrow. Lowering her voice she whispered, "The inscription reads, *To Anne…this, as my heart…Louis XIII, 1615.*"

"No!" Cristabel gasped. "Truly? The King of France…to Anne of Austria?"

Claire shrugged—even as she smiled with beaming delight. "It cannot be proven…not without my giving it over to the French. Yet, what else could it mean? Furthermore, Trevon acquired it from pirates who had only just plundered a French ship. Therefore, I like to imagine that it is what it appears to be."

"Astonishing!" Cristabel breathed. "Purely fascinating!"

Claire inhaled a deep breath—studied Cristabel a moment. "Mister Baskerville," she called.

"Yes, ma'am?" Baskerville asked, approaching.

"List two pieces of eight under Trevon's bounty from this treasure hoard," she explained. "I am gifting them to Miss Albay...for I can see that she is truly appreciative of their origins and travels...just as I am."

"Oh no, ma'am!" Cristable argued, attempting to return all the pieces of eight she held to Claire. "I cannot possibly..."

"This one," Claire interrupted however, pressing the worn coin marked 1739 into Cristabel's palm. "And this one," she said, placing a more recently minted coin with it. Claire smiled, knowingly. "If you could only have one...which one would you choose?"

Cristabel smiled. "The worn one...without pause."

Claire nodded. "Mister Baskerville...mark two pieces of eight to Trevon's share of these spoils."

"Yes, ma'am," Baskerville chuckled.

Claire giggled then took Cristabel's free hand in hers. "Now, darling...help me find some sweet trinkets to give as gifts this Christmas, will you?"

"Of course," Cristabel said, still studying the coins in her hand. Navarrone's mother was enchanting! The moment of their first meeting she had fancied her very soul had begun to adhere to the woman's spirit— yet now—now she was assured of it. They were, as Thomas Gray had written in 1751, *kindred spirits*—and she was overwhelmed with a sudden feeling of having found an eternal friend. The mother of a privateer she may be—yet Claire Navarrone was a diamond—a rare gem of greater worth than any other that had ever lingered in the crown jewels of France.

Still clasping the two pieces of eight in her hand, Cristabel smiled as she began to sort through the gold, silver, gems and jewels cached in the ramshackle house boat. It was the very stuff of dreams—the treasure, the pirates—and most of all, Trevon Navarrone. She thought of the handsome privateer captain and her mouth began to water for want of his kiss—her body aching to be in his arms. It was the stuff of fantasy—all of it.

❧

In a lowered voice of conspiratorial tone, Trevon Navarrone said, "I have an errand for you, James Kelley."

"Aye, Cap'n," James whispered.

Navarrone smiled as he saw the boy's eyes illuminate with pride and excitement.

"It is a secret errand, lad," he began, "and one that may require patience. You are the only man for this errand and it is of profound importance."

"Yes, Cap'n," James said smiling.

"I have been musing, James Kelley," Navarrone explained. "This conspiracy looming where Cristabel is concerned…it taxes my mind greatly…as some intricate riddle or puzzle in need of solving."

"Aye, Cap'n," James agreed. "I can well see your frustration."

"Cristabel Albay is worried for her mother…along many venues does her worry meander," Navarrone said. "I would see one venue eliminated…that being her mother's misconception that her daughter is lost or dead. Yet, I pause in communicating this to Mrs. William Pelletier."

"For her husband is a traitor," James Kelley offered.

Navarrone chuckled. "You are a wise young man, James Kelley. Yes…part of me fears that Cristabel's mother may not keep silent…that she might reveal, even without intention, that Cristabel is alive. Yet, another part of me owns suspicions that Lisette Albay Pelletier may be more our kin than even her daughter realizes."

"How so, Cap'n?" James inquired.

"Cristabel revealed to me…under the influence of the devil rum…" Navarrone paused—chuckled at the memory of the proper Miss Albay sloshed to the wind. "She rather inadvertently revealed that she and her mother regularly visit Marie Blanchard's shop."

James Kelley's own brows arched—a smile donning his face as understanding began to wash over him.

"It is patriots and friends that frequent Marie Blanchard's," James whispered.

"Exactly," Navarrone said, smiling. "You are a clever lad."

"You're thinking Cristabel's mother knows her husband is a traitor…and is perhaps gleaning information that she then shares with fellow patriots, who frequently nibble on Marie Blanchard Biscuits."

"Yes," Navarrone confirmed. "That is why I want you to dress as a tattered and destitute orphan boy and give this note to Marie Blanchard," he said handing a letter sealed with wax to the boy. "Then wait for Lisette

Pelletier to appear. I am thinking she may be frequenting Marie's shop even more regularly in hopes of gleaning news of her lost daughter."

"Aye, Cap'n," James Kelley said. "It would seem reasonable."

"That it would, lad. Therefore, when Marie indicates to you that Lisette Pelletier has arrived, go to Cristabel's mother and feign begging for coins, and place this in her hand." Navarrone offered another letter sealed with wax to the boy.

"Aye, Cap'n," James said accepting the letter. "And I'm to stay…"

"Until you have completed this errand," Navarrone interrupted. "Then you know how to send our men a signal…and one of them will sail you back to us. Very well?"

"Very well, Cap'n," James Kelley agreed.

"Do this, James Kelley…do not fail me…and I will reward you very well."

"Aye, Cap'n. I will not fail you."

"Then go now," Navarrone ordered. "Fergus is waiting for you on the shore…he will direct you from there."

"Aye, Cap'n," James Kelley said, fairly leaping to his feet. The boy began to leave—but paused, turning back to Navarrone. "I owe you my life, Captain Navarrone…and I will not fail you."

"And I know I can trust in you, James Kelley," Navarrone said. "As I would trust my own brother, lad."

James Kelley smiled—sighed with pride and joy. "Aye, Cap'n."

Navarrone watched the boy go—hoped he would be careful and that his suspicions were correct where Cristabel's mother was concerned. He was risking near all he was and owned—the safety and lives of all those who depended on him in order to ease her mind over her daughter. He closed his eyes and silently prayed that he was not wrong in his strategies and trusts—prayed that he would not fail as he had failed once before—as he had failed Vienne.

≈

Cristabel stared at the two silver pieces of eight resting in her palm. She found Claire's interest in the older coin wildly contagious. In truth, Cristabel had spent the remaining hours of the afternoon in wondering where the coin might have traveled—what sights it may have seen. The more recently minted coin was lovely as well—shining and fresh—the artistic imprints on it detailed and quite lovely. Yet, Cristabel found that her heart was in full agreement with Claire's—the older coin was far more interesting—far more a treasure.

"I see my mother has infected your mind with her whimsical tales of the souls of commonplace objects."

Cristabel smiled as she turned to see Navarrone standing behind her. He wore a slight grin of amusement and appeared weary. Yet as ever—he was breathtakingly handsome.

"She makes a fascinating point, don't you think?" she asked.

Navarrone smiled—shrugged broad shoulders as he held one hand toward her. Rather unwillingly—for she somehow feared he may claim them for himself—Cristabel placed the two pieces of eight in his warm palm and watched as he considered them.

"Yes…she does," he admitted as his eyes narrowed and he studied the oldest coin. "One's attention is always drawn to the more weathered coin…is it not?" He chuckled and returned the coins to her. "I am glad to know my mother has corrupted you in some virtuous manner. Perhaps it will atone for the manner in which I endeavored to corrupt you…in which I still endeavor to corrupt you."

"In the first of it," she began, turning and lifting the lid of her trunk, "I am entirely incorruptible."

"Entirely incorruptible? No one is entirely incorruptible," he chuckled as she carefully placed the cherished pieces of eight in one corner of the trunk. She smiled—grateful that James and Navarrone had maneuvered her trunk into the upper tier of the tree house. Having her trunk near did comfort her somewhat.

"And in the second…you would not dare to endeavor to do anything improper to me with your mother so close at hand."

"Are you so certain, love?" he asked.

"Very," she said. Yet, considering him a moment she added, "At least I think I am certain." For in truth she was not so certain. In truth, she was hopeful that he would endeavor to corrupt her—but only a little.

Again Cristabel silently chastised herself for allowing such ridiculous and romantic musings to amble through her brain. Quickly she straightened the top layer of clothing in her trunk. Smiling she said, "I know your reasons for ransacking the contents of my trunk, Captain Navarrone. Still, I do wish you would at least have left the sprigs of…"

Cristabel paused—for a startling understanding had instantly begun to wash over her. She could not believe she had not thought of it before.

"What is it?" Navarrone asked. He took hold of her shoulders, turning her to face him. It was obvious by his curious and rather concerned expression, that he sensed her disconcertment.

"The sprigs of lavender," she whispered.

Navarrone's frown grew more severe. "Sprigs of lavender?" he asked.

"Y-yes," Cristabel stammered. "I-I am so very used to seeing them…whenever Lavinia prepares my trunk."

The girl appeared far too unsettled—had instantly grown pale. Trevon tightened his grip on her shoulders and asked, "Who is Lavinia?"

"One of the servants…a servant girl w-who lingers in Richard's employ," she whispered.

"Richard's servant?" Trevon inquired. "Why ever would she be attending to you?"

"Richard always and ever has her attend to me. I-I'm very fond of her. There's a certain lack of pretentious attitude I admire in her. Yet…yet if it was Lavinia who prepared this trunk…Lavinia who prepared my trunk in anticipation of my abduction…"

Trevon could see the pain and returning fear welling in her eyes—and he felt the need to comfort her somehow.

"This Lavinia prepared your trunk, love," he said. "It does not mean she knew for what purpose she prepared it."

"B-but…" she began.

"Furthermore, it may indeed reveal something further to us concerning this ambiguous treason swirling about you," he continued. "It is true that after our meeting with the governor we know Richard is somehow dabbling in your step-father's treasonous activities…but now I am led to wonder if it was not, in truth, Richard himself who orchestrated your abduction and passage aboard the Chichester." He paused—for tears brimmed in the girl's eyes—disappointment and fear the like he had never before seen in her before owned her countenance.

"What is it?" he inquired. "Is there something else?"

She shook her head—yet his heart felt as if some bloody dagger had been plunged into his bosom as he watched tears spill from her violet eyes.

"I-I cannot believe it all," she confessed in a whisper. "I-I dwelled in that house with William Pelletier as my step-father...agreed to marry a man I do not even care a wit for...and yet...they endeavored to..."

"It is all in your past, love," he interrupted. He was surprised—in truth astonished—for Cristabel Albay had thus far weathered more than some men could manage—but here she stood before him, weak and vulnerable—wounded and frightened. "And I'll see them hang for what they did to you...and for their efforts to betray this country," he growled.

"But my mother...she thinks I am dead...that I have abandoned her to a life of further misery with William Pelletier." Panic seemed to wash over her and she reached out, desperately fisting the fabric of his shirt in her small hands. "She is all alone and in the hands of traitors!" she cried.

He must settle her—was desperate to soothe her.

Taking her face between his hands he brushed the tears from her cheeks with his thumbs, saying, "All will be well with your mother, Cristabel."

"No! No she..." she began as near hysteria began to overtake her.

"Hush, now, love," he assured her. "I have sent word to your mother concerning your safety and well-being. She will be comforted."

Though tears still spilled from her lovely eyes, the expression of panic began to abandon her pretty face.

"Y-you sent word?" she asked.

"Yes," he assured her. He felt his own anxiety begin to lessen as she calmed.

"Why?" she inquired in a whisper. "Why would you wish to give her comfort?"

Navarrone smiled. He would not tell her that he wished to comfort the mother who had given birth to such a beautiful, brave young woman. He would not tell her his heart was tender toward her—that he had grown protective of her—wildly protective. It was too much for a pirate to reveal. He was certain she would see it as weakness in him.

Therefore, he simply answered, "I would not want to witness my own mother suffer in vain over me...thus I would not wish to know yours is in unnecessary pain and grief. You have showered the wealth of the

Chichester upon me, love…handed me treason and traitors to best. I would be ungrateful to my tempting little prisoner if I did not offer some sort of remuneration."

She grinned. "I have no doubt that you're babbling off some sermon of morality…yet, I am too weary…too relieved in knowing my mother will be comforted to make sense of it."

He chuckled. "If you are too weary to take my sermons to heart, then perhaps you should retire, love."

"Perhaps," she agreed, releasing the fabric of his shirt—smoothing the wrinkles she had caused with her warm palms. Her touch was far too invigorating and Navarrone released her—straightened his posture and stepped back from her.

"I bid you sleep well then," he said.

The pirate bowed in slight, and Cristabel smiled—charmed by his gallant gesture. He had sent a message to her mother! It was far more than could ever be expected of a pirate—even a privateer. She was assured that her growing admiration of Trevon Navarrone's character was not so perfectly ill-placed, after all. She thought of his compassion and consideration—affection and love toward his mother. She thought of his philanthropic attitude where distributing plunder to poor houses and asylums was concerned. She thought of his treatment of James—of his treatment of his entire crew for that matter. Furthermore, she realized that, though he may have been brutal and threatening toward her, he had never truly harmed her. Rather he had thrilled and delighted her more often than not.

The privateering pirate Trevon Navarrone was more hero than anything else—a patriot—fighting for the country's safety under the guise of piracy. It was indeed a ruse of sorts—for what pirate captained his ship with such camaraderie and trust, and respect of his men? What pirate did not violate a young woman when given the chance? What pirate kept his mother in such safe comfort? Furthermore, what pirate would care enough for his prisoner to offer her own mother comfort?

Cristabel smiled as she thought of her own pirate ruse—of dressing as James to attend the meeting with the governor. She mused that Navarrone the Blue Blade was not so very different than she—and her heart swelled—accepted what it had been fighting to accept. Cristabel was drawn to Navarrone—like a moth to a candle flame. She craved his attention—his conversation—his affections—and in those moments she did not experience guilt in owning such thoughts toward him. In those moments she saw him for what he truly was—a hero—a patriot—a champion.

"I will leave you to your sleep then," he said. He turned to leave her, but paused. Looking back over his shoulder to her he warned, "But remember, love…you remain my prisoner…a woman associated with traitors and you are my means to thwarting them. So do not attempt escape. You would become lost in the swamps and perish…and the Pelletiers would continue in their treachery. Do not let my mother's kindness to you veil the truth of the reasons for your presence here."

"I may be motivated by defiance on occasion, Captain…but I'm not entirely asinine," she said, somewhat offended he would think her so ignorant as to attempt to escape from such obvious and complete isolation.

He chuckled. "I see I've pricked your tender little pride once more," he said. "You know what is said of pride, don't you, love? Pride goeth…"

"Before the fall," she interrupted. "I well know it." Her eyes narrowed as she glared at him. "I cannot fathom why it is you chose a life of piracy…when you seem so much better suited to that of a preacher."

He laughed then, and his smile lit up the night like the stars in the heavens.

"Oh, I own too many sinful desires where you are concerned to ever fathom becoming a preacher, love," he said. "Thus, keep a weary eye about you as you sleep…for my mother's close proximity will not stay me from coming for you if the preacher precedes the pirate to slumbering."

"I bid you goodnight then, Reverend Captain," she mocked.

Navarrone's smile broadened. "Goodnight then, Sister Temptress."

As she watched him stride from her, Cristabel experienced the overwhelming desire to rush after him—take hold of his arm and demand his attention—to kiss him! She gritted her teeth—clasped her hands tightly at her waist to keep from running to him. She listened to him descend the stairs leading to the main tier of the tree house before she exhaled the breath she had been holding.

"I would be locked away in the furthest basement corner of the asylum if my thoughts could be read," she whispered to herself. "A pirate? What hope is there in loving a pirate?" Cristabel gasped—her hands moving to cover her mouth. Love? Had she truly spoken the word in reference to Navarrone? It was madness! Surely it was proof of literal lunacy!

Quickly she turned toward the small bed, collapsed upon it as waves of dizziness and fatigue overtook her. She knew any woman would be drawn to Trevon Navarrone—but to consider allowing oneself to fall in love with him—insanity!

"I have become a lunatic pirate woman!" she breathed as the memory of the villain she had run through for the sake of James Kelley washed over her. She briefly wondered where James Kelley had gone to. She had not seen him since the afternoon. Still, her thoughts quickly returned to Navarrone—to the goose flesh racing over her arms as a vision of him lingered in her mind. She thought of the kisses they had shared in his cabin—and her mouth watered for want of tasting his again. A sudden and near consuming aching to be held by him began in her arms—spread through her bosom and stomach. Tears welled in her eyes as an internal echo whispered through her being—*I love him*!

All at once Cristabel's emotions were too great to bear. As her tears escaped her eyes to trickle over her cheeks, she thought of her mother—hoped she would find comfort from the message Navarrone had sent. She thought of the treasonous traitors that had been surrounding her for two years. She thought of her dead father, missing him with excruciating pain of loss. She thought of James Kelley—wondered where he dallied—hoped he was well and happy. She thought of Trevon Navarrone—the pirate Navarrone the Blue Blade—and it was her undoing. Her weeping turned to sobbing and she prayed for sleep to take her—to ease her mind—that she would find her strength renewed by morning.

Brushing tears from her cheeks, Cristabel's contemplations lingered for a moment on the two pieces of eight gifted her by a pirate's own mother, and now cached safely in the trunk Lavinia had prepared for her. She mused that she was now more akin to the older and worn silver coin than she was the new one. Her weathering had begun with her father's death—continued until she found herself the prisoner of a pirate she had fallen in love with. She wondered if her new weathering was as evident on her face as the coin's was.

"Trevon Navarrone," she whispered, choking on her own emotions. "I am as much yours as the treasure in the house boat...for you have plundered my heart as you plundered the Chichester's riches."

# Chapter Eleven

"Thank you, boy," Cristabel's mother whispered. "And tell your captain...he is correct in his estimations of me...as well as in his estimations of my husband, William Pelletier."

"I will, ma'am," James said, offering a smile of assurance.

The bell at the door tinkled, indicating another patron who favored Marie Blanchard's pastries had entered the shop.

James glanced up to the elderly baker woman. No one must suspect he was not the homeless orphan he was pretending to be and Marie Blanchard knew it as well. Thus, taking hold of her broom, she forced a frown at him.

"Out with you, boy," she growled, swishing the broom at him. "I have no time for beggars to be bothering my patrons. Out!"

"Is everything in order?" the tall man who had only just entered the shop inquired scowling at James.

"Oh, he doesn't mean any harm, I'm sure of it," Lisette Pelletier said. "Here boy...take this."

James nodded and mumbled, "Thank you, ma'am," as Cristabel's mother pressed a silver coin into his palm.

"Now, off with you before you unsettle anyone further. Very well?" Lisette encouraged.

"Yes, ma'am," James said. "Thank you, ma'am."

"Out with you, boy...be on your way," Marie said, waving one hand in a gesture of dismissing him.

James nodded to Marie Blanchard—thought what a perfect patriot she was—for no one would suspect her of such secretive doings. Her white hair and blue eyes gave her the look of an angel—even for her weathered and wrinkled appearance. He nodded once more to Cristabel's mother—thinking he knew then just how Cristabel would appear with twenty more years to her name—for her mother was as beautiful as Cristabel was—simply more matured.

The male patron growled with impatience and James took his leave of the shop. Once he had turned onto another street, he chuckled. Success! He had delivered Captain Navarrone's letters—both the letter to Marie Blanchard and the one to Cristabel's mother! No other wonder in the world could compare to the joy that leapt to Lisette Albay Pelletier's face when she read of her daughter being alive—and safe. James knew he would never forget the look of pure happiness in her eyes at having read the news. Oh, certainly it had been plain obvious to James that Cristabel's mother wished to speak with him further—to inquire after details of where her daughter was and how she had come to be taken and then rescued. Yet, the woman was wise—as all patriots must be—and she simply scribbled a short response to Captain Navarrone's letter. Lisette had, in fact, handed the letter of response to James only moments before the other patron of the shop had entered.

It had been four days since James had ventured out to complete the errand Navarrone had asked him to undertake. He had traveled to New Orleans—waited for his best opportunity to contact Marie Blanchard first, and then Cristabel's mother. Yet now the errand his captain had asked of him was finished—and pride swelled within his young bosom. He had not failed his captain—he had not failed Cristabel. Her mother now knew she was alive and safely guarded. James would return to the hidden community of pirates and their families knowing he had endeavored to do his captain's will—and succeeded. Perhaps Captain Navarrone would truly forgive him for having allowed Cristabel to accompany the away crew to meet the governor.

James Kelley shoved his hands into the tattered front pockets of the worn trousers he wore as part of his disguise. He would seek out his fellow crew members awaiting him at the docks—and return to Captain Navarrone—triumphant and ready for a new errand.

As he sauntered along the streets of New Orleans, James Kelley began to whistle—for his heart was happy, and his hopes high once more.

❧

"Yet, how do you know they will keep their word?" Cristabel asked, dipping her head back into the water. The water was refreshing. She felt as if her skin and hair had not been properly bathed in years! Still, she was wary—for she could not believe that the men who dwelt in the secreted pirate community were gentlemen enough to honor rules—rules such as not visiting the fresh water bathing pool on certain days.

"They may be pirates, darling," Claire explained with a smile, "but we women keep them lined up just as they should be where these sorts of things are concerned."

"And their days to bathe here are in opposition to ours?" Cristabel asked.

"Yes," Claire confirmed. She smiled—her eyes fairly dancing with mischief. "Therefore, you must be wary to well-remember which days to visit the bathing pools and which days not to…else the innocence of your eyes be lost."

"Indeed," Cristabel giggled. Again, she dipped her head back in the water—savored the feel of freshness over her skin.

It had been five days since The Merry Wench had dropped anchor in a small hidden bay—and Cristabel had relished every moment of them. Navarrone's mother was delightful—so very like her own mother—kind, loving, attentive and considerate. She enjoyed Claire's company and conversation. Yet, it was Trevon Navarrone's company and conversation that Cristabel savored. The pirate Navarrone the Blue Blade was yet severe at times—for he and the crew had been laying plans for their next voyage as well as discussing strategies to reveal William Pelletier's treason to the Governor.

Still, even for all the concerns he bore—even for his obvious desire to best William and Richard Pelletier (and any other man who dared to involve himself in treason)—there was a certain manner of calm that had begun to settle over Navarrone. Oh, he was ever the leader of his men—ever the strategic genius and thoughtful admiral of war. Yet, his brow was not so consistently puckered with worry—his voice more often the deep intonation of allure rather than the growl Cristabel had grown accustomed to while aboard The Merry Wench. It was often he sat with Cristabel and his mother at the small table in the tree house, sharing humorous stories of his childhood, or adventurous tales of his privateering expeditions. He was yet guarded in her company—Cristabel was not naive enough to think he was not. Still, he was all the more attractive, all the more fascinating in his current condition, even than he had been (and would be) in his pirate-captain-at-sea circumstance.

Furthermore, with each passing day—with each passing hour and moment—Cristabel found herself deeper and deeper in love with him! It was as if he were some sort of handsome quicksand of perfect masculinity—drawing her deeper and deeper into the smoldering warmth of his eyes. The beguiling knowledge that his kiss was more desirable and satisfying than any confectionary wonder often consumed her thoughts—caused her mouth to water for want of his again.

Cristabel knew that the dream of lingering in the pirate community with Navarrone would end—that she must awaken and face the truth—the reality of all that had transpired before. Yet, she in constant pushed such thoughts of consequence and future from her mind—determined to bathe in Trevon Navarrone's attention for each precious moment allowed her.

Cristabel finished her bath—toweled, dressed and combed her hair. She did not braid it into a plait, however—for she enjoyed the feel of liberation wearing it down allotted her.

"Do you feel quite refreshed, darling?" Claire asked as she sat in brushing out her own hair.

"Oh, yes!" Cristabel chimed. "Bathing always offers such renewal and vigor."

"Indeed, it does," Claire agreed. She smiled at Cristabel, suggesting, "Why not allow yourself a little wandering on the shore. I often enjoy meandering there…searching for sea glass on the sand…or tiny creatures to observe."

"Is it allowed?" Cristabel asked—for she had not been to the shore since The Merry Wench had dropped her anchor in the bay upon arrival.

"Occasionally," Claire answered. "I know there are others who have gone today…therefore, Trevon must've granted this day as one when we can venture there."

"I do not want to provoke him," Cristabel began.

"Oh, you won't," Claire assured her. "I would not send you out if I did not think he would approve." She smiled—winked at Cristabel and added, "What's good for the pirate is good for the pirate's prisoner, eh?"

"Very well," Cristabel giggled. "If you're certain it would be all right...for I am terribly bored with no horizon to view. The trees conceal everything so perfectly. I feel as if I am lingering in a hole or some such thing."

"I understand perfectly," Claire said, nodding with emphatic understanding. "I sometimes think I might go mad if I have to live out the entirety of my life here...even for its ethereal beauty. Thus, take your stroll...enjoy it. But please do not tarry too long...else Trevon begins to worry you have endeavored to escape him."

"Of course," Cristabel said. "I will return soon. Thank you, Mrs. Navarrone."

Claire smiled, attempting to restrain her pride in her own cleverness. She knew Trevon was at the shore—that he had gone there for respite and thought. Yet, Claire was impatient with her son. It seemed as if there were certain things in life that he leapt into—fearless of harm or death being the possible consequence. Yet, in other venues, he paused. It was as if Trevon feared pain more than death—and though Claire knew why this was so—she had grown impatient with him where Cristabel Albay was concerned.

Therefore, she saw only one road to take—she must intervene on his behalf. Hence, she sent Cristabel out to unwittingly find him—hoped Trevon's good sense would own him for once, and that he would finally weaken enough toward his lovely prisoner to admit to himself he was keeping her for very different reasons than he professed.

"Let us hope, however, that your father's chivalry is well-founded in your character today, Trevon Navarrone," she whispered to herself as she watched Cristabel disappear into the line of trees that would lead her to the shore and Trevon. "For I would not wish the pirate in you to compromise your restraint where your prisoner is concerned, boy."

Still, Claire smiled—for she knew Trevon's heart—and it was ever so good.

❧

Trevon closed his eyes. As the sun warmed the shore, the rhythm of the surf lulled him to rare tranquility. He savored the feel of the sand beneath his feet—between his toes. The air was fresh and zestful—untainted—so unlike the stale, stagnant vapor of New Orleans. He could hear the distant call of gulls—imagined fish and other creatures of the sea frolicking in the cool depths beneath the water's surface. For long moments, Trevon knew a measure of serenity. His mind was uncluttered—temporarily void of worry, strategizing, anger or frustration. As his soul found respite, he felt his strong body begin to relax as well. He mused he would like nothing more than to lay on the warm sand forever—lulled by the breeze and the calm cadence of the gently breaking waves.

Yet, void-mindedness never lingered long for Trevon Navarrone's sake. As a vision began to form in his thoughts, the pirate Captain Navarrone the Blue Blade, permitted himself to indulge in a luxury he rarely allowed—abandoning reality to linger in fantasy—and Cristabel Albay was there. As the sun and sand soothed him—as the savory air filled his lungs—as the soft waves lapped at the shore—he thought of Cristabel. In his mind he could see her vividly—clothed as he secretly preferred her—in her long chemise—her corset worn over it. Trevon envisioned Cristabel wandered along the shore—approached the place where he lay. In this yearning visualization, her long, dark hair feathered on the wind—an alluring smile donning her sweet, pink lips. He imagined her smile was meant for him—an invitation to kiss her—to own her. Oh, if he were another man in another life—he would move the moon and stars in the heavens to own Cristabel Albay's favor—to win her heart—to bed her as his wife. Yet, he frowned—for he was not another man—and he owned no other life. Thus, nearly as quickly as it had begun, Trevon Navarrone's alluring daydream was ended.

He moved one hand from behind his head—rubbing at the sudden burning in his eyes.

"Does your head pain you, Captain?"

At the sound of her melodic voice, Trevon opened his eyes, shading them from the sun's intensity with one hand.

"A bit, love," he answered. His mouth began to water at the sight of Cristabel standing over him. "Only a bit." He grinned as she sat down next to him—burying her toes in the sand.

"You've had too much sun today, perhaps," she suggested.

"Perhaps," he agreed.

He watched as she gazed out to the sea, and smiled.

"It is a lovely space in which you all linger here," she sighed. "No noise...no strangers. I can well see why everyone loves it so."

"It is our haven," Trevon said. "Jean Lafitte prefers excitement, and risk. Perhaps if he had been less indulgent, he would have been left to his smuggling and exploits in Barataria. As for me and my men...we enjoy our solitude. And yet...often I still long to be somewhere else."

"Where?" she asked—and he wished he had not spoken his thoughts aloud.

He shrugged. "It's of no importance."

"Tell me," she pressed, however. "Where would you rather be...right this moment?" She glanced up into the sky. "The sun is warm...even for the fact it is autumn elsewhere. It seems to me a man of the sea would prefer a warm climate. So tell me...where is it you long to be, Captain Navarrone?"

Trevon sighed. What harm could there be in answering her question? "Salem," he mumbled.

"Salem?" she asked, smiling at him. "You mean home."

He chuckled—amused by her insight. "Yes."

Cristabel felt a warmth swelling in her heart—an empathy of understanding. Though she had never been to Salem—though she had never been farther north than Charlotte—she knew what it was to long for the place of one's youth. When her mother had married William Pelletier, he had insisted they leave Charleston for his home in New Orleans. Cristabel had wept bitter tears over many long nights in missing her true home. She missed the fragrance of the flowers there—missed the kind people she had known. She missed the feel of the South Carolina grass beneath her feet—missed her father and the happy life she and her mother had shared with him.

"Then tell me about your Salem," she said. "Tell me what it feels like to be there."

Trevon's smile broadened. "Why?" he asked.

Cristabel shrugged. "I have never been there...yet I have heard much about it. Is it truly as beautiful in the autumn as everyone claims it to be?"

Navarrone sighed, "Yes...indeed it is."

"Then tell me of it," she insisted. "Tell me why it is you would rather be in Salem."

He grinned at her and she smiled in return—for she knew he would tell her.

"The days are cool and crisp," he began. "Scenes of harvest are everywhere in the outlying country...shipping and trade at the waterfront." He paused, wistfully smiled and said, "Though I prefer the fields and open spaces of the outlying farms."

"As would I," she told him.

"In the autumn, the leaves of the trees begin to change," he continued, "and it is as if one awakens one morning to find himself bathed in a pageant of color...as if during the night some master painter dipped his brushes into a palette of crimson and gold...orange and plums that no mere mortal imagination could conjure," he said. Cristabel sighed—contemplative—wondering what such variances of colors in the trees might inspire in herself were she to witness them. "Everywhere there lingers comforting aromas upon the air," he continued. "Kettles simmering with warm, hearty stews...the sweet essence of apples as they are pressed to juice. Pumpkins lay in fields, round and plump...sheltered among their lavish, green vines spread over the earth...and looking like fanciful orbs of orange treasure."

He closed his eyes a moment, and sighed. Cristabel's smile broadened when she saw his smile broaden.

"Fanciful orbs of orange treasure," she repeated, exhaling a dreamy sigh of her own. "Why, Captain Navarrone...you're a poet and a pirate!"

Trevon chuckled. "Not a poet, love...just a pirate who would linger forever in a field of ripening pumpkins if he could. All the gems and gold in the world heaped up together, would not be so beautiful to me as a field of pumpkins...the rows of corn stalks reaching high...the colors of the leaves in the trees when summer has given way to autumn."

"You *are* a poet, Captain," Cristabel giggled.

He chuckled. "I suppose I should tell you the bad of it as well."

"The bad of it?" she prodded—curious.

"In the autumn, as the sun begins to set, the tombstones in the cemeteries cast long, ominous shadows," he began. "As darkness descends, the spirits of the dead begin to rise and wander the earth...especially the spirits of those wrongly accused in the trials...the spirits of those who were hanged...or met death by more gruesome means."

Cristabel's eyes widened, and Navarrone had to bite his tongue to keep from laughing—for the expression on her face was not so much that of trepidation—but delighted curiosity.

"You're lying, of course," she said—though he knew she hoped he was not.

"Yes, love," he chuckled then. "I am lying...though there are stories that abound...and there are those who claim to have seen spirits lurking about in the shadows or beneath the full moon."

"Ooo! Then tell me a story of shadows and full moons!" she breathed. "Something deliciously frightening and gruesome!"

Trevon laughed—entirely amused by her interest. "Is it not enough for you to know that I am descended of one who was hanged as a witch?"

Cristabel's violet eyes fairly sparkled with anticipation. "So you are a pirate...descended of a witch?"

"I suppose that I am," he answered. He studied her a moment—enraptured by her beauty and charm. "Therefore, why is your smile that of such delight? You should be trembling in the presence of a pirate who is progeny of a witch."

"In the first of it," she began, "you are a privateer...not a pirate. And in the second...the women of the Salem Witch trials were not truly witches. Therefore, I do not see how you have any claim to intimidation through your piracy or ancestry."

"So, to you I am merely a simple man on the shore," he said. "Not so unlike your traitorous Richard might be."

He chuckled when Cristabel rolled her eyes. "You are always unlike Richard...*very* unlike Richard...unlike any man," she whispered. He chuckled and she smiled at him. "Yet, you do seem somewhat dissimilar to your average demeanor today. How is it you are so varying today, Captain?" she asked. "What is the difference between the pirate captain Navarrone, and the simple man on the shore?"

"A pirate would simply ravage you, love," he said, smiling at her. Cristabel blushed and was pleased. "But the man on the shore…he would endeavor to charm you…seduce you with tender flirtation void of dominant virility…perhaps beg a pristine kiss."

"Would he indeed?" she asked, still blushing. "And this man on the shore…how is it that he could so easily mollify the rogue within him?"

Trevon chuckled. "I did not say it would be done with ease…only that it could be done."

"Pff!" Cristabel puffed with amused disbelief.

"Are you doubting me, love?" he asked. He was yet smiling—but she could see playful indignation in his countenance.

"Vastly!" she answered.

Cristabel giggled as Trevon gasped in pretense of offense. Dramatically he put one strong hand to his bosom.

"My lady!" he exclaimed, still feigning assault. "You plunge a dagger of insult into my heart!"

Cristabel rolled her eyes—simultaneously amused and appalled. "Tender flirtation? A pristine kiss?" She shook her head. "You could not do it. You could not put off your demanding, dominant virility long enough to even attempt the application of either."

"You are so certain, are you?" he asked. "So absolute in your opinion that I cannot be tamed?"

"Consummately," she assured him.

"I quite like your selection of phrase there, love," he chuckled.

"There! You see? You have only just proven that my determination is correct!" she exclaimed as her blush deepened. "You could not maintain a gentleman's character for even the brief length of time necessary to…to beg a pristine kiss." Cristabel cocked her head to one side—frowning inquisitively as she seemed to consider him. "Do you even own a concept of what a pristine kiss would be?"

Trevon shrugged. "Boring?" he responded.

Cristabel laughed and Trevon fancied the sound was like that of perfectly tuned chimes.

"There you have it!" she giggled, shaking her head. "You cannot even conceive of decency!"

"Conceive. Yet another interesting choice of word on your part...and you are right there, love," he said, feigning thoughtfulness. "I cannot conceive...but you...you can. But only with my help, of course...though it would hardly be deemed a thing of decency."

"Captain Navarrone!" Cristabel exclaimed, fairly leaping to her feet. She stomped one foot in the sand and he chuckled—amused by her indignation. "You must not utter such improper implications!"

"Oh, sit down, love," he said, reaching up and taking hold of her hand. Gripping her wrist he tugged at her arm until she relented and settled in the sand next to him once more. "You know I am merely teasing you. You make it so effortless to do so."

"You are an absolute rogue," she grumbled at him. "A rakish, knavish rogue."

"Pirate, love," he corrected with a chuckle. "Pirate."

"Either way, you all sprout from the same bean," she said, shaking her head. Yet, by the scarlet on her cheeks and the smile tugging at the corners of her mouth, Trevon Navarrone knew she was not so appalled at him as she wished him to believe.

"Anyway," she sighed. "You could not be the man on the shore instead of the pirate. Your own behavior has already bested you."

"Try me then, Miss Albay," he dared her. "Give us a kiss...and I promise to be the man on the shore and not the pirate."

Cristabel studied him a moment—her lovely brows arched in an expression of ambiguity. "I would no more kiss you than I would any other blackguard."

Trevon smiled. "But you forget, love." Lowering his voice he added, "You have already kissed me." He delighted in the appearance of alarm mingled with indignation on her face.

"You kissed me, Captain!" she exclaimed.

"And you kissed me in return," he reminded her. "Furthermore...you kissed me first."

Cristabel hoped Trevon did not see the goose bumps racing over her arms. The memory of their moments together in his cabin the night after

173

settling with Governor Claiborne—the returning sensation of bliss evoked by his kiss and touch—had sent goose flesh rippling over her entire being.

She swallowed—fought to think with clarity. He was baiting her—she knew he was. Their banter was, as ever, entertaining—wonderful—yet she stood on a precipice of forfeit now. She must think—own wit and cleverness.

"I suppose…I suppose I did," she admitted. "But I only did it because…"

"Because I rouse lust in you?" he offered.

Cristabel gasped and he chuckled—amused by her astonished expression.

"Because you rouse spite in me, Captain!" she corrected him.

"Lust," he countered.

"Spite," she said in return.

He laughed and she thought his smile was the most pleasing sight on all the earth. Trevon Navarrone's smile ever sent a thrill through her—especially when she was the cause of its appearance on his handsome face.

"Lust or spite…whatever the reason…the fact remains that you did kiss me first," he reminded her.

"Yes, I did," she admitted. "Though my kiss to you was indeed pristine. Something you could never discipline yourself to apply…pirate that you are."

He shrugged his broad shoulders. "Why should I desire it…when the blending of our mouths in full passion's meld was so much the more pleasurable?"

Again she gasped—again he chuckled.

"You are the most inappropriate, ill-behaved man I have ever known!" she exclaimed.

"Then tame me, love," he dared her. "Tame the pirate in me to offering only the pristine kiss the simple man on the shore would offer."

Cristabel felt an odd disappointment well within her—for in truth, she would never see him tamed. She adored him as the roguish patriot pirate he was—loved his insinuative banter and teasing—loved him. Why then would she ever wish to change him? She did not wish it. Still, she must maintain the pretense of disapproval—else she entirely lose herself to dreaming of what her heart most wished for—to belong to Trevon Navarrone.

"There is no hope in taming a rogue such as you Trevon Navarrone," she told him as she rose to her feet. "For you are not meant to be tamed. You were born to your wild and passionate ways...to your freedom. And it suits you."

She was making ready to leave him. Trevon sensed he had pressed her too far—frightened her. Yet, he could not give her up—not yet—not until he had known the warm nectar of her kiss once more. Thus, he reached out, caressively taking hold of her ankle with one hand. Oh, it was well he remembered the tale she had told him that first night she had spent aboard The Merry Wench—the tale of the Acadians who had 'violated' her ankles. He knew how truly offended she would be at his touching the ankle—either offended or delighted—and when she did not run from him—he smiled—for it was an acceptance of sorts—an invitation.

"You're not leaving me now, are you?" he asked, still holding her ankle with one hand.

"I-I...of course I am," she managed. "I promised your mother I would not tarry...else you begin to think I..."

"Stay a moment more," he said, gently tugging on the hem of her gown. "For you have accused me of being a rogue who cannot be tamed. It is only fair that you allow me the opportunity to prove myself otherwise. Do not judge and hang me unjustly...the way the Salem magistrates judged and hanged my innocent ancestor."

She sat down promptly then—yet he wondered if it was for the sake she had decided to stay with him—or the fact that his attention to her ankle had weakened her knees. She sat opposite him—her back to the sea in facing him.

"As I said," he began, releasing her ankle—for he did not want to press her to trepidation. "Today I am but a simple man on the shore...a simple man...begging a pristine kiss from a lovely young woman of his acquaintance."

As Trevon Navarrone sat staring at her, Cristabel swallowed the excess moisture suddenly flooding her mouth. Her body was yet alive with goose flesh—the residual bliss of his having grasped her ankle. She was trembling—weak—mesmerized by the smoldering depths of his dark gaze. As he sat—one long leg stretched out before him, the other serving as support of his strong arm—he appeared quite approachable in a manner. Yet as the breeze caught his dark hair, blowing several long tendrils across his forehead to slightly shade his eyes, Cristabel was suddenly terrified! He held some dark power over her—some dangerous allure she had never experienced in the presence of any other man. It was as if his very soul beckoned hers. She felt that if she was ever to succumb to his beguiling charm, he might actually absorb her somehow—consume her very essence.

"May I kiss you then?" he asked. His voice was low—provocative—laced with some bewitching tone that echoed in her mind like a reverie. "Just one pristine kiss...politely applied?"

"Of course...if you are truly able to politely apply anything with a resemblance of refinement," Cristabel answered. She feigned calm—though her heart beat so brutally within her bosom she feared it may beat itself dead!

"I can do anything I put my mind to, love," he said, reaching out to brush her cheek with the back of his hand.

He leaned toward her then and Cristabel held her breath as he gently took her face between his hands—pressed his lips to hers—applied a sweet, pristine kiss that lingered only several brief moments. He drew away from her then, trailing one thumb over her tender lips before releasing her.

"There you are, love," he mumbled, donning a mischievous smile. "Polite and pristine...just the way you prefer it."

"I never said I prefer it, sir," she reminded him, weakly rising to her feet. "I only said you could not do it. And you have proven me wrong. Therefore, I offer my congratulations."

An odd mingling of emotion was brewing within Cristabel. She was suddenly overwhelmed with a sad sort of disappointment. Still, in the same moment, the physical effect of his kiss had sent her body into flushing warm and desirous. She wanted to cry—yet fancied giggles were bubbling in her throat.

"This? Resignation...from *you*?" he chuckled rising to his own feet. "Easy acceptance of defeat...from Cristabel Albay...the rebellious rum-drinking vixen?"

She quivered as he trailed the back of his hand over the tender flesh of her arm. He took her hand—loosely lacing his fingers with hers.

"I have only ever once partaken of spirits…out of sheer desperation of thirst imposed by you, Captain Navarrone," she said. "And I assure you…I will not be partaking of them ever again."

He grinned—ran his palm from her wrist up over the sensitive flesh of her inner arm—sending goose bumps rippling over her in waves of breathtaking tingles. She should run from him—bolt for the tree house and his mother's company. Yet, she could not move—for he had bewitched her.

Trevon moved to stand behind her. He brushed her hair to one side— trailed his warm breath along her neck and shoulder.

"Are you fond of me, love?" he asked—his voice low and again, wildly alluring.

"Of course not," she lied—barely able to speak. He exhaled a breathy chuckle and she felt his hands at her waist—trembled as they slid to her stomach and lingered.

"Why not?" he whispered and she felt him press a kiss to her neck.

"Y-you're a pirate, for one," she answered. "And you've held me captive for quite some time."

"I would hold you captive forever if I could, Cristabel Albay," he whispered in her ear. He kissed the tender curve of her jaw. "Were I a different man…a better man…I would endeavor to keep you…to own your kiss…your body and your mind. Were I a better man…I would endeavor to hold captive your heart."

Tears brimmed in Cristabel's eyes. His words were those of a lover— and they were as a dagger in her heart—for she was desperately in love with him—in love with Trevon Navarrone and not some pretended man on the shore.

"Are you not at all fond of me?" he asked.

"P-perhaps a measure," she stammered.

He chuckled again—took hold of her arm at the elbow. "Come with me," he ordered softly, turning her to face him. "Unless that daring, rum-drinking, she-pirate in you has lost her courage."

Cristabel was overwhelmed at the sight of him then. His eyes smoldered with desire—his shirt hung open—unlaced and revealing the bronzed condition of his sculpted torso. His dark hair, square jaw, strong brow—all combined to create the most attractive man of her imagination. Her attention was drawn to his mouth—and hers watered for want of his kiss.

"I-I have as much courage as I did the day you cast me from the deck of The Screaming Witch," she bravely told him—though in that moment, it was not true.

"Then come along, love…for we are too much in view of others here."

Cristabel's heart hammered—pounded—caused her pain so brutal did it beat within her. As Trevon Navarrone kept hold of her arm, leading her from the open shore and into the trees beyond, she knew she should run from him—flee whilst she was still able. And yet, he had beguiled her— and the joy she knew each time she lingered in his company was forefront in her mind—and her heart.

# Chapter Twelve

The cypress grew thick where Trevon Navarrone stopped at last. Cristabel was breathless—both from the hastily trod escape into the privacy of the trees, and from the effects of being kissed by her pirate. She gasped as he took hold of her arms, none-too-gently pressing her back against a cypress trunk.

"Now tell me, love," he rather growled, leaning toward her. "As I have only just proved to you…I can be tamed…if I so choose."

"However…" Cristabel breathed as hope welled in her heart—hope that the pirate in him was about to emerge once more.

He smiled—pleased with her prodding. "However…the pirate in me would be a far better lover."

Trevon watched as a visible, smoldering desire illuminated Cristabel's violet eyes. She was no timid lily, and as her lips parted in indication she would speak—he sensed what words would fall from her pretty mouth.

"Then loose the pirate, Captain…and prove that as well," she whispered.

"Aye, my pretty temptress," he mumbled, taking her face between his hands. His breath was already labored—simply for the euphoric sensation washing over him as he softly caressed her parted lips with one thumb. He could feel her trembling—trembled in slight himself as he felt her palms press his chest—slide under his arms—around and up his back to cling to his shoulders.

Her touch was his undoing and he took her mouth with his own—claimed her. He was ravenous for the taste of her kiss—desperate to deepen their exchange. He pulled her away from the tree and into his

179

arms—holding her to him—reveling in the feel of her soft body pressed to his own.

Where was her decorum? Where was her sense of propriety? Cristabel's mind struggled to think with a semblance of order—but there was nothing but Trevon Navarrone! Nothing but the rapturous joy of being held in his powerful arms—the wild, sublime pleasure induced by his mouth melding with hers. She thought of his words—the words he had spoken after he had kissed her as the tamed man on the shore. He had claimed that if he were not a pirate—if he were a better man—he would endeavor to hold captive her heart. Yet, Cristabel knew he could not be a better man than he was—for he was everything a supreme man should be. Furthermore, he already held her heart captive. She was his prisoner—body, mind, heart and soul!

She wondered for a moment, if he truly wanted to own her heart—or had he simply been toying with her—attempting to lure her to his will. Yet, in that very moment, he broke the seal of their lips—held her to him, resting his chin on the top of her head. She could hear his heart hammering within his strong, broad chest—could feel the trembling, irregularity of his breathing. He nearly crushed her in a desperate embrace—and it was more than carnal desire she sensed in him—it was raw emotion.

"I would own you if I were a better man, Cristabel Albay," he mumbled her into hair.

She wanted to encourage him—to tell him he was a better man—the very best of men. Yet her own powerful emotions struck her mute.

Trevon lowered his head, slowly brushing her cheek with his own—the whiskers of his burnsides, mustache and goatee deliciously chafing her tender skin. She felt his shoulders slump in a manner of defeat. Though she knew not what had turned him from kissing her as his lover to near despair, Cristabel would not lose the affections of her pirate—not yet.

"Trevon," she breathed, against his neck. "Trevon...please...I want you...I want you to...

But Trevon was recovered already. Indeed, memories of Vienne had briefly intruded on his pleasures in kissing Cristabel—plagued him at the very zenith of knowing pure joy in her affections. The truth of Vienne's demise had, indeed, distracted him. Yet, as he felt Cristabel's breath on his skin—as he felt her hands slide up and over his chest—to his neck to embrace him—he pushed aside the recollections of his greatest pain and failure. He would not let even Vienne's death keep him from being Cristabel Albay's lover for a time. Moments were fleeting—as Trevon Navarrone well knew—and he would not let this moment pass him by—he would have Cristabel's kiss for as long as she would gift it to him.

He was nothing if not determined and resilient—thus, he cupped Cristabel's chin in his hand, gazed into the sweet violet of her eyes and whispered, "Prepare yourself, love...for I have not yet begun to quench my thirst for you." He kissed her lightly—grinning as she sighed with delight and adding, "Or yours for me, it would seem."

Gasping as his mouth captured her own once more, Cristabel abandoned all timidity—allowed her fingers to be lost in the soft darkness of Trevon Navarrone's hair. She kissed him with full as much fervor and desire as he kissed her—met each ravenous demand of his mouth with the answering eagerness of her own! He would not harm or defile her—she knew he would not—for he had done nothing but protect her from the moment he had found her aboard The Screaming Witch.

The common man on the shore was gone, and in his place was the pirate Navarrone—his consummate masculinity further kindling Cristabel's feminine fervor. In mere moments more, a fevered passion overwhelmed Cristabel and she was briefly conscious of tears lingering in her closed eyes. She pulled herself more tightly to him—clutched the hair at the back of his head in trembling fists of desperation. His powerful arms wrapped around her and he lifted her from her feet as his mouth ground to hers with ravenous, amorous desire.

He set her feet on the ground—briefly broke the seal of their lips as he gazed at her with such an expression of barely restrained desire smoldering in his dark eyes that she gasped—rendered breathless by the broiling passion evident in his countenance.

She stumbled as he pushed her backward, bracing her against the trunk of the tree—his hands pressing her waist as his mouth ravaged hers! Cristabel relished his kiss a moment more—but a sudden fear traveled through her—fear of her own will being compromised—her will to resist should Trevon press their passion beyond the kiss.

It was sure he sensed her trepidation—for he paused—and though he did not release her—he drew his face in slight away from hers.

"I've frightened you," he mumbled. He frowned an expression of regret and self-loathing—glanced away a moment.

"No...I...I frighten myself," she whispered.

Still frowning, he looked back to her—inquisitively.

"I am not at all certain in this moment that I own the will to...to keep my wits about me," she awkwardly confessed.

"An impassioned pirate is a dangerous venture indeed, love," he said as his expression softened to that of understanding—of gratification in understanding. The right corner of his mouth curved into the hint of a grin as he brushed a strand of hair from her cheek. "And you are ever the genteel lady in claiming it is your will of self-control that concerns you, instead of mine."

Cristabel frowned. "But I am in earnest," she assured him.

Yet he chuckled. "Of course you are, love."

It was obvious he did not believe her—that he thought she was fearful that he would force her to intimacy beyond a kiss. She frowned—suddenly feeling quite indignant that he would arrogantly assume he knew her thoughts.

"Come," he began, turning from her. "I'll take you back to the safety of the..."

Trevon was curious when he felt Cristabel take hold of his arm, tugging on it until he turned to face her once more. She wore an expression of deep defiance, determination and desire.

"I am not finished with you yet, Captain," she rather growled at him.

Trevon's brows arched in astonishment as his lovely prisoner then reached up, taking his face between her hands and pulling his head to hers once more. She kissed him—fervently kissed him—kissed him with coaxing passion. There was a manner of seduction about her—as if she were daring him to resist her.

He gathered her in his arms at once—pulled her body tight to his as he devoured her offered affections.

He broke from her a moment—whispered, "I will not press you beyond this kissing between us," against her lips.

"I know," she breathed, trailing soft fingertips over his lips as if priming them for further passion to come.

"But I may well press you to the brink of something beyond it," he confessed.

She smiled—a purely alluring smile—and whispered, "I know."

Trevon took her then—took her in his arms—took her mouth with his—took them both on a voyage of such shared kisses of bliss and passion as to cause the very trees to tremble with rapture from the leafy limbs to their shallow, yet ancient roots.

❦

"And she was ever as happy as any woman could be, miss," James Kelley said, smiling.

Cristabel closed her eyes—sighed with blessed relief in knowing her mother would not mourn her any longer.

"And she is well? Safe?" she asked the boy.

"Yes, miss," he said, nodding with reassurance. "Well and safe she is…and much more so since reading the Cap'n's letter."

Cristabel glanced to where Trevon sat nearby, enjoying one of his mother's delicious meals. He did not look up at her—only continued to concentrate on the plate of food before him. She wanted to thank him— to rush to him, throw her arms about his neck and kiss his warm mouth. Goose flesh riddled her body as the memory of their shared tryst among the trees washed over her. She could hardly fathom it had happened. It seemed such a dream. Furthermore, there he sat—only an arm's length from her—looking as if he were nothing more than a man at a table enjoying a meal—instead of a pirate who so recently played the attentive lover to her.

Cristabel knew she could not race to him—could not kiss him. He was the captain of The Merry Wench and must ever appear in dominant control of every thing, every one and every emotion. This she understood— though he had not spoken it to her.

Therefore, since she could not thank Trevon for his kindness to her and her mother, she returned her attention to James Kelley. "Thank you,

183

James Kelley," she said, placing a hand on his forearm. "I am forever in your debt...again."

"No, miss," James said, placing a hand over hers that lay on his arm. "I am in yours."

"Very well, you two," Trevon rather grumbled. "Enough of this sentimental slathering over indebtedness to one another. You are both fortunate you do not bear the marks of the cat for the sake of your tomfoolery in the past."

James grinned at Cristabel and she bit her lip to keep from giggling.

"Aye, Cap'n," James managed.

"Find my mother, James," Trevon commanded then. "She is at the house boat and has chosen a prize for you...something in addition to your part of the Chichester treasure...my reward to you for having completed this errand."

"Aye, Cap'n," James exclaimed fairly leaping to his feet. James' eyes were purely glistening with wild anticipation. Cristabel giggled as he looked to her and said, "Have a good evening, miss."

"And you, James Kelley," Cristabel said a moment before the boy bounded down the stairs of the tree house, heading for the treasure house boat at a dead run.

"That boy is far too fond of you, love," Trevon mumbled as he pushed his plate away. He drank water from the tankard his mother had provided. "I think you may own his loyalty more deeply than I do."

Cristabel shook her head. "No. He fair worships the ground upon which you tread."

"I very much doubt that, love," he said, rising from his chair.

She felt awkward—strangely uncomfortable in his presence suddenly. She was his prisoner. He had held her captive, and intimidated and threatened her. Yet only hours before, they had stood together among the cypress sharing kisses the like only lovers share. It was a peculiar circumstance indeed.

She watched as he strode toward her—her heart's beat increasing its frantic rhythm with each step of advancement to her.

"Perhaps it would be wise for me to accompany James to the boathouse." He smiled and chuckled, adding, "Else my mother gifts him

184

the entire contents of it. She dotes on him as if he were an infant at times."

"He seems adept at evoking maternal feelings in women...for he elicits them in me as well," she said.

She smiled as Trevon took hold of her arm, pulling her to her feet and into a strong embrace. "And what feelings do I elicit in you, love?" he flirted.

Cristabel's heart began hammering—her mouth watered—her limbs tingling with delight at his touch. "I-I cannot say, Captain," she nervously stammered. "I-I cannot think of how to term them...not properly."

Trevon smiled—his handsome brows arching in approval. "Oh, I well-like that answer, love. I well-like that indeed."

He pressed his mouth to hers in an alluring, teasing manner—as if daring her to refuse him. She did not refuse him, however—and shivered with the thrill his hot, moist aggression on her mouth sent rippling through her when his kiss deepened.

"Come along, love," he said, ending their embrace and taking her hand. As he laced their fingers, leading her down the stairs from the tree house to the ground he added, "It needs be we make our way to the house boat...for Mother often struggles to keep from spoiling James Kelley."

Cristabel smiled—her heart fairly swollen to bursting with joy! She had feared the passion they had shared earlier in the day would be the end of his romantic involvement with her—that he had simply let down his guard—that once he owned his wits again, he would berate himself for softening toward her. Yet now—as he held her hand in walking to the house boat—she had reason to hope that he truly cared for her beyond simply quenching a momentary thirst.

She would not think about the truth of it all—ignore that she was a woman surrounded by traitors and treason—the prisoner and pawn of his patriotic ambition. She would linger in his approval and affections for as long as fate allowed her to. She would dream that she might find herself in the company of the secreted pirate community forever—that she would wait on the shore for The Merry Wench to return with its captain and her lover—just as the other women and children waited for their loves to return.

Oh, it was well Cristabel knew in her heart that such dreaming was folly—but in those moments she cared nothing for reality. Trevon Navarrone cared for her—at least in some regard—and she would bathe in the knowledge and truth of it—for as long as providence would allow.

⤳

As Cristabel accompanied Trevon's mother back to the tree house, Claire Navarrone shook her head—still smiling. "Trevon is right to scold me," she giggled. "I cannot keep from gifting James Kelley doubloons and gems...nor love and affection." Claire wistfully sighed. "He simply owns my heart," she added.

"I understand," Cristabel confessed. "There is something...something darling about James. One cannot quite determine it in words...but he somehow takes ownership of a heart the moment he meets it."

"Yes," Claire agreed. "He is such an angel-boy. I am so grateful...so thankful that it was Trevon who found him wandering the streets of New Orleans...instead of someone who would have abused him...exploited his innocence or endeavored to turn him to villainy."

"Indeed," Cristabel whispered—for she, too, was ever thankful it was Trevon who watched over James Kelley. Oh, it was true the pirate captain attempted to treat the boy as any other member of the crew—yet it was ever more evident that Trevon viewed James as more a sibling than anything else.

"I suppose Trevon thinks of his brother Vortigem often when James is in his company," Claire said in a lowered voice. "Vortigem was ever Trevon's hero." She smiled—lightly laughed. "Oh how Trevon followed after his elder brother. He trailed along in Vortigem's footsteps like a happy little pup. I know it nearly broke his spirit when Vortigem died of illness."

Cristabel frowned. "I-I did not know he owned a brother," she said.

"Oh, yes...my eldest child...Vortigem Navarrone. He was a patriot like Trevon and his father. He died five years past. Consumption claimed him."

"I am so very sorry," Cristabel said, reaching out and taking Claire's hand in her own.

Claire paused in walking—turned to face Cristabel. Forcing a smile, she returned Cristabel's reassurance with a squeeze of her hand.

"Thank you, darling," she said. "I nearly died myself when Vortigem was lost." Cristabel smiled and brushed a tear from her own cheek as Claire reached out and took a long strand of Cristabel's hair between her fingers. "As I nearly died when Vienne was lost."

"Vienne?" Cristabel inquired. An odd anxiety began to burn in her bosom—yet she assumed it was merely for the sake of discussing loss and mourning.

"Yes. Beautiful Vienne," Claire whispered. She tucked the strand of Cristabel's hair behind her ear—softly caressed Cristabel's cheek. "I nearly died with her," she whispered. "As did Trevon. In truth, he has never recovered himself fully."

Cristabel's stomach broiled with nausea.

"Were...were they married then?" Cristabel asked—certain the contents of her stomach would reveal themselves. It was true then! Trevon's heart had belonged to another—another woman who had once waited on the shore for the handsome pirate to return.

"Married?" Claire asked, frowning yet seeming amused somehow. "Oh no, darling. Vienne was my daughter...Trevon and Vortigem's younger sister."

"What?" Cristabel gasped.

"Yes." Claire's frown deepened. "Oh surely you have heard the terrible tale from some crew member. And her portrait hangs in Trevon's cabin aboard The Merry Wench. He keeps it there...a constant reminder of what he views as his consummate failure." Claire paused—fresh tears spilling from her eyes at the reminiscing.

"The portrait is of his...his sister?" Cristabel gasped.

"Well yes, darling. Did you not notice the resemblance?" Claire asked, brushing tears from her cheeks. "Of course Trevon owns his father's dark eyes...and Vienne inherited the blue of mine...but they favor one another all the same. Do you not see it?"

"N-no," Cristabel whispered. "I-I did not see it."

"There, there, darling," Claire soothed, gathering her into a comforting mother's embrace. "It was a terrible thing...and I am touched that you are so very empathetic. But please...please do not let Trevon find us both in tears over Vienne. It so breaks him each time he thinks of her. I would not want our weakness to distress him."

187

His sister! Trevon's sister was the woman in the painting! Cristabel was certain she would vomit—certain she might faint dead away. How could she have been so foolish? And they thought Vienne was dead? How could they think it? She lived! Vienne was as alive as Cristabel—or Trevon! Why? Why did they think she was dead? Why hadn't Cristabel told Trevon of the woman at the inn—of having seen the woman from the painting at the tavern inn—of having seen Vienne at La Petite Grenouille following the meeting with Governor Claiborne and the Pelletiers? Why hadn't she told him? Yet, she knew why. Cristabel Albay had already been falling in love with Trevon Navarrone by that night, and jealousy had kept her from reporting the presence of the beautiful woman from the painting. She had assumed Vienne had been a past lover of Trevon's—and had not wanted to sacrifice his attention to either wanting an old lover, or resenting one.

"H-how did she die?" Cristabel ventured.

Claire brushed tears from Cristabel's cheeks—took her hand and began ambling toward the tree house once more.

"She was taken," Claire began, "by pirates."

"Pirates?" Cristabel exclaimed in horror. Again the contents of her stomach threateningly churned.

Claire paused a moment—frowned. "I am astonished that Trevon has not told you what brought him to privateering."

"No, ma'am," Cristabel admitted—disgusted with herself for never having considered the matter previously.

"Well then, I must tell you…for it is all a terrible web of pain and guilt," Claire said. She sighed, and began. "Trevon was a captain in the regular Navy, like his father before him."

"A Navy captain?" Cristabel gasped.

"Yes. His advancements in the Navy were hastily made. He was well-liked and respected by his crew."

Cristabel brushed at the perspiration gathering at her temples and beading on her brow. A Navy captain? As she considered it, she could see it in him then—for he led his pirate crew unlike other pirate captains— with discipline and regular officers.

"It was near the start of the war...the Bloody British then had ten times ten the ships the states had. Trevon's ship was a full rigged ship...three masts it had...the USS Wasp."

"I have heard of her," Cristabel breathed. "She was surrendered to the British...but only after her captain had captured two enemy ships with her."

"Yes," Claire confirmed. "It was the British that took the Wasp...but it was pirates that took my Vienne."

"I feel...from the sound of your voice...that the two are somehow connected, Mrs. Navarrone," Cristabel fearfully ventured.

"Indeed, darling. They are indeed."

"W-will you tell me of it," Cristabel asked. "I understand it may be too painful and that I should not press..."

"Vienne was aboard the Wasp," Claire began. "She was engaged...to Jacob Capes...Trevon's First Mate. Trevon was against her being aboard, of course...but she and Jacob were so very desperate to be together. It was to be a short voyage...one that would well avoid the regular shipping lanes the British encroached upon. Yet, as you know, darling...pirates are not so predictable as the bloody redcoats, are they?"

"No they are not," Cristabel breathed. She was so overcome with nausea and anxiety that even her skin felt ill.

"Well...the pirates attacked in the dead of night...a ship called Victoria's Revenge...captained by Rackham Henry. There had been fog and the men of the Wasp had not seen the Victoria's Revenge approach until it was too near to properly prepare for defense. Trevon's crew battled hard. Nearly all of them were slaughtered. Trevon and two others were the only men remaining when the sun rose. Trevon was flogged with the cat until he fell unconscious."

"I-I have seen the scars, I think," Cristabel offered as tears traveled over her cheeks.

"Yes. It is purely a miracle he survived such a flogging. Most men die long before Trevon even fell unconscious," Claire confirmed. "When Trevon awoke...it was to find himself and the two remaining men of his crew adrift on the sea in a small boat. Vienne was gone...taken by the pirate Rackham Henry. One of the surviving sailors told Trevon of it...for he had been yet unconscious when Henry's crew took her."

"But he did not see her murdered?" Cristabel was driven to inquire—for she knew Vienne did not die at the hand of Rackham Henry and his crew.

"No," Claire answered. "No...but pirates...true pirates, the likes of Rackham Henry, do not keep prisoners...even women. Women are beaten and ravaged near to death...and then killed. At least women who refuse to become pirate wenches. Even then they are not kept aboard pirate ships...rather abandoned on shore somewhere to die. Yet, Rackham Henry never allowed a prisoner to live long. He set Trevon and his men adrift without rations of any sort...assuming they would not be found, and would suffer dehydration and starvation until they finally died."

"But they were found."

"Yes," Claire confirmed. "A small schooner captained by an elderly Spaniard named Don Gabriel found Trevon and his men adrift. He brought them aboard his ship, sailed them here...cared for them until they were able once more."

"Don Gabriel?" Cristabel asked. "The man who built your house? The nobleman turned pirate Trevon told me of?"

Claire nodded—smiled slightly. "Yes. He was a good man...pirate or not."

"So it was Don Gabriel who nurtured Trevon to privateering."

"Yes...and no. Trevon was furious...madly furious over Vienne's death...and the manner of it...over imagining what she must have endured before her murder."

"Mrs. Navarrone...I do not wish to..." Cristabel began—for such a tale must indeed be merciless in the pain it caused in retelling.

"I want you to know the whole of it, darling," Claire said, however. "For you may not understand Trevon's inner torture if you do not."

Cristabel nodded—thinking her own guilt and inner torture would near destroy her. Why had she not told Trevon of having seen the woman in the painting? Was this to be yet another choice that had forever altered the course of her life? She knew that it was.

"He felt overwhelmed with guilt and self-loathing," Claire continued. "He saw himself as a failure and no longer worthy to captain a ship for the Navy. Yet, he would not abandon his country to the British threat. Furthermore, he owned a deep vendetta and sense of revenge toward pirates the like of Rackham Henry. Thus, he began privateering. He begged Don Gabriel to help him...to teach him and to sail with him...and Don Gabriel did...until he died suddenly just four months ago."

Cristabel wept even more profusely than she had been weeping a moment before. Such loss! She knew her own heart—how it had nearly broken and died at the loss of her father. Yet Trevon had lost so much more—a father, an elder brother—a sister and a friend.

"I-I...in truth, I feel so sickened that I do not know if I can endure it, ma'am," Cristabel wept.

"Oh, here, darling," Claire said, gathering Cristabel into a comforting embrace. "All is well. We endure the unfathomable, Cristabel. You know that as well as we."

"You do not understand," Cristabel sobbed. "I have done...I have chosen badly...selfishly...and you cannot imagine the consequences!"

"There, there, love...hush, sweet thing," Claire soothed. "Let us both regain our self-possession before Trevon finds us so miserable and wilted. I have come to learn that it does him no good to see my agony over Vienne. He has been so happy in your company, darling...pray continue to make him happy."

Cristabel pulled herself from Claire's embrace. Sniffling, she brushed the tears from her cheeks.

"I would make him happy if I could," she whispered. "But I see now that one choice truly can change the course of a life...or two...or more."

"Whatever is the matter dear?" Claire inquired. "I know it is brutal...the story is difficult to hear...to acknowledge. But it cannot be changed...nor does it change the fact that I know you hold Trevon's heart in your hands and..."

"Would you mind terribly, Mrs. Navarrone," Cristabel interrupted, "if I were to walk alone a while before the sun sets?"

Claire sighed—obviously still thinking Cristabel's empathy for Trevon where the loss of his sister was concerned was the only thing that had overtaken her emotions. She could not know that Cristabel's self-loathing and self-disgust had added hopelessness to her soul.

"Of course, darling...of course," Claire said. "Trevon will tarry with James a while longer. Take the time you need."

191

Cristabel nodded and, without offering one more word, strode away from Claire—toward the shore of the bay where The Merry Wench was anchored.

Claire would loathe her when she discovered Cristabel's secret—and she would discover it—for Cristabel would not make the same fatal error in choice twice. She must tell Trevon of Vienne's existence—of having seen her at the tavern inn. He would despise her—hate her with such abhorrence she could not fathom—but she would tell him. He could not continue to carry the burden of guilt in feeling responsible for his sister's death, when she still lived. Furthermore, Vienne must return to her family. Cristabel's fevered mind could only guess at why Vienne had not already sought them out. She tried to imagine that it was for the sake Trevon and Claire were hidden. They lived as pirates—secretive in their community's geography. Yet, Vienne had run—escaped being seen when she had been told the crew of The Merry Wench were lingering in the tavern. It was clear she did not want to be found—for it was well-known that The Merry Wench was captained by Navarrone the Blue Blade—Vienne's own brother.

Thus, Cristabel's imagination took her mind on a journey of pirates having tortured and abused their women prisoners—women prisoners such as Vienne. Was it humiliation and self-loathing keeping Vienne from her brother and mother?

As she stumbled out of the tree line and onto the shore, Cristabel fell to her knees, gasping for breath—for anxiety and fear were consuming her—despair, regret and an ever deepening self-loathing of her own.

"I did not know, Trevon!" she cried. "I did not know! I love you and I did not know! I love you…and I will give you up to hating me that I might right the wrong I have done! I did not know!" Sobbing, she whispered, "I love you! I love you!" Over and over, again and again she whispered her confession to the breeze, to the sand—and the gently lapping waves of the sea.

# Chapter Thirteen

She heard him approaching—heard his footsteps in the sand at her back. The sun was setting—casting orange and yellow pillars across the sky—causing the clouds to appear as dark, ominous shadows of foreboding.

Cristabel surmised it had been near an hour since she had left Claire Navarrone—since she had fled in search of isolated mourning. She had wept—sobbed bitter tears of heartbreak and despair. Yet, resignation had found her at last—and she knew what must be done. Cristabel knew she must confess the truth to Trevon—tell him of having seen his sister laboring as a serving wench at La Petite Grenouille. He must be told—that he could champion her—bring Vienne home to her mother and her brother who loved and desperately needed a healing to their pain of loss.

Still, she knew that in telling him all she had seen—all she had kept from him—Cristabel knew Trevon Navarrone would never forgive her sin of omission. He was too weathered—too beaten with loss, privateering, battle and patriotism to forgive her such a thing. Yet, she could never, and would never, consider allowing Vienne to linger in the circumstances she endured. Thus, she would confess to Captain Navarrone—and he would do with her what he would. It was all she deserved.

"Mother said I might find you here, love," Trevon said, as he stepped to stand beside her. "The sun will have set soon and you might not find your way back to the house in the dark."

"There is something I must tell you," she said. She did not yet look to him—for she was afraid she would not be able to utter the truth if she did. She feared the look of disgust and loathing that would appear on his face when she told him, might literally strike her dead.

"Very well," he said—and she sensed the change in his demeanor.

Cristabel closed her eyes a moment—silently prayed for the courage to confess all to the man she loved. Yet, when she closed her eyes, such a vision of his features—such a remembrance of the bliss she had known in his arms—washed over her as a warm, summer rain. Her mouth watered and her body began to tremble. She must own his lips once more! She must know the feel of him—the scent of him. She wished to be forever haunted by his memory—by the memory of what might have been.

Turning to him at last, she gazed up into the handsome, alluring countenance and features that were those of Trevon Navarrone. His dark hair framed his face, as ever it did. Rogue raven tresses had tumbled over his forehead—shading his eyes and causing a look of mystery and allure to emanate from him.

Trembling, Cristabel reached up—took Trevon's rugged face between her hands. His eyes narrowed, yet he did not move to aggress nor evade her touch. Slowly she allowed her thumbs to caress his lips—to gently trace his mustache and goatee. She would study every detail of his handsome face—memorize the fiery smolder of his eyes—the perfect line of his nose. Her hands traveled over his temples to be lost in his hair—for she would know the feeling of the soft, dark lengths of it between her fingers once more. Raising herself on the tips of her toes, she pulled her body against his—shivered with painful delight as his arms enfolded her—as his mouth pressed the sensitive flesh of her neck. Her tears were beginning—though she had hoped to stay them a while longer.

Pressing her face to his neck, she inhaled deeply the scent of his skin—the aromas that were Trevon Navarrone—the warm spice of masculinity, the salty essence of the sea—the breath of the breeze and the comforting savor of grass and trees.

Trevon sensed an overwhelming melancholy in her—a strange, sad desperation—and it unsettled him—even worried him. He was careful not to press her—though the caressive manner of her touch caused such a near manic hunger to rise in him, he feared he may falter and aggress upon her. Still, he gritted his teeth, holding her in a firm, protective embrace—for he somehow knew she was fragile in that moment.

He desired to soothe her—to ease whatever anxiety was torturing her. He wanted to be her champion—to vanquish her unhappiness—but he knew not how.

"Cristabel," he began, "what is this?" But her mouth was suddenly pressed to his in a warm kiss of mingled anguish and passion.

Trevon's heart swelled—his emotions and bodily desire mounting to a rapturous height. Yet, he knew this was a kiss of wretchedness—of regret and longing. He must remain tender.

The kiss they shared was not brief—rather a lingering kiss of loving affection—and though it held passion barely at bay—at bay he did hold it—and Trevon knew trepidation.

Her soft, quivering lips left his mouth—drifted to his jaw—to his neck.

"I love you, Trevon," she whispered to his ear. "I would have endeavored to be your pirate bride. I would have remained here...waited on the shore each day...prayed for your safe return." He felt moisture on his neck and knew she was weeping. "I love you...I love you!" she breathed.

Trevon could scarce draw breath! She was confessing love for him? He could not fathom it at first. Furthermore, he could not fathom her despair. Was it so terrible a thing to love a man the likes of him?

"Cristabel," he whispered. "I love..."

But he was silenced by her finger pressing his lips.

He frowned as she looked to him then—tears of sheer agony streaming over her cheeks.

"Do not speak the words," she whispered—her voice breaking with suffering. "For when I have confessed the breadth of my sins...you will not feel such a thing for me any longer."

"Confess?" he asked, frowning—for what sin could she possibly confess to him that would change his heart toward her? None.

"I wish you to understand that...I meant no malice," she said.

It was madness—and Trevon had grown impatient.

"Cristabel," he said, taking hold of her arms and gazing into her eyes. "What are you rambling about? Your touch...your kiss...do you endeavor to destroy my resolve to keep from ravaging you?"

He allowed the corner of his mouth to quirk into a grin—yet her tears only increased in profusion.

"I endeavor to tell you the feelings of my heart before you are forced to strike me dead," she whispered.

Cristabel watched as his grin faded—as his strong brow furrowed with a frown.

"I would never strike you," he said. "Dead or otherwise."

She stepped back out of his reach—her heart breaking—shattering—splintering into a thousand painful shards.

"Leave off your cutlass, Captain," she said. "Please. And the dagger you wear at your back."

He took a step toward her, saying, "This is madness, love. There is nothing you could tell me that…"

He paused in his advance as Cristabel raised her palm to him.

"Please," she said. "If you are to kill me for what I am about to reveal, I want to feel your hands at my throat as I die. I do not want to die by the blade."

"Cristabel," he began again and she saw the expression of near panic on his face.

"Please, Captain," she begged, "for I have been keeping something from you…and I know that when I reveal it…you will own less mercy toward me than you do any of my traitorous acquaintances."

Trevon exhaled a heavy breath of frustration. There was nothing she could reveal that would change his heart toward her. If she was about to confess that she too was in league with the Pelletier's in their treasonous strategies—he would love her still. Nothing would keep him from her. She had only just told him she would be his pirate bride—the words had only just fallen from her lips—and he would have her. There was nothing that would stand between Trevon Navarrone and the woman he loved—nothing!

Still, she was over-wrought and he must remain patient. Thus, he removed his cutlass—tossed it to the sand some distance off. He removed his dagger sending it to join his cutlass on the shore.

"Tell me this thing that is so vile, love," he said then. "I promise that it will not change my heart."

He frowned as she took several steps back from him—as an expression of fear, panic and pain owned her pretty face. He sensed she was truly fearful he might harm her—either her heart—or her body.

"I did not know the portrait that hangs in your cabin aboard The Merry Wench is...is your sister's," she began, "I did not know it. You never spoke of her being your sister."

Trevon felt his heart burn with pain—disappointment and despair. She had discovered his weakness in failing Vienne. In that moment, he did not care how she had come by the knowledge of the circumstances of Vienne's horrifying demise—for it made no difference from whence the information came to her—it only mattered that it did. He understood then the look of dread on her face. Cristabel Albay had realized she had fallen in love with a villain—a weak man who could not even protect those he most cared for—who had lived while his precious sister had died.

"So you see me for what I am now, is that it? You see me for the weak, failing man I am," he growled. "You have no secret that will drive me from you...rather it is mine that drives you from me...for I well-see loathing of me in your expression."

"It is self-loathing y-you see, Captain," she stammered as more tears flooded her cheeks. "Not loathing of you...for you are a hero...a great man among men."

Trevon's eyes narrowed. He did not understand her rambling. What secret could she own that was worse than the one he cached? What could ever endeavor to make her think he would not love her?

"Vienne is not dead, Captain," she whispered. She must confess it all while courage still lingered in her bosom. "I have seen her. She is not dead."

Trevon frowned—such a frown as to cause Cristabel's own brow to ache with empathetic pain.

"My sister was taken by pirates, Cristabel. By the pirate Rackham Henry," he said, gazing at her as if she were mad. "She was taken and murdered."

197

"You did not see her killed," Cristabel reminded him, brushing at the tears on her cheeks. "You did not see her body or receive any word that she had truly died...did you?"

"I need no proof," he told her. "Rackham Henry has defiled and killed every woman he has ever taken."

"But I have seen her...the night you met with Governor Claiborne to discuss the Chichester. She was there...serving drink at the tavern inn...at La Petite Grenouille."

She watched the color drain from Trevon Navarrone's face as he shook his head in disbelief. "No," he muttered.

"I saw her, Trevon," Cristabel insisted. "She stood as close to me as you do now...even asked me if she could serve me."

"No," he mumbled. She could see he was beginning to tremble—see his powerful hands clench into fists.

"She asked me which ship I crewed...and when I told her...she fled at once," she continued as Trevon raked a quivering hand through his hair. "I-I did not tell you because..."

"Vienne is dead, Cristabel," he growled. "No woman could survive capture by Rackham Henry."

"As no man could survive as many lashings with the cat as you did?" she asked.

"No," he breathed. "She would have come to me."

"Y-you have been in hiding...and your mother," she reminded.

He shook his head—his scowl deepening. "It cannot be her!" he shouted, infuriated. "You did not know her! You could not recognize her from her portrait! You could not!"

"I-I did...I swear on my life that it was Vienne at La Petite Grenouille," Cristabel cried. "I am not lying, Trevon."

She gasped—stepped forward as he suddenly dropped to one knee in the sand—pressed a trembling hand to his chest as if his heart would stop.

"Vienne," he breathed—a breath—a word—a name uttered in torture.

Trevon looked up to Cristabel—his eyes narrowed—blazing with pain and anger. "How could you keep this from me?" he asked. "How could you not tell me you had seen the woman in the painting?"

"I-I was your prisoner…or have you so easily forgotten that I am aligned with traitors and treason," she wept. "You meant to put both James Kelley and me under the lash of the cat for our farce!"

"You feared me?" he asked. "You did not tell me you had seen Vienne because you feared me?"

Cristabel shook her head—angrily wiped at the tears blinding her eyes. "No," she confessed. "I did not tell you because I did not know she was your sister. I-I thought she was your lover…a lover you mourned losing. I-I th-thought perhaps she had broken your heart and left you wounded…that you would return and claim her for your own once more if you knew wh-where she was. It was obvious she was fearful of seeing someone from The Merry Wench…and I thought…I thought you loved her."

"I do love her," he grumbled. "She is my sister!"

"I did not know!" Cristabel cried, burying her face in her hands. "I did not know…and jealousy bid me not to tell you I had seen the woman in the painting."

Trevon clutched his chest—for his heart gave him great pain. In truth, he wondered if it would expire and leave him dead on the shore. He had failed Vienne—far worse failed her than even he had thought. She was alive? She lived? He felt tears well in his eyes—burning tears of the knowledge he had not kept searching for Vienne. In truth he had spent near two months in inquiring of Rackham Henry's whereabouts—his plundering—where he had sought refuge. Nothing had come to him concerning Vienne—nothing. Only assurance at every turn—from every person or place that Rackham Henry had touched—that no woman would have survived two days in his possession. Rackham Henry was known to keelhaul the women he captured and abused—toss their remains into the sea—it was well acknowledged in tale and document. There had been no hope—it was what he had been told—what he had believed. Yet now— now Cristabel Albay claimed to have seen Vienne alive. Could it truly be Vienne had been living so near—for two years?

He glanced up when he saw Cristabel collapse to her knees in sobbing. "I am sorry! I am so sorry!" she cried. "I did not know!"

Trevon stared at the woman he loved—knowing then that he should never more endeavor to have her. He was a pitiful man—weak, failing—and unworthy of such a woman as Cristabel Albay. And yet—as he studied her—as he thought of her courage, her wit—her soft form and warm mouth—he did not care so much for his own unworthiness. He would yet have her for his own—whether he was worthy of her or not. But he could not have her until Vienne was found—for he would never know one moment of true happiness without repentance of failure—without righting the unfathomable wrong he had done.

Cristabel watched as Trevon struggled to his feet. He straightened his strong back, inhaled a deep breath—his eyes still narrowed. He strode to where his cutlass and dagger lay in the sand—retrieved them—slipped the cutlass into its sheath at his hip and the dagger into the back waist of his trousers.

She stumbled backward as he strode toward her then—such a look of rage and determination upon his face, that Cristabel's hands went to her throat to defend it from his grip that would easily strangle her.

But he did not strangle her. He simply took hold of her arm in the tight vise of his powerful hand, and began pulling her along beside him toward the tree line—back toward the tree house. She had to near run to match his pace. When once she could not match it and stumbled, he paused only long enough to bend and position one broad shoulder at her waist. Hoisting her onto his shoulder as if she were no more than a sack of grain, Trevon continued his hasty march toward the tree house.

Cristabel said not a word—not one word in defense of herself—not one word to question what his intentions toward her were. Her end would be met however he chose for her to meet it. Still, he had once promised he would not kill her—and she thought he was not one to break a promise—no matter what circumstance may arise. She began to think he would simply return her to her mother—to her life with a treasonous stepfather and fiancé. After all, William or Richard might kill her upon her return as well.

It was the very first time in the entirety of her life that Cristabel felt wholly defeated. Despair was owning her—and she could not find courage or will within herself.

Trevon set her on her own feet once more as they stepped out of the trees and into view of the tree house. "James Kelley!" he roared. "James! Attend me at once!"

"Aye, Cap'n," James called from the first tier of the dreamy abode. He ran down the stairs and to his captain.

"Gather Baskerville, Fergus and three others," Trevon growled. "Have them meet with us at once. At once, do you understand?"

"Of course, Cap'n," James said, frowning. He looked to Cristabel—began to speak to her—but she shook her head in indication he should not. She could see the worry on his young brow—wondered if he would yet be so worried when he knew what she had done.

"Trevon?" Claire called from the tree house.

Cristabel looked up as the sun set, leaving all in darkness—save the warm-lit house in the ancient tree. How she would have cherished to live in it forever! How she would have slept happy in Trevon's arms there.

"One moment, Mother," Trevon called. He looked to James again—glowering as he ordered, "Now, James Kelley! I mean to have the men here now!"

"Aye, Cap'n," James said as he nodded, glanced to Cristabel once more, then hurried off in the direction of the house boat.

Again taking hold of her arm, Trevon began to fairly haul her toward the tree house. He still did not speak to her—yet she never expected he would ever utter another word meant for her ears.

"Trevon?" Claire asked as Trevon pushed Cristabel up the stairs ahead of him. "What is all this?"

Cristabel brushed new tears from her cheeks as Trevon sighed. He yet wore a frown and she knew he was considering whether or not he should tell his mother of Vienne.

"Trevon," Claire prodded. She looked to Cristabel—reached out and placed a warm palm to her cheek. Cristabel turned from her, however—knowing the woman would not feel such affection for her if she knew what she had done. Claire frowned, asking, "Whatever is the matter, darling?"

"Cristabel has told me that…that she has seen Vienne," Trevon said.

"Well of course you have seen her, darling," Claire said, smiling with reassurance as she gazed at Cristabel. "Her portrait hangs in…"

"No, Mother," Trevon interrupted. "She says that she has seen Vienne living…that my sister was one of the serving wenches at the tavern inn, La Petite Grenouille."

Cristabel watched—wept as Claire frowned a moment in considering what Trevon had told her. Quickly however, her frown faded and a smile spread in its place.

"Oh, darling…it is often one person can be mistaken for another," Claire offered.

"I was not mistaken, Mrs. Navarrone," Cristabel managed. "It was Vienne. I saw her…she spoke to me…I did not know then that she was your daughter. I..I…"

The frown that now puckered Claire's brow was that of deep disbelief mingled with wild optimism.

"I would not give you false hope, Mother," Trevon began, "but I cannot dismiss the sense that it is, indeed, Vienne that Cristabel saw."

Tears welled in Claire's eyes—yet she bravely straightened her posture. "You mean to sail and find her?"

"Yes," Trevon answered.

"Then I will sail with you," Claire announced.

"No, Mother…I think it best…"

"I *will* sail with you, Trevon," Claire stated. "Vienne will need her mother when she is found. I cannot imagine what atrocities she may have endured, and I will be there to comfort and reassure her."

"She fled when The Merry Wench was mentioned, Mother," Trevon explained. "It may be that she does not want us to…"

"Why would she not want us to find her, Trevon?" Claire asked. "Of course she will want to come back to us."

"Mother," Trevon began. Cristabel could sense his barely restrained emotions—anger, frustration, impatience. "There is certainly a reason she has not sought us out…a reason she avoided contact with anyone from The Merry Wench. We may, indeed, have to…well…rather abduct her."

"Don't be ridiculous, Trevon!" Claire scolded. She was weeping now—her hands trembling. "She will see me and know utter relief and instant soothing."

"She may not, Mother," Trevon argued—nearly growled.

"M-may I speak?" Cristabel ventured.

Claire looked to her with anticipation—yet Trevon merely glanced away.

"Of course, dear," Claire said, scowling at Trevon.

Cristabel winced—for it was painful to endure—Claire's still addressing her so kindly.

"I do not think it would be wise to force her...to abduct her," Cristabel offered. Trevon still did not look at her—simply inhaled a deep breath of attempting to calm himself. Claire did not respond either—but seemed to be waiting for Cristabel to continue. "It is nearly certain that she has been ill-treated, is it not?"

Claire winced then—wept more tears.

"Yes," Trevon mumbled.

"Then allow me to sail with you...to approach Vienne and explain your feelings and desire to have her with you...before you attempt to force her to come home with you," Cristabel suggested.

"She will come with me," Trevon said, finally looking to Cristabel. She saw the pain in his eyes—the desperation toward atonement.

"She will flee if she catches sight of you," Cristabel gently argued. "I do not know why...but she will." She looked to Claire then. "I fear the same is true of you, Mrs. Navarrone. I would go to her first...explain that your love and acceptance of her is unconditional."

"She should know it!" Claire cried out, weeping. "Vienne would know we love her...no matter what she has had to endure."

"I am certain that she does...deep in her heart. Yet why then would she flee...so desperately flee when Trevon was at her very door? It makes no sense. Why would she not have sought you before now? At least inquired after you? And Trevon would have known of such inquiries...for some person would have informed him." Cristabel paused—watched Trevon's frown deepen with pensive thought—Claire dabbed the tears from her eyes with the hem of her apron. Feeling they both understood her case, Cristabel ventured, "I could go before you...approach less...less aggressively and speak with her...explain that you want only to have her with you again...no matter what has happened to her. And then...then we must allow her the choice. Vienne must make the choice to return to you."

Oh how she prayed Trevon would agree—that he would see the wisdom of her proposal. It was certain he was lingering in loathing Cristabel for her deceit—yet for Vienne's sake, Claire's and most especially his own—Cristabel prayed he would listen to her.

"We will sail the schooner," he mumbled. "I will secure lodging for us and Vienne at the inn across the way from La Petite Grenouille." He turned to Cristabel—glaring with either self-loathing or loathing of her—she could not determine which. "You will speak with her...attempt to convince her to accompany you to us. But if she chooses not to leave La Petite Grenouille with you...then I will extract her from it by force. Do you understand?"

"Yes," Cristabel said, nodding.

"She will need a sanctuary, Trevon," Claire said then. "Her room at the inn...there must be a warm bath prepared and waiting...clean clothing...perhaps soothing oils and good food."

"We have no time, Mother," Trevon grumbled. "Even now she may have left La Petite Grenouille for another path."

"Bring my trunk with us, Captain," Cristabel said. "I have clothing...she looks to be of my same figure and approximate height. You well know that when my trunk was prepared, a fine toilette was included...scented oils and lotions. Everything a woman would need to feel clean and comfortable. Bring my trunk for Vienne."

"Yes, Trevon," Claire said. "In fact, I demand it."

"Very well," Trevon growled. "I will plan...as a mother and woman would for this...for Vienne's sake. However, I remind you both...that I will bring Vienne home. Nothing will stand in my way of it. Therefore, if all does not proceed as prettily as you women wish it to...be prepared. I will not fail Vienne again."

"Cap'n Navarrone?" Baskerville called from the ground.

Cristabel looked to see James Kelley in the company of Baskerville, Fergus and three other members of The Merry Wench's crew.

"Aye, Baskerville," Trevon called. Looking back to his mother and Cristabel he said, "We sail at midnight. Therefore, do not tarry in your preparations."

He strode away then—descending the stairs with furious determination. Cristabel heard him begin to explain matters to his men.

"You did not know the painting was of Vienne," Claire began. "Not until I told you of her this evening...did you?"

Cristabel wept once more—shaking her head with painful remorse. "No. No I did not," she answered. "I would not have kept my sighting of her a secret if I had known. I thought...I thought she was perhaps Trevon's lover and that..."

"And that you would lose him?" Claire offered.

Cristabel nodded. "Yet...in the end...one wrong choice has fatally determined that my life will take a very different path than I had begun to hope."

She began to sob as Claire took her face in her hands, smiled and said, "You made no wrong choice, darling. You could not have known it was Trevon's sister you saw. He does not place blame on you for Vienne's misery...only on himself."

"You did not see the loathing in his eyes!" Cristabel cried.

Yet, Claire smiled. "Oh yes, darling...I did. Loathing of self." Claire embraced Cristabel for a moment—yet it little soothed her. Trevon did loathe her—she had seen it in him.

"Now, darling," Claire began, releasing Cristabel and brushing tears from her own eyes. "Let us prepare...for Vienne's sake, yes?"

Cristabel nodded. "Yes, ma'am."

"We will find Vienne and she and Trevon will both begin to heal. I promise," Claire said.

Cristabel nodded once more—forced a trembling grin. Still, she wished persons would not make promises they could not keep.

"Now hurry up to your trunk," Claire encouraged. "Don your most tattered dress...for you must not appear too genteel or Vienne may flee from you as well."

"Of course," Cristabel agreed.

She turned then, hurried up the stairs to the second tier of the tree house and to her trunk. Opening its lid, she began to rummage through the clothing allotted her. She did find a dress that was perhaps far from tattered, yet a plain sort of brown fabric—simple and without embellishment. It would do—it must.

As she pulled the dress from her trunk however, her attention fell to the two pieces of eight nestled within. She picked them up—considered them for a long moment. She would bring them with her. The two silver coins were the only items she would take from the trunk. The rest she would gift to Vienne. Nevertheless, she would need the two pieces of eight—in order to return to New Orleans. She would need to pay someone—a carriage and driver or purchase passage on a schooner, in order to return. Thus, she must keep the gifts of thought and wonder that Claire Navarrone had presented to her. Trevon would put her off for good once Vienne was with him—and Cristabel would return to her mother—no matter the consequences. She would construct a tale of some sort—a lie of adventure and escape in order to protect Trevon from retaliation.

Shaking her head, Cristabel began to change her dress. She would consider how to return to New Orleans and what to tell her treasonous step-father after Vienne was safely in the care of her brother and mother once more. For now, she would simply consider what she must say to convince the battered beauty to return to her family. And Vienne must return to Trevon and Claire. She must!

As Trevon steered the schooner through the black of night, he tried to subdue his anxiety—his fearful trepidation. In truth, he still struggled to believe Vienne was the woman Cristabel had seen at the tavern inn. Yet, he had seen the sincerity in the deep violet of her eyes—and he knew she spoke the truth. Whether the woman she had seen truly was Vienne or not—Cristabel Albay believed her to be. Thus, Trevon had begun to hope—to hope as surely as his self-loathing deepened.

He glanced to where his mother sat—a comforting arm about Cristabel's shoulder. His mouth began to water at the sight of his lover—and he prayed that in rescuing Vienne at last, he might win back a part of the fondness Cristabel claimed to own for him. Still, he must prove himself first. He must demonstrate to Cristabel that he would not fail his sister again—that he could be trusted to protect anyone and everyone he loved—that he could be trusted to protect her.

As the sea sailed him closer to La Petite Grenouille—to Vienne—his mind began to strategize. If Cristabel could not convince Vienne to leave La Petite Grenouille, he would have the other men take her from it. Still, he wondered if perhaps there was something he could do while he waited for Cristabel to speak with Vienne.

As his mind mulled over the varying circumstances and outcomes of his determination to rescue his sister, Trevon attempted to ignore the trepidation causing his innards to quiver. He must find Vienne—liberate her from the life of misery she had lingered in since Rackham Henry had taken her. He must find Vienne—and then—then he must win back Cristabel Albay. He would find Vienne—and he would have Cristabel— and not man, nor devil, nor any other circumstance could keep him from either!

# Chapter Fourteen

Cristabel glanced over her shoulder to where Trevon stood leaning against a nearby building. He nodded to her with encouragement—and she was astonished that, even for her fear and trepidation about speaking with Vienne, Trevon's handsome appearance still caused a wave of butterflies to flurry in her stomach. She must convince Vienne to come with her to the inn across the way—to return to her brother and mother waiting there for her.

A room had been prepared for Vienne—comfortable, clean—a bath drawn and Cristabel's aromatic oils mixed with the water. Good food would be waiting—and most importantly, protection and love.

Cristabel could not imagine that Vienne Navarrone would not want to return to her family—to comfort and safety. Yet, she had seen the manner in which Vienne fled when hearing The Merry Wench's crew lingered in the tavern in which she labored. Cristabel's sensitivities whispered that Vienne's experience with Rackham Henry, and perhaps beyond, had caused her not only unfathomable pain and misery—but that it had perhaps destroyed her spirit—caused her to feel spoiled for any good thing— unworthy of happiness and love. Cristabel had thought long of what might have become of herself had Trevon not found her in Bully Booth's clutches—had he not thrown them both into the sea and taken her aboard The Merry Wench. Empathy then told her what Vienne must have felt when she at last escaped Rackham Henry—despair, unworthiness, fear, self-loathing. Thus, she must approach Vienne with care and understanding—calmly and with patience. She must not demand Vienne return to her family—it must be Vienne's choice—a choice that would well change the entire course of her life from that moment forward.

Furthermore, Cristabel knew that Vienne's choice might likewise change the course of Cristabel's own life. She hoped that if Vienne returned to her mother and brother—then perhaps Trevon could forgive Cristabel her failings. If she was successful in helping to reunite Vienne and her family, perhaps Trevon could find something in Cristabel to care for once more. She knew it was folly to hope for such a happy ending to it all—still she did hope—for hope was the only thing fanning her courage as she entered La Petite Grenouille.

It had been difficult to wait through the long morning—to wait until the majority of the patrons of the tavern had finally staggered away to find drunken rest in an inn room, or alleyway. Yet, Trevon thought it best to approach Vienne when there were not so many men about—when the tavern was lingering in the quiet of day. Still, Cristabel feared Vienne would not be about her labors when there were not ready customers.

She stood just within the doors of La Petite Grenouille, glancing through the gloom and near visible stench of the establishment. She saw first the woman called Celestine. She was in conversation with a man— an ugly, disheveled-looking man. The man seemed to be giving instruction and Cristabel wondered if this was the man Celestine had warned Vienne of the night Vienne fled at having heard mention The Merry Wench. Cristabel remembered how Celestine had warned Vienne that Christophe would be angry at her absence. She again wondered if this was he.

Cristabel stepped further into the room—glanced at every face seated at a table. Her hopes were beginning to quickly dwindle. She feared that Vienne had indeed left La Petite Grenouille—fearful of being found by her brother, captain of The Merry Wench. Nausea fair engulfed her—for she knew it would be her fault if Vienne had fled—none but hers.

She gasped slightly as she saw Vienne enter from another room then, however. She could scarcely draw breath—for she was again assured that it had been the very woman from the painting in Trevon's cabin that she had seen that first night. It was Vienne! Vienne was there—just beyond several tables.

Cristabel observed her a moment before approaching. The beauty that was Trevon's sister and Claire's daughter appeared tired, worn and weathered—unhappy as well. Cristabel was overcome by a sense of urgency. She must not tarry—she must not pause. The moment was upon her—and the course of her life would be decided in the next minutes—of her life, and Vienne's.

Swallowing the lump of trepidation in her throat, Cristabel walked to Vienne.

"Pardon, miss," she began.

Vienne frowned—glanced about her. Frowning with uncertainty she said, "Are you speaking to me, miss?"

Cristabel forced a smiled. "Yes. May I speak with you a moment please?" she asked.

"Why?" Vienne asked. It was obvious she was suspicious. No doubt Vienne had learned that few people were to be trusted.

"I...I am looking for work," Cristabel lied. "I was wondering if perhaps you could tell me if this establishment might be in need of another woman to..."

"Oh, do not bind yourself to this low place," Vienne whispered. "Surely you can find other means of making your way."

"Who is that?" the man speaking with Celestine shouted. "Who are your talking to when you should be working, woman?"

"J-just an old friend, Christophe," Vienne answered. "I will only be a moment more."

"Make certain of it," the man growled.

"Come with me," Vienne said, taking Cristabel's arm and leading her to a room toward the back of the establishment. "Sit here," she said, gesturing toward a chair at a small table. Cristabel did as Vienne instructed—watching as Vienne took her seat in the chair across from her.

"Why ever would you come here looking for work, miss?" Vienne asked in a whisper. "Do you not know that this is a place of pirates and criminals? Christophe does not care who drinks his beer and rum...as long as they pay for it. You would be in constant danger here...and I can tell you are yet unspoiled...as sweet as the day you were born. You must not come in here again."

There was a marked desperation in Vienne's voice and expression—and Cristabel was touched—her heart warmed by the manner in which Trevon's sister offered protection via wisdom and experience.

"If...if I confide something in you, miss...will you give me your word that you will not flee from me?" Cristabel asked. Time was waning and she knew she must hurry. Oh, certainly she wished to be soft—to ease Vienne into the knowledge that her brother and mother waiting only across the way to welcome her. Yet, Christophe was too wary and she knew she could not pause.

Vienne frowned. "What could you want to confide in me?" she asked. "I am a stranger to you."

"Will you give me your word you will not leave me...once you have heard what I must confess to you?" Cristabel asked.

Vienne studied Cristabel for a moment and Cristabel almost smiled—for the expression of curious wariness was so like that of Trevon's that it warmed her very soul.

"Very well," Vienne said at last. "Confess what you will...but hastily...else Christophe decides you are too pretty to resist."

Drawing a deep breath of courage, Cristabel began. "My name is Cristabel Albay. I was abducted from my home in New Orleans...in the dead of night...by Acadian mercenaries."

Vienne frowned. Cristabel knew painful memories were washing over her—as well as empathy.

"What has this to do with me?" Vienne asked.

"I was taken...and given over to the British," Cristabel whispered. "Put aboard a bloody British ship bound for England. We were set upon by pirates...a ship called The Screaming Witch."

"Bully Booth's ship," Vienne whispered.

"You have heard of it, then?" Cristabel ventured.

"Yes."

Cristabel swallowed—reached out and took hold of Vienne's hand that lay on the table. "Remember...you promised you would not abandon me...no matter what I confess."

"I did," Vienne confirmed—yet Cristabel saw her body grown tense.

"Bully Booth set upon the British ship...as I said...but in the midst of battle, another ship appeared. It attacked the British ship...beat back Bully Booth's crew. The captain of the third ship boarded The Screaming Witch...killed Bully Booth. He took me 'round the waist and cast us both into the sea."

Vienne's eyes were wide with astonished curiosity. Cristabel gripped Vienne's hand more firmly.

"You promised," she reminded Vienne.

"Yes," Vienne whispered—assuring her she would not flee.

"The man who saved me...he swam me to his own ship...took me prisoner...for I had been found to be a passenger of the British ship after all," Cristabel continued. "The man who saved my life...sails The Merry Wench. He is the pirate Navarrone the Blue Blade...and he is your brother, Vienne."

Instantly, Vienne pulled her hand from Cristabel's, fairly leaping from her seat.

"Please! Please, Vienne!" Cristabel begged in a whisper—else Christophe should hear them and intrude. "You promised you would not run from me! Please...I must speak with you."

"Is he here?" Vienne gasped—tears springing to her eyes to escape over her cheeks. "Is Trevon here with you?" She was near to panic.

"Please, Vienne," Cristabel soothed. "Please just listen to me...to my confession."

Vienne frowned. "Your confession? What more could you confess than to tell me you have trapped me for my brother? And you have, haven't you? You have come here at Trevon's bidding."

"I have come here of my own bidding, Vienne," Cristabel said. "Please...I have more to tell you...that I must tell you."

"Where is he?" Vienne demanded, however. "Where is Trevon? Is he already here?"

Cristabel shook her head. "No. He waits across the way. But please, Vienne...there is more I must confess. You promised you would not flee."

"That was before I knew you meant to trap me!" Vienne cried in a whisper.

"I do not mean to trap you," Cristabel said. "I mean to speak with you...to confess the great wrong I have done you and your brother."

"Great wrong?" Vienne asked. "What great wrong could you have done me? I have been wronged many times, girl...and nothing you offer can compare."

"Please...only hear me," Cristabel begged. "You promised."

Vienne glanced beyond Cristabel—out into the other room.

213

"He is not here," Cristabel said.

Vienne sat down once more. "Tell me this wrong you have done me," she demanded. "Though I warn you…nothing you could have done would be worse than the fact you led my brother to me."

Cristabel sighed—relieved Vienne had kept her promise—at least for the moment. She inhaled a deep breath and told Vienne the whole of it then. She told Vienne of being prisoner aboard The Merry Wench—of the second battle with the crew of The Screaming Witch. She told her of James Kelley, of his feeling of indebtedness, and of the pirate ruse they had contrived. She told her of William and Richard Pelletier—and of Trevon's anger. She told her then of having been in La Petite Grenouille following the meeting with Governor Claiborne—and of having recognized Vienne from the painting.

Cristabel brushed tears from her cheeks. "I did not tell Trevon I had seen you…the woman from the painting that hangs in his cabin. I-I did not know you were his sister…I thought you were perhaps a lover of his past…and I was afraid he would come for you. Thus, I did not tell him…not until your mother told me of the Wasp and Victoria's Revenge…that you had been taken by pirates…and killed."

"My mother?" Vienne exclaimed in a whisper. "How is it that you came to speak with my mother?"

Cristabel wiped more tears from her cheeks as Vienne dabbed at her own tears.

"Trevon did not know what to do with me…for he meant the Pelletiers to think me dead," Cristabel explained. "He could not return me to my mother…or to anyone else. Furthermore, he had promised not to kill me. Therefore, with no alternative before him, he sailed me with them to the bay…the hidden pirate community where the crew of The Merry Wench and their families reside. Your mother was there…and was very kind to me…even after I confessed what I had done to you and Trevon."

"Is she well?" Vienne asked. "My mother? Is…is she well?"

"She is well," Cristabel said. "Though she painfully misses her daughter."

Vienne glanced away. "She would not miss me so if she knew what I have become."

"She misses you…and loves you…no matter what you have endured. As does Trevon," Cristabel said, reaching across the table and taking

Vienne's hand. She was encouraged when Vienne did not pull her hand away—but rather squeezed Cristabel's in return.

Vienne shook her head. "No. No...I am dead to them, I am certain," she said. "Rackham Henry captured me...and I do not remember what I endured. My mind will not allow me to remember it. Though I do remember the pain...the terrible pain piercing my entire body when I awoke on the shore. A fisherman found me and took me to his kind wife. They told me they did not know how I survived Rackham Henry...but I did. I have a brief wisp of a memory...of standing on the bridge of Victoria's Revenge...of gazing into the sea and thinking death would be welcome. I somehow knew the ship was close to some shore. I remember thinking that I was a good swimmer...that perhaps I could make my way to the shore and freedom. But if I drowned in trying...it would be better than remaining where I was. That is all I remember of it." She looked to Cristabel—frowning with agony—more tears traveling over her cheeks. "Yet I know what happened...though I do not remember...I know what abuse I endured aboard Victoria's Revenge."

Cristabel wiped tears from her eyes—her heart aching for Vienne's pain—both physical and otherwise. "Did you not remember your mother and brother then either? Was the memory of those who love and miss you also taken from your mind?"

Vienne swallowed—shook her head ashamedly. "No. No...I well remember Trevon and Mother. Father and Vortigem as well." She paused, weeping. "But I could not return to them...not when I was so...so entirely ruined." She sobbed a moment—then inhaled a calming breath. "So...I found work here. Christophe is cruel...even abusive at times. Yet, he does not lay hands on his serving wenches...not in the same way a pirate does. Christophe may strike me if I do not serve well...but he does not touch me otherwise." She forced a hopeful smile. "It is not so terrible a thing to work hard here...and to be safe from...from the abuse of men. Is it?"

Cristabel shook her head—knowing she must proceed with understanding. "No, Vienne. It is not so terrible a thing."

"I could not face them," Vienne said. "I could not allow my mother to see what I have become. I could not allow Trevon to see it." She gazed at

Cristabel—wiping more tears from her eyes. "I am ruined, pretty girl. Ruined. There is no mending me…my body or my mind."

"You are not ruined, Vienne," Cristabel said, taking her hand once more.

Vienne studied Cristabel a moment—her eyes narrowing with a rather inquisitive expression.

"Are you in love with my brother then?" she asked.

Cristabel winced—struggled to keep from melting into sobs.

"I am," she admitted.

"And he is, no doubt, wildly in love with you," Vienne added, smiling a little.

Cristabel's tears increased their profusion over her cheeks as she shook her head. "No," she whispered. "For I have wronged him…in not telling him I saw you that night. I mean now to make amends in whatever small, pitiful way that I can."

"You mean to bring me to him…as your venue of repentance…that you may win him again," Vienne said.

"No," Cristabel said, shaking her head. "I mean to reunite you and Trevon…and your mother…because it is right…and will bring him happiness I can never give him."

"I cannot face them," Vienne said. "I am in ruin…broken, unworthy."

"You did nothing wrong, Vienne!" Cristabel insisted through her tears. "You are still Vienne…beloved daughter and sister. Their love for you is unconditional! There has been two years of this pain…and it was needless. Please…please come with me. Trevon has had a room at the inn across the way prepared for you. Please! You need only rise and walk with me from this painful life."

Yet, Vienne shook her head. "No! No!" she breathed as she wept. "You do not understand. I can never return. I am worn and weathered. I cannot face them…for I know what their thoughts toward me would be."

"That they love you with all their hearts and will only be glad to embrace you once more…to kiss your cheeks and see you smile!" Cristabel pleaded.

"No," Vienne said. "I am ruined…I am not worthy of happiness…or a life filled with loving people. No." She looked to Cristabel—pain so evident in her beautiful blue eyes that Cristabel's own heart near broke.

"Once you have endured terrible things, you cannot undo them. You are changed...and worthless."

Cristabel fought to keep from dropping to her knees and begging Vienne to come with her. It would be her next course—pleading with sheer desperation. She did not want Trevon to rush in and take his sister by force. Vienne had no doubt endured too much force already. She wanted her to choose to go—to realize that her family was waiting and would love her without condition.

Cristabel suddenly gasped—for inspiration was upon her. Reaching into the front of her dress, she removed the two silver pieces of eight from their hiding place between her breasts. She had brought the silver in order to purchase passage to New Orleans. Yet, now—now she knew they were meant to serve another purpose.

"Vienne," she began placing the two pieces of eight in her palm and offering them toward Vienne. "What do you see here...in my palm?"

Vienne brushed the tears from her cheeks—shook her head with not understanding what cause Cristabel could have to show her the two pieces of eight.

"Please," Cristabel whispered. "Tell me what you see."

Brushing more tears from her cheeks, Vienne answered, "Two pieces of eight. Two silver Spanish coins."

"Yes," Cristabel said. "Now tell me...which coin has the most worth?"

Vienne frowned. "What do you mean?"

"Which coin holds greater value?" Cristabel asked.

Vienne shook her head—still confused. "They are of equal value," she answered.

"But this coin is more recently minted," Cristabel said placing the new coin on the table before Vienne. "It is not tarnished or worn." Cristabel then placed the second coin on the table before Vienne. "This coin is older. It has seen travel and is weathered. It has collected soil and is not so shiny as the other coin. And yet you claim that it is of the same worth as the coin that is not so worn and tarnished."

"Yes," Vienne whispered. Cristabel saw tears renewing in Vienne's blue eyes as understanding began to enter her mind.

"Are not all God's children beloved of him?" she asked. "Are not we all of the same worth and value in his eyes?" She paused, again offering

217

the two pieces of eight to Vienne. "All pieces of eight are of equivalent worth…tarnished and worn or shiny and new…each will bring the same price…each will purchase the same wares. Each is beautiful in its own regard. The new one because it glistens…its etchings clear and strong. Yet, the weathered coin…it knows experience…perhaps ill experience. It is not so unsullied as the new coin…but it owns full as much value…is full as precious as the other."

Vienne accepted the coins—studied them. "It is a beautiful sentiment," she said.

"It is true…and it was given to me by your mother…just as the coins were," Cristabel said.

Vienne covered her mouth with one hand, attempting to silence her sobbing.

"Trevon has been weathered, too, Vienne," Cristabel said. Vienne looked up to her—an expression of astonishment on her tear-streaked face. "He has carried the burden of your death…blamed only himself for your torture and murder. He has become, as you well know, a privateer…living in isolation and without hope of happiness."

"It was no fault of his!" Vienne exclaimed.

"And it was no fault of yours," Cristabel reminded her. "It was the fault of the villains in the world and the devil who instructs them. You are a victim, Vienne. And now…now it is time to empower yourself with strength and hope. You know your mother loves you still. Would not you still love your own daughter? You know your brother loves you…that he, too, fights self-loathing at every turn." She reached out, closing Vienne's fingers over the two coins and gripping her hand. "Come with me, Vienne. Choose to walk from this wretched place of your own will! Your brother waits for you just across the way…and your mother waits to hold you in her arms once more."

"Mother?" Vienne breathed.

"Yes," Cristabel assured her. "Your mother is there. If you come with me, I am to take you to your room so that you may bathe and prepare yourself to see them. I-I explained to Trevon that you may need some time to…to prepare. But they are both there…waiting for you…loving you as much as ever they did before you were parted from them."

"But Christophe…Christophe will be enraged," Vienne offered.

Cristabel smiled. "Do you truly think Cristophe would risk provoking the pirate Navarrone? Navarrone the Blue Blade? Over a serving wench?"

Vienne smiled through her tears. "No...but he may not allow me to leave."

Cristabel smiled. "Trevon has a plan for that, too," she said. She reached out taking both Vienne's hands in hers. "If you are ready to walk with me...to simply cross the road and leave this horror behind you...then we will walk from here...and to freedom."

Vienne stood. "Then let us go now, Cristabel Albay...my brother's lover," she said. "For in another moment, my courage may be lost to me."

Without pause, Cristabel stood, taking Vienne's hand and leading her from the room.

"You'll lose a day's wages if you keep from your work any longer, woman!" Christophe roared as he strode toward them.

But Cristabel only smiled—for Baskerville already sat at a nearby table.

"You!" Baskerville called. "Inn keeper! This beer is weak. Have you watered it down then? Is that your game?"

Instantly, Christophe was distracted—glared at Baskerville and growled, "Are you accusing me, man?"

"Come, Vienne," Cristabel said, leading Vienne toward the nearest door.

As they approached their outlet to freedom, Trevon, Fergus and James Kelley entered. Cristabel heard Vienne gasp—felt her pause as Trevon looked at her.

"He only comes to offer distraction that we may escape," Cristabel said. Tears sprang to her eyes anew however, when she saw the astonishment—the mingled joy and pain in Trevon's countenance as he passed them, nodding to his sister.

"Inn keeper!" Fergus shouted. "We want drink and we want it now!"

"Vienne!" Christophe called. "Vienne...serve these men, at once!"

"Do not look back, Vienne," Cristabel said as they neared the door. "Do not look back. It is all behind you with this last step."

As they stepped across the threshold of La Petite Grenouille and into Vienne's freedom, Cristabel glanced back. Vienne looked frightened—in truth, terrified. Yet she had made a choice—and Cristabel knew it would forever change the course of both their lives.

# Chapter Fifteen

It had been hours—hours of talk and tears—of Cristabel offering Vienne reassurance and encouragement. Vienne had begged to be isolated from her family for a time—to bathe, weep and prepare herself to greet her mother and brother. Yet, a bond had been forged between Cristabel and Vienne—thus, it had been Cristabel who had spent the first hours of Vienne's freedom with her. It had been Cristabel who comforted and offered promise to Vienne Navarrone that her family would love her— and without condition—Cristabel who now endeavored to distract Vienne with the tale of how she had come to be in Trevon's possession—and beyond.

"Well, certainly he threatened to ravage me. Again and again he threatened to do it…but I quickly began to suspect he was not so brutal as he would have me think," Cristabel explained as she wove Vienne's hair into a long, ebony plait. She frowned. "Though, I do admit to owning no memory of the night I consumed the demon rum. I suppose he might well have had his way with me and I might not have remembered it."

"You would have known…whether you remembered it or not," Vienne mumbled.

Cristabel wished Vienne would allow a change in the course of their conversation—but she was far too determined to learn everything she could concerning Cristabel's experience with her brother, the pirate Navarrone the Blue Blade.

"Furthermore, I know my brother," she stated. "He does not have within him such a thing as the villainy necessary to defile women. I am glad it was Trevon who found you, Cristabel."

Cristabel felt awash with guilt—for she had escaped the terrible fate that Vienne had not. She could not fathom the nightmare Vienne had endured. She winced as her imagination lingered a moment on such horrors. Still, she shook her head—determined not to think on Vienne's past—but only to help her to move into a bright and beautiful future filled with hope and love—unconditional love.

Vienne turned in the chair in which she sat, gazing at Cristabel and smiling. "Truly, Cristabel…I am glad you were saved," she said. "I do not resent that you were, and I was not." Her smile broadened. "And I am glad it was Trevon who saved you."

"As am I," Cristabel agreed. She smoothed the long raven plait of Vienne's hair, nodded toward the looking glass and asked, "Will it do? I am not so very gifted at braiding."

Vienne returned her attention to the looking glass before her. She sighed—her smile fading a little.

"It is very nicely done," she said. "I only wish I did not look so dark beneath the eyes." She reached up, tracing her forehead and cheek with trembling fingers. "I wish…"

"You look as beautiful as ever you have, Vienne," Cristabel told her. "How else would I have recognized you from your portrait?"

Vienne smiled into the looking glass. "You are too sweet to me, Cristabel Albay. I wish I could repay your kindnesses…but I have nothing to offer."

"Of course you do!" Cristabel exclaimed.

"And what is that?" Vienne laughed.

"Well, though nothing is needed in return," Cristabel began, "for you forget that I created a grievous sin in not telling Trevon about you before…and I hope that one day you may find in it in your heart to forgive me that…still, I would like to own your friendship."

Vienne smiled and Cristabel was dazzled by the sudden light in her blue eyes—the perfect beauty of her face. She was indeed sustaining the beginnings of restoration.

"Of course! Anything else?" she prodded.

Cristabel smiled. "Well…I would enjoy hearing stories of Trevon as a child. I wish for you to tell me of what he was like as a boy. Someday…when we have ample time to sit together in light conversation."

Vienne giggled. "Done. We will find the time one day…and soon."

"Yes, we will," Cristabel agreed. "But for now…I know two people who are nearly ill with wanting to talk with you, Vienne. Do you feel ready?"

Vienne's smile faded. "Of course not," she whispered.

Cristabel knew that neither the soothing, fragrant bath, nor having her hair brushed and plaited—could have vanquished Vienne's fears of facing her family. These luxuries only made her feel more prepared in appearance to face her mother and brother—her heart and soul were still terrified of the judgment that might appear in their eyes.

"You have nothing to fear, Vienne," Cristabel told her. "Now, come." She bid Vienne stand and walk toward the hearth. "Wait just here," she said. "I will bring them to you."

Vienne frowned—terrible trepidation obviously breaking over her. Cristabel smiled. "Do I dare leave you…even for a moment? Will you flee?"

Vienne breathed a nervous giggle. "No. No I will wait for them. I will meet them now."

"Good!" Cristabel said.

Hastening to the door, lest Vienne change her mind—Cristabel left the room, closing the door behind her.

Claire and Trevon were waiting without—both with expressions of concern and anxiety.

"She is ready," Cristabel told Claire. "As ready as she can be."

"James Kelley," Trevon growled.

Cristabel smiled at James as he appeared from around one corner.

"Stand guard here," Trevon commanded. "I do not yet trust that the proprietor of La Petite Grenouille will not attempt to retrieve Vienne. Sound an alarm if anyone approaches."

"Aye, Cap'n," James said, nodding with determination.

Trevon glanced to Cristabel—but only briefly. "And do not allow our prisoner to wander far. Do you understand?"

"Aye, Cap'n," James agreed.

Tears filled Cristabel's eyes—for Trevon did not make any gesture to indicate he might have begun to forgive her in the least.

"Come along, darling," Claire said, taking Trevon's arm. "Let us see to our Vienne."

Without another word, Trevon turned the door latch and allowed his mother to precede him into Vienne's room. He followed her, closing the door behind him.

Tears flooded Cristabel's cheeks as she heard Claire exclaim, "Oh my darling! My baby! Oh, my beautiful, beautiful Vienne!"

Quickly she moved away—toward the open doors nearby leading to the inn's upper balcony. It was all so consuming—entirely overpowering. The tender, battered emotions of weeks of continually knowing joy, then despair, then joy once more had weakened Cristabel's resistance. She felt as if she might expire—or in the very least that she would never feel rested or be truly happy again.

"You all right, Miss Cristabel?" James Kelley inquired from his post inside.

Cristabel nodded—sniffled and angrily brushed at the tears on her cheeks. "Yes, James. I am well. I am simply overcome with the strain of it all I suppose."

"You need your rest, miss," James said. "Perhaps you may rest peacefully tonight...knowing all is well with the Cap'n and his sister."

"Yes...perhaps. Thank you, James," Cristabel said. The poor boy was so wholly innocent—so blind to the pain Cristabel was enduring. She supposed that his youth and inexperience left him unable to see that Trevon had spurned Cristabel—that Cristabel's heart was breaking. She did not blame James for his naiveté—for she was fully as naive at aged fourteen years as he was—far more so, in fact.

Thus, she would not press her young friend to worry. She would simply linger on the balcony and gaze at the horizon. The sun would begin to set soon. Although it seemed impossible, it was true that the day had nearly exhausted itself already. Vienne had taken many hours in preparing to meet her family again. Cristabel mused that this was yet another reason she felt such a sense of weariness—for it had been wearing to sit with Vienne—talk with her, encourage her and offer hope all the long hours it took her to find the courage to face Claire and Trevon.

Suddenly, Cristabel wanted nothing more than to simply collapse—to find respite through deep slumbering unconsciousness. Yet, it was not so thoroughly true that it was the only thing she wanted—for there was one thing she wanted more—Trevon.

❧

"I should have died before I let them take you," Trevon growled, still kneeling before his sister.

"No!" Vienne sobbed. "No, Trevon! I know the pain you feel…and the guilt…for I thought you were dead for a time…and I owned guilt for it."

Trevon gazed into Vienne's blue eyes—the eyes he had known for as long as his memory could allow. "What?" he asked. "Why would you think me dead?"

Vienne sniffled—dabbed at her red nose with a handkerchief. "I saw them beating you, Trevon. I saw them put you under the cat until your body was drenched with your own blood…until you collapsed…unconscious. But I thought you were dead…that you had been beaten to death before my very eyes. It was not until months later that I heard you had been found…and lived…that you had taken to piracy."

"I should have died, Vienne," Trevon said, kissing the back of her hand. "For a very long time I wished that I would have died. I existed with the knowledge I failed you…allowed you to be tortured and murdered."

Trevon felt his lower lip tremble as his sweet sister gazed into his eyes—smiled at him—brushed a lone tear from his temple.

"And if you had died, Trevon…you would not have saved your sweet Cristabel…and she would have known the same fate I did…worse even than mine. Furthermore, it was Cristabel who brought me to you, in the end…was it not?"

"Yes," Trevon whispered. He knew it was true—had been cognizant of it since the moment Cristabel had revealed having seen Vienne. "She is my rescuer in many ways…for she rescued you…and my heart."

Vienne giggled and Trevon frowned. It had been near two hours since his mother had left them alone—left brother and sister to begin the healing of their wounds. Two hours he had lingered in her company—and it was the first time she had laughed.

"So you set sail in search of traitors and treason…and found your true love instead. Is that it, brother?" Vienne asked—her eyes bright with merriment in teasing him.

225

Trevon breathed a chuckle as he stood. He raked a weary hand through his hair, shaking his head.

"I am not worthy of her," he sighed. "She deserves a better man than I will ever be."

"In the first of it, you are the best of men, Trevon," Vienne said. She stood, taking hold of his arm and smiling at him. "And in the second…we are none of us perfect. No one is without fault…or damage. Whether physical, emotional, or both…we are all of us human."

Trevon frowned as Vienne reached into the small pocket at the waist of her dress. Holding her hand toward him, she opened it to reveal two silver pieces of eight lying in her palm.

"Your Cristabel gave these to me, Trevon," Vienne explained. "She told me the tale Mother told to her when first she gifted them to her." She took his hand, depositing the coin into it. "But only after she had told me her own tale of them at La Petite Grenouille. And now…I give them to you…with my tale to tell."

"You women and your coins," Trevon chuckled.

"You know our mother, therefore you know she dotes on the older coin because it has known adventure and experience," Vienne said. "Cristabel dotes on it, for to her it is an example of the worth of souls…that each person God has placed on the earth is of equal value…not matter their worn and tattered condition. I give them to you now with this contemplation…who would love better, Trevon? A youthful, naive man who has no experience in hardship, loss and agony…or the man who knows the value of love?"

Trevon shook his head. "I am not a coin, Vienne."

"Exactly. You are a man…a man who can love Cristabel as she deserves to be loved…passionately, desperately…a man willing to give his life for her." Vienne paused—brushed a tear from her cheek. "There are not so many men like you in the world Trevon. Cristabel seems a strong, passionate young woman. Only a strong, passionate man could know how to love her as she must be loved. Likewise, the same is true of you." Vienne pointed to the newer coin. "View this coin as Cristabel…young, fresh, shining and full of hope and desire." She pointed to the worn coin. "What better companion than this worn and weathered coin…to protect her through life…to keep her fresh and untainted, eh?"

Trevon sighed—shook his head and smiled. "You women and your coins," he repeated. "Will a coin ever be simply a coin in your eyes?"

"No. Never again," Vienne said. "Not after today."

Trevon fisted the coins in his hand. "Still, she was purely disgusted with me for my failing of you," he mumbled, frowning. "I may not be able to win her heart."

Vienne shook her head. "You were disgusted with yourself, Trevon...and needlessly," she told him. "Furthermore, you already own her heart, darling. So do not waste another moment in claiming it."

"I cannot leave you," Trevon said—wild with wanting to seek out Cristabel.

Vienne smiled. "I will be here when you return. Send Mother in if you are worried that I will flee...though I will not. I am returned to you and Mother...and I will not be parted from either of you ever again."

Trevon nodded. Taking Vienne's face between his hands, he pressed a firm and loving kiss to her forehead. The pain he knew at having failed her would never leave him. Vienne's soul would be scarred forever as well. Yet, they were together—two worn pieces of eight who were still of worth.

"I go then," Trevon began, "though I may not survive it if she will not have me."

Vienne smiled. "She will have you, Trevon. The love she owns for you is easily visible...and nothing could keep her from you now." She giggled, adding, "And I shall have a sister at last!"

"Do not be too hopeful, Vienne," Trevon warned—anxiety and trepidation churning within him. "She may not..."

He was silenced as Vienne placed a hand over his mouth. "She loves you, Trevon...far more than even a ship loves the sea." She released him. "Now go to her. She has been suffering miserably. Champion her once more in ending her torment."

Trevon sighed. Inhaling a deep breath, he summoned his courage—the same courage that attended him in battle—allowed him to best traitors and pirates. He shook his head, thinking he was far more fearful at the thought of confessing his love to Cristabel and facing rejection, than he was at battling an angry mob of pirates in preservation of his life.

"Very well," he said, at last. "Here…take your bloody coins." He deposited the coins into Vienne's hand, smiling and adding, "For in a moment, I hope to have my hands otherwise occupied."

Vienne giggled, playfully slapping his arm in a manner of scolding. "You truly are a pirate, you dashing devil."

"I'll have Mother come to you," he said, turning and striding from the room. He paused, looking over his shoulder to her once—for he could scarce believe she was there—alive and with him. "We move forward, Vienne…yes?"

"Yes, Trevon," she said, smiling and offering a nod of reassurance. "Only forward."

Cristabel rose from the chair in which she had been sitting. From the inn's upper balcony, she had watched the sun set—slowly sink into a horizon of tall cypress and pine. The stars now twinkled in the night sky—the moon a brilliant, full and glowing orb of warm luminance. She knew she should have taken advantage of the hours Claire and Trevon had spent in conversation with Vienne—that she should have fled while the chance was allowed her. Yet she did not wish to do disservice to James Kelley. He had been set as her guard and she would not allow him to fail at his task. Furthermore, she was in need to know that all was well—that Vienne was soothed—assured that her mother and brother did, indeed, want her back in their warm embraces. She would see that Vienne was comforted and did not attempt to flee—attempt to return to the morbid, horrible life she had led since escaping Rackham Henry.

Yet now—now the cover of darkness had fallen—and Cristabel began to feel restless—as if the opportunity to escape was slipping away. She thought of the two silver pieces of eight she had gifted Vienne—knew they had been bartered to purchase far more than her own passage to New Orleans—and she was glad. Still, she wondered how she would make her way to her mother.

"Cristabel."

She gasped at the sound of his voice—whirling around to face him— her heart wildly pounding within her bosom. Cristabel swallowed the uncomfortable lump of trepidation that leapt to her throat at the sight of Trevon Navarrone. He stood on the balcony now—there—just before her—as handsome and alluring as ever he had been before—more so. She quickly studied him for a moment. He looked weary—yet his expression was void of the simmering anger that often burbled just below the surface of his countenance. A breeze caught the fabric of his white shirt—billowing it and causing that the laces at the front of it should loosen and give way to reveal his bronzed and sculpted torso.

Cristabel stepped back as he approached—for he was intimidating—even for all that had passed between them. She frowned when he, unexpectedly, dropped to one knee before her.

"I've come to beg your forgiveness, love," he said, bowing his head. "I have been a wounded, hateful man...self-loathing and bitter." He looked up to her then, and she near melted at the warmth in his eyes. "But you have changed me...softened my heart...healed my soul."

Cristabel stepped back from him—overwhelmed by sudden hope—yet fearful of it as well. He had hardly spoken a word to her since the moment she told him of having seen Vienne—hardly a word. And now he lingered before her on bended knee, professing she was his healer? She could make no sense of it, and she began to take another step back from him.

She gasped, however, as Trevon reached down, gripping her right ankle to stay her, and she began to tremble. His touch was overpowering to her senses—his firm, yet somehow non-threatening grip—the warmth of his hand against her flesh. Instantly, tears welled in her eyes—fro she wanted only to be in his arms. She wanted his forgiveness for her ill choice in not having told him of Vienne—wanted to own his heart as fully as he owned hers.

"A moment before you told me of having seen Vienne," he began, gazing up at her, "you claimed to love me. Is it true? Even after you knew of my failing Vienne two years ago...even knowing I am a coward...that I should have died rather than let her be taken...even then did you mean what you said?"

Cristabel grimaced as tears escaped her eyes. Quickly she thought of the choices she had made—choices that had endangered others or herself. It was as if an inspiration had overcome her—for she suddenly understood that no human being could know the consequences of each and every choice made. She understood then, that the best that could be done was to choose as wisely as one could, then hope and pray for the finest result. As she gazed into the handsome, nearly pleading expression on Trevon's face, she knew she must risk her heart once more. Only by risking it—by again confessing that she truly did love him—only then might she have a chance to win his heart—truly win it.

"Yes," she managed to answer in a whisper. "But you did not fail her."

He exhaled as if he had been holding his breath in anticipation of her response to his inquiry.

"And you?" he asked, caressing her ankle. "Have I failed you, Cristabel Albay?" He shook his head, breathed a disbelieving chuckle. "I took you prisoner...threatened to despoil you in order to glean information...placed you in danger and kept you captive in the solitude of the bay."

"You are a patriot," she offered. "You were only trying to uncover treason and wickedness that you may vanquish it."

"At first," he said, again caressing her ankle. She quivered with delight as his hand traveled up the length of her calf in a slow caress, coming to pause at the back of her knee. He pulled her knee toward him, placing a lingering kiss to it. Even through the fabric of her dress she could feel the warmth of his kiss. "But I kept you...because I wanted you for my own," he confessed, smiling up at her. "I would not have ransomed you to Richard Pelletier, Cristabel...even if he was a good and honest man. I had decided to keep you by the time we met with the governor."

"What?" she breathed—too overcome by his intimate touch to utter anything else.

He released her leg then, placing his hands one on each of her ankles—only over the fabric of her dress instead of on her skin. Slowly, his hands traveled up the length of her body—along the outside of her calves and legs—to her waist—to her back. The gesture weakened her knees and she melted to him as he pulled her against him then, softly kissing her cheek.

"I was falling in love with you by then, you see, love," he whispered, kissing her opposite cheek. "And I could not give you up. It worked well to my advantage that Richard is a conspirator...for I knew you did not love him...as you first told me the night you were tankard up on the rum."

"I-I did?" she asked, rendered breathless by his attention, his touch—by his very existence.

He grinned a mischievous grin of owning secrets. "You did."

"Wh-what else did I tell you that night?" she ventured.

His smile broadened and she was discomfited. "You asked me if I seduced many woman."

Trevon chuckled at the astonished and horrified expression washing over Cristabel's face as she gasped.

"I did not!" she argued.

"You did, love," he said, pulling her body more tightly against his.

"And what did you answer?" she asked. She was breathless in his arms. He could see that she wanted him to kiss her as desperately as he wanted to kiss her. Yet, he would assure himself further of her affection and love for him first.

"I told you that I did not seduce women to my bed...and you confessed that it would be preferable to be ravaged by me than by Bully Booth," he said.

"I did?" she gasped. He adored the bashful blush that rose to her cheeks.

He could not torture her longer—nor keep from her. "You said you would endeavor to be a pirate bride, Cristabel," he began. "Is it true? And if it is...would you consider being the pirate bride of Navarrone the Blue Blade?"

She burst into sobbing then—burying her face against his shoulder and weeping bitterly. He could feel the release in her—the release of restrained heart ache and fear.

"Marry me, love," he whispered, kissing the top of her head as his own heart hammered brutal within his chest. "Marry me and I swear I will never fail you...never. I would die before I would fail you."

"Do not speak such things!" she exclaimed, covering his mouth with her hand. "Never speak such words!"

Trevon could see he had truly upset his little vixen—and he would not be the cause of any more distress to her.

"Very well, love," he said, taking her face in his hands. "It was needs be that I find Vienne...before I could allow myself to have you. Do you understand that? I hated myself for what happened to her...I did not blame you for any of it...only myself. I was certain you must loathe me for my weakness…and I could do nothing but seek her out…attempt repentance and restitution. I…"

"I never thought ill of you for what happened to her, Trevon," she interrupted. "Never."

He sighed—for he could see the truth of it in her eyes. It had been his hatred of himself that had caused him to think she would not want him.

"Will you be a pirate bride then, love?" he asked once more. "My pirate bride?"

"Yes," she breathed as more tears streamed over her pretty cheeks. "Oh, yes! Yes! I love you!"

"And I love you, Cristabel," he whispered as his mouth descended to hers.

Oh, such a kiss it was! Cristabel's soul took flight to the heavens as Trevon bathed her in the euphoric bliss of his attentions to her mouth. His arms were banded around her—as if he meant never to release her again! Did he truly mean to marry her—to take her to wife? Yet, as the passion of their exchange increased—she knew that he did. He loved her! Trevon Navarrone loved her! It was unfathomable—yet true!

How had they come to this—to such fiery passionate love? How had they come from captor and captive, to being lovers? Yet, she did not care in those moments. In those moments all there was in the world was Trevon—his handsome strength, his wit, his wisdom, his patriotism—his love.

Cristabel was startled from her rapture by the sound of gunfire—and nearby. Trevon broke from her at once, drawing cutlass as he turned from her. There was a scream from within the inn—from Vienne's room.

Trevon glanced around—his attention quickly falling to a small alcove on the wall of the balcony.

"Stay here," he commanded, frowning. "The dark should hide you well against the wall." He pushed into the small alcove and turned to leave.

"No, wait!" she cried in a whisper.

"It is the keeper of La Petite Grenouille…no doubt come for Vienne," he said, frowning. "Stay here, love…all will be well soon enough."

But as Cristabel watched Trevon disappear into the inn, her heart pounded with fear and trepidation. How could all be well when Vienne was being threatened?

It was because she did not stay where Trevon had told her to stay. It was because she ventured from the safety of the darkness and the alcove to peer in through the doors leading to the inn that they found her. Cristabel understood this the moment a hand was placed over her mouth from behind—the moment she turned to see two faces she recognized.

As she struggled—fought to keep from being bound with rope—a cloth wrapped around her mouth to silence her—Cristabel sobbed. The two men tying her hands and feet—the two men who mercilessly pushed her over the railing of the balcony to fall into a wagon full of straw—were two men she had seen before. As they leapt over the railing to land beside her in the wagon and hold her down—horror engulfed her—for these were two of the men who had first abducted her from the house of her stepfather.

Struggling—crying out though the cloth binding around her mouth—Cristabel watched as the wagon lurched forward—gazed up at the balcony where she knew Trevon would return to find her gone. She knew Trevon could not hear her—even if she had not been gagged he could not have heard her—for the ruckus in the inn was loud enough to mask her weeping and muffled cries.

# Chapter Sixteen

Trevon tightened his grip around Christophe's throat. "Tell me where she is!" he roared. "Tell me, or I'll slit your belly open and string out your guts while you watch!"

He was infuriated—mad with anger! Fergus was tending to Baskerville's wound while the other men kept guard over Vienne and his mother. Trevon had sent James Kelley to knocking on doors through the town in search of information concerning who had taken Cristabel and where.

"All right! All right!" Christophe choked. Trevon did not immediately release his hold on the inn keeper, however. The proprietor of La Petite Grenouille had already abused his sister—now he had helped someone abduct Cristabel. Therefore, Trevon owned no mercy for him—only wished to continue tightening his grip around the villain's neck.

"Release me! Release me and I'll tell you all I know," Christophe whispered.

Exhaling a heavy sigh, Trevon did release his grip around the man's throat. Yet, he quickly pulled the dagger from its sheath at the back of his waist, pressing the blade to his gullet.

"Speak, or die, inn keeper!" Trevon growled. "And I warn you...tell the truth...all of it...or I will make good my threat to open your belly!"

"All right! All right! Hold your blade, pirate!" Christophe panted. He paused, however, and Trevon pressed the dagger blade more firmly against his throat.

"Speak! Now!" he ordered.

Christophe held up a hand to stay Trevon's blade—nodded and swallowed hard.

"All right...all right," he began. "She was recognized when she came into La Petite Grenouille to steal my serving wench."

Trevon cut a small wound in Christophe's neck with the tip of the dagger. "That serving wench is my sister, man! Whom you abused and held captive with fear! Proceed carefully here...or you will die!"

"Yes, yes! Of course," Christophe stammered. "Your woman was recognized by an Acadian that frequents La Petite Grenouille. I heard him tell another that he had seen her before...in fact that he had taken her from her home...and been paid well to do so. He left soon thereafter and a wealthy man returned with him."

"William Pelletier?" Trevon offered.

"I do not know! He was a youngish man...perhaps your age," Christophe panted. "He approached me and offered me near a barrel of money to help him capture the girl once more. I could not deny him...for he would have killed me I am certain."

"Where did they take her?" Trevon shouted. "Where?"

"I do not know! I do not!" Christophe cried, beginning to sob. "I only know that the place was not far off...for I heard them say that much."

"Perhaps...p-perhaps the old house where we met before, Cap'n," Baskerville grumbled as Fergus endeavored to clean the wound in his shoulder.

Baskerville had stepped in front of Vienne in time to take a ball in the shoulder. It was eternal gratitude Trevon felt toward his friend for such a sacrifice—yet, his thanks would have to wait. Cristabel had been taken—by Richard Pelletier no doubt—and he could not fathom what the man might do to her.

"Perhaps," Trevon agreed. "Baskerville...see that mother and Vienne are safely returned to the schooner." He looked to Fergus then. "Fergus...set sail with my mother, my sister and young James Kelley. Then send the other men to accompany Baskerville to the old house where we met Claiborne concerning the Chichester."

"Aye, Cap'n," Fergus agreed.

"You're not going alone, are you, Cap'n?" Baskerville asked. "Pelletier may well have men other than the Acadians with him. You cannot go alone."

"You and the others will attend me soon enough…but I cannot wait," Trevon explained.

"And what am I to do?" Christophe asked as Trevon sheathed his dagger once more. "What will happen to me?"

"I don't give a damn," Trevon growled as his fist met with the man's jaw, rendering the proprietor of La Petite Grenouille unconscious.

❧

"Richard…Richard, please…" Cristabel begged. "I don't understand. We were to be wed…how can you do this thing?"

She tried to call upon greater courage—yet it was difficult, considering the circumstance. In truth, she had managed to muster more courage in facing Bully Booth and all that had happened before The Screaming Witch had attacked the Chichester—before Trevon had rescued her and thrown them both into the sea. Now, however—now she was not so naïve. Vienne's tale of abduction and torture had frightened her—had taught her how very fortunate she had been—how blessed and watched over. What woman could hope for even one miracle in a lifetime—and Cristabel had already known two—rescue at the hands of the pirate Navarrone the Blue Blade, and finding true love with a man only heaven itself could have blessed her with.

Thus, now—as one of the Acadians who had again abducted her, slipped a rope over her wrist—a separate rope over her other—she knew she could hope for no further miracles. Still, she silently prayed for them, even as two men forced her to where two large posts were sunk into the ground apart from one another.

"How can *I* do this thing?" Richard asked. "How can *I* do this thing? You are the one keeping company with pirates, Cristabel."

Cristabel frowned. "Better pirates than traitors," she could not keep from mumbling.

"Do you know what you have cost me?" Richard asked, striding toward her.

Cristabel's terror heightened as the Acadians began to stretch her between the two posts outside the house where Trevon had so recently met with Governor Claiborne. She watched as Richard reached to his back. He seemed to struggle in removing something from the waist of his

237

trousers. She gasped—shook her head as tears again filled her eyes at the site of the cat of nine tails in Richard's hand.

"I cost you a fiancé," she told him. "That is all. You will easily find another."

"Well, I *will* easily find another…that is true," he said coming to stand before her. "But you cost me much more than the trifle of a fiancé. A woman is effortlessly replaced, Cristabel. But the same is not true concerning wealth and position."

Cristabel knew he referred to the treasure Trevon and his crew had plundered from the Chichester. Yet, as far as position was concerned, she did not understand him.

"Position?" she asked. "And what have I to do with your wealth and position?"

"There was a great wealth of treasure aboard that British ship the pirate Navarrone plundered…gold, silver, gems, jewels," he said. His eyes narrowed as he looked at her. "Not to mention the price you would have brought. It is full obvious Navarrone the Blue Blade plundered you along with all my riches."

"You had me abducted…delivered to the enemy!" Cristabel accused—for she knew assuredly now—it was Richard who had orchestrated her abduction—just as Trevon had begun to suspect.

"I did," Richard admitted. Cristabel winced as the two men tightened the ropes, stretching her arms up and out.

"You meant to have me sold," she accused.

"Of course not, darling," Richard said, frowning at her as if he took offense. "That is my cousin William's trade…not mine. I meant to offer you and all the wealth aboard the Chichester to King George…to purchase my way into the Empire and the King's good graces…to prove my loyalty was placed where it should be…and not on these revolutionary shores."

Cristabel cried out—grimaced as Richard's sudden anger caused him to lash the ground with the tails of the cat.

"And now…now you have ruined me!" he shouted. "My wealth is in the hands of pirates and I have no means to purchase my way into the British Empire! For that…you shall pay dearly, Cristabel Albay. I shall take my revenge from your flesh…just as I was led to believe the pirates had done."

"Richard, please…I beg you, listen to me," Cristabel began.

"Silence, wench!" he roared. "For that is what you are, are you not? A pirate's wench?" He chuckled. "Captain Navarrone must own all the charms that are told of him, indeed…if he managed to woo you into being his wench."

"Richard…only wait…" she stammered through her tears.

"And since he has already defiled you…I want nothing from you but to see your blood spill, Cristabel," he interrupted however.

She winced—trembling with fear as she saw him strike the ground with the tails of the cat once more.

"Cut her bodice at the back…and her corset stays," Richard ordered. Instantly, Cristabel felt the cool blade of a knife slip beneath her corset and chemise. She gasped as the knife tore through the fabric of her chemise—through her corset stays and dress. She felt the cool, moist air upon the flesh of her back and began to sob.

"Richard…I beg you…please do not do this thing!" she cried. "I will talk with Captain Navarrone. I am certain he will return your treasure…in exchange for my life."

"It is far too late for that, Cristabel," Richard growled. "Don't you see…the British will come for me. King George will send men to assassinate me, for I have not kept my promise to him to return with riches…and you. Someone must pay for this disservice to me…someone must know the lash of the cat, bleed and die. I will see your flesh hang in strips from your body, Cristabel Albay…for you deserve nothing less for what you have done."

"Only a coward would beat a woman to death for something a pirate did."

Cristabel looked up—wept to a near frenzy at the sight of Trevon.

"Trevon! Trevon!" she cried—nearly screamed, so frantic was she. At first, it was pure relief and hope she knew at seeing her lover there before her. He was there—Trevon—strong, handsome and she knew he could cut Richard down as a knife through cream. Yet, in the next moment, she realized he was alone. None of his crew attended him—not Baskerville, nor Fergus—nor even James Kelley.

Quickly she glanced about her—horrified when she counted full ten men attending Richard. Trevon was greatly out-numbered, and she was helpless to assist him.

"Captain Navarrone," Richard said, smiling. He chuckled—studied Trevon from boot to brow. "Has the pirate lover come to beg mercy for his wench then?"

"I beg mercy from no one," Trevon growled. "Not from presidents, kings...traitors or cowards."

"You lied to me that day...here...with Governor Claiborne," Richard said. "Did you know of the Chichester's treasure then?"

Trevon's eyes narrowed. "I had possession of Cristabel then, yes."

"Trevon...please...I will not see you..." Cristabel began.

"Oh, yes!" Richard exclaimed. "Your lover has come for you, Cristabel. He has told me I should not beat a woman for something a pirate did." Richard looked to Trevon then. "Is the pirate then willing to be flogged to save his dirty wench? Flogged to the death?"

"No! No!" Cristabel breathed as she saw Trevon draw his cutlass and drop it to the ground—as his dagger joined it. As he then stripped himself of his shirt, tossing it to the ground as if he never meant to retrieve it again, Cirstabel cried, "No, Trevon! No!"

Trevon Navarrone strode to where the villains had tied Cristabel between two posts. Baskerville and the others should find them soon. He had left word at the inn for his crew to investigate the old house where they had previously met with Governor Claiborne—for one of the serving wenches at La Petite Grenouille knew the house was owned by a man named Pelletier. She had revealed the information after having seen Trevon render Christophe unconscious. Thus, Trevon's intuition had whispered to him that Cristabel had been taken there. He only hoped Baskerville and the others had received his message.

Trevon knew he could endure a brutal flogging with the cat—for he had endured it before. Furthermore, this time he would die before he allowed the villain to harm someone he loved. He would die under the cat before Richard could harm Cristabel further.

Silently he prayed for Baskerville and the others to be quick. For it would not matter if he survived the flogging or died—if his crew did not arrive in time to save the woman he loved from harm.

"No, Trevon! Please!" Cristabel cried as he moved to stand behind her.

Reaching up, Trevon used the slack in the ropes that held Cristabel's wrists—twisting his own wrists to stretch his arms out and above his head. Placing his chest against the tender flesh of her soft, bare shoulders and back, he silently swore to himself that not a mark would be put to her.

Richard chuckled. "You expect me to believe you have the strength and fortitude to keep your own hands bound? That you will endure being flogged to death without being restrained?"

"Do your worst, traitor," Trevon growled.

"Trevon no! Please, Trevon!" Cristabel sobbed. He felt her body go slack as she weakened under the force of so much terror and misery.

Bending to place his lips to her ear, he said, "I love you, Cristabel. Know that. If you are sure of nothing else in life…know that I love you."

"Trevon!" Cristabel screamed as Richard made his way to stand behind them. "No! Richard! Do not do this thing! I swear I will kill you with my own hands if you harm him!"

"Your hands are bound, darling," Richard reminded her. "Now watch your pirate lover die for the sake of your weakness."

Cristabel screamed as she heard the crack of the cat's tails—felt the force of Trevon's body being struck.

"I love you, Cristabel," Trevon whispered once more.

"Stop it! Stop it! Richard! Stop! I will kill you…I swear it!" Cristabel cried.

She glanced up—saw Trevon's hands tighten the ropes more firmly around his wrists a moment before the snap of the cat tails and the force of the lash reverberated through his body and into hers.

"No! No!" Cristabel cried. Why had Trevon come? Why was he being beaten instead of her? She could not fathom it, and felt for a moment as if she might faint. But she could not—she would not. She would not leave Trevon to endure the torture meant for her.

241

"The others will be here soon, love," Trevon whispered to her from behind. He kissed her ear a moment before the tails of the cat tore his flesh once more.

"I see you bleed like any man, Navarrone," Richard chuckled.

"Kill him, Trevon!" Cristabel cried. "Let go of me and kill Richard!"

"There are too many others, love," he said. "One might harm you before I could run them all through." He kissed her ear again and she felt the perspiration on his face as he buried it against her neck a moment.

Again the cat struck—and again Trevon made no sound—only absorbed the brutal blow with the strength of his own body. Cristabel felt him tremble for a moment—knew the pain must be excruciating. She thought of the scars on his back—evidence of having endured such torture before. She could feel the moist, hot perspiration the pain was drawing to his chest against her back and shoulders—again she screamed at Richard that he should stop.

Thirteen lashes with the cat—thirteen strikes of nine tails tearing into his flesh did Trevon endure. Cristabel well knew it was thirteen—for she felt the force of the cat each time Richard brutally applied to his flesh.

"I l-love you, Cristabel," Trevon breathed again. It seemed his professing of love following each blow was his focus—what kept him conscious—and alive.

Yet, Cristabel would not allow him to die for her sake—to be beaten and abused—his body and mind scarred with pain only to save her life. She would not be the cause of his death.

Thus, at last, she produced a long, piercing scream. Over and over she screamed.

Richard paused in whipping Trevon for a moment.

One of the Arcadians mumbled, "She's gone mad, in the end of it."

Richard then came around to stand before Cristabel.

"Shh, love," Trevon panted in her ear. "The men will be here. I have great endurance in me yet."

But Cristabel did not quiet herself.

Richard now stood before her, smiling—the cat of nine tails still held in his hand—dripping with blood.

"Mad is it?" Richard asked. "So, your lover's pain has driven you mad?"

242

Cristabel glared at the villain. "You bloody coward! King George would never have admitted you to the British Empire. He does not bode well with cowards who must beat a woman for vengeance. There is no honor in that."

"I am not beating you, darling," Richard reminded her. "I am beating your lover...who is a filthy pirate to the boot."

"The crew of The Merry Wench will arrive any moment...and you...all of you," she said, nodding to the mercenaries surrounding her and Trevon. "All of you will be dead...for you dare not cross blades with them...just as Richard Pelletier is too cowardly to meet the pirate Navarrone blade to blade."

"I am no coward," Richard growled. "Navarrone is the coward...for he does not even attempt to escape."

"That is because he is a champion," she hatefully sobbed. "He would rather die than allow a woman to be abused. You are a coward...a treasonous, traitorous coward who is afraid to meet a pirate blade to blade. King George would never have accepted you into his fold, Richard! Coward!" she cried, spitting in his face.

Fury turned Richard Pelletier's face crimson as he wiped her saliva from his cheek.

"Coward? Fearful of a bloody pirate? Never!" Richard roared.

Cristabel knew Richard well—and it was well she knew his temper. Once aggravated, he did not think with clarity. She only hoped the crew of The Merry Wench would arrive to save their captain before he was dead by either the cat, or the cutlass.

"Come pirate!" Richard goaded Trevon. The villain tossed aside the cat, drawing his own cutlass. "Come then! Meet me with a blade and let me run you through. Let Cristabel watch you die before I bury the same blade in her heart!"

"Sir," one of the Acadians began.

"Silence!" Richard shouted. "Let no man interfere here! You will not be paid if you do! I will vanquish this bloody pirate alone!" He gestured to Trevon again. "Come then, Navarrone the Blue Blade. Gather your cutlass and meet your death."

"You only face him because he is near to death from the flogging!" Cristabel accused.

243

Richard's brows arched. "But he is Navarrone the Blue Blade. His skill with a blade is legendary…and surely no mere flogging could harm a legend."

Cristabel felt Trevon straighten—looked up to see him unwind his hands and wrists from the rope. She wept as she saw the blood trickling from his palms and wrists—for he had held so tightly to the ropes during his flogging that they had cut into his flesh.

She gasped—sobbed as Trevon staggered from behind her to stand before Richard. The blood and torn flesh at his back were so plethoric—so gruesome—she wondered that he was still alive, let alone conscious.

"Trevon!" she breathed—suddenly overcome with a feeling of dizziness. "I'm so sorry. I-I…Trevon…no!"

"Give him his cutlass!" Richard shouted. When not one man moved to do as he ordered, Richard growled, picked up Trevon's cutlass and flung it toward him to land at his feet. "Pick it up, pirate!" He laughed—amused with himself—blind with fury and arrogance. "Let us see this Blue Blade they tell of."

"Trevon!" Cristabel breathed as Trevon struggled to bend—struggled to grasp the hilt of his cutlass. "Trevon no!" What had she done? In attempting to save him from death by means of the cat, she had only just sent him to die by the blade.

Glancing over his shoulder to her, Trevon winked at her. "Our men will be here to claim you, love. Just keep from harm until they arrive."

He turned to Richard then—nodding toward one mercenary, then another. "You are all dead men," he called to them. "The crew of The Merry Wench will have their revenge upon you for your deeds here…and your conspiring with traitors! Pray they slice your throats quick…instead of putting you under the cat yourselves…or keelhauling you." His speech was labored and breathless.

He turned to Cristabel then, quickly took her face in one hand. "Now, give me one last drink of you, love." He kissed her—his mouth open, moist and demanding—hot and impassioned.

"Your last drink it is indeed, pirate!" Richard raged. "Now die…you dog!"

244

Cristabel screamed as Richard lunged and Trevon turned to meet him. Trevon was weak—brutally battered and wounded. What had she done in provoking Richard further?

She gasped then as Trevon quickly took hold of Richard's wrist—of the hand with which Richard wielded his weapon. Holding Richard's wielding hand high overhead, Navarrone the Blue Blade then plunged his cutlass into the villain's chest. Trevon's triumph took less than an instant, and in the next moment, Richard Pelletier staggered backward—an expression of pure astonished disbelief on his face. He fell to the ground then—exhaling his final breath.

At that very moment, Baskerville and the men from The Merry Wench appeared. James Kelley was with them, and Cristabel watched as, shouting, they attacked the mercenaries. Struggling, she tried to free herself. She could not—she knew she could not—yet she was desperate to protect Trevon—for she knew he was yet in danger.

Trevon Navarron was weak—trembling with residual pain from the flogging—and from loss of blood. Cristabel was not yet freed and safe, however. Thus, he called upon what strength was left him, pulled his cutlass from Richard Pelletier's body and ran it through the guts of an advancing mercenary.

He looked up in time to see James Kelley vanquish a foe—and the thought quickly flittered through his fevered brain that he had ordered Baskerville to see the boy stayed aboard the schooner and out of harm's way. Still, he could not be angry—should not—for the boy was helping to defend Cristabel.

In mere moments the mercenaries were beaten. Most were dead. Those who had survived were struggling to escape. Richard Pelletier was dead—and Cristabel would be safe.

Turning to her then, Trevon staggered to her. He knew he would not have the strength to reach up to untie her wrists—and raised his cutlass intending to cut the ropes from the poles and free her.

"Trevon! Trevon! You are so injured, Trevon!" she sobbed. "You must be attended to at once! Baskerville! Baskerville! Hurry! He will die if we do not hurry!" She paused, gazing at him with inquisitiveness and desperation. "Cut these ropes, Trevon! Hurry!"

Yet, Trevon Navarrone paused. In truth, he felt his body was ready to give up the ghost. He knew William Pelletier would still be a danger to Cristabel and her mother. She was not so entirely safe as he first thought she would be—and he was in no condition to champion her.

"You are well, love," he panted. "Well and safe from harm…for now. But I am not well…I do not know if I will survive this…for I fairly sense my body dying."

"No! No, Trevon! You will be well! I will help you to be well!" she cried. "Untie me, Trevon! Please! Why do you pause?"

"James Kelley," Trevon called. "Hurry here, boy."

James was there at once. "Aye, Cap'n?"

"I gave orders that you were to stay aboard the schooner," he said.

"Aye, Cap'n. I disobeyed the order," James bravely answered.

"I see that," Trevon panted. He could feel the darkness of unconsciousness at the threshold of his mind—sensed The Reaper himself was near to him. "But now I give you an order that you must not disobey, James."

"Aye, Cap'n?"

"Stay here with Cristabel," Trevon said. He was weak—his knees nearly numb and he dropped to them in the grass.

"Trevon! No! Please, Trevon!" Cristabel screamed.

"Once we have gone…have had ample time to sail…untie her and take her to her mother's house," Trevon instructed. "I will have word sent to the Governor explaining what happened here…to Richard Pelletier…and that William Pelletier is a trader in human flesh and a traitor. Stay with Cristabel and her mother until they are well, James Kelley…until you are certain they are safe."

"Aye, Cap'n," James Kelley whispered.

"No! No, Trevon!" Cristabel cried. "Do not leave me! I love you! I love you! We are to be wed! You cannot leave me!"

Trevon struggled to stand. The effort near killed him, he knew. Yet, she must not know how close he was to death—she must not. If he died, he would have Baskerville send word—for he would not have her haunted the way he had been haunted when Vienne had been lost. Still, he would not have her watch him die—he would not leave her with that vision. Furthermore, if he lived—if he somehow managed to survive and heal—

then he would come for her. He would find her, marry her and live in wondrous simplicity and impassioned love with her. But he must survive first.

"Hush, love," Trevon whispered, taking her chin in one trembling hand. "I will come for you...you know I will come for you. If I am able I will come for you. Know that, Cristabel. But I cannot allow you to linger in this pirate's life any longer. It is a danger to you...in ever so many ways."

"Trevon," Cristabel sobbed—desperate to touch him—to hold him—to know he would be well. "Please do not leave me...please! I will be no further trouble to you...I promise it! I will be safe now. Richard is dead. Please let me come with you. Please!"

"I will come for you, love," Trevon whispered. She could see the weakness in him. The pallid condition of his face—the absent smolder in his eyes—he would die if he was not attended to immediately! "I will come for you. If I live, I promise I will come for you. And if...if I do not come...if I cannot...I will send Baskerville to you...with my heart sealed in a box so that I may ever be with you."

"Trevon no!" she sobbed, struggling in a vain attempt to free herself. "Do not leave me, Trevon! No! Do not!"

"Keep her safe, James Kelley," Trevon said, aside to James. "No matter what comes to pass."

"Aye, Cap'n," James mumbled—his lower lip trembling with restrained emotion.

A strange dizziness began to overtake Cristabel. She would lose him! She would lose her lover! Trevon may die from the wounds inflicted him by Richard's cat of nine tails. She did not want to live if Trevon was to die!

"I love you, Cristabel," he said, pressing his mouth to hers in one last kiss. It was driven and moist as ever his kiss was. Yet, it was weak and his lips were cold. "Wait for me, sweet pomegranate," he mumbled. "Wait for me...or for Baskerville. Either he or I will come to you...I promise."

With panicked desperation, Cristabel looked to James. Trevon would not listen to her—for he was too weakened to think with clarity and reason.

"James!" she cried. "Do not let him leave without me! Please! He needs me!"

"Aye, miss," James said—tears welling in his eyes. "But I have my orders. I will do as my Cap'n commands me."

"Good lad," Trevon said as Baskerville stepped up to place one of Trevon's large arms about his shoulders.

"No! No! Trevon! Do not leave me!" Cristabel cried as Navarrone the Blue Blade turned and began to stagger and stumble away. "No!" She was suddenly breathless—dizzy. And then there was only darkness.

"I will not survive to see the bay, Baskerville," Trevon mumbled. The pain had already numbed his arms and legs—yet, he could feel the warm blood streaming over his back. "Find the nearest doctor to attend me."

"Aye, Cap'n," Baskerville said.

"And Baskerville…"

"Aye, Cap'n?"

"If I expire…go to Cristabel and tell her. Do not let her linger in not knowing my fate."

"Aye, aye, Cap'n Navarrone," Baskerville said.

"I love her, Baskerville…I would die for her," Trevon Navarrone whispered a moment before the black of unconsciousness overcame him."

"Aye, my Cap'n," Baskerville mumbled. "Aye."

# Chapter Seventeen

Cristabel Albay gazed out over the horizon. The sun was nearly set. Soon it would dark and another day would have ended without word of Trevon Navarrone.

As ever it did at eventide, Cristabel's anxiety heightened. She silently reminded herself that Baskerville had not come to her—that if Baskerville had not come, then surely Trevon was alive.

The war with the British Empire was at an end—the final battle having took place in New Orleans. It was rumored that Colonel Jackson had bartered with Governor Claiborne to issue pardons to all privateers who had fought to defeat the British during the Battle of New Orleans. In the darkest corners of her mind, Cristabel wondered if the crew of The Merry Wench had been soldiers in the battle. She wondered if perhaps Trevon had survived the wounds of the flogging—healed to good health only to die in battle under Colonel Jackson. Perhaps Baskerville had been killed and was unable to come to her as well. Yet, she would not give up hope. After all, she knew the kind of warriors that were Trevon, Baskerville and all the crewmen of The Merry Wench. Thus, she surmised that Trevon was not dead—only delayed in coming to her.

She reminded herself that it would, indeed, take longer for Trevon or Baskerville to reach her and her mother in South Carolina as well. William Pelletier had been arrested and hung for treason shortly after James Kelley had returned Cristabel to his home in New Orleans. And though his estate fell to her mother, neither Cristabel nor Lisette wished to linger in a city that had wrought them with such pain and fear. Thus, they had returned to South Carolina—purchased a home near the seashore—now lingering in quiet waiting.

"Come inside, darling. Won't you?" Cristabel's mother said, placing a comforting arm around her daughter's shoulders.

"In a moment, mother," Cristabel said. "I'll watch for the green flash first."

Lisette sighed. "Very well," she said, kissing Cristabel's temple. "But do not tarry too long…else James will worry that you are despairing."

Cristabel smiled at her mother. "Dear James Kelley," she sighed. "He is like a brother to me now. I hope he will never leave us."

"I wish for him to remain as well," Lisette said. "Yet he is restless over Claire Navarrone…and his shipmates. I can see it growing in him daily. It may be that he cannot bring himself to settle in with us forever."

"I know," Cristabel said. "Still, I do not want him to leave."

"Nor I. Therefore, do not linger too long. He is always comforted with your company once the sun has set. It settles his anxiety, as well as yours."

"I know, Mother," Cristabel said. "I know." And she did know. Cristabel knew that her mother so encouraged James and Cristabel to soothing one another for the fact it gave them both hope. Whenever Cristabel and James were in conversation—in reminiscing of their meeting and adventures aboard The Merry Wench—each was reassured that nothing could triumph Navarrone the Blue Blade—even the brutal beating of the cat of nine tails Richard Pelletier had inflicted.

Still, even for all James' assurances—even for all Cristabel's assurances to James—she wondered why Trevon had not come. Her deepest fears whispered that he did not truly love her as deeply as he professed. Yet her faith told her that no man would take such a beating or stare death in the face unless he loved the woman he championed. Therefore, Cristabel continued to hope—to watch the sea and the horizon for The Merry Wench and Trevon Navarrone.

The sun set and the sky flashed green. Yet again, The Merry Wench had not sailed toward the shore.

"Come, darling," Lisette said. "Your dinner will be cold."

"Very well," Cristabel mumbled.

She turned, accompanying her mother back into the house. She caught the scent of the herbs in her mother's small garden—of thyme and rosemary—and of peppermint. Her mouth began to water and she knew that no matter where life found her in the end, the scent and taste of peppermint would ever send her thoughts to Trevon—to the kiss of the pirate Captain she would love for all eternity.

❧

Cristabel held her breath. Something had awakened her—the quietest noise—as if someone was in the room and had exhaled a sigh. She opened her eyes, sat up in her bed, and peered into the shadows. Clouds lingered before the moon outside, allowing no light to penetrate the windows of the room. There was only complete darkness.

"Wh-who is there?" she called as panic near over took her. She was suddenly awash with fear—for the memory of being abducted from her bed once before, came to her full and terrifying.

There came no answer from the dark—yet she fancied she heard footsteps—the sound of boots on wood. "Who are you?" she asked, her heart hammering with dread.

"I've come to ravage you at last, love," came the voice Cristabel had only dreamt of hearing once more.

"Trevon?" she gasped, leaping from her bed. "Is it you? Truly?" She could not believe he had come—thought certain she as dreaming. Rubbing her eyes she peered into the shadows once more—saw the outline of a figure standing in her doorway.

All at once a candle was lit and flickered to life. Tears swelled and spilled from Cristabel's eyes as she saw the illuminated face she so dearly loved. He was there—Trevon—handsome, powerful and alluring—his dark hair having tumbled over his forehead to hide one eye.

"Trevon!" she cried, collapsing to her knees. "Oh, Trevon!"

Quickly Trevon strode to her, gathering her weakened body from the floor and into the strength of his embrace. Cristabel wept into his shirt—his shirt that smelled of the warm spice of masculinity, the salty essence of the sea—the breath of the breeze and the comforting savor of grass and trees—his shirt that smelled of him!

"You're alive!" she sobbed. "Are you well?"

"I am," whispered his beloved voice in response. "But only for the sake that I was determined to have you, Cristabel Albay. I promise…it was our love and my desire that found my life spared."

"And you've come for me?" she asked, clutching the fabric of his shirt in desperate fists—for she yet feared she was only dreaming.

"Aye, love," he answered. "If you'll still have me. If you still wish to be a pirate bride...then I am fair mad to be your pirate groom, love."

"Oh, yes!" Cristabel breathed. "Yes!" She looked up to him then, still clasping the front of his shirt in her fists. "Kiss me," she whispered. "Kiss me so that I will know you are truly here and that I am not dreaming. Kiss me as you've never kissed any woman before, Trevon Navarrone. Kiss me now!"

"I've already kissed you as I've never kissed any woman before, love," he chuckled. "But if it's proof that your pirate still lives that you desire..."

He took her mouth with his then, and Cristabel's heart swelled to near bursting! Tears streamed from her eyes to mingle with their kiss—their heated, moist, impassioned kiss! The sense of his kiss—the taste of it— sent her emotions rising—her body to thrilling. He was there! Trevon was there—and she bathed in his affections—shared his desire.

It was all too soon that he broke the seal of their mouths. Cristabel was desperate for him to continue kissing her—yet she realized her breath was rapid and irregular—as was his.

"Your bed lingers too close for my will to resist you to be maintained long, love," he chuckled. "Thus, come with me...for I mean to sail you to our new life."

"Our new life?" she asked, warm and comfortable in his arms.

"Yes, love. We are done with privateering...you and me...everyone," he began to explain. "The families have been relocated from the community near the bay. It is only the small remnants of the crew that now sails The Merry Wench...Baskerville and me...Fergus and only a few others. We will sail her to our new life...in Salem...then set her adrift to whatever fate finds her."

"Salem?" Cristabel asked, smiling.

"Aye, love," Trevon said. "Baskerville and Vienne have wed already...and Mother is near beside herself with wanting to embrace James Kelley. They all await us aboard the Wench...your mother, too. James is speaking to her now...and I'm certain she will come with us."

Cristabel smiled, embraced him tightly. "Then let us not delay," she said. "Not one moment longer."

"Aye, love," Trevon said, kissing her once more. "Come with me and I will make you a life of such happiness as heaven itself...this I promise you."

Cristabel sighed—returned his impassioned kiss with her own fervor. She paused, however, giggling.

"Baskerville and Vienne?" she asked.

Trevon shrugged as he brushed a hair from her cheek. "Indeed. And you will be astonished at how well suited they are to one another."

"Then take me, Captain Navarrone," she breathed, against his mouth. "Sail me, wed me and ravage me...for I have waited the whole of my life for you...you bloody pirate!"

"Aye, love," Trevon mumbled. "As I have waited for you."

Their mouths were blended then—as triumph and love consumed them.

# Epilogue

Trevon Navarrone smiled—chuckled and leaned the handle of the hoe he had been using to remove the weeds from the garden. He watched as Vedette and Raphael scampered toward him hand-in-hand. He could not believe his little girl was already aged four years—could not believe Veinne's son was five. Time moved faster than he would have liked it to. And yet, it ever seemed a lifetime since the pirate Navarrone the Blue Blade had disappeared—since he and Cristabel had wed and started their life of happiness in Salem.

"Daddy!" Vedette called as she and Raphael tumbled to a giggling halt at his feet.

"Yes, love?" Trevon chuckled.

"Daddy...may we choose a pumpkin yet?" Vedette asked. "Mother says if you will carve a face in it today...she will place a candle in it to glow through the night and then make it into pies tomorrow. Please, Daddy! May we choose just one?"

Trevon chuckled. Vedette had been begging for Trevon to carve a face in a turnip or pumpkin ever since the previous month when he had told her the old Irish tale of Stingy Jack. He had explained several times that the pumpkins in the field must ripen well before they were picked. Though no one knew that Trevon Navarrone and his wife Cristabel would never want for wage or money, still they lived the life of a common farmer and his family. Certainly the riches they cached meant they would never suffer for want of necessity—even for want of luxury if they had so chosen. But the simple life is what Trevon and Cristabel most wished for. Thus, the pretense of needing a good crop to sell at harvest time or for winter stores must progress.

Still, as Trevon gazed into the pleading, violet eyes of his daughter, he knew he could not refuse her again.

"Very well, love," he agreed, laughing when Vedette and her cousin hugged with delight. "Just one. The biggest one you can find. I will carve the face in it for tonight and your mother can makes pies tomorrow. Just one now."

"Yes, Daddy! Just one," Vedette giggled as she and Raphael skipped toward the pumpkin field.

"Uncle Trev," Raphael called, having paused in his skipping.

"Yes? What is it, boy?" Trevon asked.

"My daddy says there is a new family in town. They are speaking with him now...and he thought that I should tell you," Raphael explained.

Trevon frowned—a familiar discomfort traveling up his spine. "Thank you, lad. Now run along with Vedette...but be careful. Have James help you with the pumpkin."

"Aye," Raphael said.

Trevon dropped his hoe near a row of corn stalks and hastily strode toward the houses. If Baskerville had wanted Raphael to tell him of the new family—then it may be he had been recognized.

As he approached the front of the houses—one shared by he and Cristabel and their children—the other by Vienne, Baskerville and theirs— he saw two men and two women standing steeped in conversation with Baskerville, Vienne and Cristabel.

"Hello," he said as he approached. "I'm Trev Navarrone." He offered his hand to first one man and then the other, nodding to the women before exchanging worried glances with Cristabel and Vienne.

"Navarrone, is it?" one man asked.

"Aye," Navarrone answered.

"I am Zachary Sutton and this is my wife Abigail," the man offered. He gestured to the man and woman also in attendance—they were younger in age and the resemblance the younger man boar to his elder, assured Trevon that they were father and son. "This is our son John and his wife Molly. We have recently come here from Rochester."

"Welcome," Navarrone said.

Zachary Sutton frowned—studied Baskville and then Trevon a moment.

"Trev Navarrone" Zachary Sutton inquired. "Are you perchance, Trevon Navarrone...also known as Navarrone the Blue Blade?"

Instantly, Navarrone chuckled, shaking his head as if utterly amused.

"Aye," Baskerville chuckled as well. "And I can be your quartermaster...Captain."

Cristabel and Vienne both forced amused laughter as well. Yet Zachary Sutton smiled above his frown.

"Oh, forgive us Zachary," Trevon said, sighing with mirth. "It is I am always astonished when people inquire of me as to whether I am that privateer we all knew as Navarrone the Blue Blade some years past. It flatters me in truth. Yet, I can tell you, however...I am only a simple farmer...one who loves this country and the beauty of Salem."

Zachary smiled—as did his wife and the others. "Forgive me, sir," he said. "Abigail is always telling me my imagination is over active these days."

"There is nothing to forgive, sir," Navarrone assured the man. "As everyone else, I like to believe the pirate Navarrone's ship was not abandoned to the sea as some believe it was."

"Yet it was found by Jean Lafitte," Zachary's son, John suggested. "Empty and sailing of her own will."

"Yes...yes it was," Trevon said. "But I like to think The Merry Wench was not sailing of her own will...but rather that Navarrone the Blue Blade and his faithful privateering crew were sailing her still...only unseen."

"Do you mean to say...sailing it as ghosts?" Abigail Sutton inquired.

"Exactly, Mrs. Sutton," Trevon assured her. "It's a much more intriguing notion to think the captain and crew of The Merry Wench were somehow vanquished by death and continued to sail their ship as ghosts...than it is to think they simply vanished and became shop owners and farmers. Do you not agree?"

Again the Sutton's all smiled—obviously amused by Trevon's tale.

"Indeed," Zachary said.

"You see, Abigail," Cristabel offered. "You husband is not the only man here in Salem with too great an imagination."

"I am glad to hear it" Abigail said.

Trevon glanced to Cristabel—caught the glimmer of delight in her eyes.

"We'll be off then," Zachary Sutton sighed. "We are simply out and about to greet our new townspeople. Enjoy your day."

"And yours," Baskerville offered as the four newcomers strolled away.

The moment the Sutton's were distant enough to be deaf to conversation, Vienne giggled. "Oh, Cristabel! My mother will purely delight in hearing of this! As will yours," she said.

"Indeed they will," Cristabel agreed. It was not the first time townspeople had inquired of Trevon if he had once been the pirate Navarrone the Blue Blade. Ever did he deny it—ever did both Cristabel's mother and Trevon's find humor in such goings on.

Trevon smiled as Cristabel nodded. The sound of her giggle sent a thrill to warming his heart, and he knew he must have her alone for a time. He thought of how similar Vedette was to her mother—how it was said young Vortigem so looked like his father Trevon—even at only two years—and he bathed in delight that it was so.

"Does your mother have Vortigem?" Trevon asked his wife.

"Yes," Cristabel assured him. "I am certain she is spoiling him with too much honey."

"Then come with me, love," Trevon said, taking her hand. "The leaves are just turning. Let us have a walk and linger beneath their beauty. They will be gone all too soon this year."

He watched as Cristabel's eyes warmed—twinkled with love and anticipation.

"But wait, Trevon," Vienne said as Cristabel and Trevon turned to leave. "Have you seen Raphael?"

"Yes. I relented and sent him and Vedette in search of the larges pumpkin in the field that I may carve a face for them in it tonight," he answered. "They had orders to have James accompany them."

Suddenly, there skipped along the air the sound of children's laughter. Trevon chuckled when he heard James' laughter as well.

"Oh, there they are," Vienne said, standing on the tips of her toes and gazing toward the pumpkin field.

"Then Cristabel and I will return shortly," Trevon said. He paused, sighing as he smiled at Baskerville. He placed a hand on his friend and brother-in-law's shoulder. "It's a good life, is it not, my friend?"

Baskerville nodded. "Aye, Cap'n. That it is."

"Come along, love," Trevon said then.

As he and Cristabel approached an ancient oak whose leaves had blushed crimson, he asked, "And do you feel the same as Baskerville? Do you feel it's a good life for us? Are you happy?"

He knew what her answer would be—yet sometimes he still feared he had not been a good enough husband to her.

Cristabel paused—turned to Trevon. Wrapping her arms about his neck, she smiled up at him.

"I could never have imagined such happiness, Trevon," she whispered, "or such love and passion as I have known with you."

Trevon smiled. "And you do not miss the adventure of being a pirate?"

Cristabel giggled—kissed his chin and shook head. "No. Never," she told him. "And anyway…you have not changed, you know."

Trevon frowned. "What do you mean? I am a farmer now. In secret a sinfully wealthy farmer…but a farmer is still far different than a pirate."

"It is only your occupation that has changed, my darling," she said. "Not you. You are still as wild and untamed as ever you were, love. You still thrill me as thoroughly as you did when first you kissed me."

Trevon grinned. "You mean when first I kissed you and you put a dagger to my throat, vixen?"

Cristabel kissed his cheek—a breathy giggle escaping her.

"I only pulled the dagger because I feared…" she began.

"That I would ravage you?" he quiried.

Yet, she shook her head. "No…for fear that I would allow you to ravage me."

Trevon smiled—took her mouth in a moist, impassioned kiss. He felt something brush his face, and broke the seal of their lips to glance up into the limbs of the ancient maple. A large ruby leaf floated down, caressing Cristabel's forehead.

"It appears autumn is nearly spent, love," he said.

He smiled as Cristabel placed a warm palm to his cheek. "Fear not, my love," she said. "It will come again. And if you become impatient in waiting for its return…" She lowered her voice and added, "You have my permission to slip into the root cellar and unearth some of the rubies planted there. You can imagine they are autumn leaves…let them sift through you fingers and bring you joy."

Trevon tightened his embrace of his wife. "There is nothing more beautiful to me than you, Cristabel Navarrone. Nothing of more value than Vedette and Vortigem...and their beautiful pirate-bride mother. I love you."

"And I love you, Navarrone the Blue Blade," she whispered.

He kissed her then—there beneath the ancient Salem maple—as soft drying leaves fluttered down about them like a rubied, autumn snow...

# Author's Note

As I was growing up, there were a few movie genres that I always, always adored. Every weekday I'd rush home from school in time to watch *Dialing for Dollars*. *Dialing for Dollars* was the 'afternoon movie' type show (not to be confused with the *After School Special* type). At the beginning of the show, a 'host' would give the viewing audience a secret word and number (I think it was called 'the count and the amount'). Then the 'host' would select a phone number out of a bowl and dial it. If the person who answered the phone had been watching the show, they would know 'the count and the amount' and would win whatever the 'amount' was! It was totally exciting! A real nail-biter! Because, if whoever the 'host' dialed didn't answer, the amount of money would go up! I'm telling you, you've never known such wild anticipation! (Note of interest: Years later—after I was grown up and married with children—I was checking in at the airport one day and my travel agent guy was none other than the old *Dialing for Dollars* local host! I was totally star-struck, and told him so. He smiled and seemed flattered when I told him that I had watched him almost every day for years. The places you bump into celebrities, right?)

However, having told you all that pointless trivia for the sake of nostalgia, I must tell you that the main reason I rushed home to watch *Dialing for Dollars* was for the movies! Back in the olden days (you know—the 1970s and 80s) there weren't a lot of movies on TV. Usually just like *The Wonderful World of Disney* on Sunday nights and something on Saturday night maybe. But good ol' *Dialing for Dollars* was perfect for this life-long movie buff!

Certainly, there were particular movie genres that interested me more than others. For example:

261

1.  Anything romantic! Especially old 40s and 50s musicals!
2.  Anything set before, during or after the Civil War. (With the exception of *Love Me Tender*...Hello!? Elvis dies in that one!)
3.  Anything with cowboys who were tough, cool, and capable of surviving no matter what the odds. (The old Clint Eastwood spaghetti westerns were my favorite!)
4.  Anything with a Christmas theme (especially any and every version of Dickens' *A Christmas Carol*—though *Scrooge* starring Albert Finney is my ultimate favorite!).
5.  Old black and white monster movies—the classics—but especially anything *Dracula* or vampire-themed.
6.  Egypt and mummy movies. (Deliciously frightening!)
7.  Tarzan movies (but *only* Johnny Weissmuller ones).
8.  (Of course, I loved movies like *Puf-n-Stuf*, too (based on the Saturday morning Sid and Marty Kroft wonder—but I don't think that applies here because I can't really see how Jack Wild (Jimmy) and Witchiepoo inspired any characters or scenes in any of my books. But hey—the night is young—so you never know!).

On *Dialing for Dollars*, there were movies about insane brides locked in dungeons and plagued with leprosy—Fred Astaire and Ginger Rogers movies—movies based on the scandalous works of Tennessee Williams. There were silly movies and sad movies—giddy movies and scary movies—classic movies and not-so-classic movies. Yet, looking back, there was a sad, sad, sad lack of pirate movies!

The same is true today! I mean, other than this century *Pirates of the Caribbean*, what pirate movies have there been of late? Especially good pirate movies?

I've always loved the whole pirate thing. Only in *my* mind, the pirates were the good guys—you know—the Robin Hoods of the sea, if you will. Furthermore, I have wanted to write a pirate book forever! Yet, I couldn't quite get past how to make a pirate a good guy. They were pretty bad blokes in real life. Still, I wanted to write a pirate romance. So I chewed on the idea for a couple of years—sort of like a cow chewing her cud—you know what I mean? I'd think about it—think, "Hey! I can write a pirate book!"—and then think, "But how can I make him a hero?"

Ironically, the answer was standing right in front of me—just like he always does—Kevin!

It's true! The whole time I was mulling over how in the world to write a pirate book and have a moral pirate hero—there was Kevin! Once again, Kevin provided the perfect inspiration for romance! Now, obviously Kevin is not sailing the seven seas as a pirate. However, he is ethereally handsome and was born and raised in New Orleans, Louisiana. Why is the New Orleans, Louisiana part important? One answer: The historic Battle of New Orleans and Jean Lafitte!

When Kevin and I were first married, he used whistle and/or sing a song entitled *The Battle of New Orleans*. He had learned it in school as a child in St. Bernard Parish—the very Parish where the Battle of New Orleans took place during a series of battles culminating on January 8, 1815 (120 years to the day before Elvis was born, by-the-way). Anyway, I began to think about the pirate Jean Lafitte. Jean Lafitte made his home in and around New Orleans and Barataria Bay, before and during the war of 1812. I knew Jean Lafitte had played an integral part in the success of The Battle of New Orleans, but couldn't quite remember the story. So, off to a selection of pirate information books I did go!

It was while researching Jean Lafitte (for he's been hailed a hero in Louisiana history) that I discovered the difference between regular pirates and privateers. And with that—voila! Inspiration was upon me! Privateering—Letters of Marque! At long last, I had my venue for a good, moral, pirate hero! And all thanks to Kevin, New Orleans and Jean Lafitte. Naturally, it would require a bit of creativity on my part—but hey—it could happen. And so, I was off on *The Pirate Ruse* adventure!

I've actually been to the Chalmette Battlefield (the site of The Battle of New Orleans) several times. It's a very intriguing place—swathed in history and balmy New Orleans air. Spanish moss drips from the limbs of large trees—cannons mark the battle lines of long ago. There's an old mansion there on the grounds—the Malus-Beauregard House—built in 1830 and wildly inspiring! A cemetery is also part of the Chalmette Battlefield historical park—with soldiers from the War of 1812, Spanish-American War, Civil War (including Buffalo Soldiers), both World Wars and even Vietnam interred there. The mighty Mississippi River runs parallel to the battlefield and you have to walk up a flight of stairs to get to it—

which always wigs me out. It seems so unnatural to walk *up* to the water. But that's New Orleans—resting about 11 feet *below* sea level! It's a fascinating place to visit—slathered in history, mood and mystery! Wonderful!

Hmmm—I was just thinking of another little something that contributed to my inspiration for our hero Trevon Navarrone. My dear friend (to whom this book is dedicated) sent me a little something fun awhile back—a YouTube clip of a kissing scene in a Spanish mini-series starring Puerto Rican-born pop star Chayanne as a vampire named Gabriel! I know what you're thinking about now—"How in the blue blazes did a Puerto Rican-born pop star playing a vampire in a Spanish mini-series inspire anything for Trevon Navarrone?" Well, let me say this—it's all in the facial hair styling! Yep—that's what inspired Trevon's facial hair and sideburns. Let me tell you this—you never know what's going to flip a switch in my head and turn on a light.

I'm so random! From *Dialing for Dollars* on TV when I was kid, to Kevin's elementary education in music/local history in St. Bernard Parish, to Jean Lafitte and the Battle of New Orleans, and on to a Puerto Rican-born pop star with cool facial hair! Sometimes I'm astonished at how many venues of inspiration converge to cause a story to begin playing out in my mind.

Now you know I cannot do an author's note without getting a little sappy and sentimental, right? And here it comes! Vienne. I have a philosophy I try to live by—and though I do not claim to be perfect in living it—not by any means—I do try to keep ever conscious of it. I try to have it right there at the forefront of my mind and apply it always. As I said, none of us are perfect and we all make mistakes and I make more than most people! However, when it comes to this way of thinking that I have, Vienne is an example of my feelings on this point: That we should always, always treat someone as if it might be the worst, most painful, tragic day of their lives, and we just don't know it.

We do not know what someone is dealing with. Whether they're smiling or not, we should wonder if perhaps there are tears behind that smile and treat them accordingly. Very few people I know let the world see what they're truly feeling—and I think that's the way it should be—for the most part. For me, wearing a heart on a sleeve and endeavoring to bring everyone else down with despair, stress and problems doesn't do the world any good. I save my anxieties, worries and stress for my poor, dear, heroic husband and a handful of very close friends.

I can tell you this—Vienne endured nearly unimaginable pain and trauma. She was worn and weathered—hurt and damaged. Yes, she is a fictional character—but there are people enduring similar horrors every day. Vienne represents to me the Post Office clerk, the checker at the grocery store, the UPS man, my neighbor…any person in the world and every person in the world who has known excruciating sorrow, trials and pain. Vienne also represents those of us who simply deal with the everyday hurts and worries. We're all weathered to some degree—like an old silver piece of eight. Yet each and every one of us is of value, and should be treated as kindly and with as much compassion and understanding as possible. Don't ask me about literal murderers, crazy dictators, etc. I'm just talking about regular every day people. Vienne represents them to me—and I would put forth this—if we came upon Vienne working at the Post Office and looking as if she might be a little fatigued—how would we treat her, knowing what we know? I guarantee we would treat her well—with compassion and understanding. We would *not* gripe at her because the line waiting to buy stamps is too long—or because she informs us that we've used the wrong kind of packaging material and need to start over, right? Therefore, I strive to see everyone I meet as Vienne. I'm sure I fail miserably a lot of the time—but I hope I don't fail as much as I feel I do.

And now that I've babbled you to boredom and tears AGAIN—let's move on to a few snippets—but only after I thank you for sailing out aboard The Merry Wench with me! I hope you've enjoyed my first attempt at a pirate romance! I had fun with it, and learned a ton! So let's set sail for more adventure soon, shall we? After all, who doesn't love a good swashbuckler?

### The Pirate Ruse Trivia Snippets

Snippet #1—"Richard!" Okay…another secret revealed. Every time I hear the name, Richard, or think of the name, Richard, or write out the name Richard—I think of the movie *Somewhere in Time*. If you're old

265

enough to even remember this movie, you'll know that it was like THE romantic movie of the early 1980s era. It had a profoundly beautiful soundtrack (which my college roommates and I used to listen to on Sundays or whenever we needed some relaxation). If you're not familiar with the premise of *Somewhere in Time*, it's about this guy who goes back in time to find this woman, and they fall in love, and on and on—but at one point he reaches into his pocket and pulls out a penny from the future and it snatches him away from the woman and back into the present. As he's being stripped away forward in time, Elise (the heroine) screams, "RICHARD!" (the hero's name). My friends the Groovy Chicks and I, often used to yell, "RICHARD" and reach out like Elise did when she was trying to grab her true love! It's just a weird little, non-important, trivial side-note. If you haven't seen the movie, watch it! It's not my favorite—but I LOVED it when I was a teenager!

Snippet #2—The 'Cristabel drinks the rum' scene in *The Pirate Ruse* was one thing I included based on historical accuracy. Water stored on board ships at the time in which *The Pirate Ruse* is set, rapidly became foul and undrinkable. On the other hand, beer, rum, brandy and other liquor had a 'shelf-life' of nearly forever—thus mariners stored barrels of it in their vessels—especially beer—even aboard naval vessels.

Snippet #3—Currently my dream vacation destination is Salem, Massachusetts! I cannot wait to visit there! Can you imagine the history? The leaves in autumn? I've been to Boston and it's awesome—but now Salem is my goal!

Snippet #4—Jean Lafitte was a pirate and privateer who operated in and around the Gulf of Mexico in the early 1800s. His smuggling operations were based in Barataria Bay and New Orleans, Louisiana. Without getting into all the political and historical details, he was forced out of Barataria Bay in September of 1814, but was granted a full pardon after his invaluable insight ensured a positive outcome for America at the Battle of New Orleans. He went on to more piracy, of course, and obituaries written of him date his death as February 5, 1823—though there are still speculations about the accuracy of this.

Snippet #5—Letters of Marque were very real—and they were issued by the United States at the time of the war of 1812.

Snippet #6—Don Gabriel's name was a subconscious thingy on my part— at least at first.   As I previously mentioned, from the very beginning I imagined Trevon Navarrone's 'look' to be very similar to that of Chayanne's character in a Spanish mini-series called, *Gabriel.* My friend Sheri had e-mailed a YouTube kissing scene to me from Gabriel.  I found the 'look' wildly intriguing and perfectly suited to how I similarly imagined Trevon to appear.  However, it wasn't until I was rereading *The Pirate Ruse* and noticed Don Gabriel's name that I realized how much that little ol' YouTube clip had influenced by subconscious.  Another Marcia-goofy-ism!

Snippet #7—Percy Shelley's heart. Yep—it is a morbid tale.  Percy Bysshe Shelley (the poet) was born in 1792.  He lived a terrible, scandalous life— but we won't dwell on that.  His second wife was named Mary.  Now, just before his 30th birthday, Percy was sailing in his schooner and was set upon by a storm.  Percy Shelley drowned.  When his body washed ashore, it was cremated right there on the beach—in keeping with quarantine laws of the time.  Well, as the cremation began, a man named Edward Trelawny, reached into Shelley's body cavity and snatched out his heart before it burned.  Percy Shelley's wife, Mary, kept Shelley's heart for the rest of her life.  It was eventually buried with the body of their son, Sir Percy Florence Shelley.  Interestingly enough, Percy Bysshe Shelley's wife, Mary, was indeed, Mary Shelley—the author of the gothic novel, *Frankenstein.* Therefore, if you thought, for a moment, that Trevon's telling Cristabel he would have Baskerville bring his heart to her in a box if he died, was a little too gruesome—I guess that's just history and the gothic novelist coming out in me.

To my husband...
*My Hero Inspiration!*

# About the Author

Marcia Lynn McClure began writing novels as Christmas gifts for her closest friends. She weaves her tales of love, life, laughter and adventure around those compelling, romantic moments which most appeal to a woman's romantic and loving heart. Gazing out her window into the surreal beauty of the New Mexico desert, she writes her stories inspired by life and imagination. Blissful in the company of her wonderful husband, two sons, a daughter, son-in-law, and grandson, Marcia continues to captivate readers with her own, unique writing style and adored stories.

Visit www.marcialynnmcclure.com to order books and e-books by Marcia Lynn McClure.

## Weathered Too Young
Historical Romance, 304 Pages

Lark Lawrence was alone. In all the world there was no one who cared for her. Still, there were worse things than independence—and Lark had grown quite capable of providing for herself. Nevertheless, as winter loomed, she suddenly found herself with no means by which to afford food and shelter—destitute.

Yet, Tom Evans was a kind and compassionate man. When Lark Lawrence appeared on his porch, without pause he hired her to keep house and cook for himself and his cantankerous elder brother, Slater. And although Tom had befriend Lark first, it would be Slater Evans— handsome, brooding and twelve years Lark's senior—who would unknowingly abduct her heart.

Still, Lark's true age (which she concealed at first meeting the Evans brothers) was not the only truth she had kept from Slater and Tom Evans. Darker secrets lay imprisoned deep within her heart—and her past. However, it is that secrets are made to be found out—and Lark's secrets revealed would soon couple with the arrival of a woman from Slater's past to forever shatter her dreams of winning his love—or so it seemed. Would truth and passion mingle to capture Lark the love she'd never dared to hope for?

## The Windswept Flame
Historical Romance, 280 Pages

Broken—irreparably broken. The violent deaths of her father and the young man she'd been engaged to marry, had irrevocably broken Cedar Dale's heart. Her mother's heart had been broken, as well—shattered by the loss of her own true love. Thus, pain and anguish—fear and despair— found Cedar Dale, and her mother Flora, returned to the small western town where life had once been happy and filled with hope. Perhaps there, Cedar and her mother would find some resemblance of truly living life— instead of merely existing. And then, a chance meeting with a dream from her past—caused a flicker of wonder to ignite in her bosom.

As a child, Cedar Dale had adored the handsome rancher's son, Tom Evans. And when chance brought her face-to-face with the object of her childhood fascination once more, Cedar Dale began to believe that perhaps her fragmented heart could be healed.

Yet, could Cedar truly hope to win the regard of such a man above men as was Tom Evans? A man kept occupied with hard work and ambition—a man so desperately sought after by seemingly every woman?

## Beneath the Honeysuckle Vine
Historical Romance, 304 Pages

Civil War—no one could flee from the nightmare of battle and the countless lives it devoured. Everyone had sacrificed—suffered profound misery and unimaginable loss. Vivianna Bartholomew was no exception. The war had torn her from her home—orphaned her. The merciless war seemed to take everything—even the man she loved. Still, Vivianna yet knew gratitude—for a kind friend had taken her in upon the death of her parents. Thus, she was cared for—even loved.

Yet, as General Lee surrendered signaling the war's imminent end— as Vivianna remained with the remnants of the Turner family—her soul clung to the letters written by her lost soldier—to his memory written in her heart. Could a woman ever heal from the loss of such a love? Could a woman's heart forget that it may find another? Vivianna Bartholomew thought not.

Still, it is often in the world that miracles occur—that love endures even after hope has been abandoned. Thus, one balmy Alabama morning—as two ragged soldiers wound the road toward the Turner house—Vivianna began to know—to know that miracles do exist—that love is never truly lost.

## Saphyre Snow
Historical Romance, 250 Pages

Descended of a legendary line of strength and beauty, Saphyre Snow had once known happiness as princess of the Kingdom of Graces. Once a valiant king had ruled in wisdom—once a loving mother had spoken soft words of truth to her daughter. Yet, a strange madness had poisoned great minds—a strange fever inviting Lord Death to linger. Soon it was even Lord Death sought to claim Saphyre Snow for his own—and all Saphyre loved seemed lost.

Thus, Saphyre fled—forced to leave all familiars for necessity of preserving her life. Alone, and without provision, Saphyre knew Lord Death might yet claim her—for how could a princess hope to best the Reaper himself?

Still, fate often provides rescue by extraordinary venues, and Saphyre was not delivered into the hands of Death—but into the hands of those hiding dark secrets in the depths of bruised and bloodied souls. Saphyre knew a measure of hope and asylum in the company of these battered vagabonds. Even she knew love—a secreted love—a forbidden love. Yet it was love itself—even held secret—that would again summon Lord Death to hunt the princess, Saphyre Snow.

## A Crimson Frost

Historical Romance, 296 Pages

Beloved of her father, King Dacian, and adored by her people, the Scarlet Princess Monet endeavored to serve her kingdom well—for the people of the Kingdom of Karvana were good, and worthy of service. Long Monet had known that even her marriage would serve her people. Her husband would be chosen for her—for this was the way of royal existence.

Still, as any woman does—peasant or princess—Monet dreamt of owning true love—of owning choice in love. Thus, each time the raven-haired, sapphire-eyed, Crimson Knight of Karvana rode near—Monet knew regret—for in secret, she loved him—and she could not choose him.

As an arrogant king from another kingdom began to wage war against Karvana, Karvana's king, knights and soldiers answered the challenge. The Princess Monet would also know battle. As the Crimson Knight battled with armor and blade—so the Scarlet Princess would battle in sacrifice and with secrets held. Thus, when the charge was given to preserve the heart of Karvana—Monet endeavored to serve her kingdom and forget her secreted love. Yet, love is not so easily forgotten...

## The Highwayman of Tanglewood
Historical Romance, 293 Pages

A chambermaid in the house of Tremeshton, Faris Shayhan well knew torment, despair and trepidation. To Faris it seemed the future stretched long and desolate before her—bleak and as dark as a lonesome midnight path. Still, the moon oft casts hopeful luminosity to light one's way. So it was that Lady Maranda Rockrimmon cast hope upon Faris—set Faris upon a different path—a path of happiness, serenity and love.

Thus, Faris abandoned the tainted air of Tremeshton in favor of the amethyst sunsets of Loch Loland Castle and her new mistress Lady Rockrimmon. Further, it was on the very night of her emancipation that Faris first met the man of her dreams—the man of every woman's dreams—the rogue Highwayman of Tanglewood.

Dressed in black and astride his mighty steed, the brave, heroic and dashing rogue Highwayman of Tanglewood stole Faris' heart as easily as he stole her kiss. Yet, the Highwayman of Tanglewood was encircled in mystery—mystery as thick and as secretive as time itself. Could Faris truly own the heart of a man so entirely enveloped in twilight shadows and dangerous secrets?

## The Visions of Ransom Lake
Historical Romance, 295 Pages

Youthful beauty, naïve innocence, a romantic imagination thirsting for adventure…an apt description of Vaden Valmont, who would soon find the adventure and mystery she had always longed to experience…in the form of a man.

A somber recluse, Ransom Lake descended from his solitary concealment in the mountains, wholly disinterested in people and their trivial affairs. And somehow, young Vaden managed to be ever in his way…either by accident or because of her own unique ability to stumble into a quandary.

Yet the enigmatic Ransom Lake would involuntarily become Vaden's unwitting tutor. Through him, she would experience joy and passion the like even Vaden had never imagined. Yes, Vaden Valmont stepped innocently, yet irrevocably, into love with the secretive, seemingly callous man.

But there were other life's lessons Ransom Lake would inadvertently bring to her as well. The darker side of life—despair, guilt, heartache. Would Ransom Lake be the means of Vaden's dreams come true? Or the cause of her complete desolation?

## The Touch of Sage
Historical Romance, 272 Pages

After the death of her parents, Sage Willows had lovingly nurtured her younger sisters through childhood, seeing each one married and never resenting not finding herself a good man to settle down with. Yet, regret is different than resentment.

Still, Sage found as much joy as a lonely young woman could find, as proprietress of Willows' Boardinghouse—finding some fulfillment in the companionship of the four beloved widow-women boarding with her. But when the devilishly handsome Rebel Lee Mitchell appeared on the boardinghouse step, Sage's contentment was lost forever.

Dark, mysterious and secretly wounded, Reb Mitchell instantly captured Sage's lonely heart. But the attractive cowboy, admired and coveted by every young, unmarried female in his path, seemed unobtainable to Sage Willows. How could a weathered, boardinghouse-proprietress resigned to spinsterhood ever hope to capture the attention of such a man? And without him, would Sage Willows simply sink deeper into bleak loneliness—tormented by the knowledge that the man of every woman's dreams could never be hers?

## The Whispered Kiss
Historical Romance, 256 Pages

With the sea at its side, the beautiful township of Bostchelan was home to many—including the lovely Coquette de Bellamont, her three sisters, and beloved father. In Bostchelan, Coquette knew happiness, and as much contentment as a young woman whose heart had been broken years before could know. Thus, Coquette dwelt in gladness until the day her father returned from his travels with an astonishing tale to tell.

Antoine de Bellamont returned from his travels by way of Roanan bearing a tale of such great adventure to hardly be believed. Further, at the center of Antoine's story loomed a man—the dark Lord of Roanan.

Known for his cruel nature, heartlessness, and tendency to violence, the Lord of Roanan had accused Antoine de Bellamont of wrong doing and demanded recompense. Antoine had promised recompense would be paid—with the hand of his youngest daughter in marriage.

Thus, Coquette found herself lost—thrust onto a dark journey of her own. This journey would find her carried away to Roanan Manor—delivered into the hands of the dark and mysterious Lord of Roanan who dominated it.

## The Time of Aspen Falls
Contemporary Romance, 272 Pages

Aspen Falls was happy. Her life was good. Blessed with a wonderful family and a loyal best friend—Aspen did know a measure of contentment.

Still, to Aspen it seemed something was missing—something hovering just beyond her reach—something entirely satisfying that would ensure her happiness. Yet, she couldn't consciously determine what the "something" was. And so, Aspen sailed through life—not quite perfectly content perhaps—but grateful for her measure of contentment.

Grateful that is, until he appeared—the man in the park—the stranger who jogged passed the bench where Aspen sat during her lunch break each day. As handsome as a dream, and twice as alluring, the man epitomized the absolute stereotypical "real man"—and Aspen's measure of contentment vanished!

Would Aspen Falls reclaim the comfortable contentment she once knew? Or would the handsome real-man-stranger linger in her mind like a sweet, tricky venom—poisoning all hope of Aspen's ever finding true happiness with any other man?

## Dusty Britches
Historical Romance, 307 Pages

Angelina Hunter was seriously minded, and it was a good thing. Her father's ranch needed a woman who could endure the strenuous work of ranch life. Since her mother's death, Angelina had been that woman. She had no time for frivolity—no time for a less severe side of life. Not when there was so much to be done—hired hands to feed, a widower father to care for and an often ridiculously lighted-hearted younger sister to worry about. No. Angelina Hunter had no time for the things most young women her age enjoyed.

And yet, Angelina had not always been so hardened. There had been a time when she boasted a fun, flirtatious nature even more delightful than her sister Becca's—a time when her imagination soared with adventurous, romantic dreams. But that all ended years before at the hand of one man. Her heart turned to stone...safely becoming void of any emotion save impatience and indifference.

Until the day her dreams returned, the day the very maker of her broken heart rode back into her life. As the dust settled from the cattle drive which brought him back, would Angelina's heart be softened? Would she learn to hope again? Would her long-lost dreams become a blessed reality?

## The Heavenly Surrender
Historical Romance, 261 Pages

Genieva Bankmans had willfully agreed to the arrangement. She had given her word and she would not dishonor it. But when she saw, for the first time, the man whose advertisement she had answered...she was desperately intimidated. The handsome and commanding Brevan McLean was not what she had expected. He was not the sort of man she had reconciled herself to marrying.

This man, this stranger whose name Genieva now bore, was strong-willed, quick-tempered and expectant of much from his new wife. Brevan McLean did not deny he had married her for very practical reasons only. He merely wanted any woman whose hard work would provide him assistance with the brutal demands of farm life.

But Genieva would learn there were far darker things, grave secrets held unspoken by Brevan McLean concerning his family and his land. Genieva Bankmans McLean was to find herself in the midst of treachery, violence and villainy with her estranged husband deeply entangled in it.

## Shackles of Honor
Historical Romance, 349 Pages

Cassidy Shea's life was nothing if not serene. Loving parents and a doting brother provided happiness and innocent hope in dreaming as life's experience. Yes, life was blissful at her beloved home of Terrill.

Still, for all its beauty and tranquility…ever there was something intangible and evasive lurking in the shadows. And though Cassidy wasted little worry on it…still she sensed its existence, looming as a menacing fate bent on ruin.

And when one day a dark stranger appeared, Cassidy could no longer ignore the ominous whispers of the secrets surrounding her. Mason Carlisle, an angry, unpredictable man materialized…and seemingly with Cassidy's black fate at his heels.

Instantly Cassidy found herself thrust into a world completely unknown to her, wandering in a labyrinth of mystery and concealments. Serenity was vanquished…and with it, her dreams.

Or were all the secrets so guardedly kept from Cassidy…were they indeed the cloth, the very flax from which her dreams were spun? From which eternal bliss would be woven?

## The Fragrance of Her Name
Historical Romance, 366 Pages

Love—the miraculous, eternal bond that binds two souls together. Lauryn Kennsington knew the depth of it. Since the day of her eighth birthday, she had lived the power of true love—witnessed it with her own heart. She had talked with it—learned not even time or death can vanquish it. The Captain taught her these truths—and she loved him all the more for it.

Yet now—as a grown woman—Lauryn's dear Captain's torment became her own. After ten years, Lauryn had not been able to help him find peace—the peace his lonely spirit so desperately needed—the peace he'd sought every moment since his death over fifty years before.

Still, what of her own peace? The time had come. Lauryn's heart longed to do the unthinkable—selfishly abandon her Captain for another—a mortal man who had stolen her heart—become her only desire.

Would Lauryn be able to put tormented spirits to rest and still be true to her own soul? Or, would she have to make a choice—a choice forcing her to sacrifice one true love for another?

## An Old-Fashioned Romance
Contemporary Romance, 272 Pages

Life went along simply, if not rather monotonously, for Breck McCall. Her job was satisfying, she had true friends. But she felt empty—as if party of her soul was detached and lost to her. She longed for something— something which seemed to be missing.

Yet, there were moments when Breck felt she might almost touch something wonderful. And most of those moments came while in the presence of her handsome, yet seemingly haunted boss—Reese Thatcher.

## Romantic Vignettes-The Anthology of Premiere Novellas
Historical Romance, 296 Pages
### Includes Three Novellas:
### The Unobtainable One

Annette Jordan had accepted the unavoidable reality that she must toil as a governess to provide for herself. Thankfully, her charge was a joy—a vision of youthful beauty, owning a spirit of delight.

But it was Annette's employer, Lord Gareth Barrett, who proved to be the trial—for she soon found herself living in the all-too-cliche governess' dream of having fallen desperately in love with the man who provided her wages.

The child loved her—but could she endure watching hopelessly as the beautiful woman from a neighboring property won Lord Barrett's affections?

### The General's Ambition

Seemingly over night, Renee Millings found herself orphaned and married to the indescribably handsome, but ever frowning, Roque Montan. His father, The General, was obsessively determined that his lineage would continue posthaste—with or without consent of his son's new bride.

But when Roque reveals the existence of a sworn oath that will obstruct his father's ambition, will the villainous General conspire to insure the future of his coveted progeny to be born by Renee himself? Will Renee find the only means of escape from the odious General to be that of his late wife—death? Or will the son find no tolerance for his father's diabolic plotting concerning the woman Roque legally terms his wife?

## Indebted Deliverance

Chalyce LaSalle had been grateful to the handsome recluse, Race Trevelian, when he had delivered her from certain tragedy one frigid winter day. He was addictively attractive, powerful and intriguing—and there was something else about him—an air of secreted internal torture. Yet, as the brutal character of her emancipator began to manifest, Chalyce commenced in wondering whether the fate she now faced would be any less insufferable than the one from which he had delivered her.

Still, his very essence beckoned hers. She was drawn to him and her soul whispered that his mind needed deliverance as desperately as she had needed rescue that cold, winter's noon.

## Daydreams
Contemporary Romance, 216 Pages

Sayler Christy knew chances were slim to none that any of her silly little daydreams would ever actually come true—especially any daydreams involving Mr. Booker, the new patient—the handsome, older patient convalescing in her grandfather's rehabilitation center.

Yet, working as a candy striper at Rawlings Rehab, Sayler couldn't help but dream of belonging to Mr. Booker—and Mr. Booker stole her heart—perhaps unintentionally—but with very little effort. Gorgeous, older, and entirely unobtainable—Sayler knew Mr. Booker would unknowingly enslave her heart for many years to come—for daydreams were nothing more than a cruel joke inflicted by life. All dreams—daydreams or otherwise—never came true. Did they?

## Love Me
Contemporary Romance, 243 Pages

Jacey Whittaker couldn't remember a time when she hadn't loved Scott Pendleton—the boy next door. She couldn't remember a time when Scott hadn't been in her life—in her heart. Yet, Scott was every other girl's dream, too. How could Jacey possibly hope to win such a prize—the attention, the affections, the very heart of such a sought after young man?

Yet, win him she did! He became the bliss of her youthful heart—at least for a time.

Still, some dreams live fulfilled—and some are lost. Loss changes the very soul of a being. Jacey wondered if her soul would ever rebound. Certainly, she went on—lived a happy life—if not so full and perfectly happy a life as she once lived. Yet, she feared she would never recover—never get over Scott Pendleton—her first love.

Until the day a man walked into her apartment—into her apartment and into her heart. Would this man be the one to heal her broken heart? Would this man be her one true love?

## Desert Fire
Historical Romance, 199 Pages

She opened her eyes and beheld, for the first time, the face of Jackson McCall. Ruggedly handsome and her noble rescuer, she knew in that moment, he would forever hold captive her heart, as he then held her life in his protective arms.

Yet, she was a nameless beauty, haunted by wisps of visions of the past. How could she ever hope he would return the passionate, devotional love As her family abandoned the excitement of the city for the uneventful lifestyle of a small, western town, Brynn Clarkston's worst fears were realized. Stripped of her heart's hopes and dreams, Brynn knew true loneliness.

## To Echo the Past
Historical Romance, 180 Pages

As her family abandoned the excitement of the city for the uneventful lifestyle of a small, western town, Brynn Clarkston's worst fears were realized. Stripped of her heart's hopes and dreams, Brynn knew true loneliness.

Until an ordinary day revealed a heavenly oasis in the desert…Michael McCall. Handsome and irresistibly charming, Michael McCall (the son of legendary horse breeder Jackson McCall) seemed to offer wild distraction and sincere friendship to Brynn. But could Brynn be content with mere friendship when her dreams of Michael involved so much more?

## Born for Thorton's Sake
Historical Romance, 175 Pages

Maria Castillo Holt...the only daughter of a valiant Lord and his Spanish beauty. Following the tragic deaths of her parents, Maria would find herself spirited away by conniving kindred in an endurance of neglect and misery.

However, rescued at the age of thirteen by Brockton Thorton, the son of her father's devoted friend, Lord Richard Thorton, Maria would at last find blessed reprieve. Further Brockton Thorton became, from that day forth, ever the absolute center of Maria's very existence. And as the blessed day of her sixteenth birthday dawned, Maria's dreams of owning her heart's desire, seemed to become a blissful reality.

Yet a fiendish plotting intruded, and Maria's hopes of realized dreams were locked away within dark, impenetrable walls. Would Maria's dreams of life with the handsome and coveted Brockton Thorton die at the hands of a demon strength?

## Divine Deception
Historical Romance, 205 Pages

Mistreated, disheartened and trapped, Fallon Ashby unexpectedly found the chance of swift deliverance at the hand of a wealthy land-owner. The mysterious deliverer offered Fallon escape from unendurable circumstances. Thus, Fallon chose to marry Trader Donavon, a man who concealed his face within the dark shadows of an ominous, black hood—a man who unknowingly held her heart captive.

Yet malicious villainy, intent on destroying Trader Donavon, set out to defeat him. Would evil succeed in overpowering the man whose face Fallon had never seen? The ever-hooded hero Fallon silently loved above all else?

## Sudden Storms
Historical Romance, 180 Pages

Rivers Brighton was a wanderer—having nothing and belonging to no one. Still, by chance, Rivers found herself harboring for a time beneath the roof of the kind-hearted Jolee Gray, and her remarkably attractive, yet ever grumbling brother, Paxton. Jolee, had taken Rivers in, and Rivers had stayed.

Helplessly drawn to Paxton's alluring presence and unable to escape his astonishing hold over her, however, Rivers knew she was in danger of enduring great heartbreak and pain. Paxton appeared to find Rivers no more interesting than a brief cloudburst. Yet, the man's spirit seemed to tether some great and devastating storm—a powerful tempest bridled within, waiting for the moment when it could rage full and free, perhaps destroying everything and everyone in its wake—particularly Rivers.

Could Rivers capture Paxton's attention long enough to make his heart her own? Or would the storm brewing within him destroy her hopes and dreams of belonging to the only man she had ever loved?

**The Prairie Prince**
Historical Romance, 214 Pages

For Katie Matthews life held no promise of true happiness. Life on the prairie was filled with hard labor, a brutal father, and the knowledge she would need to marry a man incapable of truly loving a woman. Men didn't have time to dote on women—so Katie's father told her. To Katie, it seemed life would forever remain mundane and disappointing—until the day Stover Steele bought her father's south acreage.

Handsome, rugged and fiercely protective of four orphaned sisters, Stover Steele seemed to have stepped from the pages of some romantic novel. Yet, his heroic character and alluring charm only served to remind Katie of what she would never have—true love and happiness the likes found only in fairytales. Furthermore, evil seemed to lurk in the shadows, threatening Katie's brightness, hope, and even her life!

Would Katie Matthews fall prey to disappointment, heartache and harm? Or could she win the attentions of the handsome Stover Steele long enough to be rescued?

**A Better Reason to Fall in Love (E-Book)**
Contemporary Romance (Excerpt…)

> *"Boom chicka wow wow!" Emmy whispered.*
>
> *"Absolutely!" Tabby breathed as she watched Jagger Brodie saunter past.*

*She envied Jocelyn for a moment, knowing he was most likely on his way to drop something off on Jocelyn's desk—or to speak with her. Jocelyn got to talk with Jagger almost every day, whereas Tabby was lucky if he dropped graphics changes off to her once a week.*

*"Ba boom chicka wow wow!" Emmy whispered again. "He's sporting a red tie today! Ooo! The power tie! He must be feeling confident."*

*Tabby smiled, amused and yet simultaneously amazed at Emmy's observation. She'd noticed the red tie, too. "There's a big marketing meeting this afternoon," she told Emmy. "I heard he's presenting some hard-nose material."*

*"Then that explains it," Emmy said, smiling. "Mr. Brodie's about to rock the company's world!"*

*"He already rocks mine…every time he walks by," Tabby whispered.*

## The Tide of the Mermaid Tears (E-Book)
Historical Romance

She took two more steps and paused—squeezed her eyes tightly shut andEmber gasped as she looked forward up the shore to see a man struggling in the water. He was coughing—spitting water from his mouth as he crawled from the water and onto the sand. As he collapsed face-down on the shore, Ember lifted her skirt and ran toward the man, dropping to her knees beside him.

"Sir?" she cried, nudging one broad shoulder. The man was stripped of his shirt—dressed only in a pair of trousers—no shoes…

Ember shook her head, rolling her eyes at her own foolishness.

"Sir?" she called again, nudging his broad shoulder once more. The man lay on his stomach—his face turned away from her. "Are you dead, sir?" she asked. Placing a hand to his back, she sighed with relief as she felt he yet breathed.

"Sir?" she said, clambering over the man's broad torso.

The man coughed. His eyes opened—his deep blue eyes, so shaded by thick, wet lashes that Ember wondered how it was he could see beyond them.

"Sir?" Ember ventured.

He coughed, asking, "Where am I?"

"On the seashore, sir," Ember answered.

## Kiss in the Dark (E-Book)

Contemporary Romance (Excerpt...)

*"Boston," he mumbled.*

*"I mean...Logan...he's like the man of my dreams! Why would I blow it? What if..." Boston continued to babble.*

*"Boston," he said. The commanding sound of his voice caused Boston to cease in her prattling and look to him.*

*"What?" she asked, somewhat grateful he'd interrupted her panic attack.*

*He frowned and shook his head.*

*"Shut up," he said. "You're all worked up about nothing." He reached out, slipping one hand beneath her hair to the back of her neck.*

*Boston was so startled by his touch, she couldn't speak—she could only stare up into his mesmerizing green eyes. His hand was strong and warm, powerful and reassuring.*

*"If it freaks you out so much...just kiss in the dark," he said.*

*Boston watched as Vance put the heel of his free hand to the light switch. In an instant the room went black.*

## The Light of the Lovers' Moon (E-Book)

Historical Romance

Violet Fynne was haunted—haunted by memory. It had been nearly ten years since her father had moved the family from the tiny town of Rattler Rock to the city of Albany, New York. Yet the pain and guilt in Violet's heart was as fresh and as haunting as ever it had been.

It was true Violet had been only a child when her family moved. Still—though she had been unwillingly pulled away from Rattler Rock—pulled away from him she held most dear—her heart had never left—and her mind had never forgotten the promise she had made—a promise to a boy—to a boy she had loved—a boy she had vowed to return to.

Yet, the world changes—and people move beyond pain and regret. Thus, when Violet Fynne retuned to Rattler Rock, it was to find that death had touched those she had known before—that the world had indeed changed—that unfamiliar faces now intruded on beloved memories.

Had she returned too late? Had Violet Fynne lost her chance for peace—and happiness? Would she be forever haunted by the memory of the boy she had loved nearly ten years before?

**Sweet Cherry Ray (E-Book)**
Historical Romance (Excerpt...)

*"Cherry glanced at her pa who frowned and slightly shook his head. Still, she couldn't help herself and she leaned over and looked down the road.*

*She could see the rider and his horse—a large buckskin stallion. As he rode nearer, she studied his white shirt, black flat-brimmed hat and double-breasted vest. Ever nearer he rode and she fancied his pants were almost the same color as his horse, with silver buttons running down the outer leg. Cherry had seen a similar manner of dress before—on the Mexican vaqueros that often worked for her pa in the fall.*

*"Cherry," her pa scolded in a whisper as the stranger neared them.*

*She straightened and blushed, embarrassed by being as impolite in her staring as the other town folk were in theirs. It seemed everyone had stopped whatever they had been doing to walk out to the street and watch the stranger ride in.*

*No one spoke—the only sound was that of the breeze, a falcon's cry overhead and the rhythm of the rider's horse as it slowed to a trot...."*

**Kissing Cousins (E-Book)**
Contemporary Romance (Excerpt...)

*"It won't change your life ..." he said, his voice low and rich like a warm drink laced with molasses. "And it sure won't be the best kiss you'll ever have," he added. Her body erupted into goose bumps as his thumb traveled slowly over her lower lip. "But I'll try to make it worth your time ..."*

**The Rogue Knight (E-Book)**
Historical Romance

An aristocratic birthright and the luxurious comforts of profound wealth did nothing to comfort Fontaine Pratina following the death of her beloved parents. After two years in the guardianship of her mother's arrogant and selfish sister, Carileena Wetherton, Fontaine's only moments of joy and peace were found in the company of the loyal servants of Pratina Manor. Only in the kitchens and servant's quarters of her grand domicile did Fontaine find friendship, laughter and affection.

Always, the life of a wealthy orphan destined to inherit loomed before her—a dark cloud of hopeless, shallow, snobbish people...a life of aristocracy, void of simple joys—and of love. Still, it was her lot—her birthright and she saw no way of escaping it.

One brutal, cold winter's night a battered stranger appeared at the kitchen servant's entrance, however, seeking shelter and help. He gave only his first name, Knight…and suddenly, Fontaine found herself experiencing fleeting moments of joy in life. For Knight was handsome, powerful…the very stuff of the legends of days of old. Though a servant's class was his, he was proud, strong and even his name seemed to portray his persona absolutely. He distracted Fontaine from her dull, hopeless existence.

Yet, there were devilish secrets—strategies cached by her greedy aunt and not even the handsome and powerful Knight could save her from them. Or could he? And if he did—would the truth force Fontaine to forfeit her Knight, her heart's desire…the man she loved—in order to survive?

LaVergne, TN USA
05 April 2011
222986LV00009BA/40/P